The Trade

Colby Marshall

The Trade
©2013 Colby Marshall
All Rights Reserved

ISBN 978-0-9888777-2-6

Visit Colby online:

www.ColbyMarshall.com

STAIRWAY≡PRESS

The Armchair Adventurer

An Armchair Adventurer book
STAIRWAY PRESS—SEATTLE

Cover Design by David Zampa, www.pensivedragon.com
Interior image www.mipan.orgfree.com via iStockphoto.com

www.stairwaypress.com
1500A East College Way #554
Mount Vernon, WA 98273

For Ashlee,
Because Everything Happens For a Reason

PROLOGUE

THE WORD "SOCIOPATH" doesn't scare me much since I've known for quite some time that I am one. For someone who is starting to tap his potential, however, here are my fundamental truths:

Liars aren't made. They're born. But a lot of talented liars think because they're born liars they're good at it. Lying is a craft to be practiced and shaped every bit as much as painting or writing. Or acting.

The second truth is the eyes. Your eyes can betray you faster than your tongue. Why do you think so many poker players wear sunglasses?

The last truth is the most important of all. It's a rule, so pay close attention.

Don't lie to another liar. Because he knows the rules of the game, too.

CHAPTER 1

A RAT SCURRIED across Liza's foot.

She blinked twice to help her eyes adjust to the darkness. What the hell was this place, and how did she end up here? She'd been walking through Central Park on her way home—

Her right hand swatted her left arm.

Fire! Fire!

When her palm connected with her bicep, she realized there were no flames. She'd be engulfed if there were. The sensation of her arm on fire didn't make sense.

Stop burning so I can think for a minute!

Maybe then, she could figure out where she was.

She wanted to roll onto her side, but the bottom half of her body refused. Her legs were disconnected from her brain.

Liza's mind lit like a stick of dynamite.

The baby!

Her hands shot to the bulge that had been growing in her tummy for the past eight and a half months.

Heat seared from her arms and up her neck as her hands reached her stomach. The bump was gone. She fingered the bottom of her shirt and lifted it a few inches. Her face prickled. What she felt reminded her of the time when she was little and her mother had let her pull the insides out of the Halloween pumpkin.

She closed her eyes and bit her lip hard. In the darkness, she could tell the thick, viscous substance coating her fingertips was her own blood. White noise rushed in her ears as answers jarred into place. Tears formed, dribbled down her cheeks, and streamed off of her nose into her mouth. She opened her eyes again.

She'd cut through the park on her way home like she did every day. James had told her to call a cab. The stories on the news had him worried. She'd promised she would, but when the time came, she'd toddled toward the subway. They'd already discussed breaking into her childhood piggy bank. The baby was only a few weeks away. Cab fares wouldn't help a thing.

Halfway through the park, the sky had burst. People around her scattered like pillbugs under a lifted rock, but running wasn't an option for her. She couldn't even see her feet, much less force them to a jog.

Liza had waddled and tried to wrestle an old brochure from her purse to hold over her head for cover. She'd looked up right in time to dodge a man in a suit passing her.

He seemed to glimpse her out of the corner of his eye. His pace slowed.

"Would you mind holding this?" he'd said as he extended his black umbrella. "I'm losing my notes."

The man made a show of stuffing papers down in his briefcase, but nothing was falling out. He didn't want her to refuse his umbrella. When he was finished, Liza offered it back to him, but he waved her off.

"You're headed for the subway, right? You can carry it for me," he'd said.

She'd thanked him.

Nice people still exist in the world.

Now, as she lay in the suffocating blackness, she tried to remember what happened after that. It was all so fuzzy, like the noise in her ears.

Think, Liza. Think!

Her skin recoiled as something scuttled up her pants leg. She squinted, her eyes burning.

"Help me," she whispered. Her voice came out with a sound like crackling paper. God, she was so thirsty. "Help me!"

A face burned bright in her mind for a second before it died out like a cigarette butt on the pavement. Another memory crashed over her: a knife slicing into her arm.

Come on, brain!

The faces of riders as she had drifted in and out on the subway. "You've had some day, haven't you, honey?" the voice had asked.

Liza's eyes flew open. It wasn't white noise pounding in her ears.

"Help me!" In her head, she screamed louder than ever, but her voice was so weak, it didn't manage to make an echo against the walls around her

The clamor built, and the darkness thinned. "Someone!" she gasped, even though she knew no one was coming.

Trash glowed around her feet, and an old Metro card blew across her chest. She was in the spotlight, her scarlet hand finally lit up for her to see.

"I'm sorry, James," she whispered as the train thundered toward her. "I'm so sorry."

CHAPTER 2

"I'M MOVING AS fast as I can, *Morton*," McKenzie McClendon huffed as she jostled through people toward the subway tunnel. A few months ago, she'd have been demoted to the police blotter if she'd called her boss at *The Herald* by his first name. Amazing how uncovering an assassination plot could boost you overnight from glorified slave to corner office with a view. It had turned out to be a lot lonelier up there than she'd imagined it would be.

Her high-heeled boots clacked against the sidewalk as she strode faster. She caught a glimpse of herself in the reflection of a store window. Her auburn hair blew in the wind, split ends screaming for a trim. One day she'd have time. Maybe.

"I'm on my way into the subway station now, so I'm about to lose the signal. Be there soon," McKenzie said. She clicked the "end" button on her phone.

That's for all the times you sent me to cover ribbon-cuttings at Whole Foods.

She didn't bother to take off her sunglasses once she reached the platform. Better to go unrecognized these days. She hopped on an R train and took a seat. Before, all she'd wanted was the front page by-line. By the time the initial hearings were over, all she wanted was her anonymity back.

The doors closed, and the subway rocked towards Manhattan. She grabbed the pencil tucked behind her ear, opened her notebook to a fresh page, and tapped the eraser in a slow drum roll against the paper. Next to her, two women chattered about the very same thing for which McKenzie's editor had called: another body had been found.

"The police should really release details about where they found her," one said.

The other woman clicked her tongue. "They're doing it on purpose. Don't want people scared to go out. They did say she was like the others. Sliced like deli meat."

"I don't even like to run errands anymore," the first woman whispered. "I can't imagine how scared they must've been. I won't even chop onions with a paring knife. I'm that afraid of cutting myself. I use a mini-processor."

"I doubt you have anything to worry about," Tongue Clicker responded. "You're not pregnant."

McKenzie jotted the word on her page.

"What kind of person gets off on killing pregnant women?" Mini-Processor girl wondered.

Tongue Clicker grunted. "The same kind who can leave a girl on the edge of the roof of the Edison Hotel butchered to a pulp. Even if she hadn't bled to death first, if she'd rolled over another inch, the fall would've killed her. It's sick."

McKenzie scribbled: *He doesn't kill them outright.*

This murder marked the fourth body in two months. All of them in their third trimester, all of them gutted at the womb. McKenzie scratched another couple of notes: *Mommy issues? Desperate for a child?*

The subway squealed to a stop, the doors opened, and the gossipers exited the train. Good thing having a baby was about as far down her to-do list as burning off her own fingerprints with battery acid.

The prescribed ten seconds passed, and yet, the doors stayed open.

What now?

A moment later, the robotic voice of the Metropolitan Transport Authority crackled through the speakers. "Ladies and

Gentlemen, we are being delayed because of an earlier incident. Please be patient."

Whoever said patience was a virtue had never worked as a journalist. Patience meant waiting, and waiting meant she might miss an important story. She hopped off the seat, left the train, and trotted up the stairs to higher ground.

The second she reached street level, "I Can't Get No Satisfaction" bleated from her phone. She ripped it from her pocketbook.

"Morton, the damned subway is delayed. I'm coming as fast as my Stuart Weitzmans will allow me. I'd be faster if I didn't have to answer my cell every two seconds." She ended the call. Dang, she'd grown some balls.

As she scrambled into a cab, the Rolling Stones taunted her again. Maybe she had pushed her boss too far, but unless he had hired Inspector Gadget to drive this cab, the constant phone calls weren't helpful.

"620 Eighth Avenue, please," McKenzie told the cab driver before she jammed her finger into the green button. "What?"

"McKenzie? McKenzie McClendon?"

McKenzie pressed the phone harder against her ear. The caller was obviously not Morton Gaines. "This is she," she said.

The man replied, but his voice was muffled by static and his own slurring.

"Could you repeat that?" she asked.

"Do you remember me? I'm Jonas Cleary. We went to school together."

McKenzie held back a gasp. Remember him? She'd ended up in the back of a Cherokee Blazer with him after their junior prom.

"Rings a bell. It's, um, nice to hear from you?" She was unable to stifle the way her voice hitched up at the end, a question.

What the hell?

"You're reporting now, right? For the *New York Herald*?"

7

"That's right." It was the same answer she gave anyone who asked her about the *Herald*. It was no secret dozens of other papers had been trying to steal her out from under the *Herald*, so it was only natural for people to be curious. No way she would tell them she wasn't about to go anywhere, that even she wasn't confident she wasn't a one-trick pony.

A one-trick pony who gets everyone around me in trouble.

Plus, on her previous career-making story, she'd had help.

"I need you to do something for me," Jonas said, his voice jolting her back to the moment.

Oh, perfect. That's all I need.

Not only was she running late, but she didn't have an angle for this new story. Now, her high school sweetheart called in between tequila shots for a favor. People sure had come out of the plumbing systems these past few months.

"Look, Jonas, I don't know how you got my number, but I'm in a rush today. Maybe you can tell me how to reach you, and we can catch up sometime when things are less hectic. Maybe when your blood alcohol level is less than ninety percent. I have a deadline, and I—"

"I know. That's why I'm calling you," he slurred.

Though his words teetered on the slope of incoherence, the next statement shook McKenzie from annoyance to rapt attention. "You're writing about the serial killer, right? The guy who kills the pregnant women? I think...I think he killed my wife."

CHAPTER 3

AS MCKENZIE PULLED out a chair across from Jonas at the Jersey diner, she was already having second thoughts. The liquor on his breath would catch fire from across the table if she lit a match.

Never walk away from a possible angle.

She sat down.

"McKenzie. 'S good to see you. You look exactly like I remember. Same copper eyes, same auburn hair. I guess it's a little shorter now, though, right? But you're mostly the way I remember."

She wished she could say the same. Jonas had aged three decades since they'd crossed the stage to receive their diplomas. His dark-as-night hair hadn't changed much, though it had to have been months since he'd had it cut. His broad shoulders were similar, but he'd gained a few pounds around the middle to even them out. His eyes were sunken, and the white sliver of a scar snaked down his right arm.

Still, she wasn't here for a high school reunion. "Thanks, Jonas. So, you said on the phone you wanted to talk about your wife."

Jonas grunted and plunked his coffee mug back down on the table. "You don't mess around, huh?"

"Time isn't your friend when you report for one of the biggest papers in the country."

Jonas shifted in his chair, his right hand twisting the thin gold band on his left. "Noelle would probably tell you that if time isn't your friend, you should make some new ones. She was like that. Even if it took an extra thirty minutes, she'd walk rather than take the bus."

His laugh sprinkled McKenzie's arms with goosebumps. "In fact, she used to tell me cabs would shorten my life span. She'd say one day when I was watching her run around from my wheelchair, I could blame the lack of exercise and air."

"What happened?" McKenzie whispered.

"The freaking air got her killed is what happened. She was taking one of those mommy and me yoga classes. Walked to and from it every day. Found her in an alleyway not too far from the gym."

McKenzie swallowed the lump in her throat. Even as she said, "I'm sorry," the words felt wrong. None would feel right.

Jonas' fists clenched the napkin in his lap. "You're sorry. You're sorry, and I'm still here with a dead wife and no one to listen to me."

"Whoa, now," McKenzie said, "You called *me*, remember? *You* wanted to talk to *me*."

The guy who'd pinned a corsage on her awful, magenta prom dress now hung his head and blew out a deep breath. "I know, I know. I'm sorry. I'm frustrated out of my mind, okay? That's why I called you. You've got clout. Maybe if you did a piece on it, they'd look into it harder."

"Why do you think the Cradle Robber has anything to do with your wife? I made a few calls on my way here, Jonas. I know this isn't your first theory."

Jonas' dilated pupils met hers. His nostrils flared. "Look, I know everyone thinks I'd rather have a fifth of gin than go to therapy. They're probably right. And yes, I've been down to the police station one or two times when a woman's been murdered. But damn it, this time it isn't the Jack talking. I know it's him."

Jonas banged his fist on the table with the last words.

McKenzie flinched. Other patrons shot glares at them.

McKenzie lowered her voice to a whisper. "I'm listening to you now, so stop raving. Tell me what you know. How did they find her?"

His chest rose and fell with another slow breath. The tension in his shoulders eased marginally. "*They* didn't find her anywhere. I did. Went looking for her when she didn't come home. Gibb was nowhere to be found."

"Gibb?"

"Our son."

McKenzie nodded, a knot forming in her stomach at the mention of the little boy who'd been kidnapped. Still, she couldn't help but notice this case already had an obvious difference from the Cradle Robber murders: the child had already been born. No need to harp on that yet. "How did she die?"

The napkin Jonas had been tying into a knot was now ripped cleanly down the middle. "Not how you'd think, considering how she was cut."

"She was stabbed?"

"No, she was *cut*. Everywhere. Gashes all over her body. She didn't bleed to death, though. The coroner's report said cardiac arrest. That fucker scared my wife to death."

McKenzie winced but shook the mental image. *Stay in the game.* "Excuse my wording, but there wasn't anything weird about the death? The killer didn't leave her in a way that killed her *later*? That sort of thing is this guy's signature."

"No, James Bond, he didn't tie her to the conveyor belt at the rock quarry. But I do have a reason for being sure it's the same guy."

"And…?"

Jonas slashed invisible marks over his left thigh. "They said on the news all the women have been found with some type of symbol carved in their arms. The M.E. reported a gash on Noelle's leg that was shallower and less haphazard than the

11

others."

McKenzie frowned. "The symbol thing is a rumor."

"Some rumors are true."

It was a stretch at best, desperation at most. "Listen, Jonas, I'm not sure I can help you. I'm sorry about Noelle, but if the FBI had any reason to believe her murder was connected to the new ones, they'd be all over it by now. They run violent crimes through their systems to determine if they're similar. If their cross-referencing database hasn't connected Noelle to the Cradle Robber's victims, then chances are she's not."

Jonas shoved back from the table, which sent the coffee mug crashing on its side. Hot liquid scalded McKenzie's lap.

She shrieked, jumping up and grabbing the napkins on the table to mop at the mess. He threw his hands in the air. "Right. Because the Feds know *everything*, don't they McKenzie? They solve all the crimes in the world, right? You should know better than anybody—to be the one to die, that's one thing. But to be the one left behind, to be the one who can't follow, that's another. And to know my son could still be out there somewhere…"

Jonas' voice boomed louder until it echoed off the diner walls. He leaned forward toward McKenzie, a vein pulsing in his throat, his face purple with fury. The diner owner ambled out from behind the bar as others in the restaurant stared, transfixed.

"I don't really give a damn what the Feds are doing," Jonas shouted, "but the least *anyone* can do is listen. You don't know what it's like to find your wife in an alley, slashed almost beyond recognition. I know exactly what I look like to everyone, McKenzie. I even know what I look like to you. But you don't know what it's like to lower your mouth to your wife's to give her mouth to mouth and smell on her lips the garlic from the lunch you had together at the corner bistro. To feel how cold they were. It ripped my heart out, McKenzie. Ended my *life!*"

The owner had reached their table. "Maybe it's a good idea

for me to walk you outside for a bit of fresh air, sir," the guy said. He placed a firm hand on Jonas' elbow.

Jonas jerked away, straightened his jacket, and threw a five dollar bill onto the table. "Never mind. I'm leaving."

He stormed away, kicking the wall before he reached the exit. As he pushed the swinging door, he turned back to the diner owner. "By the way, fresh air can get you killed."

"Where in the name of all things sacred have you been?" Morton Gaines asked. He waddled behind McKenzie through the *Herald* office.

"Visiting an old friend."

"You're kidding me."

"Morton, I was tracking down an angle for the story. It turned out to be a wash. A guy I dated in high school thinks the serial killer offed his wife a couple years ago. But apparently that's been his take on every murder suspect brought in since his wife died." McKenzie paused for a second at the water cooler and poured herself a drink. "Are alcoholics more obsessive than sober people?"

"I don't know. Probably. Forget that for now, McKenzie. We have other things to talk about, like how they released the name of the girl found in the subway."

"It's sad how he's still hoping—expecting—the cops to find his wife's killer. The file is probably collecting dust somewhere—" McKenzie stopped. "Wait. She was found in the subway?"

Morton nodded. "Finally, you listen to me. Yes. What was left of her after the L Train, that is. We'll have to wait for the autopsy report to be sure, but the impact of the train is probably what killed her."

"Jesus Christ."

"Yeah, I'm almost positive Jesus wasn't around for this."

"And the fetus?"

"Taken out, but gone like the others," Morton supplied. "I'm telling you, one day they're going to find this guy's house with a bunch of dead babies in the freezer. Pleasant thought."

"About to make me puke," McKenzie choked out. "I hope when they do, they kill the asshole on sight. Probably be better than he deserves, but we'd be rid of a baby killer. Come to think of it, that was one weird thing about this guy's story. His wife was killed, and their baby was taken. Granted, the wife wasn't pregnant when she was murdered. The kid was already born. Still, they never found the child. "

"Right. So, if old lover boy isn't a good angle, then what is?"

Damn good question.

"I thought I'd see if any local obstetricians can sit down with me and explain what someone would need to know to cut a baby out of a woman. I don't know if this sicko kills the moms and then the babies later or some screwed-up woman or couple who can't have kids is killing off the moms to snatch the kids. Either way, an OB might have a clue who could pull this off."

CHAPTER 4

DIRK HARRIS EASED his motorcycle into a parking spot. He glanced at his watch and grinned. One o'clock. Somehow, he'd finished the job, dealt with a problem, and still had time to go home to shower and shave.

Hot damn.

He lifted off his helmet. In its reflection, he caught a glimpse of the black wavy hair matted to his forehead. He tossed it out of his face and plunked down the helmet. Adrenaline still ripped through his veins as he dismounted the bike and strode toward the main entrance. His only regret was that the setback meant he hadn't been able to hang around and watch. Watching was his favorite part.

Dirk passed through the double doors and made a left toward the Staff Only entrance. With a quick scan of his employee access card, the door buzzed and unlocked. At the nurses' station, he slid a stack of folders off the counter and wandered down the hallway. A surgeon moonlighting as an ER doc. Such a do-gooder, he was.

He rolled his head in slow circles as he reviewed everything again. At least the next could come sooner now. Discipline was important, of course, but could he help it if things hadn't gone entirely to plan?

Everything happens for a reason.

A short blonde nurse sidled up to him. The smell of cheap watermelon body splash tickled his nostrils as he glanced down at her. She was about the same height as the girl this morning.

"Dr. Harris, we need you in exam three. Looks like a clean break in the kid's right arm, but we should probably take care of him first. He's screaming like a howler monkey."

Dirk's mind filled with the shrill squeal the girl had let out as he dug his knife into her flesh. He shot the nurse a grin. "Maybe we ought to give his mother a break and put him down."

She giggled. "Dr. Harris, behave yourself!"

He chuckled and winked. "I'll do my best."

In his thirty-seven years on this earth, Trevin Worneck had probably swallowed his own weight in pills. Now, he dumped an arbitrary amount of Xanax into his palm and threw the handful back with a sip of black coffee. He wasn't gonna make it.

This was supposed to make things *easier*, not harder.

Ollie buzzed in on the intercom. "Mr. Worneck, the Petersons are here to see you."

He slammed his head to his desk and jabbed his finger in the general direction of the intercom button. "Did they bring rum?" he mumbled.

"Sir?"

"Send them in, Ollie."

Trevin tapped his head against the mahogany a couple of times for good measure. Maybe if he had a giant welt on his forehead, the blasted Petersons would be afraid he had something contagious and leave sooner. His grandmother had once told him people who cursed weren't intelligent enough to structure their thoughts in a more positive way. His grandmother had never been buried in the pile of steaming shit he was now.

"Afternoon," Rodney Peterson said as he stepped through the door. His wife trailed behind him, meek.

Trevin stood and extended his hand. "Good to see you both."

"Trevin," Sarah Peterson greeted him with a tight smile.

He gestured to the chairs across from him and watched Rodney plop his stocky frame down between the arms. Sarah perched daintily on the chair's edge as though it might bite her. Even though her graying tea-colored hair was perfectly coifed and sprayed, she brushed an invisible strand behind her ear.

"What can I do for you kids today?"

Sarah's thin smile lingered while Rodney took the lead, as usual. "We've found a good situation. The girl is young, but she's had a hard life. She appreciates the thought of having someone to take care of her for a while."

Trevin's brow furrowed. "Over eighteen, of course?"

"I'm not a moron, Worneck," Rodney shot back.

At Trevin's sharp look, Rodney conceded. "I'm sorry. This has been a stressful few months. It's getting to me."

A dry laugh escaped the young lawyer's throat. "Tell me about it."

Rodney scrunched his nose, confused, then shook his head. "Anyway, after talking to her, we're pleased with her thoughts on the process, what she feels her role would be, and the head on her shoulders in general. She's agreed to a closed adoption."

Trevin nodded. Thank God the Xanax was starting to kick in. It wasn't much, but at least the vice squeezing his lungs was letting up. "Brilliant. How far along is she?"

"Twenty-eight weeks," Sarah whispered.

"Superb," Trevin answered reflexively.

He choked down his sarcasm and forced a grin. "That's great, folks. All I need is some basic information, and I'll draw up the paperwork."

CHAPTER 5

"DR. SCHWETZER WILL be with you shortly, Ms. McClendon," the receptionist said.

At two-fifteen, McKenzie was right on time for the meeting she'd set up, but she couldn't complain. The obstetrician had not only been kind to squeeze her in on such short notice, but the business of birthing babies didn't allow for perfect scheduling.

"Thanks," McKenzie replied.

On her way to an empty chair she passed a dozen other women in the waiting room, all of them in varying degrees of pregnancy. One couple had a newborn in a carrier at their feet. They probably all thought she was pregnant, too, but not yet showing.

Or, I'm here to pick your doctor's brain about how a psychopath would go about stealing your babies from inside your bellies.

She snagged *Avid Housekeeper*—the juiciest magazine on the lobby table—and settled in next to a girl with a smattering of freckles across the bridge of her nose. If it wasn't for the bulge of her belly that made her look very much grown up, McKenzie would've figured her as pre-pubescent.

The girl nodded toward McKenzie's magazine. "Not exactly *Time*, huh?"

At this, McKenzie glanced at the girl a little harder. Her ears were pierced three times each, her dishwater blonde hair pulled into a sloppy ponytail. Kinky curls framed the youthful face.

This girl reads Time?

McKenzie's gaze fell to the book in the girl's lap: an open copy of *Pride and Prejudice*.

"They could stand some new reading material," McKenzie answered. "This thing is from April two years ago."

The girl nodded, but her gaze shifted to McKenzie's stomach. "Pregnant?"

Images flashed into McKenzie's mind. Her Uncle Sal. Levi.

As if I could do something as simple as have a family.

Losing Pierce and Levi was one thing, but her *own* child? Impossible. Besides, it wasn't like her love life was booming these days. She didn't exactly have a dad-to-be lined up. The closest to it was Noah, and whether he was father material or not was questionable at best. And that was if they were even a couple. At this point, she had no clue what they were.

McKenzie shook her head. "Nah, just meeting one of the doctors. What about you? When are you due?"

"About two months to go," the girl answered. "Not a minute too soon. After that, I can relax some."

"If the baby cooperates, you mean," McKenzie mused.

The girl smirked. "Not mine. I'm having the baby for another couple."

McKenzie's ears perked up. "Like a surrogate?"

Entrapment, McKenzie. You know surrogacy contracts are illegal in New York.

"Not exactly—"

"Ms. McClendon?" the receptionist's call cut the girl off.

"Yes," McKenzie called, standing. She turned to face the freckled pregnant girl. "Good luck."

"Likewise," the girl said, her focus returning to her book.

McKenzie followed the receptionist through the corridor and into a dim office. The lady gestured to an armchair across from the doctor's desk. "He'll be right in."

Pictures covered the soothing blue walls of the study, Christmas cards bearing photos of infants. She could still remember the first Christmas card she'd gotten where her cousin Levi was featured front and center, his dark head poking out of a red-wrapped box in front of the Christmas tree. His mother would never again take his Christmas card picture.

The father of the baby of the girl in the subway this morning wouldn't even *see* the child, much less send out Christmas cards.

Jonas had been alone for two Christmases now.

"Ms. McClendon." The doctor's greeting broke her thoughts.

"Dr. Schwetzer." She offered the white-haired man her hand, which he took into his firm grip. "Thank you for taking the time to talk with me today."

"Of course," he replied. He pushed his glasses further up the bridge of his thin nose. "Have a seat. I hear you're working on an article about the Cradle Robber."

"Floundering for an angle would be more apt. Do you mind if I record our interview?"

"Oh, not at all, not at all," he replied, his gaze on McKenzie's hand-held voice recorder. "I'm happy to help."

She clicked the record button, then set the device back into her purse. "What sort of knowledge would it take to remove a fetus from a woman? From what I understand, the victims that aren't mangled from their—um—*true* causes of death are stitched up from where he's—" McKenzie's voice trailed. No words would sound right. "From where he's done what he's done. He cuts out the infants, then moves the victims to the location where they themselves die."

Dr. Schwetzer sat forward in the leather arm chair and perched his chin atop his fist. "Yes, yes. But honestly, anyone who's taken a few sewing classes could manage that."

"What about the actual—is cesarean the right word in this case?"

The doctor shook his head. "I don't know that there *is* a word for this particular case, my dear. But to answer your question, I'd say a great deal depends on how *rudimentary* the procedure is."

Hard to get more information when you only know half the story.

"The police haven't released details on the removal of the fetuses, but for the sake of speculation, let's say he cuts out the fetus to *torture* the mother but not kill her. How much medical knowledge would it take to excise the baby without the mom bleeding to death?"

The doctor shrugged. "The knowledge of how to operate a chainsaw? It would be different if we thought he was *delivering* these fetuses rather than *removing* them, but he's a serial killer, not a nursemaid."

"Could you expound a bit?" McKenzie coaxed.

"I apologize," Dr. Schwetzer said. He took off his glasses and rubbed the bridge of his nose between two fingers. "An anatomy class or two, and the perpetrator could probably see his way around any immediate complications. Then again, don't bet your mother's jewelry on the classes. If he planned on killing the women anyway, he could've learned by trial and error."

"Makes sense," McKenzie agreed. "We don't know if they've been consistent or become cleaner as they go."

A visible shiver rippled through Dr. Schwetzer's body. "Hate to think what that means for the fetuses."

McKenzie's jaw clenched. "We'll assume he doesn't use a chainsaw for now. What sort of pain are we talking about if it's a 'normal' cesarean?"

Dr. Schwetzer grunted. "Let's just say epidurals and Demerol are standard because they're needed. C-sections are common, but they're still major surgery. He'd have to have the women knocked out or restrained in some fashion. For them to still be alive and transported to a second location, the surgery would have to be somewhat well-executed. That doesn't leave much room for squirming."

McKenzie tried to focus, but her cell phone vibrated in her

purse again. This was the third time it had rung. Something was up.

"I'm sorry, Dr. Schwetzer, but I have to take this," she said, fishing in her purse.

"Of course," the doctor replied, though annoyance was written on his face. He pushed back from the desk. "I'll take my next patient in the meantime."

He exited the room in a huff and slammed the office door behind him.

"Shit," she muttered. God help the bastard screwing up a cooperative interview. She punched the pick up on her cell.

"I realize you're taking certain liberties with me these days, McClendon, but let's not forget that cell phone of yours is on the company dime."

"Right, Morton," McKenzie replied. She swallowed her retort about how many company dimes he'd spent on Oreos the past couple of years. "Article interviews must take a backseat. I'll answer on ring two next time. What's up?"

"Save the tone, McClendon. One of my contacts from the NYPD called. They found another body."

"Already?" she gasped. "You're kidding."

"Sorry to say I'm not. But it isn't another woman," he answered. Her boss took a long pause. "It's an infant."

CHAPTER 6

EVERITT CROSSED ANOTHER block toward the two-story brownstone on the Upper West Side. The stone pathway to the townhouse seemed to take hours longer than it should after her long afternoon at the doctor's office. Settling into bed for her first night in her new home sounded perfect. Her thoughts strayed back to this afternoon's examination.

She propped her feet up into the stirrups and let her legs fall open. Sure, she hadn't had to have a pelvic exam today, but unfortunately, they didn't make the ultrasound tables for anything besides showing off your hoo-hah.

Oh, well. Might as well let anyone take a peek who wants. I'll never look the same after this.

"Everything's been going well, then?" Doctor Schwetzer had asked. He touched a gloved hand to her belly as he squirted warm jelly onto her stomach.

"Well, I can't see my feet when I stand up, and I pee more than a five-year-old after a six pack of soda. Other than that, yeah."

"All normal," he said. "The joys of being pregnant."

"Oh, bliss," she said. A tiny dot blipped rapidly in the center of what looked like a Rorschach ink blot test on the black and white screen. The heartbeat.

"Where's the head?" she asked. She'd loved puzzles ever since she was a kid, but this one she couldn't figure out.

The doctor used the hand not sluicing the transducer over her belly to outline a body. As he did, the picture in the clouds that was the kid's

nose finally clicked in Everitt's brain. Against her will, her legs trembled.
She pressed her palms against her knees. "Cold in here."
"Still don't want to know the sex?" the doctor asked.
"Nope," she replied, though she did request a printout of the
ultrasound. They'd probably like that sort of thing, after all.

Now, she clutched the printout in her hand as she approached the door of the prewar townhouse. Before she had a chance to knock, the cherry wood flew open to reveal Sarah Peterson. "Everitt! Where have you been? We've been worried sick. I told you we would pick you up at the doctor's office, but then you weren't there. What happened?"

Everitt rolled her eyes. Two months with these people ought to be a blast. "I told you there was no need for that. I took the subway."

"But, Everitt, dear," Sarah simpered, "I told you we'd take care of all of your expenses until the baby is born. That does include travel."

"I know," Everitt replied. She pushed past Sarah into the dark foyer. "But it isn't necessary."

Damn, this woman was weird. "Oh," Everitt said, remembering the paper in her hand, "I brought home a keepsake for you guys."

She held out the ultrasound image, which Sarah slowly took from her fingertips. The prim lady stared, unmoving, at the picture for a full minute. Finally, her mouth curved at the edges.

"Beautiful," she whispered.

CHAPTER 7

MCKENZIE SPENT THE hour after she left Dr. Schwetzer's office trying every contact in her God-forsaken Blackberry, but no one had information on the dead infant some poor old lady had found on the subway. The baby had been inside a zipped duffle bag. The woman who found it had been taken to the hospital to be treated for an anxiety attack. Other than that, there wasn't much to go on. The police wouldn't acknowledge a possible connection to the Cradle Robber, even though everyone with a TV or radio suspected it.

Now, she had her source from the NYPD on the line. Missy Cambridge was usually a sure thing, but even *she* was giving McKenzie the run around.

"Missy, I realize you can't tell every reporter who calls, but it *will* leak somehow. You know it, and I know it. When it leaks, you have to think about what kind of damage it'll do to your investigation if it's put out by someone who doesn't actually research and report accurate information. I'll sit on it until you tell me I can move, I swear. Just let me be prepared."

Never mind that I already signed a lease on a new apartment for twice my current rent based on that raise I was promised.

Guaranteed promotion or not, McKenzie wanted this article. She was no one-trick pony. Plus, that little voice in her head reminded her day in and day out of what she'd sacrificed for this job.

Morton stood in her office doorway chewing a fingernail. His eyes narrowed, calling her on her bullshit, as on the other end of the line, Missy shut her down, too.

Hang up before you start cussing.

"Fine, Missy. Fine. I appreciate your time. Give me a call if anything changes."

She slammed her phone down and shoved back from her desk. If Missy didn't come through, she'd have only one more source who might be able to help her. It would *not* come to that point. She wouldn't let it. To get to that source, she'd have to call *him*. "I'm going home. I can't think here."

"Whatever you need to do," Morton replied. "But I need something on this ASAP, McKenzie. Like, at three o'clock this past afternoon, ASAP. I know I already told you about the promotion, but don't think I can't change my mind."

"It's tattooed on my forehead," McKenzie shot back. She snatched up her purse and headed out the door.

Apparently almost dying for a story wasn't enough for Morton, nor was her managing to drag her friends and family into harm's way. Maybe he'd prefer it if she'd toss a few more loved ones under the bus for every story she was assigned. Too bad she was fresh out.

Her neck burned as Levi's sweet little face popped to mind. How insulting to his memory would it be if everything that had happened in her pursuit of her last headline-making story had occurred just so she could go back to writing sidebar stories? Embarrassment she could handle. But the knowledge her cousin had died in her pursuit of her career would haunt her forever if she didn't at least maintain the place she'd managed to get him killed trying to attain.

McKenzie leaned back in the papasan chair and flipped her phone over three times in her hand. If Pierce were still here, this problem wouldn't exist. A computer hadn't been made her former roommate couldn't hack. Sometimes, she still half-expected him to come waltzing through the door, trying to get her to taste some disgusting new kind of fish he'd bought at the corner market or trying to talk her into going to karaoke night at some skeevy bar. But no, he was in the ranks of the people who'd laid down their lives for her stupid career.

At her feet, her hundred-pound Great Dane rolled onto his side.

"I'm aware this is a bad idea, Carbon, but it's not like I have more attractive options."

The dapple dog blinked at her lazily, then plopped his head onto the hardwood.

"Don't give me that. I'm *not* in a rush. I just know better than anyone that all it takes to lose your place as the top dog is one nosy reporter with one lucky-ass, random lead."

Carbon lolled his head onto her foot.

"As long as you realize this is a last ditch effort."

She punched send on her cell and closed her eyes. His voice would hit her ears any second now.

On the third ring, right as she was ready to chicken out, he picked up. "Whoa! Mac. Not a call I was expecting today."

"Well, *Lieutenant Hutchins,* it's good to hear your voice, too."

McKenzie had spent the most significant and terrifying moments of her life with Noah Hutchins last year, but she found out soon after he moved away that his wise-assery didn't translate well over long distances. The calls had become fewer and further between, to say nothing of the visits.

"To what do I owe the pleasure, Mac?"

Deep breaths. He might not say no right away.

"I need Jig."

"Right. And after I put you in touch with her, I'll chop off my nuts and send them on over, too."

Of course.

He'd never told her how exactly they knew each other, but from the way Noah and Jig talked, it didn't take Stephen Hawking to put that puzzle together. Still, Jig was the only person McKenzie knew of who could dig up the sort of information she needed on the dead infant.

"Noah, I'm onto something here, but I have no access. You of all people should know how much that sucks."

"I appreciate your predicament, Mac. I really do. But surely a big name reporter like you has plenty of contacts."

"If Pierce were still alive, we wouldn't be talking. But he's not. My best friend could've helped me, but he died trying to help you find the truth when it mattered most to you. Now I need the help of the only other computer genius I know. I wouldn't call if I didn't need this. Believe me."

There was a long pause on the other end before Noah spoke again. "Look, Mac, even if I tell you how to contact her, there's no way of telling if Jig would talk to you. That's not me being an asshole. It's the truth."

"Well, lucky for you, this time it won't be your problem."

CHAPTER 8

"PATIENT IN RENAL failure, coded during dialysis. Ambulance is four minutes out."

Dirk nodded to the nurse. "Size seven and eight trach tubes ready in two, then."

"Yes, sir."

Dirk turned to the sink to scrub up, stomping the pedal below the sink for sterile foam soap. Normally, he wouldn't scrub his hands, but he did have four minutes and something to decide. *Hurry, hurry, little girl.*

The motion sensor activated the faucet. Dirk held his hands under the barely tolerable hot water. He smoothed suds on the backs of his hands, between his fingers, his fingernails while the tune of "Happy Birthday" played in his head. To think, some surgeons only washed their hands for nine seconds. Then again, even the good ones didn't clean up quite as thoroughly as he did.

"Happy birthday, dear someone. Happy birthday to you."

He took his hands out of the stream of water, and the faucet shut off. Too bad for the dialysis patient. Some days you got the fast nurse, other days she didn't make it back soon enough.

Dirk called for the patient's chart. A nurse shoved her way through the activity of the busy ER, and the folder found his hand. He ducked around the corner, already skimming the open file, though he didn't read a single word.

Ever since he could remember, he'd been a brilliant mimic. At eight, he could listen to his next door neighbor's Spanish and reproduce it perfectly regardless of the fact that he didn't know what the words meant. He could watch his cousin practice karate kicks and copy them so well that all the kids in his homeroom thought he took karate, too. This talent extended to everything he needed: dialects, demeanors—human emotions.

He produced a paper from his lab coat, a paper he kept ready every day, just in case. One quick swish with his pen, and he was back amongst the fray in the ER right in time to see the EMTs crash through the door with the dialysis patient.

Dirk dropped the file on a counter and rushed toward the gurney. "What measures have we taken?"

An EMT with a mustache and goatee answered. "Regular procedure with calcium chloride, plus an amp of sodium bicarb. Got her back for a minute, then she crashed again."

"Right," Dirk said. He touched a hand to her throat to check for pulse, breath. "Get me the ET tubes—"

"Dr. Harris…"

"ET tubes. Now!"

A tech at his side put the tube into his hand. He tilted the patient's head back and opened her mouth, depressed her tongue with a finger.

"Dr. Harris!" the nurse called again, this time louder. Panicked.

Hand still holding the tube poised at the patient's mouth, Dirk wheeled around. "What?"

It was the same nurse who hadn't made it with the tubes before he was finished washing his hands. She piped up again, timid. "Dr. Harris, I don't know how I missed it, but there's a DNR on file."

He widened his eyes, adopted the face of shock mixed with anger. "Are you sure?"

The young brunette's head bobbed up and down, and her eyes filled with tears. "Yes."

Dirk let the trach tube fall out of his hand. He bit his lip hard and looked at the floor. "What time is it?"

"Six-fifteen," a tech replied.

"Time of death, six-fifteen," he whispered. Then, for emphasis, he added, "Fuck!"

As Dirk trudged away from the gurney, one of the nurses he'd worked with a long time caught stride with him and laid a hand on his shoulder. "Dr. Harris, I know that must've been difficult for you."

Oh, really, now?

"That's my Mom. But for the grace of God, that's her." He said it, because he knew it was what the nurse wanted to hear. He said it, because the statement would keep him treading through the status quo.

He said it, because it was so easy to make all of them believe.

CHAPTER 9

CUP OF COFFEE in hand, Carbon snoring on her feet, McKenzie flipped the page of her high school yearbook. The Jonas Cleary at the cafe was like a specter compared to the one pictured on page eighty-seven. Then again, she'd changed quite a bit from the smiling, vivacious girl on page ninety. She glanced at her reflection in her computer monitor. Yep. Eyes more sunken, something missing behind them. Or maybe something added, like the knowledge of what it feels like to lose someone. Loss could change a person.

Maybe after this serial killer story died down, she'd have some time to do some more digging into Jonas' wife's case, see if she could turn up anything. Levi flashed in again, his limp form staring up at her the way it had after he'd died. Questioning. Accusing.

She shook the thought away. McKenzie wiggled her mouse to wake up her desktop monitor. The chances of this attempt going well were about as good as the chances of Morton Gaines becoming the new spokesman for Weight Watchers. She'd been stalking her Skype all evening, but Jig's icon remained unavailable. Nevertheless, she opened Skype one more time.

Her heart leapt into her fingertips at the sight of the green light. Her fingers flew faster than her thoughts.

Jig?

A solid sixty seconds went by before the pencil on the screen signified Jig was replying.

> *to what do i owe the pleasure, mckenzie mcclendon?*

What the hell?

> *How do you know who I am?*

The pencil moved again.

> *lmao. because i'm a wizard.*

McKenzie replied again, wary of boring or pissing off Jig.

> *You're the only person I know of who can help me.*

Before she could send the next thought on her mind, Jig had already replied.

> *i'd love to commiserate with you that noah hutchins followed his—erm—sniper rifle—to greener pastures, but i happen to know the ammo wasn't that powerful...*

McKenzie half-choked on her coffee, then hit backspace to clear what she'd written. She typed again.

> *It's not that, though I'd love to share war stories with you sometime. I'm looking for information on the infant who was found in the New York subway.*

Then, as an afterthought:

> *The autopsy information.*

The pencil icon hesitated before moving.

> *you and every other reporter in the country.*

McKenzie tapped her fingers on the edge of the keyboard.

> *Fortunately for me, not every other reporter in the country has been indirectly introduced to your*

internet handle before.

No hesitation of the pencil this time.

ha. i like you.

This was a delicate balance not to be upset. Jig was the most skilled person she'd ever found at ferreting out hidden information. Even better than Pierce had been. She was also the most evasive, prickly, and secretive. Still, McKenzie's impatience won out.

Does this mean you'll help me?

McKenzie knew what was coming even before the response displayed on the screen.

what's in it for me?

Of all times to have not prepared for a quiz.

Um. A steak dinner and my eternal gratitude?

The response came instantly.

eternal gratitude for one story? wow. talk about making a deal with the devil.

Christ. This must've been how Alice felt talking to the Caterpillar in Wonderland.

Is that a yes?

Jig started typing again, stopped, then typed some more. Finally, the answer materialized.

this better be a damn good steak.

CHAPTER 10

"TREVIN, THERE ARE other ways to work through this anxiety. Relaxation techniques. I can get you in to see a massage therapist. We'll find you meetings—"

The young lawyer's hands shook like a Parkinson's patient. It had taken him months to find a doctor liberal enough to write prescriptions for benzodiazepines like they were Tic Tacs, but now here she was, preaching the same crap he'd come to her to escape. "Dr. Kettleman, I don't need an NA sponsor. I need you to fucking *help* me."

The psychiatrist rested her chin onto her cappuccino colored pointer fingers. "I'm *trying* to help you, Trevin."

Trevin stood and paced. He had far more important things to do besides beg his psychiatrist for drugs, even if this visit would make those later chores easier. "I thought you understood this. I came to you because you understood."

Dr. Kettleman swallowed hard. "I have a better understanding than most doctors on this front, Trevin, which is why I've given you so much leeway up until now. But don't you think it's time you confronted this? You'll have to at some point, you know. There *will* be an intervention. It's all about whether or not you choose to do it on your own terms."

Trevin wheeled to face her, his neck hot. "Is that a threat? Every single thing I have said in this room is protected by doctor-patient confidentiality. God help me, I will slap a lawsuit on you so fast—"

"Trevin! Trevin. It's not a threat. I'm simply saying that something like this isn't conducive to normal life. It won't go unchecked forever. Something in your life will intervene."

He collapsed onto the couch and gripped its edge. Sweat from his palms slicked wet prints on the leather sofa. *You have no fucking idea.* "I don't need a lecture, Dr. Kettleman. You and I both know I'll get what I need whether you help me or not. It's a matter of if I get *other* things in the process."

Her shoulders sagged as she reached for the drawer that held her prescription pads. Good people were pretty predictable. Push the right buttons, and the shell of the "supposed to" side would crack and expose the center of compassion.

"Thank you," Trevin muttered. He accepted the prescription for a box of clean needles.

She gave a half-hearted shrug. "I want to see you back here in two weeks. I only hope you'll be ready to let me help you in a different way before it's too late, Trevin."

He shook the woman's hand but ignored the warm, it'll-be-okay smile that came with it.

It might already be too late, Dr. Kettleman. I need to get my ass out of here so I can find out.

Why had he thought this was a good idea? Fuck his job. Fuck Ollie at his office with her blue hair and her watermelon Bubblicious. Fuck the Petersons. How was it possible that something so fucking complicated could become exponentially worse overnight?

And now, he'd made it to the one place that could make him even more anxious than he already was.

Trevin had left Dr. Kettleman's and gone straight to the PATH station. During the fourteen minute train ride to Jersey, he'd repeatedly rehearsed his back story to make sure he knew his plan. Yet somehow, now that he was about to walk into the main administration building of the Hudson County Juvenile Detention Center, he still had no clue what he was doing.

He'd already worked out how he would gain access to the files. Or rather, how he *hoped* he'd get his hands on them. Whether or not it would work was another story entirely.

Maybe I should say I need a liver transplant instead of a kidney. I probably do need one, or will. Wonder how my liver's doing these days? Too bad I don't really have a brother. I know the perfect person who could obtain the liver from him for me.

Trevin smiled at the woman behind the counter and hoped she didn't see him wipe his sweaty palms on his trousers.

"Can I help you?" she asked, returning his warm smile.

"I sure hope so, ma'am," he said, letting his accent become a tad Southern around the edges. "You see, I'm in a bit of a mess, but I'm hoping you'll bear with me for a second. My brother and I—our parents died in a car wreck when we were little. I was adopted, but my brother stayed in foster care. I know he was adopted by another family some time later. And now, well, frankly," he cast his eyes downward, sad, "I need to find him really bad. I need a liver transplant, and he's my only living relative that I know for sure would be a match, see. I don't even know if he'd be willing, but I have to try."

The middle-aged Puerto Rican woman gaped at him, engrossed. "How can I help?"

"Well, one of the only things I've been able to find out about my brother is that he was here for a while. His foster parents' neighbors heard through the grapevine that he'd gotten into trouble and was sent to juvey after his new family adopted him. They didn't know his adoptive family's name, and the foster parents have long since moved. I know the year he was in juvey, and I actually tracked down a guy who was in detention the same year he was who remembers a contraband smuggling incident involving a guy he said matched my brother's description."

The woman now had her head cocked, eyebrows furrowed in confusion and disbelief. He'd better wrap this up, and quick, before she shut him down. "Long story short, if I could somehow look at the files from that time period and find that incident, I could find my brother's current name. Then I'd know where to start looking for him."

She was already shaking her head. "I'm sorry, sir, but you can't walk in here and access those files. Juvenile records are sealed for privacy, sir. Now, if you can get a court order to release them, then it might be possible for me to help you, but—"

Trevin leaned on the counter and dropped his head into his hands. After a few long deep breaths and a fake sob or two, he looked up at her with pleading eyes. "Please. I don't have time to file for a court order. Miss, I'm dying. If I don't get that transplant soon, my kids won't have a dad."

Whoa, Trevin. Bringing in non-existent spawn. Nice!

He added, "I have to find my brother before it's too late."

She glanced at her watch and licked her puffy, red-coated lips. Her gaze shifted from side to side. "What years did you say he was here again?"

"It would've been 1988-1991," Trevin called as she turned her back to walk into the room behind her. He smoothed his hands over the top of his head. *Was this actually about to work?*

A second later, the clerk returned and motioned for him to follow her. Trevin walked around the desk and tagged along behind her through a large conference room into a smaller, windowless area lined with shelves and filing cabinets all the way to its ceiling. On the wooden table in the center of the room was a box full of folders.

"Take your time," she said, "but if you're caught, I'll swear you broke in through the window."

Then, she looked around the room at the lack of windows, winked, and pulled the door to.

Holy shit. This was actually about to work.

CHAPTER 11

A WATCHED COMPUTER never receives messages, so both McKenzie and Carbon jumped when her desktop dinged with the sound of an incoming e-mail. Her stomach fluttered as she clicked her inbox.

Her eyes darted back and forth across the page until she was about halfway down. She slipped a hand underneath her hair and rubbed her neck. What now?

> *McKenzie,*
>
> *I apologize for how I acted the other day. I know I didn't make it easy for you to listen to me, and in acting that way, I put you in an awkward situation. I'm not proud of what I've turned into, but I'm moving on as best I can. Anyway, I hope you won't hold it against me if we run into each other again. Thanks for meeting up with me.*
>
> *Best,*
>
> *Jonas*
>
> *P.S. And now I'm sorry for this awkward, rambling e-mail.*
>
> *P.P.S. I'm also sorry for apologizing so much.*

So, the Jonas she remembered *did* still exist somewhere behind those bloodshot eyeballs. She really should've given him more benefit of the doubt. After all, he had lost his wife and kid. What had she expected? A completely normal, happy-go-lucky guy with a Labrador?

The memory of attending her little cousin Levi's memorial service surged forth in her mind. Levi's mother, screaming in her face. "Was it worth it, McKenzie? Was my little boy's life worth the front page? How dare you show your face here after you made him just one more stepping stone on your career path. If it wasn't for you, we wouldn't be here at all!"

The woman had been a ghost of herself, furious and hollow all at the same time. And Jonas had lost not only his son, but his wife, too. They'd gone out one day and never come home.

McKenzie revisited the open browser tab where she'd been browsing Noelle Cleary's Facebook page. It had turned into something of a tribute page after her death, but her own photos and posts lingered. A status of "making an all-organic dinner for the boys," a picture of their little family in front of a mantle full of framed photographs.

A tiny plop told McKenzie she had a new Skype message. Jig was back.

> *against my better judgment, i have some information for you. anything specific you were hoping for, or should i unleash everything with reckless abandon?*

The whole report *did* sound good. But then again, so did keeping Jig's trust.

> *Connected to one of the dead pregnant girls, I'm guessing?*

McKenzie waited for Jig's response.

> *of course.*

Oh, I forgot. I have to ask if I want to know something.

How did they connect...him? Her?

The pencil pushed on the screen as Jig responded.

> *her. one of the drugs found in the baby's tox screen matched a drug in the mother's.*

For a second, McKenzie's fingers froze. Then, they unstuck and flew across the keyboard.

> *Drugs? As in, plural? The police only said one drug had been found in the women.*

The pencil moved again.

> *well, they would, wouldn't they? there was only one drug of note in the other victims.*

McKenzie drew a sharp breath.

> *Okay, Jig. Steak and dessert.*

Jig typed back.

> *cheesecake?*

A woman after my own heart.
McKenzie typed.

> *Is there anything else?*

A few seconds later, Jig's response flashed up on the screen.

> *well, now that i know cheesecake is involved...yes, there's been a little development with the baby being found. the victims were drugged with propofol. one detail the po-po haven't released to the public is that they can't find an injection site on any of the victims. now, call me crazy, but that's a problem.*

McKenzie knew from past experience that there was only one

thing to do in this situation besides dangle a lame bribe: unconditionally pander to Jig's God complex.

So, what've you spotted that the cops haven't?

There was barely a pause before the pencil moved again.

> *haha. you jest. i shall bite, tho. when the cradle robber's victims were printed, pathology noted that their palms were extra oily. standard, really, with murder victims. anxiety can cause profuse sweating prior to death. so, this palm thing was something no one looked at twice until today, when traces of dimethyl sulfoxide were found in the infant.*

McKenzie's brow wrinkled.

> *Dimethyl de-who-be-what?*

As if anticipating the question, Jig's response almost overlapped McKenzie's query.

> *dimethyl sulfoxide, or dmso. the agent has been tested for use in products like nicotine patches, seasick patches, pain patches. ok, mckenzie. for the game point, what do all of these medical supplies have in common?*

McKenzie typed back.

> *Patches.*

Jig's pencil moved.

> *ding ding ding! winner, winner, winner!*

McKenzie ignored the banter.

> *So, this DMSO stuff somehow makes the drug able to be delivered...through the skin?*

After a few seconds, a short paragraph appeared from Jig.

> *yes. basically, it makes the skin uber porous while also having the rare talent of being able to carry other drugs across membranes into the body. this is why they want to use it in seasick patches, etc. it's a transdermal delivery system.*

McKenzie cocked her head, considering the implications.

> *Why aren't needles out of business if this stuff exists?*

Jig answered:

> *does my profile list me as a medical doctor somewhere i don't know about?*

Actually, McKenzie had no idea what Jig did for a living. She wasn't sure she wanted to know, but she was almost positive she wouldn't find out if she asked.

> *Sorry, sometimes I forget you don't know everything.*

Jig's response was lightning quick.

> *whoa! i said i wasn't an m.d. i never said i didn't know everything. my guess would be that the transdermal aspect depends on the dosage and what part of the body it needs to reach, etc. it isn't used as much as you'd think it could be, so obviously it's not all that reliable.*

Then, as McKenzie was typing her next question, Jig said:

> *at least, that's what google says.*

McKenzie wrote back.

> *Right. And my supposition would be that the FBI isn't planning to release this information any time prior to the next coming of the Messiah?*

McKenzie could imagine the smirk on the face of the woman she'd never seen.

> *heh. would you?*

Jig was right, of course. If McKenzie was the FBI, she'd keep that little fact tucked away as long as she could. Telling people in New York City not to touch anything a stranger gave them would be like telling the entire city that breathing the same air as pigeons would cause cancer. Talk about mass panic.

Before McKenzie could say anything else, though, Jig sent more.

> *hope it helps. by the way, friendly advice: don't get too google-happy with that info. let's just say between the two of us that ever since your little escapade last year, your records are about as private as a prison shower, threat to national security you are and all. and don't think i'm not going to take you up on that steak dinner. i'll be in touch.*

Then, a beat later, Jig added:

> *figuratively speaking, of course.*

CHAPTER 12

DIRK ALWAYS FOUND the airport refreshing. People so busy coming and going that they were too frazzled to notice anyone else. The general population people-watched in the same way tourists watched animals at the zoo: to observe them in their native habitat. The airport wasn't so much a habitat as it was a waiting room in between them. Therefore, everyone kept their eyes to themselves.

It amused him to know that as in every other aspect of life, he was in the minority.

Still, in case anyone *was* watching, he'd perfected the art of blending in. He sat inside the Mexican restaurant near his gate at LaGuardia, scarfing a burrito, black suitcase on wheels parked at his side. Ethnic cuisine at six in the morning: not okay. Not to mention the food tasted like something he'd swallowed and thrown up a couple of times. He really should pay more attention to details like this next time.

No sense worrying over that now, though. Not when Tahlia Roman sat two booths away with her own luggage. She was the important part.

Her left hand rested on her swollen belly as she downed her Pepsi gulp by gulp. Every time she set her glass down, she would return to the needlework in her lap.

How anyone working for Skylight Airlines bought her seven months pregnant story, Dirk would never know. The airline had strict regulations against women flying within a month of their due date, and the fact that hers was closing in was about as subtle as an onion sandwich. All the better for him, though. Made for a fun challenge.

She took the final bite of her taco, then started on the last of her chips. Showtime.

Dirk grabbed his tray in one hand and his suitcase handle with the other, barely hanging onto his Pepsi bottle by the top. He wheeled his luggage toward the trashcan, but as he passed Tahlia's booth, he let his suitcase brush hers just enough that it tipped toward her.

"Oh, gosh! I'm so sorry." He dropped his tray onto her table and picked up her bag.

She laughed politely. "No harm, no foul. I need to move along anyway."

The girl scooted to the end of the booth and clutched the sides of her own tray. Dirk stretched his hand toward her. "Let me get that for you."

"Thanks," Tahlia replied.

Dirk set his Pepsi on the table before picking up both trays and ushering them to the garbage bin. He got back right in time to offer her a hand. "Need a little help?"

The girl grasped his palm and used it to hoist her top-heavy frame out of the booth. "Moving up and down was easier when my circumference and height weren't the same thing."

"Probably easier to move around the airport, too. Where's your gate? I'll help you with your bags."

She smiled but shook her head. "Thanks, but there's no need. I'm really not far."

Tahlia heaped the skein of yarn on the table into the handbag she was crocheting with it, then picked up her carry-on bag and the needlework and started toward the door of the Mexican joint.

"If you say so," he said, but he followed behind her with his own things in tow.

Time for the clincher.

Dirk gestured to the bag she was knitting. "It's a cool skill you have. My wife loves that kind of stuff. She's been looking for a bag like that forever."

At this, Tahlia stopped and faced him. "Oh, yeah? I sell them on my website, if you think she'd want to look."

"No kidding?" he replied.

Hook, line, sinker.

Do you have any cards on you?"

She glanced in the direction of her sandaled feet. "No, I don't. I actually had some new ones printed up, but they had a typo in the web address. I'm having them redone."

Gee. Who could have predicted that?

"Bummer," he replied. His mouth twisted to the side as if he were pausing to think. "Maybe I can give you *my* card, and you can e-mail me some information about the bags. I really would like one for my wife. Her birthday's coming up."

"Sure. I'd love to."

Dirk stood in the middle of the terminal and made a production of rifling through his briefcase, half-dropping things as he went for the non-existent business cards. Finally, he thrust a stack of papers toward her. "Would you mind holding these?"

"Yeah. Sure. No problem."

When Tahlia took the papers, he extended a folder and his Pepsi bottle. "Thanks. I'd *have* to put them all the way in the bottom, wouldn't I? Bad planning."

A few seconds later, Tahlia squeaked. Her free hand grabbed his arm, and her weight swayed into him.

"Oh, oh, oh," she mumbled. Her feet steadied, but she shook her head hard as she leaned away from him back onto her own feet. "Sorry. I felt so dizzy all of a—"

His capable arms caught her smoothly underneath her armpits as she toppled backward. "Steady, there, now. Surely you didn't have anything stronger than Pepsi in your condition?"

Her next words came out feathery and slurred. "I don't feel

so good."

Dirk reached around her waist and snugged her against him. For the next few minutes at least, he needed her trust. "Don't worry. We're going to find you some help, okay? Walk with me as best you can. I'll do the rest."

CHAPTER 13

MCKENZIE BOLTED UPRIGHT in her bed, drenched in sweat. She looked around, defenses up as though she were about to battle some unknown enemy lurking in the shadows.

Then she heard Carbon's snores from the floor and realized she was only in her bedroom. She must've fallen asleep while trying to figure out how the heck to research DMSO.

She lay back against the cool pillow, catching her breath from the nightmare that had awoken her. She focused on retracing the train of thought she'd been following before she drifted off.

If the FBI wasn't releasing the information, the last thing she needed was for them to get word she was on to the story. She'd known they were probably watching her, but something about having confirmation soured her stomach.

Finally, she threw the covers off and padded to the computer desk again. DMSO wasn't the only thing she could search. Her current city in the online yellow pages was set in another state, but that didn't matter.

She punched in the number of the first listing and responded to each prompt from the automated system. Talking to a live human being was imperative.

"Pharmacy," a voice said.

"Can you tell me what dimethyl sulfoxide is used to treat?"

A long pause. "Pardon?"

"Um—you see, I found out that my daughter has a bottle of it. She swears it's not a street drug, that the doctor gave it to her, but she, uh, won't tell me what it's for," McKenzie blurted.

Shit.

Then, she added, "Please. I'm worried."

"Ma'am, it's not possible for me to give out information about a specific patient's prescriptions—"

"Oh, no! I'm not asking about her by *name*," McKenzie cut off the pharmacy tech. "I'm asking about the *drug*. Surely you can tell me what the drug is?"

Another long pause. "Dimethyl sulfoxide is used as a topical analgesic or for swelling, especially in conjunction with interstitial bladder infections. It can also be used as a dietary supplement." A moment later, the technician spoke again, her voice lower. "It's nothing she's addicted to. Nothing to fret about."

McKenzie thanked her and ended the phone call. Bladder infections certainly lent credibility to the already prevalent idea that a doctor—chiefly an OB/GYN—could be the Cradle Robber. An OB/GYN would see a lot of bladder infections and know how to extract a fetus. Still, narrowing the list down to OB/GYNs or those with similar knowledge wasn't exactly groundbreaking. There had to be other angles on the DMSO.

After a short Google search on bladder infections, McKenzie was ready to move again.

Next listing, please.

This time, she asked for the pharmacist directly. When he picked up, she launched into her spiel. "I was prescribed a medication for cystitis, but I need to check with you to make sure it doesn't contain dimethyl sulfoxide. I was prescribed something with that years ago when I had a bladder infection, and I found out I'm allergic."

"Of course," the pharmacist answered. "What's the medication?"

"Vistaril," she parroted from the website on her screen.

"No, ma'am," he replied. "Vistaril is an antihistamine. It tends to reduce urinary frequency, which is probably why your doctor prescribed it. You're safe as far as allergies are concerned."

"Oh, okay," she replied, then quickly went on. "Is it only a certain drug that contains that DMSO stuff so I can avoid it, or is it an ingredient in a lot of things? My mom couldn't remember if it was a generic version of a drug I was prescribed that I was allergic to or an ingredient in a drug."

She could hear the clicking as the pharmacist typed on his computer. He was probably using Google just like Jig. After a moment, he said, "Actually, it's both. It can be used in generic, but for cystitis, the brand form is Rimso-50."

"Rimso-50. Great. I—"

Before she could ask another floundering question, the pharmacist interjected. "But you're probably reasonably safe here, since most doctors warn you when they prescribe that drug. It has a nasty side effect—gives off a pungent garlic smell. That can be a big deal breaker for people."

"Are there—"McKenzie almost jumped into the next question she'd scripted for herself when her brain caught up with his words. "Wait. Did you say garlic smell?"

The pharmacist laughed. "Yeah, I know. Odd, isn't it? But yes. Dimethyl sulfoxide produces both a garlic odor and garlic-like taste in patients."

"Thanks." She hung up as the pieces crashed in—asteroids hitting. Serial killer. DMSO. Garlic. Jonas. Noelle.

Jonas had smelled garlic on Noelle before he gave her mouth to mouth. He'd assumed it was from their lunch at the Italian restaurant, but what if it had been from *this?*

Oh, God.

Deep breaths.

She opened her Skype and typed a single question, one that hadn't seemed important before but that now felt key. The computer wiz wasn't online, but maybe Jig would reply when she got back.

It was no more than three seconds before Jig's reply popped

up on her screen.

Bitch has been hiding from me.

The subway infant was the *exception,* not the rule. She was the only baby that had been found. Gibb—a year old at the time Noelle was killed—hadn't been found. Signs pointed to Noelle's murderer being the Cradle Robber, only she hadn't been pregnant at the time. This was exactly why she had typed the question to Jig:

> *What did they determine to be the cause of death of the infant?*

Now she stared at the reply, mouth gaping. If Jig's information was correct, she had a new angle all right. Pregnancies weren't the killer's thing. Not directly, at least.

The face of the surrogate in Dr. Schwetzer's office flitted to mind as Jig's response glared back at her from the screen:

> *the infant's lungs weren't inflated. in other words, the baby was stillborn, not murdered.*

Good God. He didn't want pregnant women because they were his "type." He wanted them because they carried a precious cargo that gave him a profit.

CHAPTER 14

FROM A HUNDRED yards out, Jonas couldn't tell if James Kruger was crying. It wasn't the distance so much as that he'd been avoiding looking at the man as much as possible. He was all too aware of how much it sucked, the way people goggled, watching for your reaction as you put your wife into the ground.

It was probably his worst idea ever, showing up at Liza Kruger's memorial service. The cops would be scouring it for anyone who didn't belong. After all, any Lookie Lous at the Subway Girl's funeral might be something more sinister. It was both why he shouldn't have come and why he had at the same time. A common trait amongst serial killers was a need to continue to watch the grief and chaos they'd caused, the need to re-experience the power the kill gave them.

And if Liza's killer was here, so was Noelle's.

The scent of the freshly-dug earth rode the wind as the pastor said the final prayer and the crowd broke. Jonas tried to etch the faces of every mourner into his mind. A hint of smugness, some lingering pleasure might give an imposter away. So far, nothing but distress.

"I thought I might find you here."

He wheeled around to see McKenzie McClendon. "Am I that predictable?"

She cocked her head, studied him. "Maybe not so much predictable as intentional."

"Touché. I figured I'd make myself easy to find if you forgave me for the——er——*incident.*"

McKenzie kicked at the dirt with her black high heel. "You must've been confident I'd find something."

"I told you I was," he said, his blood racing. She knew something. Something he hadn't known before.

"I think you may be right. About the murders being connected, I mean."

"What changed your mind?"

She squinted. "That's a need-to-know sort of a detail."

His breath caught in his throat like a dragon choking down fire.

Control yourself.

"Who needs to know more than me?"

She raised her eyebrows. "You're a little more composed than the last time I saw you, Jonas."

He bit his lip hard and cracked his neck to the side. "I thought I'd wait until *after* the service to crack a new bottle, if you must know."

"How thoughtful."

God, he wanted to punch something. "Look, McKenzie, can we cut the shit? I'm way too sober for the tease. Either tell me why you came or leave me in peace. I have a serial killer to stalk."

"Right. Let's talk about that, actually."

"About what?" he asked.

"If we do what I'm thinking about doing, you can't have a gin bottle in your hand half the time. Alcoholics don't make reliable partners in high-stakes environments, and frankly, I'm not big enough to carry you out of the line of fire if anything goes wrong. I have enough deaths on my conscience without adding another one to it."

The line of fire? Deaths?

"I know what you saw, but I hold my liquor quite well, thank you very mu——"

"*Besides,*" she interjected, "as you've already pointed out in your perfectly constructed bait e-mail, drunk isn't the best way to make people take you seriously."

Jonas' teeth clenched. "If you weren't taking me seriously, you wouldn't be here, McKenzie. So what are we talking about doing?"

"This goes no further than you."

"I don't have anywhere for it to go," he replied.

She reached up and took off her sunglasses. "The killer is using a very specific drug to incapacitate his victims. He's also using another drug to introduce the first one into the victim. This particular drug leaves a garlic odor behind."

As sure as he was she'd dig something up, this wasn't what he'd expected. "Garlic?"

She nodded. "It would also explain how Noelle might've died of cardiac arrest. This drug helps other drugs be absorbed through the skin."

His chest tightened. "That fuc—"

"Jonas." McKenzie shoved her hands in her pockets, hair whipping in the wind. "Another thing I don't have room for is a half-cocked temper. Seriously. I understand the whole righteous anger thing. I really do. Better than you may think. But if you lose it every time you hear a new detail, we won't even make it out of the starting gate before you need me to bail you out of jail. Trust me when I say I won't."

Jonas sucked in a breath, held it. So, he should shut up and deal with it even though it felt like a rhinoceros was sitting on his chest. Check. He breathed out his next words deliberately slow, quiet. "He gave her some drug through her skin that caused her to have a heart attack?"

"Maybe. I don't know yet. If the garlic's a coincidence, it's a huge one."

"Right," Jonas said.

Keep breathing.

"And this mission you keep referring to?"

McKenzie twisted her heel into the soft dirt beside him. After a long minute, she looked up, staring into his eyes, her mouth set in a hard line. "I think your son might still be alive."

At this, Jonas guffawed. "Excuse me?"

She shoved her sunglasses back on. "Laugh all you want, but killing the babies isn't part of his M.O."

It couldn't be.

"Care to explain?"

"Jonas, I don't know anything for sure. This is all speculation—"

He cut her off. "Let's just assume for the moment that I'm hearing everything you say with all the proper disclaimers in place. What the hell is it you know?"

McKenzie leaned against the fence, crossing her arms. "The subway baby wasn't killed. It died of natural causes."

"And your point would be?"

"If the same guy murdered Subway Girl and Noelle, then maybe he had the same plan for your baby as he did for the Subway baby."

"Liza," Jonas muttered. "Her name was Liza."

"What?"

He gestured toward the graveside service. "Liza."

"Oh," McKenzie stammered. "Right. Liza."

Stop being a blithering idiot.

"Yeah. Okay. Back to his intentions with Gibb. What are you saying those were, exactly?"

"Again, all speculation, but they've found one baby. Out of all the women, they've found *one.* That one happens to have died naturally."

"You're telling me this guy is running some kind of nursery for his victims' kids? He kills their moms, then rocks a dozen babies to sleep?"

"More of an orphanage," McKenzie said. "I interviewed an OB/GYN today. I met a girl in his lobby—a surrogate. That's what I think she said, anyway. Point is, she popped into my head when I heard the baby died of natural causes. What if the other kids haven't been found because he's using them for something?"

This chick bitched at me for being drunk. She's gotta be smoking some of the best crack the Big Apple has to offer.

"For what? Selling them as slaves? I know about human trafficking and all that, but I'm pretty sure they're a little older than womb-age, McKenzie."

"Thank you, smartass, but I'm not talking about human trafficking, at least not the way you're referring to it. I may be talking about the black market, though."

Jonas frowned. He'd follow this backass maze of McKenzie's thought process way better if he had a double scotch right now. "You think my son was sold on the black market?"

"Lots of couples are desperate to have kids, Jonas. Many are willing to cut legal corners to do it, too. If my hunch is right, it could be a way to find your son and maybe even find who killed Noelle."

It was ludicrous, but at the same time, how could he turn her down? No one else had been willing to help him. Maybe someone finally believed him.

"But, McKenzie, if the police couldn't find Gibb when he was first kidnapped, how do you figure *you* can find him? Even if he wasn't killed, there's no way to trace him."

She tipped her sunglasses down on her nose and peeked at him over the frames. "There was no way to trace him back then. There might be now."

CHAPTER 15

EVERITT STARED OUT the window at the suburban yard. As if sleeping wasn't hard enough with the baby kicking her in the kidneys every three minutes, she had to have cabin fever on top of it. She would fake a heart attack if it meant the Petersons would take her to the hospital. Anything for some fresh air. Until she'd come to this place, she hadn't been aware mothballs were made anymore. Now, she smelled them on her clothes, her bedspread, her bathrobes, drapes, and everything else cloth in this house.

Everitt left the window and climbed into bed. She lay back, staring at the ceiling and thinking. Sarah Peterson was nice enough, but every time Everitt mentioned leaving the house, the woman sidestepped with some explanation for why it wasn't needed, was a bad idea, or could be taken care of in a manner that didn't involve moving. Everitt wasn't exactly in a position to argue.

She rolled onto her side and pulled open the drawer of the nightstand, one of the only pieces of furniture besides the bed. A Bible rested in the otherwise bare drawer.

She hadn't known the Petersons were church types, but it made sense. Sarah and Rodney's less than intimate side hugs definitely made them seem like the "we-only-have-sex-on-Thursdays-and-on-Valentine's-Day" sort of couple.

It might be the only available book to read, but even as bored as she was, the Bible didn't sound like pleasure reading. She was pretty sure there was a lot of stuff about unwed mothers. If she ever did get to sleep, she'd rather not have nightmares about being stoned to death or saying hello to Satan. She closed the drawer, pushed herself off the bed, and headed into the hall.

Time for escape attempt number fifty-seven.

For such a homey couple, the townhouse didn't feel lived-in. Not a lot of pictures or knick-knacks, heavy damask draperies that hadn't been dusted since the place was built. Oh, well. They'd gotten so old they couldn't have kids. They were bound to be a little depressed.

Everitt turned the corner, then ducked back out of view. Sarah was on the phone.

"Felicia, you have to stop passing along our names to everyone you meet. I was happy to work with you, but it's attracting way more attention than you want it to." Sarah's voice sounded so different than the one Everitt was used to. This one was low, almost a growl. "I understand that, *dear,* but just see to it it's the last. Goodbye."

Everitt peeked around the door to see Sarah sit down at the table. She gathered up the mail, squared it into a neat pile, then sorted it into separate stacks.

What the heck was that all about?

Still, Everitt knew better than to ask. Sarah was about as likely to give her an answer as she was to fall for Everitt's next getaway try.

"You know, I should really go by the old place and pick up my mail. Bills and stuff I have to pay," Everitt said, entering the kitchen.

Sarah looked up from the stack of envelopes and stared blankly at Everitt for a moment. Then, she smiled. "No worries, dear. I already had your mail forwarded to our address."

Everitt's heart galloped a beat.

Could she do that?

Her mind momentarily blanked. "I thought you had to do that in person," Everitt stammered.

"Oh, no. You can do it online. I figured it'd save you all that walking. It's a long way to go for a girl in your condition."

Everitt forced down her retort. Sarah was only trying to help. It was just...Jesus. She said the word "condition" like pregnancy was Alzheimer's disease or a clubfoot.

Remain calm, and don't say, "Thanks, grandma."

"Thanks. That was nice of you."

Sarah returned her attention to her mail. "I was thinking we'd order in Chinese for lunch. How does that sound?"

"Awesome," Everitt replied as she turned her back on Sarah.

How many delivery places for Chinese are there in New York City? We'll have to go out for groceries or a nice sit down restaurant meal sometime, surely.

She closed the door to her room and drew back the lace curtain over the window. Why couldn't Sarah understand walking might be *good* for a pregnant person? She shook her head in exasperation.

Everitt dropped the curtain and turned back to the bed. She retrieved her cell phone from between the mattress and box springs. Even now, she wasn't sure why she'd hidden it. The Petersons said she could bring all her clothes and possessions when she moved in, and they hadn't banned cell phones in that decree. But while she might not have a shred of *maternal* instinct, she did have *people* instinct, and her gut told her to hide the phone.

The bed groaned underneath her.

Jesus Louisas, this thing has seen better days.

Her chest tugged as she flipped the phone on.

Ignore it, girl. You need this money.

She'd be in deep shit if she went back on the deal with the Petersons. Drug money wasn't an issue—she'd quit the junk cold turkey when she realized she could make way more money as a surrogate than she could on the street corners in thigh high boots. Then again, sucking the cocks of sleazy husbands cheating on their wives had been why she started that junk in the first place. The problem was she'd gotten knocked up all on her own *before* she found a couple who needed a surrogate.

Then, she met the Petersons. They'd agreed to pay her expenses—as well as compensate her as a surrogate if they were allowed to adopt her baby. All she had to do was sign the paperwork. The only other option would be lying on her back in a cheap motel, and even if she wanted to go back to that, she couldn't. Johns didn't want pregnant girls—at least none she'd be alone with without a can of mace, handcuffs, and a machete.

Everitt had to have some human contact other than Grandma Sarah downstairs or she'd lose her mind. Maybe she could inhale the cleaner under the bathroom sink to induce labor. Maybe one of those weird-smelling aroma therapy candles Sarah lit in her room at night to create a "calming environment for the baby" would send Everitt over the damned edge soon. The baby was fine in its warm, womb-juice cocoon.

She scrolled through her contact list. Shame she didn't have anything to say or anybody to say it to. Still, knowing someone was on the other end of the phone might keep her from chewing off her own hand. Her mom was a no, as was her dad. The couple of girlfriends she had would be "working," and their pimps got pissed if they used their cells too much. Really, the only person she could text would be Zan.

Definitely not my first choice.

Still, better than nothing. Maybe.

> *Hey. Just letting you know I moved in with the couple who's adopting the baby until it's born.*

Everitt left out the part about compensation for surrogacy. He hadn't wanted anything to do with her or the baby anymore, but she'd bet that if he found out cash was involved, he'd be back in her life before you could say, "Da-Da."

In case you wanted to know. BTW, I'm a little stir crazy here. Ppl are nice, but I wouldn't be surprised if they own stock in Denta-Grip and a mothball company.

Then, just before she closed her phone and squeezed it back beneath the mattress, she sent one final text:

Need to get away from Old Lady Poly-Sure for a while. Can u think of any good excuses?

CHAPTER 16

ACRID SMOKE FILLED the airplane cabin, thick and oily with toxic fumes.

"Don't worry, baby," Gertie Plymouth said in the calmest, cheeriest voice she could muster. She pressed her palm against five-year-old Alaina's back. "We're just gonna go where the nice flight attendants tell us."

Alaina's thick little hands clutched the straps of her purple backpack, blonde curls bobbing as she shuffled down the aisle. "But what about your suitcase, Gamma?"

"They'll bring it to me later, sweet pea."

"Shit!" someone screamed. The man behind Gertie shoved her hard, the heel of his hand painful between her shoulder blades. Everyone jostled, tried to move fast in a line that wasn't budging at all. A woman up ahead cried hysterically, gasping, "I can't breathe!"

Gertie had avoided flying for sixty-five years of her life, because she feared things exactly like this. In her imagination, these nightmares always involved falling out of the sky rather than beginning after the plane had already landed. Surely they were okay. They were on the ground, right? Still, they sat on top of four hundred tons of metal and heated fuel.

And there was smoke in the cabin.

Over the sobs, grunts, and panicked fray in the coach cabin of the 747, a flight attendant hollered, "Listen up!"

Behind her, two other attendants worked around the door.

The people jammed in the plane aisle got quiet.

"Folks, we're about to deploy the emergency evacuation chutes. When I do this, I need everyone to do a couple of things for me. Cross your arms over your chest—" as she said this, she brought both arms across her torso to demonstrate, "—and keep your heels up when you jump. Most important, jump! When it's your turn at the door, fall right onto the slide. Keep moving. That way, we can evacuate everyone as quickly as possible."

Before Gertie's mind could process the information she'd just heard, the side door of the plane opened, sunlight burning her eyes. The line moved rapidly in front of her. Gertie's feet urged her forward.

"Go!" the attendant shouted, and it was only then she realized she was at the door. Gertie stared at her like she was speaking a foreign language. How did she do this again?

When Alaina hopped onto the slide, arms tucked over her body, Gertie's brain kicked in. "Alaina," she squeaked, then leapt out behind her granddaughter.

God, please don't let her be hurt!

No need to worry. In the panicked blur as she slid, Gertie saw one of the grounds crew members scoop up Alaina at the bottom of the slide and set her to her feet.

Wind rushed Gertie's face, and she reached out thankfully to the man standing there to help her up. Ambulances wailed while crew members shouted, trying to direct the distraught passengers away from the scene.

"The tire blew on the landing," a nearby woman told someone next to her. "It started the fire."

Gertie leaned in to catch what the people were saying, all the while looking around to find out where she and Alaina needed to go next. Most people, shocked and nervous, did the easiest thing. They stood rooted in a giant clump just past where they cleared the slide.

She felt tugging on her pants leg.

"Gamma?" Alaina said, yanking her trousers.

Gertie reached down absent-mindedly and patted her granddaughter's back. "Hang on a minute, baby. Gamma's trying to see what we need to—"

"What's that?" Alaina asked, pointing.

But Gertie had already seen what her granddaughter was gesturing toward. In a quick swoop, she grabbed Alaina and hustled in the other direction, holding her grandchild's face to her shoulder. "Oh, that's just probably just part of the wreckage. We have to move over here so we can make sure we're all ready to pick up our luggage and leave when the crew says it's okay."

Gertie's voice sounded shrill in her own ears. She couldn't help it, though.

In the name of all things holy.

She'd seen what Alaina had seen, probably what caused the shoddy landing. At the tail end of the plane, EMTs and police ran toward the very thing she was desperately trying to move her granddaughter away from.

Underneath the back wheel of the plane lay a woman's torso.

CHAPTER 17

DIRK WOULD BE the first to say he was pretty good at what he did. Still, no amount of practice could make certain things perfect. Too much depended on individual people. Thus, he'd learned to swing whichever way the wind blew and tailor his reaction to have, well, an equal and opposite reaction to whatever came up.

Which was exactly why now, as he knocked on Bonnie Ethridge's door, he stiffened his posture and readied his defense. He'd been seeing the chick for six months, but he never knew what mood she'd be in. Today was no exception, but he was still riding too high on the adrenaline rush from his latest jaunt to fret about Bonnie being pissed.

The door flew open, and the brassy blonde yelled, "Where the hell have you been? We were supposed to have lunch forty-five minutes ago."

Dirk stared into her eyes without blinking. "Look, Bonnie, I've had a long morning. I don't need this."

Her pupils constricted and her already skinny lips thinned into finer line. All those movie stars using up the collagen of the world, yet women like Bonnie ran around looking like a bad anime character with giant doe eyes and a comically tiny mouth.

She tapped her toe, arms folded in the classic "I'm a bitch, and I won't apologize for it" stance. "You've had a hard morning. Ha! *You* have. Never mind that I was fired day before yesterday, or that my computer crashed this morning—which, by the way, you never responded to my text. I need the number of the guy who fixed yours—"

Dirk's eyes slid out of focus as Bonnie droned on, her voice morphing into a sound akin to Charlie Brown's teacher. He'd gotten there as fast as he could, what with making the drop. Sure, she didn't know that, but her ignorance wouldn't ruin his good mood. Not when he could still hear Tahlia Roman's wheezes, her pleas as his knife sank into her. Fresh drops of crimson beading up on her onyx skin...

He forced the breath of an angry rhinoceros out of his nose. "You're not the only one with a hard life, Bonnie. I do the best I can. Most guys wouldn't be able to afford this place I'm taking you. I can because I work hard all day, but obviously that doesn't enter your head."

Her glare could've withered an entire vineyard from a mile away. Backing down was not in the cards.

On to Plan B.

As if they'd been waiting for their cue, the tears welled in his eyes. The anger from a moment ago melted like ice on the July pavement. "I'm sorry, Bonnie. It's only...I was on my way home when Mom called. My uncle had a stroke. He's in intensive care now. They don't know what the damage is yet."

The tension in her shoulders slackened, and her hand found his. "Oh, Dirk. I'm so sorry. Which hospital is he at? Should we go? Is your Mom okay?"

Of course she is. She has peach gummies. They're her favorite candy.

"No, we don't need to go anywhere. They're out of town. She'll keep me posted," he replied, wiping the non-existent snot from his nose with his sleeve. "I'm kind of numb right now. I feel like I can't help no matter how much I want to."

Bonnie's bird-like arms encircled him in a puny hug that made him want to hurl. "I know, sweetheart. Sometimes life just isn't fair."

He squeezed her back. It would be so easy to break her.

Then he leaned away, still in her embrace. "What do you say we head out for lunch? I could stand to get my mind off things for a while, and we still need to talk about what happened with your job. You haven't had a chance to tell me why the bastards laid you off."

Her reedy arms released his torso, and she shrugged. "Not much to tell. I know good and well it's only because I make that bitch in the front office jealous. She hasn't been my weight since she was five. She's made up shit I've supposedly done wrong and tattled on me since I started..."

Dirk let his mind drift back to checking in at the airport under an assumed name and using a fake ID to pass through the joke that was security. The white noise of Bonnie's complaints beat against his brain, nothing more than raindrops on a window pane. It didn't matter that he wasn't listening anymore. She *felt* like he gave a rat's ass that her boss gave her the ax. Her thoughts had successfully been steered away from his being late, and best of all, she felt sorry for him finding out his poor uncle might die. Chances were good he'd get laid tonight. It was always a bonus when his facades made for little pay-offs in the end.

He opened the cab door for her, the caring, attentive boyfriend. In reality, he'd much prefer to run a couple miles to drain off energy rather than take the pipsqueak out to eat.

Patience. Play this role for now so you can play the next one later. Who knows? Maybe lunch will turn into research.

CHAPTER 18

MCKENZIE WATCHED AS Jonas stuck the key into the lock of his brownstone. They'd left Liza's memorial to come straight here after McKenzie convinced him he could spend his time better with her than by waiting for a serial killer at Liza Kruger's gravesite.

"I'm a little weirded out by this," Jonas said.

"What do you think social media is for? Stalking officially replaced baseball as America's favorite pastime a few years ago."

That pastime made McKenzie think finding Gibb might be possible. As the gut feeling that Jonas' son might be alive had shaped, the more McKenzie had ignored that little voice in her head refusing to get involved. One child had already died because of her ambition. She couldn't bring back Levi, but maybe she could bring back Gibb.

The more the idea took root, the more she'd thought about what she could possibly use to make it happen. The picture on Noelle's Facebook page of the family in front of the Christmas fireplace had popped into her mind. Specifically, what had been on the mantle behind them.

Jonas stepped inside and motioned McKenzie to come in as well. The small home still suggested a woman's touch. Lacy eggshell curtains adorned the living room windows, hummingbird figurines perched on the end tables. Only the thin layer of dust filmed over it all and the stale, unmoving air told the real story.

"Through there," Jonas said. He pointed past a salmon-colored sofa to the stone hearth.

McKenzie dropped all pretenses as her body drew her to the spot she'd seen in the photo. Atop the mantelpiece sat the framed picture of baby Gibb matted next to a clear, clean set of his tiny handprints.

She lifted the homemade memento, staring at it wide-eyed as if it were a rare historical artifact. "Noelle made this?"

Jonas rasped as if he had some of the grit on the furniture caught in his throat. "Yeah. They do footprints at the hospital when babies are born, but Noelle insisted on the handprints. She wanted to remember his hands that small one day when he surpassed her in height."

"Smart lady," McKenzie mumbled.

"Obviously not smart enough," Jonas said dryly.

McKenzie slanted a sideways glance from the handprints toward the guy who once stole a kiss from her on a high school field trip. The teacher had turned the corner away from them, and they'd kissed in the Planetarium underneath the fake stars. "Jonas, she *was* smart. What happened doesn't change that."

"Right," he said. He plopped onto the couch. "Why do you think the cops will give a damn about the handprint? I told you. Or you told me, rather. They don't listen to me. My own damn fault, I know, but they don't."

You called me. How could you still have no idea who you're dealing with?

McKenzie tucked the frame into her bag. "Lucky for you I know someone better than the cops."

As it turned out, it wasn't hard to talk Jig into meeting her in person. McKenzie invited her via Skype to have dinner. Maybe Jig was curious about Noah Hutchins' most recent love interest, or maybe she just wanted the steak she'd been promised. Either way, the mysterious chick on the other end of the computer agreed.

McKenzie hadn't told Jig that Jonas was coming along.

Ulterior motives might not make meeting the enigma any easier.

Jonas craned his neck over the hostess stand in search of someone he didn't know. "What does she look like?"

"No idea."

He shot her a glance. "Seriously? How are we supposed to find her then?"

A sardonic chortle escaped her lips. "Oh, I doubt *we'll* find her."

Sure enough, a few minutes after six, a hand with red-painted fingernails plopped down a snake-skin handbag in McKenzie's peripheral vision. "You didn't tell me you were bringing your boyfriend, Mac."

McKenzie's eyes travelled upward. She didn't know what she'd expected, but it wasn't this. The Asian woman would've barely reached five feet tall if it wasn't for the three-inch silver stilettos on her feet. The peacock feather in her hair didn't match her outfit which didn't match her purse which didn't match her shoes, but somehow none of that mattered. Her face was strikingly pretty, her skin flawless. The heart-shape of her lips was defined with perfectly-applied makeup.

No way in hell I'd sit behind a computer all day if I looked like that.

"Jig," McKenzie stated. Best to ignore the "Mac" reference no matter how much her skin crawled.

The petite girl sat down and crossed her legs. "Veronica Sims. But yes, use Jig if you want me in a good mood."

"Right." McKenzie nodded, a little shocked to finally discover the chick's name. For someone who'd seemed so intangible, Jig wasn't the most inconspicuous. "Jig, this is Jonas. He's an old friend."

"Doesn't look that old to me," she said. She offered her hand to Jonas. "Jig. Nice to meet you. Please excuse my bluntness, but what the fuck are we doing here?"

So much for subtlety.

"We need your help," McKenzie replied.

"Shocking," Jig answered, sarcastic, but she cracked the slightest smile. She picked up her menu. "This about the baby killing thing? Let's order steaks. I'm starved."

McKenzie winced but forced herself not to look at Jonas. Hopefully his temper would hold in check at the comment. Even if Jig meant no harm, Jonas was likely to start throwing the silverware at careless mentions that struck a nerve about his wife and son.

But before McKenzie could answer, Jig spoke again. "They found another one, you know."

"What?" McKenzie said, sitting up in her chair. Her breathing quickened like it did at the peak of a roller coaster just before its imminent plummet.

Jig pursed the red beak of her lips but continued to peruse the menu. "Yep. Body literally fell out of a plane in Cali. Well, half a body. Other half stuck in the landing gear, but who's counting? I'm thinking the rib-eye. What looks good to you?"

A plane?

McKenzie blinked rapidly, as if that would help her brain bring the bizarre information into focus. "Slow down, Jig. What are you talking about? What's this about landing gear?"

Jig dropped her menu and glared at her, then spoke as if McKenzie had just stepped onto earth for the first time. "Another...wo-man...was...killed." She mimed stabbing someone a la Norman Bates in *Psycho*. "He—" she signaled stabbing again, "—the killer—put her—into...the...wheel well...of...the...plane."

"You know, I'm starting to really dislike you," McKenzie said, deadpan. Then, she half laughed. "Truth is, you're a lot like my old roommate, Pierce. You'd have probably liked each other. He was a wiseguy to rival all other wiseguys."

The reference to Pierce had come out without her meaning to bring him up, but she couldn't help the thought. They'd have gotten along. Would Jig even want to do this if she'd known what had happened to Pierce?

Jig laughed amicably. "I know, I know. I'm a first rate smartass. I actually teach a class on it at the community college. You'll have to introduce me to Pierce sometime."

Although McKenzie's gut clenched, she didn't stop Jig.

Jig, oblivious, kept going. "Yes, in all seriousness, they found another girl. The landing gear kind of lopped her in half like a magician's assistant, so we'll have to wait for the M.E.'s report before we know whether she was dead or alive when she went into the wheel well. They've identified her, and she was pregnant. If I had to make an educated guess, I'd say she was breathing but minus one close-to-term fetus when he squished her into the wheel well."

Christ. This guy is unbelievably sick. Creative, but sick.

"Psychotic bastard," Jonas seethed.

"Maybe a bastard. If so, certainly one with mommy issues," Jig considered. "So, are you kids planning to tell me why I'm here, or should we stretch the suspense?"

McKenzie didn't know enough about Jig to trust her, but she had no reason to *distrust* her, either. Noah would have told her to keep details on a need to know basis. Tough. Noah wasn't here to issue orders anymore. She was her own boss now, making her own decisions. In Jig's case, the more she knew, the more she could find.

This is either a really good idea or a really bad one.

"We think the killer might be selling babies on the black market."

Jig's eyebrows arched. "Impressive leap. What makes you say that?"

Good to know the cure for Jig's wisecracks was surprise. McKenzie glanced at Jonas, who clenched his fists in his lap, eyes on McKenzie. He nodded.

"Jonas is an old friend, but I didn't tell you how we got back in touch. Jonas called me because he thinks the Cradle Robber is the same man who killed his wife, Noelle."

Jig didn't bat an eyelash. "Pregnant?"

Jonas released his tightened fists and wiped his palms on his napkin. "No. But she was out walking with our baby at the time."

The hacker's eyes narrowed, cynical. Best to head off the objection right now.

"I doubted him at first, too. Until you told me what you did about the DMSO."

McKenzie told Jig about Jonas' wife's autopsy results and how there was no explanation for the heart attack via injection or poison. Then, at Jig's confused look, she unleashed the clincher: "Jonas smelled garlic on Noelle before the police arrived."

"Interesting theory. How do you propose proving it?" Jig replied.

McKenzie's stomach knotted again. Even though the people responsible were all dead but one, and that remaining, most notorious perpetrator was now in a high security prison in solitary confinement, for her it might never be over. "Jig, I have to be honest with you. Pierce died last year during my—well, during the uncovering of the assassinations. I have to make sure you're up for getting involved with me, considering how things have gone in the past."

"I'm here, aren't I? Don't worry about me. I'm a big girl. I can take care of myself. Now, tell me how you think you can prove Noelle was connected."

McKenzie reached into her purse and pulled out the frame she'd taken from Jonas' mantle. "I thought we'd start with this."

CHAPTER 19

FELICIA ROCKWELL YANKED two more tissues from the box and passed them to Lily Ingram, who lay sprawled on the sonogram table, her paper gown crinkled and her sadly flat belly exposed. Bless her soul. She'd cried for the past ten minutes. This part of the job never did get easier.

"I don't understand," the woman sobbed. "I've done everything they've told me. I took every injection, rested more than I have my entire life. It doesn't make sense!"

Felicia covered the woman's porcelain hand with her own mahogany fingers. "Sometimes, even with today's incredible technology, we can't predict or comprehend some things. IVF is a tough road. Sometimes it works miracles, but other times—"

"Even extraordinary measures can't make me a mother." Lily yanked her hand from underneath Felicia's and rested it on her flat belly. Another tear sparkled in the corner of her eye before dribbling down her face. "This was my last chance. My last eggs...my last embryos. Victor is...gone..."

Another sob strangled in her throat, but she composed herself and went on. "Since my husband died, no one will let me adopt. So many homeless children, yet the system would rather let them suffer in foster care than let a single mother adopt them." The woman looked down at her fingers over her empty womb. "I've never wanted anything more."

Felicia closed her eyes. If only she didn't know the feeling.

"I really shouldn't be telling you this, but if you really want a baby—and I mean really want one—I might know someone who can help you," Felicia whispered.

Lily's eyes widened, hope kindling. "I'll do anything, Felicia. Anything! Is it another doctor?"

Felicia narrowed her eyes. "Not exactly."

She took a small card from her pocket and looked Lily straight in the eye. "You can't tell anyone where you got this, Lily, and for God sakes, don't go unless you're very, very serious."

That had been two days ago. Felicia pulled her coat collar up to block the wind as she exited her place of work and set off onto the New York street. Ever since she'd given Lily Ingram the business card, Felicia hadn't been able to settle down. Sarah Peterson hadn't sounded happy on the phone, and Felicia couldn't blame her. It'd been stupid, really. A gut reaction. Still, over the years, her gut reactions rarely failed her.

The fact that her gut didn't often steer her wrong was exactly why her own paranoia freaked her out even more now.

Maybe she'd head to the Jacques Torres shop inside Rockefeller Center. It was the closest of their stores to her office, and chocolate did wonders for the nerves. As she switched directions to head toward the subway station, her cell rang. The glowing face indicated it was her mother. If paranoia was genetic, Felicia definitely knew where she'd inherited it. "Mom, it's only your third call of the day. You must've slept in."

"Ha, ha," her mother replied. "You should do stand-up."

Was it her imagination, or had a man turned out from behind the corner? "Okay, okay. I'm sorry. What's up?"

"Oh, just wanted to check on you. Don't know why, 'xactly. Been thinking about you. Felt like I should call."

Felicia's steps quickened instinctively. "I'm fine, Mom. It's been a long day. On my way to pick up a box of the dark raspberry chocolates. They're much needed."

Her mother sniggered. "That's my girl."

The laughter wasn't catching, though, as behind her, the man accelerated his pace to match hers. The old saying popped into her head: just because you're paranoid doesn't mean they're not out to get you.

Shit.

She weaved in and out of the pedestrian traffic, the sound of her shoes clacking against the pavement growing louder and louder in her ears. Her eyes darted over the street. If only she could flag a taxi.

The breaths whistled hard out of her nose. No longer looking back for the man, she could feel his presence rather than see it. Tears stung the corners of her eyes. Best to hang up before she started crying.

"Listen, Mom, I'm about to go in the subway. Talk later?"

A slight pause. "Sure, baby. Don't forget it's your aunt's birthday this week. You need to call her."

An empty taxi.

Thank God.

Felicia flailed at the curb, willing the cab to arrive before the man caught up to her. "Yeah. Will do. Bye, Mom."

The taxi rolled to the curb. Felicia yanked the door handle before it came to a complete stop. "Rockefeller Center, please."

As the cabbie pulled away, her gaze flitted back to where the man had been tailing her.

No one.

Maybe she was only paranoid after all.

CHAPTER 20

THE MORNING AFTER her dinner with Jig, McKenzie rolled over and hit the snooze button three separate times on the glass alarm clock that used to be her mother's. She'd been so damned busy this week she'd forgotten what today was. She reached to her nightstand for her cell to skim her e-mails. Stupid cell phone with the damn date on the home screen. The alarm rang again. This time, she sat up and turned it off all together. She settled back into her cool, comfortable pillows. Today she was getting some sleep, and nobody was going to tell her otherwise.

When McKenzie next woke due to Carbon's wet nose poking her hand, it was past noon. "I'm coming, bud."

As if on cue, her cell rang.

Work: the one place on earth where you can count on someone being worried about you; not because they are, but because they don't want to pick up your slack.

McKenzie snatched up her phone. "Look, Morton, I forgot to put in for the day off, but I take it every year. Can you put it on some permanent calendar somewhere?"

My mom and dad died fifteen years ago today.

"Ms. McClendon," a sharp female voice responded.

"Who is this?" McKenzie snapped, embarrassed.

"This is Whitney Trias. I'm your new boss."

McKenzie squished her toes inside her heeled loafers on the elevator up to the fifteenth floor. If she put enough effort into it, she could probably force fire out of her nose and be rid of this chick from the start. She was already breathing like a pissed off dragon.

She swung the door to the *Herald* offices wide and called, "Afternoon, kids," to the front room.

"Good afternoon, Miss McClendon," a tall, thin woman replied from the back of the room.

McKenzie's glare darted toward the voice. She'd *thought* she recognized the name. Now she immediately recognized the chick leaning against a flimsy cubicle wall. *Yeah. No skin off your ass if someone's workspace implodes on them, huh?*

The woman uncrossed her arms and started toward McKenzie. The way the kinky sable curls bounced at chin-length around Whitney Trias' face made McKenzie want to rip the strands from her head one by one. Her face was so slender that if she turned sideways, it might disappear. Hadn't she ever heard of food? McKenzie cleared her throat to keep from saying something she shouldn't. Boss or no boss, it was still the anniversary of her parents' death.

Heartless.

"I'm Whitney. I'll be taking over from here."

"You're from the *Gazette*," McKenzie said, her tone flat.

The same paper that dragged my name through the mud after last year. The one that took pictures of me at my cousin's funeral with headlines screaming that Levi's mother confronted me about being in the room when Levi was killed but choosing not to prevent it so I could get the scoop. All lies.

"I am. But I'm willing to wipe the slate clean if you are."

Not on your life.

"What happened to Morton?" McKenzie asked.

Whitney tilted her head and fake-smiled. "Let's just say Morton spent more time picking up pizzas on the way to work than stories. He missed about a dozen deadlines, so the big guys upstairs thought it was time someone stepped in who actually owns a watch. Plus, he was letting all sorts of articles slip through the cracks that weren't politically correct. You know the sort."

McKenzie's chest tightened. Sure, she and Morton didn't have the best history, but he'd let the response piece about the *Gazette's* lies run. Besides, she'd been through a lot under his watch. Suddenly, the office felt off kilter, like all of the furniture had been rearranged and that comfortable chair she was used to sitting in had accidentally been thrown out in the fray.

As if you've never let a politically incorrect article be published.

"Right. Well, what can I do for you?"

Even though Whitney's face already had more Botox than an entire case of improperly canned green beans, her cheeks pinched at the edges. "Miss McClendon, we all need personal days from time to time, but procedures exist. I'm not sure how Morton Gaines handled this office, but with me, you'll stick to policies. Clear?"

What the hell?

Whitney had apparently missed a lesson or two on social interaction.

Don't do anything stupid, McKenzie.

"Look, Miss Trias, I'm sorry I didn't call in. I didn't mean to upset the status quo," McKenzie said evenly. She pushed past the editor toward her office rather than stick around and go for Whitney's throat. Taking this kind of bullshit wasn't in her contract, for Christ's sake.

Where the hell did this troll come from?

Suddenly, her heart ached. If only Pierce were still here. He'd have given her a heads up instead of her waking up to that awful phone call.

McKenzie opened her office door to see the young reporter who usually worked at the health desk plucking away at her computer keys. "What are you doing?"

The new editor's patent leather heels click-clacked on the floor behind McKenzie. "Oh, I told Kiesha she could use your computer since hers is down. She'll be out of your hair shortly. Right, Kiesha?"

Kiesha? Another reporter at *her* desk with access to *her* notes? A reporter who could potentially rip the story right out from under her? Not to mention the germs on those fingers always picking at her skin while she wrote articles about the newest bacterial dangers. "How did you get my password?"

The girl at the desk froze like a rabbit who'd just been spotted by a hungry wolf. In her hurry to get up, she fumbled her notes. "I'm done. Thanks."

"Oh, I called up to the information support center when you didn't show up this morning and told them we needed to gain access to your computer to get a lead on where you might be," Whitney replied. "Better safe than sorry. By the way, I noticed you're taking the Cradle Robber story in a slightly different direction."

McKenzie whirled around, all intentions to be pleasant and non-confrontational forgotten. As if there wasn't enough pressure on her to keep turning out stories the caliber of the previous one. "Are you kidding me with this?"

Miss Kinky Curls cocked her head as Keisha rushed out of the room. "Is there a problem, Miss McClendon?"

McKenzie closed her eyes, forced her breathing to slow, and blinked away the image of her parents' faces in her mind.

That's it.

"Other than the fact you called me in on the anniversary of the day my parents died when I was twelve, you talking to me like I'm the pigeon poop you stepped in on your way to work this morning, *and* the fact that you let someone else use my office because I was gone for *one* morning? Yes, I'd say I draw the line at you reading my notes."

Whitney turned the door knob and shut the door with annoying precision to ensure privacy. "Miss McClendon, I understand you're something of a rock star around here, and your work is commendable. You brought a valuable story to this newspaper, and in doing so, gained a lot of street cred. Now, surely you're professional enough to understand that you shouldn't allow stardom to cloud your perspective. But in case you have, let me remind you—journalism is all about being able to perform your job objectively. Everything that happened last year has to have had quite an effect on you, and we understand that. But this idea you've come up with about the black market baby trade is a bit out there. The concept is certainly *sensational*, but every article you write isn't going to be a conspiracy within a conspiracy. I don't want black market baby trade ridiculousness. I want the facts about the Cradle Robber. No more, no less. It's probably best to keep our eye on the ball. That said, I need you on board for such an important story. If you're having trouble concentrating on your work and need to take some time off, that can be arranged, but if that's the case, I need to know about it now so I can assign the Cradle Robber story to someone who can handle it."

McKenzie's neck jerked back, her eyebrows raised in disbelief. "Is that a threat?"

"It's not a threat, Miss McClendon. It's simply being realistic."

"But doesn't the public have a right to know if this story *is* about the black market baby trade?"

"The public has a right to not be subjected to wild conjecture," Whitney said. "I do *not* want this crazy baby market story in my paper, Miss McClendon."

"What if I could prove to you that I was right?" McKenzie said, her face burning with anger.

Whitney waved a hand. "Fine. If you figure out this is yet *another* McKenzie uncovered conspiracy, I can't tell you not to run it. That said, you're not about to waste my time and this company's money trying to confirm a bunch of figments of your imagination".

"But I need a little time to at least look into it. That's what investigative journalists *do*. We'd be falling down on the job if I didn't at least pursue something like this."

Whitney tapped her toe for a moment, considering. "One week, Miss McClendon. But if you can't prove your theories in a week, I'm going to publish this as a straight news story without you."

The woman turned and left her office. McKenzie picked up the ladybug paperweight on her desk. At the last second, she stopped herself from throwing it. She didn't want to have to explain the dented door.

McKenzie yanked out her cell phone. "I am *not* intimidated by you, Miss Frizz-Ease," she muttered under her breath as she typed. If Whitney thought she had another reporter in this building who could bring in the story McKenzie could, Whitney was more clueless than an NRA spokesman at a gay pride rally. She would bring in the story, and she'd get Jonas' son back at the same time.

She clicked send on her text to Jig:

Any word on the handprint?

About ten seconds later, her phone dinged:

your ears must've been burning.

McKenzie's breath caught. Jig knew something about Jonas' son. Then, her excitement deflated.

Here we go with the riddles again.

So?

Her fingernails drummed on her desk while she waited. What was the right question to ask Jig to elicit an actual response?

But this time it turned out she didn't need to think of a follow up question. Her phone alerted again, and she opened Jig's response. How was it possible for a human being to process events this rapidly without getting emotional whiplash?

found him.

CHAPTER 21

THE KNOCK ON the door jolted Jonas from the stupor of scrolling through page eighty-six of his daily "checks"—the series of chat rooms, social media sites, and forums he consulted daily in hopes of finding a lead on Noelle's killer. Jonas blinked and waggled his head back and forth.

Wake up, asshole. How do you expect to notice anything if your head isn't even in it?

He shoved back from the desk and staggered to the door. After he unclasped the bolt, he swung the door open to reveal McKenzie McClendon.

"Not a good time," he slurred. Sure, he'd called her in, but she had the worst damned timing. He'd rather douse his head with gasoline near a ninety-year-old's birthday cake than talk through plans of attack with the reporter right now. He'd been doing this for years. The cops couldn't—wouldn't—do anything unless he found something else or something happened. That's what the checks were for.

Jonas shoved the door back toward its frame, but McKenzie's palm caught it. "Jig found him, Jonas."

The words bit at his skin, slammed through his chest.

Was it possible?

Had to be the rum. The triple shot was testing him. Jonas licked his lips as he stood rooted to the spot. Finally, he choked out, "Gibb?"

McKenzie stepped over the threshold and closed the door.

The sympathy in her eyes made him want to hurl. He didn't want her damned compassion. "McKenzie, don't confuse me with a pity-case."

She twitched, then visibly shifted mode. "Got it," she said softly. Her focus drifted toward the mantle before returning to Jonas again. "I'm sorry."

He waved her off, unable to speak. He squeezed his eyes shut tight. He'd spent hours in high school writing notes on loose leaf sheets from his binder to slip into this girl's locker. It had been number fourteen, right next to Mr. Claxton's algebra class. This girl whose auburn hair used to cascade down her back over his letter jacket when they were going steady had just found his son. McKenzie had found Gibb, and here she was, standing here apologizing to *him*.

Jonas, you suck at goddamn life.

When he opened his eyes again, he lifted his rum and Coke to his lips but lowered it reflexively. After all, she'd held up her end of the bargain.

"How? Where?" he whispered.

And do I really want to know?

McKenzie stopped looking at the mantle, and her eyes met his. "Jig ran a search on the handprint. The fingerprints match a kid in Georgia. Their local police department fingerprints the kindergarten classes at all the schools in case—" her voice trailed for a second, uncertain. She took in a deep breath. "—in case of abduction."

Jonas' own laugh sounded high and foreign to him. "Thank God for the government! Always making sure her citizens are protected from the Big Bad Wolf. Kinda makes you feel warm and fuzzy inside, doesn't it?"

"Jonas—"

"Can't help it," he said through guffaws. Good thing he was drunk. If he wasn't, he'd be sure he was nuts. Normal people didn't laugh like this.

Without warning, the wheezes of hysterical laughter morphed into dry heaving, and it was all he could do to keep from vomiting. He stumbled away from McKenzie, his staggering footsteps not entirely due to the alcohol racing through his bloodstream. Despite an entire loss of muscular control, his ass found the computer chair. He hung his head and stared at his knees for a good solid thirty seconds. When he finally spoke, he ground out the words. "The rest of the details. Tell me."

He tried hard to block everything else out so he could process her reply. The kid she thought was Gibb was in Georgia. Atlanta. Something about a change in the school's name and school records. She was working on getting more information. His mind drank her words and yet begged her to stop at the same time. Too much.

At last, she finished parroting everything Jig had told her. She stood before him, her hazel eyes boring into him. Compassion. Judgment. What did he read in them?

Cold. Numb. As if all the booze in his blood had raced to his pounding heart. Through lips that felt frozen, he forced out the question he'd been holding ever since her impossible, miraculous words.

"How soon do we go?"

The flight to Atlanta took off on time. McKenzie and Jonas were en route to find out if Jonas' nightmare could finally be ending. A few weeks ago it had probably seemed impossible to him, but now, McKenzie had a chance to change that.

"What kind of a name is Blair, anyway? Sounds like something out of a bad eighties movie," Jonas grumbled as the seatbelt light finally went off. He propped his cheek on his fist on the armrest between them. "Blair is a girl's name."

McKenzie ignored him and pressed on. After all, if she bit at every comment he made, they'd land in Atlanta and have no idea what move to make.

"Blair wasn't re-enrolled at the elementary school for the new school year, nor any school in the area. The elementary school only has cell numbers on record for the Davidsons, and their address is a P.O. Box."

"Magical," Jonas replied. "In other words, they know they suck at life, so they're good at hiding it."

"A cell phone and a P.O. Box don't mean you're trying to hide. They mean you don't want to be found," McKenzie said.

"Thank you, Mad Hatter."

McKenzie rolled her eyes. "All I'm saying is that we don't know they're hiding out. They could just be private people."

"What about your computer friend? The one who found him in the first place. Can't she figure out where they are?" Jonas asked.

A smirk touched McKenzie's lips. Wasn't *that* the million dollar question? "Jig is kind of like an obnoxious house cat. She'll pay you attention only if she is in the mood, and there's no way to predict that mood."

Jonas grunted. "Brilliant."

"Ye of little faith," McKenzie replied. "Just because the United States Postal Service doesn't have their address doesn't mean *I* don't. What do you think FedEx is for?"

CHAPTER 22

"OLLIE, HOLD MY calls," Trevin said into the intercom.

He paced back and forth across his law office. He had to put everything in order. He'd been digging through the juvey records ever since he'd gotten them, but he couldn't help but worry he was missing something. They connected him to too much for him to leave anything traceable. Fuck, his head was swimming. How was he supposed to keep this under control if he was in a pile of shit stew?

The detention center records were the biggest thing, and those were taken care of. Tonight, he'd do the records in the office. He'd taken some precautions with them on paper, but it would be best to trash them. He'd put it off because of the no-burn ordinance in the state, but that was the kind of shit that would be the end of it. Fucking paper trails.

The intercom buzzed, and Ollie's voice filled the room. "Mr. Worneck, there's someone here to see—"

Trevin leapt across the desk and jammed his finger to the button. "I told you not to bother me!"

"I know, sir, but—"

She didn't have a chance to finish. Trevin's door blew open. A stocky man with a goatee and a hook-shaped scar on his neck stormed inside.

Fuck.

The man slammed the door behind him and twisted the bolt lock into place. Trevin had been so worried about the pile of steaming bovine dung the next field over that he'd forgotten to watch where he was stepping in his own.

"I'm sorry to bother you during work hours, Mr. Worneck, but we have a little business to take care of."

Trevin backed away from the man he knew only as the Jap, though the man didn't appear to be of any Asian descent at all.

"I'm closing in on the next payment," Trevin stuttered. His breath caught. His chest was about to explode. Damn, it was hot in here. If he could just get to the desk, he could reach his emergency stash.

The Jap shook his head and clicked his tongue. "You see, Trevin, you said that two weeks ago. There's a minimum payment requirement."

"I'll have it. I swear! Three more days."

"Trev, you know I don't make those decisions," the Jap replied. He settled his rear end on the corner of the desk between Trevin and the blessed bottle of Xanax. The Jap stuck a finger in the cup of pens and stirred.

"Man, do me a solid here. Just a few more days."

The Jap twisted a ballpoint pen and pulled out its ink cartridge. The shiny silver tip glinted in the office lights. The man stood and took a step toward Trevin. "I was sent here to do a job. That job is to give you a message."

Trevin backpedaled into the wall.

Fuck, fuck, fuckety fuck!

A palm pinned him against the wall. Before he had a chance to try to get away, the Jap twisted both his arms behind his back and shoved his cheek into the wood paneling. The skin of Trevin's face screeched against the lacquered wall. If he hadn't concentrated so hard on holding his bladder, he might've been able to make himself pass out.

A fire streaked through his fingertips and all the way to his spine as the metal tip of the cartridge went under his thumbnail. His knees slammed onto the hardwood, his chord of pain echoing in the quiet of the office. Tears streaked down his face like a pot boiling over. Steam licked his insides.

The Jap released him. Trevin commanded his arms to move forward to catch himself, but they didn't react fast enough. His nose smashed into the oak with a sickening crunch.

"The money, Trevin," the Jap said. "I'll be back next week."

CHAPTER 23

"YOU'RE SURE YOU want to do this?" McKenzie asked, even though she already knew the answer.

Jonas glared at her, his eyes full of venom. "What would you do?"

Without another word, she opened the door of the rental Prius and started up the walk of 1512 Darwoody Way, also known as the address of the last FedEx package sent to Hall and Melissa Davidson.

She rapped on the door three times.

Please, God, if this door opens, don't let Jonas commit a felony.

They'd been over their backstory, but if Jonas saw the people who'd bought his son the same way they'd buy a car or appliance, all pretense would go to hell.

A young black man about McKenzie's age opened the door. "Can I help you?"

Jonas coughed behind McKenzie before she spoke up. "Yes. Are you Mr. Davidson? We—" She stumbled over her words. *McKenzie. Pull yourself together, for Christsakes!* "We live at 1215. They delivered some of the Davidsons' mail to us by mistake."

She held out the phony package. What a lame cover story. How in the name of all things sacred had she not foreseen this awkwardness?

The man at the door seemed unfazed. He removed a pair of rectangle reading glasses from his pocket and examined the address on the box. "That's our address, all right, but no

Davidsons here. We moved in this summer. I guess they lived here before us. Don't know for sure. We bought the place from a relocation company."

"Oh, okay. Thanks anyway," McKenzie replied, deflated.

The man reached out and shook her hand, then turned to Jonas, but her ex was already heading to the car.

"I apologize. He got some bad news today. Hasn't been himself," McKenzie invented.

"Sorry to hear that."

When she climbed back into the driver's seat, McKenzie put the Prius in gear and backed out of the driveway, seething. "Look, Jonas. I know this sucks, but your personal pity party won't help us get one step closer to your son. Our ruses will last about as long as a reality star's fandom if you act like this. People won't tell you a damn thing if they don't trust you. If you want to find Gibb, put on your big boy britches and play the part with me."

Jonas turned toward her. From the way the corners of his mouth tightened, for a minute McKenzie thought he was about to lash out. Then, he laughed. "Did you just say, 'big boy britches'? Is the word 'britches' even a real word anymore?"

She snickered. "Yes. Yes, it is. You can find it in the dictionary next to 'jackass.'"

For a second, McKenzie could've sworn she saw in her peripheral vision the Jonas who'd stolen kisses from her in the hallway between classes. She bit her lip and nodded at his grin. "It looks good on you."

With Bridgeborrow Elementary's state of the art playground, a security guard at the door, and plenty of Lexuses in the parking lot, it wasn't a stretch to think this was a place where people who had the money to purchase an infant might send their kid.

A young woman dressed in a black track suit sat in the front office flipping through a magazine. The scent of vanilla washed over the room, and a fountain burbled in the corner. Was this a pre-school or a spa?

"Can I help you?" the grey-haired receptionist asked. She had none of the Southern drawl McKenzie half-expected based on *The Real Housewives of Atlanta.*

She stepped past Jonas toward the desk. "We're looking for a way to contact Melissa Davidson. We moved into their old house this summer, and while we were unpacking, we found some things in the attic they left behind. We haven't had much luck finding a forwarding address. The neighbors said Blair went to school here, so we thought you might have one."

The lady cocked her head and laughed, though McKenzie didn't detect a bit of mirth. "Wish I could tell you. The Davidsons didn't exactly tell anyone where they were heading. Sorry I can't be of more help," she said.

With that, the receptionist stood and busied herself neatening papers on the counter behind her. Jonas cleared his throat, and McKenzie reached behind her and grabbed his hand to shut him up. They were in the school and hadn't been asked to leave. Not exactly an open invitation to hang around and talk to folks, but better than being kicked out any day.

McKenzie dragged Jonas out of the office, but she turned to her right out the set of double doors in the atrium instead of the obvious left toward the parking lot.

Look like you belong.

"Sir. Ma'am," the security officer barked. "This way, please."

McKenzie slumped. Stupid rich people and their competent security measures. "Oh, right. I'd get lost in my own apartment if it wasn't only three rooms," she said.

The sun blinded her as they exited. Damn, it was hot here. Jonas trudged behind her, defeated. His son had been here three months ago, but now Jonas was as far away from finding him as ever.

"Miss!" a voice called from behind her.

McKenzie turned to see the woman in the black track suit

who'd been sitting in the front office. Now that they were face to face, she realized this girl couldn't be older than twenty.

"You're looking for the Davidsons?" the woman asked.

"Yes," Jonas spoke up. "Do you know how to find them?"

"You moved into their house? We've wondered what happened to them, of course. Their son Blair was in my son's class, bless his heart. We've all been worried about him."

The chick's sleek copper ponytail swished as she stepped closer. McKenzie caught the way her lips parted slightly like they were ready to drink in any words shared. A gossip. Perfect.

"Why worried?" Jonas said a little too fast for McKenzie's liking.

"Well, they left town shortly after the accident. We didn't have a chance to find out if he was okay. Did they fix the deck out back before you moved in?"

McKenzie heard Jonas' rapid breathing next to her. Time to head him off before he blew it for them.

"The deck is fixed," she said half-heartedly. Who gave a shit? "What accident?"

The chick frowned. "Blair fell through some rotted board on the deck. We went by there to see it after they left and everything. Such a mess."

Who was this "we" the woman mentioned? They went to see someone's deck? What the hell?

The girl didn't realize this was at all out of the ordinary. She kept talking.

"We always wondered if that was what really happened, seeing as how they pulled Blair out of school and skipped town right after. Really bizarre coincidence, don't you think? Bless his heart," she said again. "Hope he's okay."

"Me too," McKenzie muttered. She grabbed Jonas' hand, urging him toward the car before he could speak. She called her thanks over her shoulder as she pulled Jonas away.

McKenzie cranked the rental before Jonas had climbed all the way in. "What the hell are you doing, McKenzie? She could've known more."

She threw it into reverse and hit the gas. "She could've. You could've grabbed her by the neck and threatened her to spill it. Then, I'd be bailing your ass out of jail instead of driving toward somewhere we can find the whole story."

"I wouldn't have—" Jonas stopped mid-sentence. "Wait. What?"

"If Blair had an accident, he'd have been taken to the nearest emergency room, right?"

Jonas snorted. "Yes. But you do realize you can't get someone's medical records, right?"

"You can do a lot of things if you're desperate enough."

McKenzie mentally sorted through options as she planned her next move. For some reason, Whitney was dead set against McKenzie's take on this article. Her new boss wouldn't exactly back her up if something bad happened. Sure, she could probably get a job at any newspaper after the award winning story she'd written after last year's terrible events. But what if she couldn't turn out more stories? What happened when *they* found out she was a hack, too? What if she couldn't duplicate that success ever again?

But worse, what would happen to her sanity if she didn't find Jonas' son?

CHAPTER 24

"YES, I'M CALLING from CVS on Lexington. We had a prescription faxed over for Nexa earlier today, but I can't quite read the name. Can you spell it out for me?" Dirk asked.

"Certainly," the receptionist replied. "Let me pull up the file."

This was too damned easy. The practice with ten OB/GYNs was so large that the chance no one there used the drugstore on Lexington was miniscule. Dirk heard through the grapevine that the practice nearly always called in special prenatal vitamins for its high-end patients despite the fact that regular ones were readily available over the counter. The combination was almost a sure bet.

"Looks like I sent one for Eleanor Freed this morning. That's E-L-E-A-N as in night-O-R. Last name F as in fox, R- E-E-D as in door," she read.

He scribbled the name on his legal pad. "Perfect. Thanks a million."

It wouldn't work if he did it with every girl, but that was the beauty of the whole thing. His particular genius. He was a planner. He didn't know the meaning of half-assed, and his plans always involved a delicious degree of randomness.

After all, that was why idiots got caught. They had a pattern, and eventually someone figured it out. Police found a link between John Wayne Gacy's construction business and multiple victims. The alleged Craigslist Killer, alas, found all of his victims on Craigslist. Some people had the intellect of primordial sludge.

Dirk found his targets early, studied them to perfection. Eleanor Freed might be an option. She might not be. Either way, by the time her name came up in the queue, the drugstore employee wouldn't remember giving it to him. Even if she did, it wouldn't matter. He hadn't given her *his* name, and she'd never speak to him again. It was exactly why Dirk wouldn't get caught.

Police couldn't find a pattern if there wasn't one.

After he got off his shift at the hospital, he grabbed a cab and headed downtown. He tipped the cabbie five bucks for a five dollar ride and stepped into the crowd before pressing send on his cell.

Bonnie's nasal tone filled his ear a second later. "Dirk! Are you on the way? I need an opinion on the pink dress or the navy…"

"Hey, babe. Listen, I have to miss out on visiting with your folks tonight. I left work early to check on Decker, and he's still puking. I'm going to have to have him looked at."

"Oh, no," she whined. He knew the tone all too well: feigned concern mixed with repressed annoyance.

"Yeah. I was hoping he'd be better by now, but he's not holding it together."

He'd texted her earlier in the day about waking up to Decker's vomit on the floor, then how Decker seemed lethargic when he'd taken him out to pee before leaving for work.

"Poor baby," she simpered. "Give him a hug for me."

Gotta love her. Just the right mix of stupid and needy.

"Will do," he replied. A quick, "I love you," then he hung up without any more details about what vet he was seeing, what time he'd call later, or anything of the sort.

She'd never met Decker, of course, even though she thought she had. He'd shown her a picture of the basset hound on his cell phone, complete with lovable sad eyes and giant droopy ears. For a dog that didn't exist, Decker sure had been a great excuse on a lot of occasions.

Dirk strode into the Olive Garden in Times Square. At the hostess station, the heavily pregnant hostess asked how many were in his party.

"Two," he replied with a grin.

She grabbed the menus and led him toward a table.

CHAPTER 25

MCKENZIE AND JONAS pulled into the parking lot of Valentine Memorial Hospital at a quarter to five. If the boy had gotten hurt at the Davidsons' former home, they would have had to bring him here, the closest emergency room for thirty miles.

Jonas reached for his door handle as she put the car into park, but McKenzie clicked the power lock on her door. Like that would stop him.

"Look, I know you want to find out where Blair—" she stopped and corrected, "—where Gibb is. But trust me here. I need to go in alone."

He shrugged. "Why am I on this trip?"

She rolled down the windows, then stepped out of the car. "You mean other than that there's no way you would've let me come alone?"

"'Let'," he replied. "That's a good one."

"I'll be back," she said.

As she rushed through the parking lot, her phone vibrated in her pocket. She took it out and clicked the text open, noticing she had five missed calls. All of the calls, as well as the texts, were from her new boss. Whitney Trias must've checked her voicemail.

Every story can't be last year. This one is simple.
Stick to the Cradle Robber story.

"Screw you, too, sunshine," McKenzie muttered, shoving her

phone back into her pocket as she walked through the automatic double doors.

The inside of the emergency room bustled with people who all had the common denominator of looking like they'd either been in a gang fight or recently insulted a particularly violent chef. People held in broken bones hanging out of skin, faces sliced and bloody. In some cases, arguments continued as though there were people who'd helped each other to the hospital so they could finish each other off. From across the room a pair of crossed eyes glared at her from beneath tangled, matted hair.

Don't look. Keep your face toward the desk.

"Can I help you?" the woman wearing blue scrubs and a rhinestone nose stud asked from behind the plate glass.

"I called earlier about picking up my son's records," McKenzie said. "Blair Davidson."

"Hang on a minute," the lady said, then turned around to look on a counter behind her. She glanced around the room, then grabbed the arm of another passing receptionist. They exchanged quick whispers. The second receptionist shook her head.

The woman with the nose stud returned to the window. She had to be about forty-five. McKenzie silently thanked her best friend for talking her out of that belly button ring when she was twenty.

"We don't have a file pulled for that name," the lady said. She yanked a form out of the desk and passed it through the window to McKenzie. A red-lacquered acrylic nail tapped the bottom line. "Fill it out, mail it to this address, and we'll have the records mailed within ten business days."

McKenzie puffed out her chest. This wasn't going to be pretty. "Wait a minute. You're telling me that I call to arrange to pick up my kid's records, and because someone here didn't pull the record, I've wasted my own gas to come down here? Because you people made a mistake, I have to wait ten more days before I can take my child to the pediatric oncologist?"

The nose-ring receptionist looked down at the form as though it would help her decide what to do, clearly torn between procedure and not provoking this obviously distraught and desperate mother.

"Here," she said, drawing a quick "X" over a few lines. "Just fill these blanks out and sign, and I'll see what I can do. Blair Davidson, you said?"

"Yes." McKenzie took the sheet and fumbled with her pen to fill it out before the woman changed her mind.

"And your name?"

"Melissa Davidson," she supplied.

The woman hit a few buttons on the keyboard, then frowned. "I have here the responsible party listed as Hall Davidson."

"Hall is my husband," McKenzie blurted. "My ex-husband, I mean. We're recently divorced."

"Oh. I'm sorry to hear that," the lady answered, pausing with fingers poised at the keyboard. McKenzie could tell she was debating.

Quick, before she calls in a superior.

"Please, miss," McKenzie said, her tone quieter than the anger she'd displayed moments before. "I'm sorry I got so upset. This has all happened so fast, though, and with the divorce and Hall and everything, it takes an act of Congress to get anything done. I need these records as fast as possible. If I have to talk to Hall, I have to jump all kinds of lawyer hurdles."

The lady grunted, but the tiniest smile appeared on her face. "Believe me, I know how that is. Hang on a sec."

She stood up and left the room, returning a moment later with a manila envelope. This time, she slid the window open since the envelope wouldn't fit through the narrow slot underneath. She took the form from McKenzie, crumpled it, and threw it into the trash. Then, she handed the file folder to McKenzie. Her ice-cold hand clamped McKenzie's wrist.

"We never talked," she whispered.

"Of course not," McKenzie responded. She squeezed the woman's arm, then turned without another word.

Jonas dug through the file on his son as McKenzie drove them through I-75 traffic. He'd held this child in his arms even before Noelle had, yet he didn't know what Gibb's voice sounded like. In the doctor's notes were descriptions of the child's responses when asked on a scale of smiley face to frown how much pain he was in. He'd answered a face equivalent to level three. The kid must be tough. Try as he might, though, Jonas didn't know what to imagine when trying to picture Gibb's face.

"I still don't know how you got them to give these to you. I thought HIPAA and all that privacy junk made getting someone else's medicals records about impossible," he said, skimming the folder.

"I told them he had an oncology appointment. Kids with cancer get stuff faster than kids without cancer."

"Shameless."

"You call it shameless. I call it journalism. Anything good?"

Jonas turned the page, and his eyebrows shot to the ceiling. "Whoa, yeah. I think I found why they skipped town."

"Really?" McKenzie asked, slanting a sideways glance at him.

Jonas grabbed the steering wheel and steered her back over the dotted white line. "Dammit! I swear to God, I'll tell you. Just keep your eyes on the damned road, please!"

"Shit. Sorry," she said, as she jerked the steering wheel hard amidst the honks of surrounding traffic. The car fishtailed back into their lane.

He watched the cars careening around him. The New York City Subway system might not be that safe, but at least he didn't have to see a bunch of bat-shit crazy drivers lurch around *other* bat-shit crazy drivers while being *driven* by a bat-shit crazy driver.

"Okay. Apparently, they took—" he paused, unsure how to

refer to his son. He'd named the boy Gibb, but it almost didn't feel right to call him by his own name. Blair felt even worse. "They took him to the emergency room after he fell through some rotten boards on the back porch. The number of fractures he had wasn't normal for the accident the parents described. The hospital contacted the Department of Family and Children's Services. I'm guessing the authorities paid the Davidsons a visit. They didn't want to risk hanging around for further investigation."

"Makes sense. I still want to make a few calls when we get back. Maybe the investigation turned up something we can—"

"You can't be serious!" Jonas smacked the roof of the car. "There's no way I'm going back right now." He'd come too close. Gibb had been here. In this town.

"Jonas, they aren't here anymore. They're long gone, and we don't have a clue where. We're not about to stop looking, but I only have a few days to get the article in or my editor isn't even going to look at it. We won't need to look if I lose my job."

She might as well have slapped him in the face. "Thanks a lot."

She beat her open palm against the top of the steering wheel before clenching it again, her knuckles white. "That's not what I meant."

For about ten seconds, he'd expected to walk up to the door of the Davidsons' house, knock, and see his son inside. He'd expected to see Tonka trucks in the floor and hear cartoons in the background. Now, his mouth felt drier than the Georgia pavement, and his stomach like it was filled with rocks. *Dammit.* "I know. I just..." His neck burned. The gold of his ring reflected a hazy circle on the dashboard. Would it ever get easier?

"I just wanted it to be like a bad episode of *Where in the World is Carmen San Diego?.*"

McKenzie threw back her head and laughed. "I didn't know anyone remembered that show besides me."

If only you knew why that show is my go-to pop-culture reference. I have the worst luck on the face of this earth.

"I guess we're out of round one."

McKenzie wheezed, still laughing. "I don't know, gumshoe. We do have the medical records. Pop those back open and tell me if you can find a social security number on that puppy anywhere."

CHAPTER 26

GLORIA WAS TREADING air.

No. Wait. That didn't make sense. Her feet brushed something hard under her. It was her legs *supporting* her she couldn't feel. She cast her eyes toward her toes. Odd. Shuffling, but no weight. A dream? Was she in labor? An epidural?

She stood at a ledge. A giant staircase. "Stop," she commanded her feet.

They didn't listen, though. She plunged down the stairs. Her pulse skittered in her ears. "Please, slow down!"

Hands rested on her shoulders, heavy, supporting her, propelling her at dangerous speed. Who—

Scenes rushed through Gloria's brain: *calling that new waiter a dick for telling her boss she'd planned to duck out a half-hour early. Grabbing the bottle of merlot another waitress had put aside for her birthday. Looking for cabs, but none around. One off-duty cab at the curb. He'd turned on his light. Her lucky day.*

They reached the landing between the two flights of steps. A triple archway stretched across from her in the inky black of the night. Gold paint. She'd been here before. Where—

More flashes.

A table. The smell of latex. The taste of her sweat. Screams.

Her own.

Her deadened legs mocked her. How stupid could she be? Raised in the Bronx projects, and she hadn't thought it odd when the cab turned its lights on just for her? She hadn't blinked twice that it happened to be parked right outside her work. She hadn't noticed the cabbie looked exactly like the man she'd seated an hour before in the restaurant.

Gloria dug her heels in, but she had so little control over her legs that the action had no force. He flung her onward like a ragdoll flailing in the wind.

Cocksucker.

She'd heard about this. Don't let the sonofabitch take you to a second location. If she wasn't so numb, she'd have laughed. Too late. And if the second location was bad, what the fuck was the third?

At the bottom of the stairs, she threw as much of her weight as she could toward her rear end. If he was going to take her, it wasn't about to look like it was of her own volition. Unfortunately, no one seemed to be nearby to see it.

He bent down and heaved her over his shoulder in a fireman's carry. The stench of cheap cologne hit her nostrils. She looked down as the patterned tiles of the floor passed beneath her.

Kick, legs! Kick!

A sob wrenched from her throat, but nothing came out. She watched her hands claw at her assailant's back in slow motion, his black coat rippling with the weak brushes of her fingernails. The archways drifted farther and farther away from her.

As backward momentum carried her into the unknown, a mound of blankets in the corner caught her eye. Underneath it, a grey-headed figure stirred in his sleep.

Help! Say help! Scream! Yell!

But somehow, her voice had been stolen. Even her tears were cruelly silent. The distance between her and the homeless man stretched until he wouldn't be able to hear her even if she could call out. Her chance for help was being ripped away. She passed under a second set of archways and out of the sleeping homeless man's line of vision, her last hope.

Everitt slipped from under the covers and heaved her frame out of bed. She'd never changed into her night clothes, so she was all ready to go. The floorboard creaked under her first step. She shifted to her toes, balance wavering dangerously.

Zan hadn't replied to subsequent texts, but he'd been quick to suggest that if she wanted out, the middle of the night was when to do it. She'd whipped back a response to ask if he'd pick her up, but nothing. Still, in case he showed, she'd better be out there. She twisted the doorknob, praying the door wouldn't squeak.

It didn't.

Panic gripped every muscle in Everitt's body. She panted like a trapped animal. The door was locked from the outside.

CHAPTER 27

MCKENZIE TORE THROUGH the door of Whitney Trias' office the next morning.

"What the hell is this?"

If she hadn't seen Whitney's pointed nose twitch a bit, she might've thought the little succubus hadn't heard her. As it was, Whitney was just being her charming self. McKenzie took the tiniest of steps backward across the threshold so her toes hit the line where the carpet changed color. She rapped on the door with her knuckles.

"Yes?" Whitney said, her curls bouncing on her head as she turned to face McKenzie.

"Cute," McKenzie mumbled.

"What was that?"

"Nice suit," McKenzie smiled a malicious grin.

Talk slowly so she can keep up.

Whitney smiled back. "Thanks. What can I do for you?"

"I wanted to stop by and ask about this article," McKenzie said. She waved her morning copy of the *Herald*. The cover article about Liza Kruger and the subway baby written by a junior journalist postulated that the Cradle Robber was an infertile woman crazed by her inability to procreate. "This is *my* story."

"If you refuse to report on the angle of the article I assign you to, I will assign it to someone else. It's as simple as that."

"I *am* reporting the story I was assigned to. We've been through this," McKenzie growled.

"You took off yesterday on a random excursion to the Southeast—"

"For work."

"—that was not approved as a business trip to look into a lead you *know* I don't approve of," Whitney finished.

McKenzie took a deep breath. "Whitney, if you could please keep me updated on who is covering the story, I'd appreciate it. I'm concerned the positions stated by the different reporters will be drastically different and reflect poorly on our newspaper."

Something you wouldn't know about, considering you worked your way up through the newspaper industry at that trashy tabloid, the Gazette.

"Silly me. We wouldn't want that," Whitney said. "Next time, I hope I'll be able to find you at your desk instead of chasing angles I've made it clear I don't have any intention of putting in this paper."

"You said I had a week."

"For your angle, you do. You have a week to ensure I'll look at it and consider including it. That doesn't mean I'm going to sideline the entire Cradle Robber story until then. It's one of the most talked about news items in town. Heck, in the whole country. Surely you of all people know you don't get a monopoly on a story like that."

Is it hard for you to come in to work early in the mornings after staying out so late partying with Satan?

"Sure thing," McKenzie replied.

She slammed Whitney's door on the way out. At her own desk, she yanked out her phone to check her messages. There were six texts from Jig.

> *call me.*
>
> *you need to call me.*
>
> *are you deaf?*

or blind, as the case may be?

or, ignoring these is good, too.

yep. ignoring is definitely the way to go.

McKenzie jabbed the button to call Jig. If something had the computer wizard this worked up, it must be good.

Jig picked up on the first ring. "Tell me, what brand of idiot *are* you? Village or Polish?"

"Whoa! What did I do to deserve—"

"You filed to get Hall and Melissa Davidson's tax returns? Are you out of your damned mind?"

McKenzie's ears tingled from the high pitch of Jig's voice.

What the hell?

"Are you their H&R Block specialist?"

"Look, as far as you're concerned, I'm their H&R Block specialist, their pastor, and their damned lynch mob, McKenzie. I've been willing to help you, but if you're going to pull half-cocked moves and have my ass put on a spit—"

"What are you talking about?" This chick had always been a little strange, but this was ridiculous.

Jig let out an audible sigh. "Never mind. That's not the point. The point is, if you need to know whether the Davidsons bought a new Mercedes or donated to the ASPCA, you come to me. Period."

"Wow, Jig. I didn't know you were so generous," McKenzie replied.

"I'm not. I'm Type A."

"Did they, by the way?" McKenzie asked.

"Did they what?"

"Donate to the ASPCA? Or buy a Mercedes? I don't give a precious peacock about their taxes. I just want to find them. The kid's insurance had the dad's social security number."

McKenzie's neck burned. She was talking about Hall

Davidson like he was actually Blair's—Gibb's—father.

"No. If they're animal lovers, they're not the bleeding heart kind. But so you don't file for tax returns a decade back, I'll tell you what donation they *did* give about two years before they moved to Atlanta."

McKenzie's heart quickened. "What?"

"First, swear to me you won't request any more government information without telling me about it first."

"On the Bible," McKenzie said.

Jig chuckled wickedly. "If only that meant more to me."

"Okay. On the lives of all of the little would-be hacker children at mutant schools everywhere who might one day be my sources."

"Ah. Now that's the type of thing that makes me want to shout, 'Amen,'" Jig replied.

She paused for her always-annoying dramatic effect. McKenzie counted backwards from five. With Jig, cues nearly always meant delays. After a long moment, her patience was rewarded.

"Hall Davidson wrote a check for a hundred thousand smackers to the research department of the Greater New York City Fertility Specialists."

CHAPTER 28

"RISE AND SHINE!"

Sunlight flooded the barren bedroom before Everitt had a chance to shield her eyes. She squinted up at Sarah Peterson, who wore a plastic smile to rival any Barbie doll. Well, any Barbie who'd received her AARP card. "What time is it?"

"Six-thirty," Sarah said. She yanked the sheet and comforter back from Everitt, leaving her exposed in her oversized t-shirt and panties.

Everitt accepted the hand the woman offered to help her out of bed. Sarah's palm was dry and cool in Everitt's clammy fist. Appropriate.

As she bore down on Sarah's hand to push out of bed, Everitt burned to mention the locked door. She shot a sideways glance at Sarah. Though Sarah smiled politely, her gray eyes blasted right through Everitt's.

She already knows.

Still, Everitt wasn't ready to break the window and shimmy down the drain pipe just yet. The Petersons had to be tired of her efforts to leave the house. After all, she came up with at least a dozen suggestions a day to try to weasel a trip. They'd give in. Until then, she'd deal. Sarah was weird as hell—maybe even possessive—but they were paying her a lot of money. Worth staying.

Plus, she didn't doubt her ability to give Granny Grunt the slip if she decided the time was right. She hadn't exhausted her talents by any means.

On her feet at last, she pulled on the pair of maternity jeans Sarah had picked up from a consignment shop. "Why are we awake?"

Sarah handed Everitt an ugly, floral-printed top out of the thrift store box. "You've seemed to have a bit of cabin fever—"

"Understatement of the century."

Sarah paused for the interruption but ignored the statement. "—so I've arranged a little job for you."

"Job?" Everitt parroted. She'd come here so she wouldn't need a job. This wasn't what she'd signed up for. At the same time, it was a chance to get out of the house.

"Yes, dear. They're expecting us at eight. Best to grab a bite of breakfast and be on our way. Come on. Waffles ready in the kitchen."

"Why not," Everitt mumbled, dragging her feet behind Sarah, not bothering to muffle the scraping noise. Rodney wasn't there, of course. He was always out of the house before dawn and wasn't back until after dark. At first Everitt thought the dude was the definition of a workaholic, but after being in the place a while, she could sympathize.

As she sat at the table, Everitt noticed the newspaper to the side of her chair. The picture looked familiar.

"Juice or water?" Sarah asked.

Everitt slid the paper over. A gasp caught in her throat. It was open to the obituaries. There, in the middle of the page, was a picture of Zan.

"What's the matter, dear?" Sarah asked, her back still to Everitt as she poured syrup on the waffles.

"Can't be," Everitt whispered to herself.

Sarah brought over an antique ivory dish laden with waffles, fruit, and a handful of vitamins. "What was that?"

"Oh," Everitt replied, her own voice flat in her ears. "This obituary."

Sarah picked up the glass pitcher of orange juice and filled a pair of glasses. Everitt's gaze drifted up to the woman's face as Sarah cocked her head and said, "Someone you knew?"

Everitt's hand flitted to her belly. Zan wasn't perfect by any means. The world probably wouldn't miss him at all. In fact, it might be better off without him. Still, there was something bizarre about knowing someone you'd slept with—had your cells merge with to create something living and breathing—was dead. Seeing this was like that moment in military movies after a bomb detonated. Everything seemed still. Numb. A high pitched ringing filled her ears, effectively blocking out everything around her.

It wasn't what Sarah asked or how she asked it. It was just the same nagging that had tugged Everitt's insides last night when the knob caught because it was locked.

She already knows.

If there was ever a hole-in-the-wall salon that did not scream, "Sarah Peterson," it was Hair if You Dare. Twenty-something girls with teal highlights, a middle-aged woman with an unnaturally black, spiky bob. Sarah would have to be drunk, kidnapped, or both to have her neat little bun styled here.

Yet, somehow, this was where she'd brought Everitt to work.

Laurel Jeffries was equally unexpected. For all the modern, trendy hair-dos walking out that door, the stylist herself might've walked into the salon from a 1950's sitcom. She wore a red polka-dotted dress that fit snug at her trim waist before flaring to her knees, at which point a trim of black tulle took over.

"Oh, it's no trouble. My book's been crazy. I couldn't do one more 'do without someone to answer these phones," the hairdresser said in response to Sarah's thank you for "finding a spot" for Everitt.

"I'll be back for you around six," Sarah said. She patted Everitt's back as though she were a toddler.

Guess you don't trust me to come home on my own, huh?

"Great," Everitt muttered. This woman had serious control issues.

As soon as Sarah walked out the door, Laurel Jeffries began fussing with her own wild platinum curls in the mirror in front of her station. She twisted a section and jammed a bobby pin with a flower atop it into her head. "Sweet lady."

"Sweet" is one way to put it.

Everitt tried to ignore the sickening smell of the perm solution of the lady under the dryer and instead, leaned in toward the soapy bubbles of the shampoo still fizzling in the sink. "Have you known Sarah long?"

Laurel met Everitt's eyes in the mirror as she nodded. "A good while, yeah. A client of mine referred her to me for a hairdo for a costume party a couple years ago. She comes in from time to time."

Everitt started to say that explained a lot, but before she could articulate the thought, Laurel grabbed her hand and pulled her toward the beauty chair. "Your ends look atrocious. Put your behind in this chair. I'll shape you up."

Everitt's brain stuttered. How could someone so blatantly insult you and stun you with the truth at the same time? "I...don't I need to be working?"

Even though I didn't apply for a job. Even though I don't have a clue what I'm supposed to be doing.

Laurel nabbed a spray bottle off her counter and spritzed Everitt's hair with a cool wash of something fruity. "Plenty of time for that. Your hair doesn't have a minute to spare."

Didn't you just say you were so busy you couldn't move without an extra set of hands?

Oh, well. As long as Everitt was out of the prison cell that was the Peterson house, Laurel could cut her hair however she wanted.

"Shame about them not being able to have kids and the whole

nine yards. They're nice folks. Well, I mean, I'm assuming her husband's a nice guy. Never really met him. I can tell he must be, though, by her. Has a good aura about her and the whole nine yards."

"Rodney's okay," Everitt replied. She forced down the wince bubbling to the surface as Laurel's pick comb worked relentlessly at her tangled ends.

"Right, right," Laurel replied absently, though Everitt didn't doubt she was drinking in every word. Most people would peg Laurel Jeffries as the ditzy, harmless type, but Everitt had been around enough accidental snitches to know Laurel's true nature. Even if Laurel's head was made of marshmallow fluff, marshmallows melted.

"When are you due?" Laurel asked after she seemed sure Everitt wouldn't volunteer anything else.

"Couple more months to go. It won't be a moment too soon."

"Oh?" Laurel perked up.

If you want to read my aura, chickadee, you'll have to turn a few more pages.

The obituary photograph flashed in Everitt's brain. She'd seen a lot of people die—lost a lot of people she knew—but damn. If this woman in a party dress and dark lip-liner was her only human contact other than Sarah Peterson for the next two months, she might as well make friends with her.

"I'm not really the mother hen type," Everitt mused aloud.

Laurel continued to comb through Everitt's hair in earnest. Before Everitt could protest, she'd begun to foil pieces of it to highlight. Money to have brighter color put into her hair hadn't exactly been a luxury in her life.

Whatever you say, Laurel.

"It's not for everyone for sure," Laurel conceded.

Everitt watched Laurel's mouth in the mirror. It disappeared into itself as she folded her lips, only the drawn-in bow visible at the top. Great. Already her new "friend" had an opinion about her reproductive habits.

Go ahead, Laurel. I've known you all of twenty minutes, but I know you'll end up saying it before you finishing putting these pieces of tin-foil in my hair.

Laurel didn't disappoint. "Kids are tough, but you never know. Sometimes you're better at something than you think you are."

CHAPTER 29

"OBOE, SLOW DOWN, bud. I'm differently-abled here," twenty-six-year-old Yancy called to his dog, who'd pulled all the way to the end of his extendable leash. A dachshund had seemed like a good idea when he'd adopted Oboe at the Humane Society. A lab would run ten times faster than a guy with a prosthetic leg, but a dachshund's short little steps evened the odds.

"Oboe. Seriously. I can't move that fast yet. I'm workin' on it, but you have to cut me some slack."

The reddish wiener dog plowed against his harness, his stubby legs straining under the weight of his struggle. Damn, he was raring to go this morning.

There was something about the early morning quiet of Central Park as the sun peeked out from behind the skyscrapers that drew Yancy to it. He wasn't much of a morning person, yet since he'd moved here, he'd gotten up every weekday morning for a jog. Before the traffic was out and about, before even the early morning yoga classes arrived. Those were the times he could just run, not caring who saw him or his weird metal foot.

"Come on, Oboe. This way." Yancy yanked the leash, but the dog was determined to run down the path to the terrace. He didn't give any indication he'd heard Yancy. The dachshund wanted that bricked walk.

Fine, jerk. Take me that way.

Usually, they ran the path up by Strawberry Fields. Not that Yancy was a huge Beatles fan, but it was a nice atmosphere. The other direction held the giant fountain, a popular spot for morning exercisers and people who liked to sit cross-legged and meditate in droves as soon as daylight hit. It was also a haunt of people-watchers, but whatever. Some guys owned a cool dachshund that liked to parade them around.

As they rounded the corner where the path spilled into the circular expanse that housed one of New York City's most famous fountains, Oboe started struggling like he'd seen the neighbor's cat streaking across the back patio. His black toenails scraped the bricks as he threw every ounce of his fifteen pounds against the leash.

"Quit being such an asshole, Oboe," Yancy yelled. He pulled back on the lead as hard as he could to pop Oboe back into order.

The leash wasn't used to battling both Oboe and Yancy, though. As soon as he gave the pop, the cord snapped cleanly in two. Oboe raced off.

"Shit! Oboe, get back here," Yancy screamed.

Yancy took off after him, his metal foot clunking underneath him.

Faster, damn it!

He couldn't lose that little guy. Sure, he gave the pup a hard time. It was only because Oboe was an asshole. Oboe knew that, too. Didn't he?

Wind swept across Yancy's face as he chased the blur of burnt orange toward the fountain. He'd given the damn dog water this morning, right? Yeah. He'd done a scoop of food and a bowl of water before he put on his sneakers. It'd kept Oboe from trying to assist him in tying his shoelaces.

"Oboe!"

Still, when he stopped for a drink, Yancy'd have a chance to catch up and grab him. Yeah. Grab him and take him to the vet to have him checked for overactive thirst glands.

Before Yancy could process what was happening, he found out Oboe had other plans. He was wrong to think it was bad to have your dog break loose in Central Park. What sucked was watching your dachshund hop onto the ledge of the fountain and jump right in.

For an awful second, Yancy stopped breathing, sure Oboe would go straight to the bottom. He had no clue if the dog could swim. In the next second, though, Oboe might've been a little Jesus Christ in dachshund form. He appeared to be gliding across the top of the water, drops splashing around his feet as he ran.

In the name of all things holy...

That's when Yancy saw it. The breath caught in his chest, then thundered out in one desperate yell. Primal, guttural, different from the calling before. "Oboe, no!"

But of course, Oboe didn't listen. Yancy stopped cold. Keeping his atrocious little pest of a best pal in his sights, he whipped out his cell phone. In the last moments before the 911 dispatcher came on the line, all Yancy could think was how ironic it was that the one guy in New York City who'd do anything not to be famous owned a dachshund that just found a dead body.

CHAPTER 30

"MAC, YOU'RE TALKING about starting a shit storm for chump change, here. Identity theft. Insurance fraud. Plus, I'm pretty sure you'll go straight to hell for stealing the appointment from some sweet, clueless couple who've been waiting for it for about a year," Noah said.

McKenzie collapsed her head onto her desk, still clutching the phone to her ear. Their contacts had been fewer since he'd taken the sharpshooter job with the FBI, but this was the second time in the past week she'd broken down and called Noah. He was the only one she knew who had what she needed. What did that say about her?

She'd called to ask him for help with fake documentation. The best plan she'd come up with was for her and Jonas to swipe an appointment at the fertility clinic, posing as one of the couples desperate to get pregnant. It was a long shot, but maybe once they were in the building, they could find a lead on where else to look for the Davidsons.

"I agree, it isn't the best option, but as you pointed out, it's a year-long wait for an appointment at the Greater New York City Fertility Specialists. If my story can't wait until next year, Jonas *definitely* can't. Hall Davidson most likely still has his son, and this is our only lead. I wouldn't ask you if I could wait like anyone else, but we both know how that would go."

Noah was quiet for a moment before saying, "Point taken. I still think it's the wrong way to go about it."

"Well, what would you suggest, Double-Oh-Seven?"

"Off the top of my head?"

"That'd be refreshing," McKenzie answered.

"Pharmaceutical reps, a job applicant, attorneys representing an estate with money left to the clinic. The list goes on, but my best idea is that you walk in there as exactly who you are. I can't speak for what you plan to do once you're in, but there's nothing illegal about walking into the building. I'm sure they'd be glad to think they were about to get a nice write-up and prime publicity from New York City's premiere journalist."

Whoa. He was right.

"How couldn't I see that?" she mumbled to herself more than to him. Strange how one second, you could be clambering over people's faces trying to climb a totem pole, and the next not realizing you'd reached the top until you looked down and saw how far you had to fall.

Noah grunted. "I didn't say run with it right away. You have to think about a few things. Obviously you go in there as yourself, you lose some anonymity—"

"Some?" she interjected.

"Okay. All your anonymity. So, what I'm getting at here is that if you go as you and are planning to do something stupid, don't go alone. And when I say don't go alone, I mean take someone who *is* anonymous."

Someone like Jonas.

"Covered. Any other sage tips?"

"Yeah. Don't do anything I wouldn't do."

After she hung up with Noah, McKenzie called The Greater New York City Fertility Specialists to set up an interview. First impressions were not the receptionist's strong suit. The whiny woman insisted that due to their packed schedule, it would be impossible to accommodate McKenzie on such short notice. A quick suggestion from McKenzie that she would be writing an article with or without an interview from the clinic and that her article would be colored based on the information she *did* have was enough to change her tone. The receptionist transferred McKenzie to a superior who was thrilled to set up an appointment for her later in the day.

"You have no idea how helpful this is," McKenzie told her, snatching up her purse and tote bag containing all her notebooks and files. If she left the office now, she'd have time to wake Jonas, strategize, and maybe grab a cup of coffee before the meeting at the IVF clinic.

On her way out the door, McKenzie spied Whitney Trias lurking over the shoulder of another of her minions. She sped up, willing her new boss to continue intimidating the luckless cubicle inhabitant. This was not the time for another argument with Whitney.

Ten steps. Eight. Six.

"McKenzie."

Her steps slowed. "Yes?"

"Where are we on the Cradle Robber piece?"

"I'm on it now. Heading toward a lead."

"A *lead* lead, or an off the wall, no-chance-in-hell-it's-real lead?"

McKenzie reigned in the urge to snap. "I don't chase leads unless they're real leads, Ms. Trias."

She turned around and walked out the door, not even listening to Whitney's calls to come back, that she had something to talk to her about. The office door slammed behind her. McKenzie dashed down the stairwell. She could take the elevator down at the next floor.

Yep. You're definitely paying for this later.

Sure, Whitney might never have the guts to fire her, but of all people, McKenzie should know making enemies wasn't smart.

McKenzie had tried to call Jonas on her way to the subway to rouse him, but he hadn't answered. She'd spent the entire subway ride out trying to figure how she would get him to the door, but Jonas was already awake.

"Don't you ever check your messages?" he said, throwing the door open.

She stepped past him through the door. "Apparently you do."

"What?"

"You're awake, aren't you?" she replied.

Jonas brushed by her toward the computer desk in the living room. "Not up because you called me. I was trying to call *you*."

She flipped her phone off standby. Sure enough, she had a missed call and a voicemail from Jonas. "I must've been underground."

He wasn't listening, though. Hunched over the keyboard, he clicked open one of about twenty browser tabs running on his computer. "Look."

She did. What met her eyes when Jonas moved aside made her want to hurl the cheapo sausage biscuit she'd scarfed down on her way in this morning.

Someone up there hates me.

CNN.com was running a breaking news story about a body found by a jogger in Central Park. No details had been released yet, but eyewitnesses claimed it was a young female. Speculators were already yammering about a possible relation to the other pregnant victims and were even calling this one "Fountain Girl."

Decision time: rush to Central Park and jump into the fray of reporters sniffing the fresh blood, or stick to a track that might be absolutely nothing and go to the IVF clinic. If she went to the crime scene, she'd walk away with the exact same pictures and names as every reporter in town. Let Whitney send another reporter to nab quotes worthy of the blotter, for better or for worse.

"You think it's him?" she asked.

"No way to tell," Jonas said.

He shrugged, but McKenzie already had her eye on another

tab on the screen titled "Similarities." She stuck out her pinky next to the label. "What's that one?"

Jonas hung his head, but he scrolled the mouse over the tab and opened it. A spreadsheet sprawled across the page, every box filled with notations. Words like "blood" and "stab wounds" hit McKenzie before she could make it to the top to read the headings of their boxes. The headings were even more bizarre: height, weight, hair color, body-type, wounds, autopsy results, family, age, race, occupation, children, and place found, among others.

She was looking at a spreadsheet of the details of every female murder victim since Noelle was killed.

"Jesus, Jonas."

Jonas kept his head down, avoiding her eyes. Instead, his hand once again worked at his wedding band. "I know. It's weird. After a spouse dies, some people go to therapy. Some people find Jesus. I found newspaper articles. Can't help it. It's the only thing that makes me feel better. Like I'm doing something."

McKenzie reached over and awkwardly patted his hand. "Yeah. I switched to newspaper articles, too. Jesus is crafty."

Jonas nodded, twisting his ring once more and then looking up. "Do we have a plan?"

McKenzie smirked. "My plan is to start planning."

CHAPTER 31

"AH, YES, MS. MCCLENDON. Our director will give you a tour. We've also managed to fit you into one of Dr. Whidby's slots. He had a cancellation," the receptionist said. She cut a glance to Jonas. "I'm not sure they were aware you were bringing a guest, though. May I tell them who is with you?"

McKenzie didn't hesitate. "This is Rob, my camera man." Rob was a safe enough name. Never mind that she was from a newspaper and would've called him a photographer. Sometimes the right words didn't come out on the spot.

"Sure," the receptionist replied. "Come on back."

A door to her left opened. McKenzie and Jonas were led through a pastel pink hallway dotted with doors on either side. The receptionist stopped beside the last door. "Idanea will be with you shortly."

McKenzie moved past her into the roomy office and perched on the edge of one of the black leather armchairs across from the director's desk. When Jonas plopped down in the other, McKenzie realized she could no longer see his face—or the door, for that matter. The Ficus tree in between the two seats blocked her view.

"Is she gone?" McKenzie hissed through her teeth.

"Yeah," Jonas said, not bothering to whisper at all.

The branches next to McKenzie rustled, and Jonas' face peered through the tree where he'd made a hole. "People trying to have a baby this way already have the process reduced to a paper cup with injections as foreplay. Couldn't they at least give them a couch?"

"Actually, we do it this way on purpose," a voice with a distinct Spanish accent said.

The two branches whipped back together as Jonas' face disappeared. McKenzie stabilized it with a hand as she sized up the office manager coming around the corner.

"Sometimes, by the time a couple has reached this point, they're at odds over the process. One wants a baby at all costs, the other is more hesitant. This gives us a way to ask questions and evaluate subtle cues each gives off regardless of their verbal answers. The screening for whether or not someone is a good candidate for IVF has a strong emotional component in addition to the physical," she explained. She held out her hand. "Idanea Sanchez."

McKenzie met the Latina's green eyes. The woman was younger than she'd anticipated. Had she met her anywhere else, she'd have figured her for a print ad model rather than director of an in vitro clinic. She reached for the director's hand. "McKenzie McClendon. Say hi to my photographer Rob Rialdo."

Idanea Sanchez folded her arms across her body and eyed Jonas' camera bag but smiled warmly. "Rob." Then to McKenzie, "We will have to be careful that no people appear in photographs without written consent. Medical privacy laws are—"

"Something that won't be an issue," McKenzie interjected. "I don't intend to be sued any more than you do."

Mostly because I'd be arrested way before I'd be sued.

"So, what sort of screening is done when a couple wants to start the in vitro process?"

Idanea tucked a strand of her long chestnut hair behind her ear as she sat down behind her desk. "The doctor first meets with the couple to go over their medical histories as well as to perform an initial physical examination to determine if they're potential candidates. Then, if that's a go, we start in on the more in-depth picture, which includes things like the father's sperm count, the mother's follicle count, extensive blood hormone analysis of both. How much detail would you like?"

Little to none, actually. Let's get on with the tour.

"I'm sure I'll ask a lot of questions about the process as they occur to me. But while we're sitting down in the office, I do want to ask a few things about the administrative side of things. I assume there's a good bit of paperwork once a couple is approved to begin the process?" McKenzie asked, scribbling notes on a legal pad.

"Oh, yes."

Idanea opened a drawer and retrieved a black folder, which she passed to McKenzie.

Oh, you've done this before, haven't you?

Inside were several papers of legal documents to be filled out by prospective parents.

"It's a hot button issue, of course, those documents. What happens to embryos in every stage of the process is quite the political concern," she said.

Something about the way Idanea's eyes blazed as she said the phrase made McKenzie's ears perk up. Was she feeling her out about whether or not she was writing that particular angle?

"Is it?" McKenzie played dumb. A yard to her left, Jonas' feet shifted beside the tree's clay pot.

Idanea exhaled heavily and crossed her arms once again. "Yes, it's what seems to interest most people who have only a layman's understanding of IVF."

"I am one such individual," McKenzie replied with a smile. She wasn't about to get a thing out of this director if she didn't put her at ease. "I do plan to cover it in the article, just because, as you said, it's a question on people's minds. But I want it to be skated over in favor of letting readers in on the bigger picture. I don't want to bog down the article with the politics."

"Right," Idanea said, but she leaned back in her chair ever so slightly.

McKenzie skimmed the page for a moment before running across what she was looking for. Options for what happened to embryos in the event of the death of either parent.

"Parents select one of these three options, then?" McKenzie said, hoping she didn't sound too interested.

Since the initial introduction, Ms. Sanchez had not so much as acknowledged Jonas' presence. Perfect.

"They select an option based on the event of one of their deaths, both their deaths, or divorce. Sometimes it's the same option, sometimes it's different. Many times, in fact, it's very different in death than in divorce. In divorce it's more common they want the embryos destroyed. In the case of death, most select the first option and allow the other spouse rights to the embryos should they want them. In the event of both deaths, it's more likely they choose option two and allow the embryos to be used by other couples on an anonymous basis. At this juncture, there aren't any governmental regulations on what happens to frozen embryos if unused. It's a very personal decision."

"I understand," McKenzie replied, making a brief note on her pad for Idanea's benefit. Inside, her heart rate had picked up. "What about if the parents achieve a successful pregnancy during the first round of in vitro, but still have remaining embryos preserved?"

Again, Idanea nodded. "Common. Some people will elect to have them destroyed, others will release them to be used by other couples trying. They can continue to pay the storage fees and keep the embryos preserved indefinitely. In case they decide they'd like to extend their family again, of course."

Jonas' feet shuffled again.

"That could get pricey, huh?" McKenzie said to keep Idanea on the train of thought.

"You'd think."

Ask better questions, McKenzie.

"You said they could be stored indefinitely. Surely the clinic doesn't absorb that expense. Do patients pay monthly fees? Yearly?"

The director opened her drawer again and rifled through her papers, apparently looking for a pricing sheet. "Yearly, sometimes several years at a time. It works like any billing system. The couple pays the first storage fees while here, then we send them a bill every time the cycle comes around and it's time for the fees to be paid again."

"Do they usually keep them around until one or both dies?"

Idanea shrugged. "It varies. Sometimes they come to the next billing cycle, and what seemed like money well-spent before would now be better used toward a private school for the child or their new mortgage. In some cases, couples forget they're being stored altogether. Other couples are constantly aware of them and send that storage check in on *the* day the previous storage contract expires."

From your mouth to God's ears.

Before McKenzie could ask another question, Idanea pushed back from her desk. "Shall we see the clinic? I want to be sure you've made the rounds before it's time for your sit down with Dr. Whidby."

"Of course," McKenzie replied, standing. "This is all so informative. I can't wait to see the operation."

Showtime.

Felicia ducked into one of the exam rooms right before Idanea passed her in the hallway. No way was she about to risk the director grabbing her by the arm, saying, "Sure, you can interview one of our nurses. Oh, here's Felicia." Not that her anonymity was ever expendable, but she'd already gone insane enough to think someone was following her around New York City. She needed a low profile now more than ever.

The reporter couldn't be the one following her. She wasn't

that nuts. In fact, she knew damn well better, because she'd *prefer* the reporter.

Felicia stood behind one of the curtains surrounding the treatment table. The doors to the exam rooms always stayed closed, but when a woman was on a table with her legs splayed, that extra layer of privacy was worth the few extra dollars the drapes cost the hospital. It was a comfort to know someone wasn't about to walk in the door to a view of one's nether regions.

Luckily, the curtains were multi-functional.

"I think I have everything I need in here," the man with the reporter said. "If it's okay by you, I'll head outside and take some shots of the exterior."

"Yes, that'd be great. Thanks, Rob," the reporter replied.

Felicia peeked out to watch the reporter and Idanea make a left down the hall towards the main lab. The photographer turned the other direction toward the office, but he didn't go into the lobby. Instead, he glanced around to check if anyone was watching, then drifted into an open exam room off to the side. *What the...?*

Felicia's nerves gnawed her stomach. The reporter looked familiar. The photographer, however...

She hugged the wall and tiptoed down the hallway. Here was one ridiculous moment she hoped her coworkers would never spot. All the same, if she alerted the photographer she was there, she'd never find out what he was up to.

He closed the door of exam four behind him. Felicia couldn't see anything.

Paranoid, Felicia. He probably decided he needed some pictures of the exam rooms or something.

But why lie about it?

She hovered outside the room. If he came out, she could easily duck into the office across the hall. Well, maybe not easily. Probably. Hopefully.

Something was happening in there. Muffled sounds. He was talking to someone.

The room next door would be a better place to listen. Despite all the money spent at the clinic, the walls in the place were so thin a person could see through them if they weren't painted. Felicia's gaze drifted toward the space where another exam room might've been, but here, there was only the supply closet. This was insane.

Still, she opened the door, crouched under the bottom shelf as best she could, and pulled the door closed.

If anyone comes to restock gloves, I'll never hear the end of this.

Sitting in the dark, she listened to his voice, which she could hear a little better through this wall.

"Yes, I understand, but if I could speak with the director, I'm sure she could clarify the circumstances. Ms. Sanchez knows our situation."

He was on the phone with the clinic. In the clinic? What on earth?

"Right. No, of course, I understand. Yes, just checking on the address. Like I said, we didn't receive our last bill, and we don't want the storage contract to lapse. Hall Davidson."

That was the last thing she heard before all hell broke loose.

CHAPTER 32

JONAS HEARD IT through the phone *and* though the walls. At first it was annoying and hard to place, a rapid-fire rat-a-tat-tat like air popped corn kernels at a movie theater.

Then, through the phone and the walls, he heard screams.

He hit the floor behind the pink curtain, thrust his cell into his pocket, and crawled along the wall toward the door.

Get to cover, lock that damn door, and ride it out.

McKenzie.

Jonas sat up against the cabinets at the front wall and let his head fall against the cabinet. He squeezed his eyes shut, trying to block out the screams. This couldn't be happening.

But he'd brought her here.

You've let one too many disasters happen on your watch.

The screams became louder. Closer.

Now or never.

With a deep breath, he peeked out of the room. Judging from the yells and popping, the shooters were on the next hall, coming from the waiting area. Instinct screamed, "Go, go!" but a quieter voice—one that had saved his ass in the past—rooted him to the spot.

Listen.

More blasts. On *his* hallway.

He jumped behind the doorway right before the hallway erupted into total chaos. Doors thrown open, men yelling. Shooting. Women shrieking. Doctors and nurses ran past his room. A woman waddled behind them, a paper sheet wrapped around her naked body, her face streaked with tears. A huge belly protruded from under her makeshift robe.

Goddammit.

Jonas reached out and grabbed her by the waist. She squealed in terror and clung tighter to the drape she held around her.

"Shh! I'm not going hurt you," Jonas said. He closed the door behind them and locked it. "Tell me everything you saw."

The woman's tiny frame shook like a pine twig in a gust of wind. Christ. She couldn't be taller than Noelle. She stared at him, her lips moving but making no sound, her blonde ponytail swishing back and forth with her trembling.

He ripped his shirt off and yanked it over her head, leaving it in a heap around her neck. He took her by the shoulders and gave her one small jolt. "I need to know what's going on."

"Men," she squeaked. "Wearing masks. Breaking open doors. Shooting."

They were coming closer. She'd have been picked off for sure if he'd left her in the hall, but now he didn't have a clue what to do with her.

Trapped in a room with a pregnant lady and no McKenzie.

"How'd you get out?"

She shook so hard he was afraid she'd tumble over, she was so top-heavy. "Ultrasound room. I heard. Was alone. Left…"

Her voice skittered away, lost in fear. Blasts. They couldn't be more than a few rooms away.

"We have to get out of here. Pull the shirt on. I won't look," he said. It wouldn't help much, but at least it'd cover half of what needed covering.

She nodded. He turned his back and glanced around the rest of the room. No way out. One door that went toward the shooters. No windows. The cabinets were no use. Table. What the hell was he—

He looked up. This had to be the worst idea he'd ever had.

McKenzie ran into the hallway and ducked behind a door in one of the rooms off the laboratory area, trying to push away the images of the bodies dropping everywhere around her. She could help these people better if she stayed alive. If Noah had taught her anything, it was that bullets could go *through* the sturdiest of hiding places. All the people crouching behind desks and under tables weren't safe. The only safe place was away from these psychos.

Unfortunately, failing getting away from them, the safest thing was to find a weapon.

She could hear the men talking to each other, planning who was going where to check what. They were American. Accents? She couldn't tell. Muffled. Northern, maybe? Canadian, even? Maine?

Footsteps. One was moving toward her.

Her chest thumped. She wiped her hands on her pants, took deep breaths.

She closed her eyes, Levi's face shining brightly in her mind.

I can do this.

Closer steps. Faster.

He was right outside. Steps toward her.

She glanced toward the floor. The toe of a black boot peeked past the door.

Go.

With every bit of strength she had, she slammed her body against the metal door and into the shooter behind it. It took him off guard. He slackened his grip on the huge semi-automatic weapon he was holding, his right hand dropping off it just long enough for McKenzie to grab it with both hands.

Keep it pointed down. Away.

She wrestled hard, throwing her elbows into his gut. She was aiming them toward his more tender areas, but she couldn't get high or low enough without giving up grip on the weapon. And *that,* she wasn't about to lose.

"You fuckin' bitch," the deep voice snarled, out of breath.

She twisted her torso to the left, using the momentum to try to yank the rifle to her right, but the man caught the gun across her with his right hand. Now, trapped between the gun and the enemy, not only did she have less of an advantage, but she didn't have any room for maneuvering.

The gun pointed at the wall at hers and the gunman's left side, straight out perpendicular to them.

If you can't beat 'em, join 'em.

McKenzie let go with her right hand and swooped it under both their arms toward the back of the gun. She knocked the weapon as hard as she could at its butt. It tipped downward and toward them both.

McKenzie weaved to her right just as the weapon accidentally discharged.

The gunman yelled, let go with his right hand.

McKenzie scrambled out from between where his arm had trapped her, made a move for the door. He still had the gun. Her only chance now was to run.

McKenzie retraced her footsteps back through the area she'd previously darted away from. There were two good things about this route: it was a known quantity she could be confident wouldn't lead her to a dead-end, and the shooters had passed through here already, for better or for worse. It didn't mean they wouldn't come back, but for now, the laboratory was dark and quiet.

As she took a hesitant step around the corner back into the main laboratory Idanea had been showing her when the bullets had started flying, she skidded. She reached out into thin air, searching for something to steady her. She found bare wall, then a cabinet. She brought her other hand down to where it made sense for a counter top to be under the cabinet. Her palm grazed something sharp there. As her eyes adjusted to the dim lighting, she realized it was glass from the burst bulbs in the room.

She looked down. A dark streak smeared the floor from the corner to where her foot was planted now. Blood.

Stomach in knots, she finally allowed herself to glance around the floor of the main room. Haphazard lumps everywhere, the shapes of fallen doctors and nurses. Whether or not any were breathing, she couldn't tell.

Something scraped at her right. A tug on her pants.

She looked down to see Idanea looking up at her, her face coated in sweat and sprinkled with blood. Whether it was hers or someone else's was anyone's guess. The director grasped her own bicep.

McKenzie knelt beside her. "Are you okay?"

Idanea stared at her like she wasn't sure who or what McKenzie was.

"Idanea?"

"What's going on?" the woman whispered.

Shit. We've got to get these people help.

She tried hard to push away the other thought forcing its way through: *Find out who these people are. They're tied to the black market ring.*

"Idanea, do you have a cell phone?"

The woman nodded.

"With you?" McKenzie whispered.

Idanea nodded again. She winced, gripped her bicep harder. "Already...called," Idanea choked, winced again. "Already called 911. Police coming."

McKenzie's thoughts raced. She needed a plan. "Okay. I'm going to stay with you and help keep you conscious until they get here, okay? Just listen to the sound of my voice. Keep talking to me."

Idanea shook her head hard. "You have to help get the patients out. Pregnant women—in the direction *they* went," she

138

gasped.

Oh, God.

"Idanea, are there any guns on the premises? *Anywhere?*"

Idanea closed her eyes, squeezed them hard. She opened them again. "One. In a locked box in the security office. It's back down the hall from where we came."

"What's the code?"

"Oh, hell. Um…one-five-two-two-four. I think. It might be one-five-two-five-four. I can't think right now."

McKenzie patted the shoulder of her uninjured arm. "It's all right. I'm going to go for it. Stay here. Stay down, out of sight. If anyone comes back, be as still as you can."

"Maybe they'll hope I already got hit?" Idanea said, her voice shaky.

"Yeah," McKenzie said. "Maybe."

Let's just hope they don't double tap.

"You done?" Jonas asked. His heart thundered. With gunmen down the hall, you'd think it'd take any woman—even a pregnant one—less time to throw on clothes.

"Yes," she whispered.

A beige Formica counter ran along one wall, lined with glass jars of cotton balls and medical supplies. A small stainless steel sink was set in its center.

"Okay. We need to get you up onto the counter."

She shook her head hard. "I can't—"

"We *have* to," Jonas hissed. "Now come on."

The girl's head bobbed up and down like a doll. This would be so much easier if this woman wasn't the equivalent of a stalled car in the middle of rush hour.

He pressed his hand hard into the small of her back, urging her toward the counter. "I'm going to pick you up."

The girl re-gripped the sheet that was now around her waist concealing her still-nude bottom half. Jonas scooped her into his arms and thrust her feet toward the sink. "In."

Her bare, pink-polished toes found the metal sink bottom, and as soon as she had more weight on them than him, he let go of her legs.

"Stand up. I won't let go. Promise," he said, settling one hand on each of her calves.

She didn't look at him at all, but nodded, child-like, as she stood.

"I need you to push up the ceiling tile. I'm about to climb on the counter and lift you up through it," he said, trying to keep his voice from rising in panic as the screams grew louder. The shots thundered toward them too fast to stop. No time!

She shook her head fiercely. It was apparently the only part of her body she hadn't lost control of. "I'm pregnant!"

Jonas heaved himself onto the tiny counter beside her, and a glass jar of cotton balls went flying, as did a box of nitrile gloves. "I'm aware. I'm trying to keep you that way."

The crash of a slammed door split through the air. Close, maybe only a few doors away. A man yelled, "Is there anyone else in here?"

The girl's hands jerked to her belly, her eyes toward the doorway. She gazed upward and reached for the ceiling.

"On three. And don't think about this sheet, no matter what happens. I won't look. Just get up there. One, two, three!"

He aligned his shoulder with her rear end and heaved. The ceiling tile clicked with pressure. "Pull up as much as you can. Here comes a boost, so hold on."

She whined, whether to acknowledge him or out of reflex, he wasn't sure.

He hefted her with as much force as he could muster. Her weight shifted off of him a bit as she presumably caught hold of a beam. Her feet scrambled under her. Jonas hesitated for a second, then took his right arm from where it wrapped her thighs and moved it to her calf.

Judging from the way her balance stabilized when he switched, this was the right move. He grabbed the other calf, holding her in a bizarre acrobatic stunt. As soon as he had both calves, he realized it wasn't maintainable.

"Last boost," Jonas grunted. "Pull up to sit this time."

Another scream. This time, it *was* next door.

"Go!"

Jonas thrust upward, and miraculously, her weight came all the way off him this time. He leapt up and grabbed the only beam his hand could reach. There was only one way he was getting up there. Hanging like an awkward ornament, he rocked until he swung back and forth.

The door knob outside jostled.

Shit.

Jonas threw every ounce of his weight into one last swing. He wrapped his legs over a beam. Now, only his butt and torso remained in the room.

"Shoot it in," someone barked.

That did it. Jonas bucked his pelvis forward and kicked his right leg straight up so he wasn't hooked beneath the tile. He pounded into the ceiling beams, knocking his chin against a diagonal piece. He bit his tongue. He tasted blood, but that was the least of his damn worries.

Jonas rolled onto his belly across the wooden planks of the ceiling. A gunshot cracked below them. He pushed on the ceiling tile they'd raised with the very tip of his index finger. It fluttered down before landing in its spot as though it had never seen them.

Finger to his lips, he found the girl's eyes. Again, she bobbled her head up and down to confirm that she understood.

"No one," a voice said. Footfalls rapped on the floor beneath them.

"Then why was the door locked, moron?" another voice answered.

They needed to get away from here, but they couldn't risk

moving with the assholes right under them.

Please, God, let this work.

"Jammed? No time to play detective. The cops'll be here any minute. We need to finish this. Move."

Jonas reached to his pocket and, as fast as he could without making noise, rotated his rump so he could retrieve his phone. The first thing he did was silence it. Then, he pulled up his Twitter app. No way to call 911 without talking, telling them what was wrong. He punched the keys, willing himself not to drop the phone.

> *Greater New York City Fertility Specialists. People shooting. Send help. Not a joke.*

He tapped the send button. If it didn't go through, he would never forgive Verizon. Two seconds later, though, the little blue box blipped onto the screen:

> *Success.*

The yells swelled further down the hallway. The shooters were on the move again. To his knowledge, McKenzie was on the far side of the U-shaped hall in the direction the shooters were heading.

"I have to go find my friend," he said, pressing his phone into the woman's palm. "Use Twitter or text someone. Do everything you can think of to make sure help is on the way, but don't make any noise."

"You can't leave me," she whimpered from where she knelt on two adjacent beams, sitting on her feet. "What if they come back?"

"They won't. They're moving that way. You have to stay here. You aren't very mobile right now, and someone needs to work on calling help. I have to find someone else, but I *will* come back for you."

A tear leaked down her face. "Okay."

He scrambled to his feet and crouched like a monkey with

one foot on one beam, one on another. Shifting his weight back and forth, he managed an awkward scamper until he realized he could move better with his hands. He lowered to his rear and pressed up to his feet and hands. He crab-crawled through the ceiling, dodging beam structures. He had no clue how to get to McKenzie once on that hallway. She might not still be there. But he had to try.

McKenzie padded down the hall *toward* the gunfire. If Noah was here, he'd probably give her all kinds of hell for running into a hot zone without a proper plan in place. Then, he'd shove her inside a cabinet and tell her to hide until the danger passed.

Unfortunately for both of them, he wasn't here to run cover, and bullets could go through cabinets.

The tiny .38 special was light in her hand as she navigated the corridors, following the yells and bullet pops. The little gun from the locked box Idanea had described didn't look nearly as modern as the Glock she'd shot on the rooftop last year, nor did it have as much of a handle to grip. McKenzie passed it back and forth between her hands so she could wipe her palms anytime she stopped to listen and discern direction. This thing might be small, but it was all she had.

They had to be close. The screams of terrified people sounded shriller, the gun blasts so close every one made her jump. With every step, she mustered her will to shoot this gun if she had to. She'd killed someone before. She'd planned to never have to again. It wasn't as easy as it looked on T.V. or in movies, watching the life drain from someone.

You have to do what you have to do.

She stopped at the corner. Footsteps thudded around it, moving away. A woman's shriek.

"Please. Don't hurt my baby," a voice cried.

McKenzie's feet moved before her mind did. She rounded the corner. Aimed the .38.

She saw the pregnant woman a room's width away from the masked man, her swollen belly cupped in her hands. McKenzie's heart lurched.

She pulled the trigger.

Nothing.

The gunman raised his weapon.

"Drop it," she yelled.

She knew the command was ludicrous even as it came out, but all she wanted was the semi-automatic to turn away from his current prey and her unborn child.

The shooter wheeled around. It was like something out of her nightmares. McKenzie dove into the open doorway to her left. Fast pops sounded in her ears, causing them to ring as her hands slammed the floor. Her wrists burned with the impact as they failed to slow the force of her torso hitting the tile. White hot pain seared through her leg.

McKenzie clutched the little revolver tighter, even though for some reason it had betrayed her. She rolled over to get her face off of the pungently bleached tile, to try to get her bearings. She had to stand up. Crawl. Get away. He'd be here in seconds.

She turned back onto her belly, pushed up with her arms. But no matter how much she commanded her lower half, only one leg would push up to a knee. The other burned straight through when she tried to bend it, a blinding pain that made her forget what she was trying to do in the first place.

She let herself collapse back to the tile. Using one foot, she scooted herself like the bizarre ticking hand of a giant clock until her head was at the doorway.

Gunshots coming from a distance. Further away from where the shooter should've been if he was moving in her direction.

She glanced back toward her leg. A dark puddle pooled beneath her.

Only one exit. Nowhere to hide. Bullets moving away.

Time to get out.

* * *

The sobs below continued, the wails and shrieks. The bursts of gunfire became fewer and further between as he scuttled over the ceiling tiles toward the far hall. By the time Jonas made it there, all was quiet.

Too quiet.

He pushed through a ceiling tile and slipped out. With no counter to catch him, he landed flat on his stomach on a red Persian rug in what looked like a doctor's office. The door stood open, splintered in by a foot or bullet. He pushed to his knees and crawled adjacent to the wall even though there was no longer any gunfire.

Careful just in case, he stood gingerly, then took off his shoes. Once his shoes were off, he yanked his socks off one by one to make sure he didn't slip.

What he saw when he stepped into the hallway made his head spin. People everywhere, some on the floor, holding their arms or sides, bleeding out. Some cried softly. Others moaned. One woman sat next to the wall with her knees pulled up to her chest. She was wrapped in the same kind of paper sheet as the girl Jonas had left in the ceiling, but this one wasn't concerned with her modesty anymore. The sheet drooped from her chest, exposing a breast. She held her head in her hands, knuckles white from gripping her face.

Jonas continued down the hall like a zombie. Nurses in the clinic's signature pink scrubs dotted the hallway, doctors in white coats. He tried to avert his eyes, but they always took in too much before he was able to turn away. Some of the pastel scrubs were soaked through entirely with blood, others speckled here and there, but the brain matter splattered over the wall told the story. All of them were dead.

"Jonas."

He whipped around at the sound of his name, so soft it might've been his imagination.

McKenzie sat with her back to a wall a few feet behind him. He must've passed her over, he was so out of it. He fell to his knees at her side. God, he was so dizzy.

"We have...to get help..." McKenzie breathed.

Her bottom slid against the slippery floor. She pushed herself back up. When she did, crimson streaked across the white tile. Black dots swam before his eyes. She was bleeding.

"Help is coming. How bad?" Jonas asked.

She coughed, then grimaced. "Not bad. I'd rather overestimate it, though. And others—"

"I know," Jonas interjected before she could finish. Goddamnit! Memories of Noelle swamped him. A woman he cared about. Bleeding. Dying. And there wasn't a damn thing he could do about it. He couldn't go through this again. Bile rose in his throat, but he choked it back to offer McKenzie the only help he could. He laid his hand over her blood-soaked one and squeezed. "Hang in there, McKenzie. Help's coming."

CHAPTER 33

AT NOON, AFTER Laurel finished a hairdo that reminded Everitt of Kermit the Frog, she declared it was time for food. Up until now, it hadn't occurred to Everitt she had absolutely no money on her and no way to procure any. Still, her stomach sounded like a freight train grew inside it rather than a baby.

"No worries," Laurel said, snapping her red coat on over her dress. "I can spot you a few bucks from your coming salary. What're friends for?"

Well, "friend" was one word you could call someone you'd known a day. So be it.

They walked down the street a block to the Brooklyn Diner. Inside, a huge crowd was gathered around the TV, but Laurel bypassed it. For all of her gossipy tendencies, she was simply walking past something dramatic. Incredible.

The hostess seated them and handed them menus.

"What's going on?" Laurel asked, nodding toward the group around the television.

Laurel wasn't ignoring the gossip. She wanted the *Reader's Digest* version.

The hostess' eyes widened. "You haven't heard about that shooting at the fertility place?"

"No," Laurel gasped, complete with hand over her mouth.

"Yep. Somebody shot the place up something awful. The police didn't catch 'em, either. No clues really. Witnesses said they sounded American. They're looking into political terrorist involvement because the clinic donated to stem cell research. So activists, maybe. They mentioned mafia as a possibility, too."

"Dear Lord," Laurel replied. She glanced at Everitt, seemingly to gage her reaction, then looked back to the hostess. "Are many people hurt?"

The hostess sighed heavily. "Yeah. A lot. I think some died. They said they were notifying families before they released names, but news people already have some of them. Wish they'd leave those poor families alone for a while."

"It's horrible," Everitt murmured. Damn. How many dead people could she hear about in one day?

At the thought of Zan, her stomach rolled. She leapt out of the booth on reflex. At the alarmed reactions on both Laurel's and the hostess' faces, she blurted, "Bathroom."

A toilet had never looked so good.

She vomited twice into the bowl, then wiped her mouth with the sleeve of the awful floral maternity blouse. Morning sickness was supposed to be for early pregnancy, dang it. Then again, it wasn't the morning, and it wasn't the baby making her sick.

On her way back to the table, she stopped in for a minute with the group around the TV. The CNN reporter's voice wasn't audible over the din, but his words appeared in the closed captions below him:

> *Unconfirmed reports from eyewitnesses suggest the* New York Herald *star reporter McKenzie McClendon was inside Greater New York City Fertility Specialists at the time of the shooting.*

A small picture of the reporter filled the right-hand corner of the screen. She looked so familiar somehow.

Everitt's eyes drifted to where another crawler crossed the bottom of the screen in tiny print. Names. Shawna Immerson. Cay Monez. Jessa Sankler. Felicia Rockwell. Hayley Cromwell. Graham Height. Lisa Shoreman.

Victims.

Her stomach swished again. She backed away from the set and turned toward the table. Somehow, this was not the best lunch time programming. People were freaking sick.

"You okay?" Laurel asked when Everitt slid into the booth.

"Yeah, I'm good," she lied, not sure how to explain her sudden nausea to someone touching soft keys on her iPhone, texting to ask a friend what they'd heard about the shooting.

Laurel typed away on her phone. "I'm shocked. I can't believe someone would do something like that at a place where there are pregnant women. What is this world coming to?"

Everitt stayed silent. Most people were like that. They noticed all the horror that made it to CNN but never saw the little girls playing in the same road where broken crack pipes littered the streets. Or people like Zan, probably killed during a robbery or fight over drugs.

"I think of the Petersons and all they've been through. For all we know, if they'd gone that route rather than surrogacy, they could've been in that place today. Makes you think, doesn't it?"

Everitt cocked her head. "Surrogacy?"

Come to think of it, she hadn't told Laurel the Petersons were adopting *her* baby. Maybe she'd assumed. Or was she told that?

"Yeah. I'm glad they went the way they did, and not because of today, either. You hear all the time about those folks trying in vitro and the whole nine yards and then losing pregnancy after pregnancy. So much heartbreak. This way, they have that beautiful baby girl and another child on the way."

Everitt fought her facial muscles to keep her eyes from expanding to the size of the toilet bowl she'd thrown up in minutes before. *What. The. Hell.*

Laurel, stirring sugar into her teacup, apparently didn't notice Everitt's discomfort. With a smile, she clinked the spoon back and forth. "How is she, by the way? The other baby? She'd

have to be about two by now, right?"
   Holy. Ever-loving. Shit.

CHAPTER 34

BURN, BABY, BURN.

In the alley behind his office, flames flashed in front of Trevin's eyes, consuming the last of the paperwork that could tie everything back to him. He'd have gotten to it before now if he hadn't had to take a handful of painkillers every couple hours the past day for his nose.

Now he was finally coherent enough to manage a few tasks, and not a moment too soon. The first on the list was Ollie. The secretary hadn't done a thing wrong. In fact, she'd probably done everything right. She hadn't called the police even when she found Trevin in a pool of his own blood and sick when the Jap left. Instead, she took his pulse every minute until he came to so she could ask him what to do.

And therein lay the problem. If she knew not to call the police, something was really wrong.

He called her and told her he was sorry, but he had to let her go. He explained he was closing the office in light of recent events. She cried a little but seemed to understand. What he was planning to do if she ever found out the office wasn't actually closed was a different matter, but he was banking on her not looking into it too closely. Only psychos showed up at their old jobs after being after being let go, right? He made sure to tell her he was mailing her check and severance pay, so she shouldn't have any need to drop by. If she did, he'd explain it away. He was packing up, some bullshit like that.

His next call would be far more difficult, but it was the only way. If he didn't make another payment next week, he was screwed like a Brazilian hooker on spring break.

The formula to the phone number was straightforward enough. Always the same first digits, then the last four rotated, the final number becoming the first number of the second sequence. The others bumped down the line. Last time, he'd called the 214 area code with the last digits 9703. This time, he'd call 3970.

"Yes?"

As always, the person on the other end of the line picked up through a voice scrambler. Why, Trevin wasn't sure. It wasn't like he didn't know who the fucker was. He just didn't know *where* the fucker was.

Even so, Trevin relayed the vital information from the start: where he was, where he'd been the past twenty-four hours. Same as every time he called. The double standard gnawed at him like a rat through drywall, but unfortunately, it was one of the rules. This guy made the rules, and Trevin knew better than to stray.

After all, it was why he'd sought Dirk out in the first place.

Leaving a single detail out was about the equivalent of requesting a personal face transplant, so he told *everything*. When he came to the part about Ollie, maniacal, robotic laughter met his ears.

"You're kidding me. Seriously?"

"What?" Trevin said, defensive. He'd done what he needed to do.

"She was a loose end. Now she's a loose end you have no control over."

Heat suffused Trevin's face. He hadn't thought he'd done anything wrong. *Fuck.* "Look, I'm not as good at mind-fucking people as you. I can't handle that sort of junk."

"Tsk, tsk. Don't get your panties in a wad because you're an eternal fuckup, *Trev*. Now, what do you want? I'm busy."

Trevin swallowed hard, trying not to imagine what Dirk was busy doing, exactly. "I need you to make another move for me. Before the weekend."

"So soon?" Excitement hummed through the line, even through the distortion.

Trevin cleared his throat. He needed another hit, and bad. His toes were far too susceptible to feeling. "I told you. I gotta have more money by next week."

"Right, right. I assume my share is still the same?"

Trevin rolled his eyes. He was already trying to think of the next step, but he couldn't until he knew the details. "Of course."

"Fine. Call back in twenty-four hours."

It was always the same. A phone call, an agreement, another phone call. The only difference not lost on Trevin was that the calls were getting closer and closer to each other. He couldn't help it, though.

"Got it," Trevin responded, before he hung up the phone.

"Sorry. Had to take that. The charge nurse knows Dr. Pemberly is taking my calls now," Dirk said as he rejoined Bonnie in their red velvet seats amidst the sea of tuxedoed men, formal gown-clad women on their arms. Bonnie's rouge looked even harsher under the shimmering chandeliers than it had in the restaurant before they arrived.

"Oh, Dirk. We're so high up. Are you sure we'll be able to see?"

Bonnie wouldn't know about the refined if she was drowning in a pool of caviar. Her love of theatre extended about as far as the cocktail dress section in her closet, since that was the only thing she liked about Broadway: playing dress up.

"Front row, balcony. I promise you, they're the best in the house," Dirk replied. He squeezed her bony hand. The little thing would be so easy to crush.

She squeezed back. "I'm so glad you brought me tonight,

Dirk. You didn't have to do anything to make up for missing my mom's dinner, but I'm thrilled you did. I'm going to hit the ladies' room before curtain. Back in a flash."

"I aim to please. Take your time."

An evening enduring a Broadway play was a small price to pay to keep her from asking questions about the dog. The annoying girlfriend was entertained in such a way that didn't involve listening to her voice *or* pretending he was interested in her. Plus, he could sit back for a few hours and revel in the memories of the last one.

He'd hung back, watching her gurgle, gasp, and choke beneath the trickle from the top of the fountain. His adrenaline had been pumping so hard that had someone lit him on fire, he might've shot straight to the moon. At any second, that homeless guy could've heard her. She might've found the strength to roll over and out of the way of the stream until morning. And yet, after several delicious minutes of watching her writhe what little she could beneath the spray, her torso bucked less. The last tear pooling in the corner of her reddened eyes had slipped down her cheek. Her eyes froze, unblinking. With a final jerk of her right hand, her body stilled. Once again, he knew he and God were on the same side.

"Excuse me, sir?"

Dirk repressed his urge to lash out and strike the person who'd just interrupted his glorious reminiscing. Instead, he turned and smiled. "Yes?"

Boy, was it a good thing he had controlled that urge.

The bowling-ball belly of the woman in the row behind him hit him first. Then, he looked up to her face, which was framed in a curtain of low, raven-colored pigtails.

"I'm sorry, but I dropped my phone under your chair," she said. She bit her lip, guilty.

"Texting in a theater?" he said, but he winked at her for good measure. "Tsk, tsk."

"Checking my Twitter," she said, a rosy blush spreading over her dusky cheeks.

"Of course," he replied. Honestly. Some bitches had no couth.

He turned his back to her and reached under his seat. His fingers found the small box that was, by feel, an iPhone. Careful to act as if he was having trouble reaching it, he slid it a bit further to the front of his seat. His thumb found the button to light it. Long shot, but how often did he have this opportunity fall into his lap—or under his seat?

He leaned over under the guise of trying to see where the phone was and looked at the glowing screen. Sure enough, the Twitter app glared back at him. Quickly, he ran his fingers over the screen and clicked "My Timeline."

Come on, come on.

"Do you see it?"

Her timeline popped up. MintJulep14. It was enough.

And to think he hadn't even set out to hunt tonight.

Dirk groaned and made an extra far reach into the corner under the seat. "Almost—" he stretched his vocalization out, "—got it!"

He whipped around and pressed the phone into her palm. "Better hang on to this puppy. I hear they're expensive."

She grinned. "Thank you so much."

Dirk smiled back at MintJulep14. "The pleasure's all mine."

CHAPTER 35

"NOAH."

The name seemed so far away, it was a second before McKenzie realized she'd been the one to say it.

Light crept into her vision. People spoke in normal tones around her, but their words were too muddled. Her leg stung like she'd run into a bee hive. Or rather, like it'd run into her. Could bee hives run? Maybe. She should ask someone.

McKenzie tried to force open her eyelids for what seemed like hours. Heavy. So heavy. On the umpty-fourth try—by her count—they opened a fraction of a centimeter. Umpty-fourth wasn't a real number. It was such a silly term.

On the next try they opened a bit more before collapsing back down again.

"McKenzie?" an unknown voice said.

Something cold touched her, then her arm started to squeeze. No, not her arm. Something *on* her arm. A snake? No! She didn't like snakes!

Her eyes flew open, and her right hand lashed out with ninja-like speed to grab the intruder. It took a moment for the picture registering in her vision to catch up with her brain. Not a snake. A nurse. It was a nurse taking her blood pressure.

"Why'mye here?" she asked. Her words blending together made her chuckle. A word smoothie. What a great idea.

"You were brought here to the hospital from the IVF clinic. Do you remember anything about what happened there?"

McKenzie squinted. The lights burned her eyes. IVF clinic. Article. No. Not article. Pretend article. Jonas. Davidsons. Men yelling. Blood everywhere.

"I got shot," McKenzie answered.

The nurse ripped the blood pressure cuff off her arm. "Yes, dear. I'm sorry to say you did. Now, you try to rest. I'll be right back after I let the doctor know you're awake. Do you want me to let Noah know?"

What? Why would she say that?

"How do you know Noah?"

"He's in the waiting room. Since he isn't family, we couldn't let him back without your consent. Would you like to see him?"

Didn't make any sense. Noah here? She didn't need him! But God, his arms would feel so good.

"'kay," McKenzie breathed. But she didn't want to shut her eyes. It'd been hard enough to make them open up in the first place.

Shooting. People shooting. Seemed crazy. What had happened?

Jonas.

"Wait," McKenzie yelped.

In a flash, the nurse was back at her side. "Does something hurt, hon?"

"No. My friend. He was there, too. Jonas. 'see okay?"

The nurse smiled. "Hon, I just told you. Your friend's in the waiting room. He's fine. Thought you said his name was Noah, but Jonas. That rings a bell. You want to see him?"

McKenzie's heart unclenched and deflated at the same time. "Please."

She closed her eyes again. One minute Idanea Sanchez had been showing her the lab where they froze embryos. The next minute people were screaming and falling, slipping in puddles of blood.

"Knock, knock," Jonas said, rapping on the open door of the

ER room.

McKenzie smiled, glad to see he was in one piece. "Hey."

"How are you, rockstar?"

She laughed, but then coughed. How could a laugh hurt in your thigh? Jesus.

"Heck if I know. No one's told me anything. Asking me more questions than giving me answers. You got any?"

Jonas dragged a chair with a rounded back toward her bed and sat down. "Someone shot up the IVF clinic."

McKenzie stared into his eyes, then down to her leg, which was bandaged and in a brace. "And you said you never went to school to be a detective." She giggled at herself. He'd never said that, had he? "Do we know who? Or why?"

Jonas stared hard at McKenzie. Was she supposed to remember something? Had she asked a stupid question? Didn't he know her brain was squishy right now?

"Jonas, help me out here. I'm drugged. Slugged and drugged. Get it? Slug? Bullet?"

"McKenzie, they were probably there because *we* were."

Crap.

"But how could anyone have known—"

Jonas' chin dropped a couple of inches. "*We* knew enough to get there, didn't we? What makes you think whoever we're looking for isn't capable of the same thing? They're capable of killing people and selling babies."

"Touché. Here comes the next dreaded question. How— ah—*known* is it that I was in the building at the time of the shooting?" Damn, her head was killing her.

"Depends how *known* you consider being the main breaking news story on three national channels to be," Jonas answered.

McKenzie pressed her head against the crisp white pillow and stared at the equally white ceiling. Her nostrils flared as she huffed out a breath.

They better give me some more drugs soon, because if they don't I'll scream so loud all the patients within three floors of me will think this hospital uses the bite-the-towel method for surgeries.

"Dandy."

"You're telling me. Worst part? I didn't get anything on Hall Davidson before it all went down."

McKenzie laugh-coughed again. "I personally think the *worst* part would be that I got shot, but whaddoo I know?"

"You know what I mean."

"Yes. I do, actually. Because I swear to God, if someone's gonna shoot me for a story, I'd damned well better land said story. In fact, I want it now worse than I did before. Those sons of bitches tried to kill me."

Jonas glanced over her leg. "Lucky for you they were bad shots. Bullet to the thigh from what the front desk would tell me, which wasn't much. It missed major arteries, though. You popped your knee out of joint. But, you'll live. Unlike some of the others."

McKenzie met his grave eyes. "Many?"

He nodded. "I don't know a number. But a lot."

"Shit."

"Yeah."

She grunted, then beat her head against the pillow in frustration. Her vision swam. Now she was shot and broken, and they'd lost their anonymity. The clinic was the only good lead they had. Now it would be closed. No way the staff would talk, either. Not after what they'd been through. "What in God's name do we do next?"

Jonas strode to the window and stared out. "We'll wait until they release you from the hospital, for one thing. Then, we'll hopefully be able to find another lead, and we can—"

The phone at McKenzie's bedside shrilled.

"Want me to pick up?" Jonas asked.

McKenzie shrugged. "Sure. If it's my editor, tell her I'm in a coma."

"Hello?" Jonas said as he lifted the receiver.

He listened for a minute, his eyebrows narrowing. "May I ask what this call is regarding?"

Jonas listened some more. As he did, he frowned, scrunched his eyebrows.

Finally, he took the receiver from his ear and covered the mouth piece. "I think you need to take this."

McKenzie accepted the phone from Jonas with no idea what to expect. She brought it to her ear. "McKenzie McClendon."

Only breathing greeted her for a long moment. Then, a girl's voice.

"I'm not sure if you remember me, but we met recently in Dr. Schwetzer's lobby. The OB office? I...I saw you on the news. Or about you, rather. I called because I...I didn't know who else to call. I hear you were working on a story about the black market baby trade."

"How did you hear—"

But the girl didn't let McKenzie ask. She kept talking.

"I heard you were, and I...I need help. I think the people adopting my baby might be...I think they're involved."

CHAPTER 36

"LET ME GET this straight. You think the people adopting *your* baby are involved with the Cradle Robber?" McKenzie McClendon's voice sounded weak but skeptical.

This wasn't going to be easy.

"Not exactly," Everitt replied. She sank to the floor in the tiny bathroom at the back of the hair salon and gripped the cordless phone in her hand.

"What do you mean then?"

Unless someone had lived Everitt's life the past few weeks, explanations would fall short. "I mean they're involved in the trade. The black market trade. I think that's why they're adopting my baby."

The reporter was silent on the other end of the line.

Please believe me. Someone has to believe me.

"What makes you say that?" McKenzie asked.

Everitt exhaled. She wasn't sure she could answer that question, but there was no judgment in McKenzie's voice. She had a chance to make her case.

"They...I found out this couple adopted another baby, too. They didn't tell me about it, and they don't have another kid."

"What's your name?"

"Uh. Shannon," Everitt said, not knowing why she lied.

McKenzie apparently knew it for the lie it was, too. "All right then, *Shannon*. Sure. That sounds a little weird. But it doesn't mean they're involved in the black market baby trade.

161

There could've been an accident they don't like to talk about. No offense, but I think you're jumping to conclusions."

"Please," Everitt said. God. How to make this famous reporter believe her? McKenzie McClendon was the only live human Everitt had spoken to in weeks that wasn't associated with the Petersons. Her only shot at telling someone she couldn't leave the house. Telling someone who might believe a wild theory.

She was her only shot at telling someone who could maybe find out what the hell was going on.

The hospital monitors beeped on the other end of the line, registering McKenzie's vitals. Finally, she responded. "Do you have any proof?"

"No. I just know it," Everitt breathed.

More beeping, the countdown for judgment to pass.

"I can't help you if you don't give me your real name, Shannon."

Rustling.

Quick. Before she hangs up.

"They pay surrogates," Everitt blurted out, before her courage deserted her.

Please don't let anyone be outside this bathroom.

"What?"

McKenzie was back on board, as Everitt expected. Any reporter worth her salt would know about the recent court battle over surrogacy in New York and how the state didn't recognize compensated surrogacy contracts. Everitt knew this detail would clue her in that something about the Petersons wasn't on the up and up.

"Yes. The kid before—" Everitt's voice trailed, "—mine. They used a surrogate. Paid her. I...I was thinking you could use it, even if it's not your main story. Maybe it would open up the black market angle for you some. Give it some depth."

"How do you know they're involved with the Cradle Robber?" McKenzie asked.

Everitt shifted onto her knees, whispering even lower. "It takes too long and too much money to get surrogates like me. If there's not enough supply to meet the demand, the only other way would be using the Cradle Robber's method. Do you seriously think there are *multiple* black market baby rings in this city?"

McKenzie half-laughed. "It *is* New York."

Still, she seemed to be considering. Everitt didn't speak, afraid of disrupting the spell she was trying to cast.

"Can you meet with me? Tell me about it in person?"

"I…I can't. I can't let them find out I'm talking to you."

"Give me some names then, something to look into, Shannon. I can't help you if you don't tell me a few details. After all, you're not even telling me your real name."

Footsteps sounded outside the bathroom. Everitt's heart scampered. She clicked the off button on the phone. For a second, she sat staring at the phone in her hand.

A knock on the door. "Everitt? Everitt you in there, hon?"

"Just a minute, Laurel!"

She stood, flushed the toilet, then ran the tap while she stuffed the phone under her shirt and tucked it into her baggy maternity pants.

She needed evidence to call the reporter back. Then, maybe McKenzie would believe her.

CHAPTER 37

"WHAT WAS THAT?" Jonas asked when McKenzie handed back the receiver.

"Another one of you people," McKenzie replied. What was it with people thinking that because she wrote for a newspaper, it meant she could solve all their problems on a hunch?

Jonas cocked his head, his eyebrows quirked into a question.

"Nothing," she murmured.

Solve Jonas' wife's murder, find his son, figure out the entire New York baby underground, uncover illegal surrogacy plot, and find a serial killer. Avoid people who might want to kill me. Easy, right?

"It was a girl who claims the couple adopting her baby is involved in the black market."

"And?" Jonas leaned forward.

"And this could have nothing to do with anything we're looking into at all. Period."

Jonas rolled his neck, which popped the whole way around. He met her eyes. "Because we have so many *more* leads?"

"In case you haven't noticed, Jonas, I'm in a hospital bed at the moment."

"I'm not."

Once upon a time, someone else in McKenzie's life had the same intensity. No way Noah Hutchins would've let a lead go unchecked. Jesus Christ running laps in Phoenix.

"How do we get hold of New York adoption records?"

* * *

Dirk both loved and hated short notice. It was a pain in the ass, but still, it meant sooner rather than later. Everything happened for a reason.

Either way, it meant the time for planning would be skimpy, but that couldn't mean halfway done. Fuckups would plan less with such a timetable, but Dirk knew what they didn't. A shorter time frame meant more planning. Meticulous planning. The kind that wouldn't come back to bite you in the ass.

It also meant not changing your regular schedule any more than you would alter it on a daily basis, which is why Dirk went into the hospital for his shift instead of having someone cover for him. Staying in and having the extra prep time wouldn't help a bit if he raised any red flags. Fortunately, he wasn't that stupid, unlike some morons he knew.

That was why, as soon as he attended to his first errand, he slogged his way through morning patients, including a teenager with a torn ACL, an eighty-year-old with strep throat, and a guy whose only real problem was that he needed to get off the couch and away from his thirty-year-old Atari.

He listened to the heart of a six-year-old girl with a chest cold. It had lasted for months, and now she'd spiked a high fever.

He couldn't wait to pick through his files. But for now, he had to concentrate.

"Let's get that blood work to the lab. With luck, we'll have an answer for you in about twenty minutes," he told the pretty mother, who sat to the side biting her fingernails.

The nurse left the room to enter the blood work in the computer while Dirk stood looking over the file, waiting.

Back in the next three minutes, I'll tell them about the crackles I hear in her lungs so they can admit her for pneumonia. If not, a prescription for Robitussin, and they're on their way.

At two minutes and forty-six seconds, the nurse came back through to let Dirk know the lab was backed up, but that she put a rush on the blood work. It would be back in ten.

Looks like it's Suzy Q's lucky day. Maybe she'll grow up to cure cancer.

Once the little girl was safely in a room upstairs being set up with IV fluids, Dirk was finished with rounds. "I'm heading up to my office to do some paperwork," he told the nurse.

It could hardly get better than the last one. Gloria Jeter. Watching her choke as the water dribbled out of the mouth of the angel atop the fountain, one constructed with the Gospel of John in mind. He smiled, enjoying the shiver running down his spine. Positively delicious. In the biblical story, an angel blessed the Pool of Bethesda with healing powers. Magnificent. And if that wasn't good enough, he'd watched that jogger on the news almost wet his pants during his interview. His face was so red you'd think he'd been caught peeing in the healing fountain.

Now, Dirk locked the door of his office and dug through his locked file cabinet until he came to the file for Phoebe Thompson. He pulled the folder as he had done so many times before and then settled at his desk to peruse it. These were important decisions.

Dirk ran his finger down the list of names inside Phoebe's folder. Some weren't ready. Others weren't possible yet, because he didn't know enough. He smiled as he read over Gloria Jeter's name, which was now crossed out. He made it all the way to the "R" section before he finally found a suitable candidate. Pregnancy close to term. Easy to access. Knew enough of her habits to get her alone.

Sorry, little lady. Advance notice, and you're the only one who fits. There has to be a reason.

CHAPTER 38

"STOP. CALLING. ME!" McKenzie screamed. She punched ignore on her cell again.

Jonas had agreed to wait until the following day to start looking for leads on "Shannon's" surrogate couple so they could to figure out where to start. In the meantime, the hospital released McKenzie to the comfort of her own apartment, which had no cooks, help buzzer, or security guards.

So she'd asked Jonas to stay the night.

Now, the sun leaked through her bedroom window, creating a warm patch on her blue comforter. Jonas' frame hunched over on one of her kitchen stools that he'd dragged into the bedroom. "You know, she's going to fire your ass."

"I have a doctor's note," McKenzie replied. Weren't there laws against firing someone for a disability? Even if it was temporary, being shot had to qualify. She'd have to look it up. "How long have you been sitting there creepily watching me?"

"Long enough to know you still sleep with one leg out of the covers."

The air suddenly felt cool on the leg—the unshot one—that was exposed up to mid-thigh. She yanked it under the bedspread, even though she didn't have anything Jonas hadn't seen before. "Some things never change. So, what's on your mind?"

"Adoption records. You?" Jonas said.

McKenzie winced as she shifted. The pain meds had worn off in the night. "Same."

"You okay?"

He was already standing to fetch her pain pills.

"Yeah, I'm super. So, adoption records. Obviously if they were easy to obtain, everyone would have them."

"Adopted people, anyway," Jonas replied as he handed her two white tablets.

"Right. What we need is a name." McKenzie swallowed the pills with a swig of water from the bottle on the side table.

Jonas' eyebrows furrowed. "Couldn't we have Jig trace the call to the hospital?"

"You have to have a trace on something to trace a call."

"Ah. Good point," he replied.

McKenzie closed her eyes but opened them right away. It might be awhile before she could do that without picturing blood spurting from a nurse's throat. Until then, no eye-closing. "Maybe we could obtain phone records for the hospital. If Jig can't do it, it'll involve a lot of red tape. Might give us a starting place, though."

Her cell rang again, then a third time. Surely Whitney didn't expect her in her office the day after a bullet wound?

"Hi, Whitney. So sorry I didn't call in and that I've been missing your calls. I was kind of recovering from a shooting spree—"

"Yeah. Really not your office, though I bet they're calling you about the same thing."

It took a few seconds for McKenzie to realize it was Jig. Man. She really had to stop answering the phone assuming she knew who it was. "I was just thinking about calling—"

"You might wanna call them, by the way. Your office. Tell 'em you're on your way so they don't send someone else," Jig said, cutting her off.

Pain meds and Jig did *not* mix. "What are you talking about?"

"It's all over the news, McKenzie. Broke about ten minutes ago. New Cradle Robber victim. But this one's alive."

CHAPTER 39

FIRST, MCKENZIE CALLED Whitney Trias to tell her she was on her way to interview the Cradle Robber's latest victim. She fudged a detail or two, sure, but she felt no need to let Whitney know Rory Nathaniel hadn't actually agreed to the interview yet. The brownie points would roll in once she succeeded—however the hell she was planning to do that—and in the meantime she needed a break from Whitney breathing down her neck, reminding her she had only a certain number of days, hours, and minutes before her lead wouldn't so much as be looked at even if it turned out to be true. Whitney had been so sure this story had nothing to do with the black market baby trade that you'd think she herself was the Cradle Robber and knew she was working solo.

Next, McKenzie ignored Jonas' increasingly annoyed looks and questions of "what the hell is going on?" and called a car service to come pick them both up. She'd brief him on the way. No time to lose.

After she hung up the phone with the car service, Jonas stopped whispering and shouted instead, "Tell me."

"I'll tell you if you help me out of this bed and into some clothes. And please, refrain from seducing me. I'm under the influence of opiates."

"I swear I will dislocate your *other* knee if you don't spill it," Jonas grunted as he half-lifted her to a sitting position on the edge of the bed. He turned to her closet and yanked out the first pair of

169

black trousers he saw.

He handed her the pants without looking at her. She pulled them onto her bare legs. Coaxing them over the brace on her knee wasn't easy, but she managed. Pulling them up presented a problem. "Uh, Jonas. Gonna need a little more help here."

Jonas jerked his eyes toward the ceiling when he saw her pants at her thighs underneath her polka-dotted underwear. "I'm trying so hard to be a gentleman, and you don't even warn me."

"Look, I was this naked when you sat me up. You were just so busy bitching about your lack of info that you didn't notice."

"So talk," he said, still eyeing the ceiling but hugging her at her rib cage to pick her up enough for her to slide her slacks up. "I heard the part about the Cradle Robber having another victim. What do we know?"

McKenzie fastened the buttons of the pants and pointed to a white blouse in the closet. "That one, please. Yeah. So, pregnant chick was reported missing by her husband yesterday even though they told him they couldn't file a missing person's for twenty-four hours. Then, she turned up in a freezer van in Connecticut. The driver stopped to make a delivery—his first one since Yankee Stadium. Found her in there, bleeding and in shock, but alive. Called 911. She's alive."

"Minus a baby?" Jonas asked.

"Apparently."

"Son of a bitch. The dude is one demented bastard. So what? We drop by the hospital with flowers?"

Don't ask questions I don't have the answers to yet, will you? I'm focusing on the upkeep of my delusions.

"Jig said she's refused interviews so far, but she's only been found by one reporter at this point. That one stumbled upon her because they somehow made it to the hospital as she was brought in. Otherwise, reporters are camped at every hospital from here to Delaware, but all those are hoping to stumble on her, too."

"Of course," Jonas said. "The media's real good at treating

victims with respect. Oh, wait. Did I say respect? I meant ruining victims' lives."

"Agreed. All reporters should be covered in pig blood and fed to a school of piranha. Either way, if we want to see what she knows, we'll have to delay the executions until later. Thanks to Jig, I have her name."

Surprised she could totter on her crutches under the influence of pain medication, McKenzie made it out the door, but handed Jonas the key to lock it on the way out so she didn't have to balance. At the sound of the bolt, the image of the gunmen burst forth in her mind. Her chest clenched.

She fished through the purse strapped across her chest. Wallet, lip gloss, Tylenol. Hairbrush. Bingo. She pulled the brush out.

"Haven't you groomed enough?"

McKenzie ignored him and plucked a strand of hair from the bristles. Jonas gawked as she stuck it in the door jam.

"If it's not there when we get back, we probably ought to leave again."

CHAPTER 40

"RORY? PUMPKIN?"

Maybe if she lay still facing the wall, Bryce wouldn't realize Rory was awake. She'd already talked to the Feds, and doctors and nurses constantly flitted in and out, never giving her a moment of peace. Sure, her husband didn't mean any harm, but she needed time to process it all. Or time to *not* process it. Maybe that was it. She needed to be allowed to not think for a while.

Her baby was gone. Nothing she could do could change it. The police told her they'd look for her baby girl. Rory and Bryce had found out the gender at sixteen weeks. They'd bought gallons of petal pink paint and a brand new, top-of-the-line crib. The nursery walls bore stenciled kittens dancing ballet.

Honestly, Rory was more scared of them finding the baby than not. At least if they didn't, she could fool herself into thinking things weren't that bad.

"Pumpkin," Bryce whispered again. This time, he shook her shoulder the tiniest bit.

Rory sniffed, not bothering to wipe away the tear dribbling down her cheek. "Yeah?" she said, her voice ending on a choke.

"Pumpkin, there's a news reporter outside asking for an interview. You're probably not up for it, but she does know your name. I'm not sure how she found out. Says she can't tell her sources. Still, since she's here...well, at some point have to talk to the media. Release a written statement or something. But still, we have to decide."

Media.

Rory was so tired, but she couldn't argue. "Who is it?"

"It's McKenzie McClendon. That reporter from the *Herald*. I'll tell her you're not taking interviews. It's fine, hon. You need rest. We'll make a statement later in the week," Bryce said softly, brushing her hair behind her ear.

Rory couldn't bear the thought of weeks of reporters knocking on her door, begging for interviews. It was too much. If she gave one exclusive, it'd be done. "Who'd you say she was?"

"McClendon. McKenzie. *The New York Herald.*"

The name tickled the back of Rory's brain for a minute, then she remembered. "Wait. Isn't she the one who was shot? The one at the in vitro clinic? I saw it on the news."

Bryce ran his hand down her head, petting her. "Yeah, I think so. She's on crutches, too."

Rory rolled over and looked up at Bryce. His eyes were red, his neck blotchy. She could tell he'd been crying every time he left the room, though he'd never do it in front of her.

"I want to talk to her," Rory said. "I have to say something eventually. Maybe she'll be more understanding than most."

Bryce frowned, then ran his finger under the tear on her cheek. "Hon, you don't have to talk to anyone."

More tears welled up in Rory's eyes. "Bryce, the baby's gone. I'm lying here with nothing to do but think, hurt, and cry. What else am I supposed to do?"

When Jonas walked into the hospital room, the scene hit him harder than he could've imagined. Bryce Nathaniel sat in a corner chair, his flushed face the outward sign of his raw nerves. A modest flower arrangement adorned the sill. Across the room, a small woman lay in the bed, monitors clipped to her finger, her chest. Pencil fine gashes streaked her face, her dishwater blonde hair damp and plastered against crusty cuts covered in salve. Her red-rimmed eyes spoke louder than any words.

Still, Bryce Nathaniel's eyes said something Rory's did not. Jonas recognized it only because it was something he'd never had. Relief.

McKenzie hobbled straight toward Rory. "Ms. Nathaniel, thank you so much for speaking with me. I'm so sorry for everything you've been through."

Jonas dragged an extra chair behind McKenzie as he watched the pained look that crossed Rory's face.

"You as well," Rory said.

McKenzie sat down, not bothering to introduce Jonas. Rory didn't seem to notice or mind, and that was just as well. If he opened his mouth right now, he might sob.

"I know these questions may be hard. If you don't want to answer anything or need a break, say the word," McKenzie said.

Rory pushed herself up in the bed, then looked at her hands in her lap and nodded.

"Before I ask questions, though, maybe you could tell me anything you'd like to say in your own words. Sometimes, that's the easiest way to start."

Rory let out a mirthless laugh. Tears trickled from the corners of her eyes. "I'm not sure how to start."

McKenzie sat forward in the chair, leaning on her crutches. "Start with the first thing you remember."

Bryce spoke up from where he was seated. "We were in Grand Central Station. We stopped by the bathrooms and planned to meet outside in the food court. I came out, and she was gone."

Rory's teeth snagged her lip, chewing a scab there. "I told the police the same thing. I know I went to the bathroom. The next thing I remember is waking up in the van." Her hands drifted to her flat belly and hovered above it.

They shouldn't be here. This wasn't right. But Rory was Jonas' only chance. His only opportunity to find out something about the man who did this to her.

To him.

174

To Noelle.

The woman stared at her stomach. The silence hung heavy as a shroud in the room, broken only by the relentless beep of the monitors.

McKenzie waited a moment, but when Rory didn't say anything else, said, "Do you remember last entering or exiting the bathroom?"

Rory shook her head. Her cheeks looked sunken. "I know I went in. I don't know about coming out."

"Did you eat or drink anything? Remember any funny tastes?"

"In the bathroom?" Rory replied, confused.

"Right," McKenzie replied.

"Or smells?" Jonas piped up.

His neck burned when both Rory and Bryce looked up at him as if noticing him for the first time. "I'm sorry. I'm Jonas. I'm helping McKenzie with her article."

"Smells are a good thought. Any weird smells?" McKenzie asked.

Rory twisted her hands together. "It was a bathroom. I might've. Nothing that sticks out."

Jonas' chest heaved.

Of all the times to stop carrying a flask.

How the hell could she not remember something? She was the one person alive in the world, probably, who'd suffered at the hands of this bastard and lived to tell about it. If she could give him anything, one detail to latch onto, Jonas could find the son of a bitch. He could bring him to his knees.

"I know it goes without asking, but I'll ask anyway. Do you know if you spoke to anyone in the bathroom or on your way there?"

The woman shook her head, and the monitor taking her heart rate sped up the slightest bit. "I'm sorry."

"There has to be something," Jonas blurted.

This time, it was McKenzie who shot a look at him that could kill the Cradle Robber.

Rory burst into tears. "There isn't! I don't remember anything. Everyone wants me to know, and I don't. All I know is that I woke up freezing cold and bleeding, my mouth so dry that I couldn't scream for help. My baby—" She stopped. Hiccupped. "My baby was gone. I can't do anything to anything to help anyone, no matter how much they want me to."

McKenzie opened her mouth to speak again, but Bryce Nathaniel stood from the corner, swooping in like an overgrown gargoyle. "I think that's enough."

"I'm sorry," Jonas muttered. It was too late, though. He'd done the damage.

Rory sniffled quietly, then rubbed her nose with her forearm. "No, it's fine. I'm fine. I just need some sleep. I'm so confused. I thought I could get this over with. I...I'm so tired."

McKenzie stood, taking her cue. "It's all right. I understand. Thank you for taking the time to talk with me, Ms. Nathaniel."

"Rory," she said, managing the weakest smile Jonas had ever seen. "You can call me Rory."

"Rory. We'll leave you to rest. Thank you again. And thank you, Bryce," McKenzie replied.

She held out her card to Rory's husband. Bryce glared at her, unspeaking. When he didn't accept the card, McKenzie nodded.

McKenzie set the business card on the table beside the hospital bed, then turned back to Rory. "If you want to talk again, on or off the record, please call."

"I may," Rory replied, eyeing the card, then her arm, then her stomach. So much upheaval. This girl clearly didn't know what she wanted at all right now. Jonas knew all too well what it was like to have no idea what would make you feel better.

"I'm sorry," Jonas said again, this time louder.

I am. I really am.

The girl gazed at her hands. "It's okay. Really."

Little blue veins glowed on Rory Nathaniel's hands, the

scrapes stretching across their lengths. Her nails were clear, glittery. Noelle's had been mauve the day he held her in the alleyway, willing her to come back to him. He would find the Cradle Robber if it killed him.

CHAPTER 41

MCKENZIE HEADED FOR the hospital elevator. Jonas hovered on her heels.

"Wait. We're leaving? Just like that? McKenzie, she's the only lead we have."

"No, Jonas, she's not. She's distraught and can't tell us anything right now. Let her heal up a bit. Until then, let's chase leads we *can* pursue, like who knew we were at the IVF clinic, how they knew it, and why they didn't want us there. The Davidsons have your son. The clinic is our only connection. Got to call Jig."

Screaming at a traumatized attempted murder victim won't help unless your fondest wish is jail time or a restraining order.

The tips of her crutches squeaked on the linoleum hospital floor as she hobbled her way toward the elevator. Jonas caught up to her. "You said yourself we can't go back to the IVF clinic. For one, the place is closed. It's in shambles and a high profile crime scene. Investigators are all over that place fingerprinting and retrieving bullets and blood and God knows what else. Two, since we're probably the 'why' the place got shot up in the first place, no one will talk to us."

McKenzie groaned. Frustration gnawed at her. "They wouldn't murder nurses one by one like a Mexican drug cartel unless they had some serious crap to hide. We might find people from the clinic who'll help, who'll talk to us."

Jonas jammed his finger on the elevator button. "What about

the director? Idanea Sanchez? Did she make it out?"

McKenzie had to think for a minute. "I don't know. I read some lists of names of people injured, but I can't remember. It was so long, and I was recovering—hell, *am* recovering myself. Still, I think she's as good a place to start as any. Let me see if I can find an address."

She whipped out her Blackberry and punched the numbers for information. As she waited for it to ring, she frowned. "We better be prepared for anything. I doubt we'll get a warm welcome."

Dirk careened his motorcycle through the streets of the city, not bothering to slow for the twists and curves in the road. This was bad on every level. Worst of all, there wasn't a damn thing he could do about it. Yet.

He'd seen the news, of course. It was inescapable. Every channel he switched to blared, "Cradle Robber's latest victim survives," or, "Newest victim may help authorities locate the killer terrorizing New York." It was the buzz at the hospital, and as soon as he'd crossed the threshold at Bonnie's house, the twit was already starting in on her own speculations about the whole situation.

"Maybe she'll remember something. Can you believe she lived through it? In a van freezer? She must've been terrified. This guy is a sicko."

He'd had to get out of there if he didn't want to kill Bonnie right that minute. All it took was suddenly "remembering" a file he forgot to update, and he was on the road, travelling nowhere, pissed as hell. Nothing had gone right in the past twenty-four hours.

A pigeon waddled in the road a half block away. Dirk gunned it. The bird ran into the dip between the road and the curb, a place it had learned was safe. Dirk swerved to plow into it. His tire caught it just as it was spreading its wings to flee. The bird tumbled left into an oncoming taxi. He didn't make mistakes, damn it.

Dirk would do a lot of things to make sure he stayed in the clear. He would court loathsome creatures like Bonnie, tend to the tedious visiting his mother once a week. But there was one thing he would not do, he knew, as he parked his motorcycle in front of the 9th precinct police station.

He would not be made a fool of.

CHAPTER 42

"CAN I HELP you?"

The eyes of the frazzled lady behind the glass looked dead, hollow. Overworked and underpaid. Just the right combination to buy Dirk's good guy routine. Good people were always willing to see the best in others.

Dirk half-smiled, half-frowned, a man down on his luck. "Actually, yes. I feel really dumb for coming here, but I've been looking for him all morning and no luck. I know this isn't where I need to be, but I thought maybe you'd have some ideas. This is the first time he's ever been lost—"

"Your son? We can get an Amber Alert started right away, sir, yes, you're in the right place."

Her hand was already on the telephone when Dirk put his hand through the window and touched her wrist. "No, no. No, Ma'am. God, I'm sorry. I feel like an idiot. It's my dog. He pulled out of his collar this morning, and I can't find him anywhere. I'm sorry. I shouldn't have bothered you with this."

Dirk hung his head and turned away, walking toward the exit. He'd only taken a couple of steps when the woman's voice called from the window.

"Sir? Nothing to be ashamed of. You're right. The police department doesn't handle that sort of thing, but I can give you some numbers of animal groups and humane societies who can help you spread the word."

He turned around and forced his face to show what he'd

learned was the look of relief and gratitude. "Really? Gee. Thank you so much. That'd be helpful."

"Sure. Let me run to the back and grab a few fliers," she said. She turned and entered a room behind her, still within earshot of the front desk.

The TV was on CNN. The newscasters were again talking about the Cradle Robber victim who lived. They were currently interviewing a doctor about how long the victim could've survived in the van freezer.

As the lady returned with the pamphlets, Dirk stared at the TV. "God. Such a mess. I hope she'll be okay. Someone broke into my cousin's apartment not too long ago when she wasn't even at home, and it was weeks before she could sleep again. I can't imagine how that girl feels."

The lady leaned through the window and propped her elbows on the counter to glare at the TV with him. "I'd be a basket case for the rest of my life, I'm sure. Hopefully they're giving her something for anxiety. I know she had police protection at St. Alphius, so maybe she was able to rest for a few days."

Dirk chuckled deep inside, but on the surface, he kept his stoic, concerned visage. He accepted the lost dog information he wouldn't use even if he had a dog, which he didn't. Stupid, stupid people. "Well, let's hope they catch the bastard. I don't know what this world's coming to." He lifted the fliers and smiled. "Thanks for these. You've been a huge help."

CHAPTER 43

"WHAT THE HELL are you doing here?" Idanea Sanchez screeched when she saw McKenzie and Jonas standing at the door of her Greenwich townhouse. "Actually, never mind. I don't care."

She shoved the door, but Jonas caught it and pushed back.

"I can call the police, you know," Idanea said. Her pale lips pursed so tight they looked as if they might pop off. "In fact, I think I will."

"Will you please talk to us? All we want to do is talk," McKenzie said. The woman acted as if it had been McKenzie who had come in and shot up the clinic.

Jonas spoke up. "Remember, Idanea, McKenzie was shot in the clinic, too."

"Too? What do you mean, 'too'? Of course they shot her. She's the reason they came into my clinic firing and torched every record in our office. She's the reason half of my friends and colleagues are dead," Idanea cried. Her clenched fists and bulging eyes made it obvious her tension rivaled that of McKenzie's last three run-ins with Whitney Trias combined.

Torched the records? McKenzie took a deep breath. Just because the records were gone didn't mean the trail to the Davidsons had to go cold.

"I haven't done anything wrong, Idanea." McKenzie caught the sound of her own raised voice despite fighting for control. She hated her loss of restraint. But here she was, a bullet hole in her thigh, on crutches, and in a knee brace, and this woman blamed her for the death of her friends

"Oh?" the Latin beauty replied coolly. "So, coming into my clinic on false pretenses when in reality, you were doing a piece on the *black market baby trade* doesn't qualify as *wrong* in your mind?"

Touché.

"Okay, you're the second person to say that. How does everyone seem to know what McKenzie is writing about?" Jonas asked.

McKenzie glanced at Jonas. That was a damn good question.

The director of the IVF clinic rolled her eyes, but she backed into her apartment and allowed them to pass. "How could they *not* know? It made the front page of the *Gazette* yesterday."

"What?"

This explained a lot. Granted, the *Gazette* wasn't exactly known for its journalistic integrity. Most days they ran as many articles about the latest celebrity break-up rumors as they did about actual news. Either way, the fact the *Gazette* ran the piece at all didn't make sense. Who wrote the article? If Idanea was right, and the clinic had been shot up because of McKenzie, it meant two things. First, the perps had to have known what her article was going to be about before the *Gazette*'s coverage of the shooting. Second—and most important—the perps were worried as hell.

"Idanea, if someone didn't want me in the clinic, they must've thought I'd find something."

Shaking now, Idanea fished a box of cigarettes out of her purse and tipped one out. She held it between her lips and picked up a lighter off the coffee table. "I had been trying to quit, but being shot in the arm isn't great for anxiety."

McKenzie looked to Idanea's arm, which was in a sling. "Trust me. I understand."

The Latina let out a dry, maniacal laugh. "Do you,

McKenzie? My people are dead or hurt so bad they'll never recover. I've lost my job. My friends don't come near me, and you're in my house pumping me for info. Did you see what they did when they thought I was talking to you before? How do I know they won't find me and put a bullet in my head instead, like right after you and this bozo of yours leave?"

"I'm terrified, too, all right? But if they're after me, I want to find them first," McKenzie said. All the people in her life who'd been hurt because of her tenacity, and this woman thought she didn't know pain.

Idanea sucked in smoke, held it, then blew it out in a long, thin stream. She flicked ash off her cigarette onto the carpet.

"Off the record. All of it," McKenzie said.

"Yeah, right," she said, puffing smoke in McKenzie's face.

"I mean it, Idanea. I need to know what they thought I'd find. It might help us figure out who did it."

"That's what the cops are for, Nancy Drew," Idanea replied. She turned her back, pacing.

Jonas cleared his throat from the doorway. "Police don't fix everything. Trust me."

Idanea threw her head back in a fit of mocking giggles. "What? They didn't recover the gin bottles stolen from your car?"

Jonas stepped over the threshold, and McKenzie willed him to not move toward the Latina. "They couldn't solve my wife's murder."

Idanea's laughter died on her lips, her face grave. "Oh. I'm sorry."

"You don't have to be sorry. Just help us," Jonas said.

Idanea rolled her head around to stretch her neck, then took a long puff from her cigarette. Tears welled in her eyes. "I don't know why they didn't want you in the clinic. They had to think you'd talk to someone who knew something bad. I never suspected there was anything but legitimate in vitro fertilization going on there. We just wanted to help struggling couples conceive. Now, even if we're able to re-open, people will be scared to come to us."

A sob tore from the director's throat. Her head drooped as she covered her face with her free hand. "I didn't know. So they couldn't have cared you were talking to me. Who else were you supposed to talk to? Mostly doctors and nurses were killed. The only other person you were scheduled to talk to was Dr. Whidby. He's dead."

At this, Idanea's sobs spiraled into uncontrollable wails. She sniffled and moaned, taking drag after drag on her cigarette every time her crying slowed. "He was my friend. I'd worked with him for years to start this clinic. It was a dream we both shared, a place that could research better ways to help people. That's all we ever wanted."

McKenzie put a hand on her shoulder and squeezed. What if this was her fault? Had it really gotten to the point where it wasn't enough to kill off her *own* best friends and family for her career? Now, she was taking others' away from them, as well. She had never wanted any of this. Last year, it had been all about her and her career, but this time she wasn't even really chasing a story. She was just trying to bring home Jonas' son. But how could she blame this woman for hating her? Hell. *She* hated her, too.

"Idanea, I have just one more question, then I'll leave you alone," she whispered. Surely the Davidsons would contact the clinic to find out about their embryos. The facility had to have records somewhere besides at the building in order to keep all of those embryos straight. No way would a place like that let so many precious potential lives sit without their owners being able to claim them. For some people, those were their only chance at children.

"What?"

"Do you know anything about Hall and Melissa Davidson? They were patients at the clinic several years ago. I know they gave some hefty donations. They may also have embryos still in storage at the facility."

Idanea smirked as she shook her mane of shiny black hair. "Not anymore, they don't. The gun fire in the lab hit the storage units and escalated their temperatures. In other words, it wasn't only doctors and nurses and staff hurt in the shooting. Hundreds of people lost potentially viable embryos."

CHAPTER 44

THE SECOND THEY left Idanea's townhouse, Jonas slammed his fist into a trashcan. "They're gone. The embryos are gone. The only lead we had on the Davidsons."

McKenzie suppressed the urge to reach out and touch him. "They lived in New York for years. There have to be other traces of them, Jonas. We'll find them."

"It all goes back to the damned Cradle Robber. We need to find him first. Find him, we'll be able to find Gibb. I know it."

"You don't know that. We're on the right track. The IVF clinic and the black market trade are tied. We can follow the IVF trail. There still have to be records somewhere. People we can talk to."

Jonas sped up, all but racing down the sidewalk to where they'd parked the car.

McKenzie had to hop and swing herself through her crutches to keep up.

Jonas shook his head. "Or, we pursue Rory Nathaniel. She can tell us way more than the IVF clinic. Anyone there who could have told us anything is dead. Even if there is some magical set of records elsewhere, do you really think they'll let us within miles of it? Besides, the Cradle Robber isn't killing women in the IVF clinic. He's leaving them in fountains and freezer vans and in the path of subway trains."

In past years, this would've been a no brainer for McKenzie. The living, breathing victim would be the far more interesting story because of the personal interest. The exclusivity. Journalists would be swarming over both stories, the victim who survived the Cradle Robber and the IVF clinic. But now that the IVF records were gone, McKenzie had the exclusive no one else could get, too. Rory. But if she couldn't get Gibb back, all the triumphant stories on earth would feel just like the one last year: hollow. Success wasn't much when everyone you might've enjoyed it with was gone. "I know you think finding the Cradle Robber is the way to go, but staying on the IVF Clinic angle has the best of both worlds. The Davidsons are tied to the clinic, and so is the Cradle Robber. We have every reason to believe the IVF Clinic could lead us to your son."

Jonas wheeled around to face her, fuming. "Which part of, 'lost embryos' didn't you understand?"

"They'll have to notify people storing embryos there about what happened. They'll have to find names somehow—"

He held up his hands. She stopped speaking. "McKenzie, unless they're on Mars or Saturn, the Davidsons'll hear about the shooting. They're skittish. What makes you think the shooting won't make them run faster and harder than before? Let alone that a reporter is working on a story about the black market baby trade."

He was right. The Davidsons had to be on their guard. Still, her reporter's gut said start at the shooting. Listening to that gut had gotten her the biggest story of the century last time. She had no reason to ignore it now.

"Maybe that's the next step, then. We need to know who at the *Gazette* knows what we're doing and how they know it," McKenzie said.

The sound of Papa Roach's metal song "Last Resort" bit through the air. Jonas dipped into his pocket. He hit the answer button on his phone and barked, "This is Jonas."

McKenzie watched while he listened. He focused on a leaf at his feet. His gaze flashed to McKenzie once. She turned her attention to spot of cracked paint on a nearby bench, pretending not to listen.

"Right," he said from behind her. "I could. Yeah. I could meet you there. About an hour? Yeah. Uh-huh. I need to finish some business right now, but then I'll be on my way. Sure. Thanks for calling."

When she was sure he was finished, she turned around. "What's up?"

He poked his cell back into his pocket. "Job interview. Few and far between these days, so I'd better go. Meet back up later tonight?"

McKenzie nodded. It might not be bad to have a few hours to dig on her own. "Text me when you're finished. I'll see if I can hunt down our cowboy at the *Gazette*."

This is the only way.

Still, although McKenzie had come to terms with its necessity on the way here, she wanted to kick her own ass as she stepped into Whitney Trias' office.

"What brings you by, McKenzie?" Whitney asked.

"Look, Whitney, can we be upfront about this for a minute? You don't like me, and you'd probably sell your own grandmother if it meant you could fire me without losing some of the best stories this newspaper sees. I dislike you, but I love this job. I get more exposure in this paper nationally than I could anywhere else. We both hate it, and we both suck it up anyway. So can we quit the power struggle?"

"What do you want, McKenzie?"

McKenzie hadn't realized the word "want" could sound so malicious.

Time for plan B.

She shrugged, palms up. "Worth a try. How about a temporary truce for the sake of this story? I know you didn't want me taking the Cradle Robber story in this direction, investigating the black market baby trade, but I'm obviously close enough to the truth that someone's trying to kill me. You know as well as I do the powers that be are watching you the way high rollers watch the long shot horse. I want to keep my job, sure. But I bet you want to keep yours, too."

Whitney's beady eyes narrowed as she scrunched her nose. "I'll give you one thing, McKenzie. *Only* one thing. I like your bluntness. But McKenzie, give it a damned rest, already. Even if something insane happened at the IVF clinic, it doesn't mean it's connected to the Cradle Robber. Your story is the Cradle Robber. So do it."

"You're saying we're not going to cover a massacre at a well-known reproductive center?" McKenzie shot back.

"No," Whitney said, returning her gaze to the stack of papers in front of her. She initialed the sheets one after the other, approving stories to go to print. "I'm saying *you're* not going to cover it."

None of this made sense. The woman clearly had the ambition to work her way to where she was now. Why wouldn't she want her top investigative journalist to cover a mass killing in Manhattan today? Particularly when they had the exclusive, on-the-scene angle of a reporter who'd been in the direct line of fire.

"Whitney, what the hell do you have against this story?" McKenzie asked, throwing her hands up as her voice rose. "People need to know the truth. It might be ugly, but it's our job. We give people information, and we expose shady shit. I don't care if the IVF Clinic is so prestigious that the leader of every country from here to Timbuktu was created in a test tube there. We have a responsibility to report what happened. And if what happened is connected to the Cradle Robber, so be it. Why don't you want me to tell the world about this insanity?"

Whitney bolted up from her desk. "Because I think you're doing more harm than good," she cried, her voice midway to a scream.

McKenzie was taken aback. That kind of screech didn't match Whitney's buttoned down shirt, her neat pencil skirt, and smart heels. She couldn't stand Whitney, but the editor usually oozed professionalism.

"Whitney? What are you talking about?"

Whitney wiped at her eyes, trying to stop the mascara from leaking down her face. She looked down, her cheeks reddening.

"Whitney, what's going on?" McKenzie asked, this time a little softer, her voice a mix of shock and concern.

"Why the hell can't you just leave it alone? Listen to someone else for a change? Take someone else's feelings into consideration? You never stop to consider the harm your relentless search for a story can do to innocents." Whitney stretched her neck from side to side as if to ease the tension there, then drew a deep breath and blew it out slowly, gathering the tatters of her shredded composure around her like a suit of familiar armor. "I didn't want you to write the article from the black market baby trade angle because I didn't want you to draw more attention to it. So many happy families are trying from day to day to live normal lives and not run from the way they ended up together. I should know."

McKenzie's heart fluttered. "What?"

Whitney nodded, plucking a tissue from the box on her desk and sitting cross-legged on top of the furniture. "I was adopted illegally. I don't remember anything about my birth parents. They sold me as a black market baby when I was only a few months old. I was adopted by a couple who couldn't have kids and was having trouble adopting traditionally because of their age."

"Whitney, I had no idea."

"It might not be right, but if it wasn't for underground adoption, many people wouldn't be able to have kids: single mothers, gay couples, people with disabilities, single fathers. My own parents. It's a lot harder for them to adopt. But instead of letting them, instead of being more flexible in their criteria and more open to the possibility of a less-than-perfect but still loving family and home, they'd rather just keep kids orphans and in foster care for years and years. And most of *those* situations are far worse than the black market babies'. At least the ones bought on the black market are wanted."

"Whitney, that still doesn't make it right, taking people's kids away."

"Don't you think I know that? I'm just afraid. Afraid law enforcement will start cracking down on people who have used the system. When you start turning over rocks like the Cradle Robber and having things like this come out, nobody is going to be open minded about them. They'll always be on the sides of the people who didn't sell or buy a baby, because those terms alone make the people willing to pay any price for a child sound like crooks. Evil ones. If the black market baby trade starts being investigated and torn apart, not only could my own family get in trouble, but tons of kids would be stuck *in* homes instead of *at* home where they belong."

McKenzie couldn't help but agree, but at the same time, this black market trade was the same one breathing life into a monster ripping babies out of women. It had to be exposed.

"All of those kids deserve homes, Whitney, just like you did. But these babies the Cradle Robber is taking, they don't deserve to never know the parents who loved them and wanted them. And the parents don't deserve to lose their families, either. The black market trade is what gave rise to the Cradle Robber. Until it's exposed, it's doubtful he can be caught."

Whitney didn't speak, just looked at her feet, a tear forming in the corner of her eye. "What do you need?"

McKenzie's heart skipped a beat.

Finally.

"Whitney, who do you know at the *Gazette?*"

CHAPTER 45

"I'LL BE BACK in about three hours, pumpkin," Bryce said, pecking Rory on the forehead.

Her husband had asked her over and over and over again if she wanted him to call someone to stay with her while he went to the office to tie up some things that were getting out of hand in his absence, but she insisted she'd be fine. She'd go nuts with him constantly in the room with her, let alone some stranger. He meant well, but something about the way he watched her as if he expected her to explode at any second made her feel even more anxious than she already was.

She needed to be normal for a while. To sit and do things she'd do on any other day. But mostly, Rory needed a chance to go through her own thoughts without being examined like a zoo animal on display. She needed to be free to cry, laugh, or scream without anyone around to notice.

Once she heard Bryce close the door on his way out, Rory stood and headed straight to the computer to pull up the internet. Bryce, overcome by throes of protectiveness, had kept her from going anywhere near the internet, television, or any other outlet for news of her abduction. As if her wanting to see it was unhealthy. But for her, it was something like needing to look at yourself in the mirror after a bad accident. Sure, it might hurt, but somehow, it was more comforting to *know*.

She read several articles about herself, though none gave her name, and it was true: the media didn't know much surrounding her ordeal. The hype was mostly about how the Cradle Robber's most recent victim was alive and how, hopefully, she'd be able to point authorities in the right direction.

Yeah. No pressure.

Rory also perused a few tidbits about the shooting at the IVF clinic. The thought of contacting McKenzie McClendon again to talk was tempting. To be part of the Cradle Robber investigation, to help catch him, was worth more than anything she could give. She wanted to do everything she could to tell them more about what had happened to her and her child.

She hadn't contacted the reporter again, though. She didn't have anything new to tell McKenzie since the last time they'd talked. Besides, she hadn't had a chance to sort through the muddled swamp of thoughts inside her head. Then there was the man who'd come with the reporter to interview her at the hospital.

They'd never introduced the guy. At first, she'd thought he was McKenzie's assistant, but the outburst he had made...he must have more to do with it than they'd let on. He seemed far too emotionally invested for a bystander.

Rory clicked through write-ups about the IVF clinic shooting. Sure enough, on the third site, she found Jonas Cleary. He wasn't McKenzie's assistant at all. He'd been one of the victims at the clinic during the shooting.

Rory wasn't sure what made her do it. But she'd never been one to ignore her natural curiosity. With a few clicks, she was looking at a page full of articles about Jonas Cleary. Apparently, his wife had been murdered years ago at the same time his son was abducted. Holy smokes. No wonder the guy was distraught. This had to have hit him really close to home.

Which was why she'd done what she did and was now lying on the sofa, resting and thinking. Thinking and resting. This had to be the longest week of her life. The hardest part was no one seemed to understand.

That's when the doorbell rang.

When the door opened in front of Jonas, Rory Nathaniel met his eyes. She'd looked small in the hospital bed, but today, she seemed even shorter, barely five feet. God, she was pale.

"May I come in?" he asked.

She nodded and smiled a tired smile. "Sure." Rory gingerly stepped aside.

Jonas followed her through the foyer and front hallway into the living room. The antique furniture and fine oil paintings that adorned the room told Jonas that despite their young ages, Rory and Bryce Nathaniel must be doing all right for themselves.

"So, is Bryce around?" Jonas asked, seating himself on a lime green chaise lounge chair. It was fine if the man wasn't home, after all. Jonas wasn't doing anything wrong. It did make him slightly uncomfortable, though.

Rory sat tailor-fashioned across from him in a striped chair. She threw an afghan over her legs and picked up her cup of tea. "He had to go in to work today. The office is in a shambles without him. I'm sorry to bother you, by the way. I...well, I was lonely, if I'm being honest. I started reading on the internet about the clinic shooting, and it linked me to an article about you, actually. I...I'm so sorry to hear about what happened to your wife and son."

Jonas hung his head. "Thanks. Me too."

Rory looked down into her teacup. "It's actually why I called you. I...ever since I woke up in the van, everyone's been treating me like I'm some sort of freak. Like I'm about to spontaneously combust or have a nervous breakdown at any second. I really wanted to talk to someone who could relate. Who'd talk to me like a normal human. Then I found out your story and thought that maybe...you'd understand."

"I guess you called the right guy."

She nodded and sipped her tea. "How do you...how *did* you

start to pick up the pieces? I mean, I know it's not that easy, and I know it has to be different for everyone. Still, I can't...I know it's only been a couple days, but I have no idea what to do with myself. How did you...move on?"

Jonas nibbled one of the cookies Rory had put on the coffee table. It looked like Rory was experiencing the same thing he had after Noelle's death: lots of well-meaning neighbors bringing over plates of store-bought goodies. Nothing like sweets to cure the grief of a murdered loved one.

He met Rory's eyes. "I didn't."

She licked her lips. "Oh."

Just because you don't have hope doesn't mean you should bring this girl down to that place, too.

"I'm sorry. I didn't mean to sound like there was no life after this. Keep in mind, your situation is a lot different from mine. You have a husband. Family."

Rory looked at him as though she'd been slapped across the face. "Oh, I see. I'm *lucky* because at least I didn't lose my spouse *and* my child, huh?"

The heat of embarrassment flared under Jonas' skin. "That's not what I meant, Rory——"

But she was already on her feet, hands in the air. Her ashen face grew splotchy with patches of angry color. "Look, Jonas, I called you because I wanted to talk to someone who understood. But if you're going to talk to me like I should be grateful for what I have right this instant, you might as well leave."

He stood, but didn't move to leave. This girl needed him. Hell, she *was* him. Hysterical, furious, confused. She didn't know what to do with herself, and she hadn't yet had days and weeks and months to learn how to channel that horrible energy into something adequately life-destroying.

"I didn't mean that, Rory. I'm sorry. I really am. Trust me, I *do* understand. I shouldn't have said what I did. It's just that it's hard, thinking about everything. Your situation brings up so many thoughts and feelings I wish I'd never had."

She exhaled hard as she collapsed back into the chair. She pulled the blanket tight around her shoulders. "It's okay. I shouldn't have pushed you to talk about it."

"You didn't," Jonas replied. "But I want to."

Rory sniffled a little into the blanket. "You found her, didn't you?"

Noelle's face drifted in front of Jonas' eyes, lifeless, cold. He'd begged her to come back. Told her he would do anything to make it happen. "Yes. I did."

"When I woke up in the freezer, I thought I was already dead," Rory said. Her voice sounded as far away as Jonas' mind. "It wasn't long before I realized the baby was gone. I started to scream and beat on the sides of the van, but no one heard me. I knew it was over. I wouldn't make it out. Then somehow, after what seemed like hours, the van stopped. The back opened. The driver yelled and came in. He picked me up, I remember, took me outside. It was so warm in the sun."

Jonas stared at the coffee table, unable to look at Rory. "He saved you."

"I suppose so, yes."

Jonas grunted. "Must be nice to be able to do that for someone."

Rory blew her nose into a napkin. "What do you mean?"

At this, Jonas looked at her, imagining what the driver must've thought when he opened the back of his truck. Shock, that there was a bloody woman in his van. Terror that she was injured. Relief when she was alive.

"He saved you. It's something I've regretted for years of my life. That I couldn't save them."

Why was he talking to a total stranger about this? This was ridiculous. The look in her eyes made him feel like he'd known her much longer than a few days.

"Jonas, you couldn't have done anything differently. Don't

get me wrong. I've been beating myself up, too, trying to think of how I could've been smarter or faster or…anything to keep what happened from happening. But I've also realized if I treat it that way, I'll probably go crazy. If I'm not already."

Rory sat crying into her hands, rubbing her face on her sleeve. After a long moment, she spoke again. "I know better than you think, you know. I couldn't protect someone, too."

She gazed down at where her belly was flat underneath the spread of the afghan. Jonas could only imagine what it felt like to know only days prior, there had been a new life growing there. "He didn't cut the baby out of me, you know."

Jonas cocked his head. Actually, he *hadn't* known this. "Oh?"

"No. The doctors think the drugs he used to kidnap me caused me to go into labor. I don't remember it at all. But somehow, knowing that hurts even worse. It feels—" she wailed, a sob racking her entire tiny frame, "—like I *gave* the baby to him. Voluntarily."

A flood of tears surged down Rory's cheeks. She clutched her belly as though she'd drunk poison.

Jonas said nothing for a few minutes while she cried. He knew how much she needed to.

"Did you know what it was going to be?" he finally asked.

Rory managed to smile. "A girl."

Jonas winced, then smiled back. "She was beautiful, I'm sure."

He said that because he knew she didn't want to hear, "I'm sorry."

"Thank you," she replied softly. "I appreciate that."

CHAPTER 46

"NESSA! LONG TIME no see, love," Whitney simpered as she opened the office door without knocking. It had been a recurring theme since McKenzie and she had entered the *Gazette* building.

McKenzie's boss walked around the desk to where the tall ribbon of a black woman stood, plastic grin affixed in place. The two shared a half-hug and exchanged a little side air-kiss.

"Whitney. It's been too long. How have you been?" the woman replied, her voice charged with enough energy to rival a Red Bull.

McKenzie stood in the doorway propped on the godforsaken wooden sticks slowing her down these days. When Whitney was done with this weird sorority girl moment, surely she'd introduce her.

"I'm well. Did you make it to the San Diego State alumni picnic? Wow, those college days seem so far away, don't they?"

Don't they?

"They certainly do. I didn't make it to the picnic this year, unfortunately. Too busy around the office." The woman's focus drifted to McKenzie. The chick *had* to have noticed her before now.

Thou shalt pretend to be happy to see your old classmate before you acknowledge a non-worthy, non-former-Greek in the room.

"I'm McKenzie," she said, sticking her hand out toward the woman. The lady eyed her crutches, then her, but said nothing.

"Oh, I forgot. Nessa, this is my head reporter, McKenzie McClendon. McKenzie, this is my good friend, Nessa Earley," Whitney said, the beauty queen smile affixed firmly to her face.

"Nice to meet you, Ms. Earley."

"Oh, call me Nessa. All my friends do," she said as she shook McKenzie's outstretched hand.

Friend. Kind of like how you and Whitney are good friends. Okay, then.

"Nessa," McKenzie said. "Lovely to meet you."

"You as well." Nessa nodded to the crutches. "Were you in some sort of accident?"

"You could say that," McKenzie replied.

Nessa wasn't too interested. She turned back to her old chum. "What brings you by, Whit?"

Good thing neither of them was paying her any attention, because McKenzie had to thrust her fist into her mouth to stifle her laugh.

Whit.

"As I'm sure you're aware, Nessa, the Galloping Gossip wrote a piece in the *Gazette* that insinuated McKenzie was at the Greater New York Fertility Specialists researching an article. The suggestion may have made her a target, and she's been thrust into a huge police investigation. The detectives could come ask the questions, but I know how that'd make *me* feel. Source protection flies out the window. You suddenly have to make a lot of decisions about cooperating with police versus lawsuits. We newspaper folks have to stick together. I thought maybe you could give us the information we—and the police—need without involving the cops. That way, if it turns out to be nothing, we haven't wrecked your whole operation."

Nessa's mouth turned down at the corners. "What exactly is it 'the police' need to know?"

"They need to know who wrote the article. No one knew what I was writing about," McKenzie said.

"Someone knew," Nessa replied.

McKenzie cleared her throat to keep her rude retort in check.

Whitney chimed in. "*Thought* they knew, Nessa. And whoever thought that may have some connection to the shooters. If the theories are right and the shooters wanted McKenzie, they had to know about her and what she was working on *before* the shooting. The *Gazette*'s piece came out *after* the shooting. Ergo, the person who wrote the article is the only one who could've blabbed."

Nessa yawned. "It's a stretch, Whitney. A big stretch."

Whitney shrugged and smiled. "If you'd rather the authorities contact you to discuss it, we can arrange that. Come on, McKenzie."

She strode past McKenzie toward the door, her heels silent on the plush carpet. McKenzie turned to follow.

Damn, Whitney. I didn't know you had it in you.

"Wait," Nessa said from behind them. "Okay, okay. I'll take you to talk to the Galloping Gossip."

CHAPTER 47

WHAT HAD HE fucking done to deserve this?

Trevin pulled out drawer after drawer in his desk. Surely somewhere in this God-forsaken office, a gracious little Xanax or a beautiful Valium would lie there, spilled from one of his quick trips into his stash. But no. The goddamned bottle chose to go empty on the day—of all days—he needed to close the baby adoption.

The couple signing the papers had exchanged a few furtive glances Trevin was sure he wouldn't have noticed before the media hype surrounding Rory Nathaniel. As it was, every extra pause between sentences, any extra blink, and Trevin was ready to leap from his desk, declare that he had a personal emergency, and run out on the whole thing. If it wasn't for the $100,000 he could now put towards the "Trevin Doesn't Want to Spend Tonight at the Bottom of the Hudson" fund, he probably would've.

Damn it! Why don't I have a fucking emergency stash?

A rap on the door made him look up from his drawer search, a mix of fear and adrenaline shooting up his spine. It wasn't the Jap.

A man dressed in khakis and a red polo stood in the doorway. "Mr. Worneck?"

"Yes." Trevin replied, his lawyer-voice clicking on. "Can I help you with something?"

He hadn't yet advertised for new help. Anyone could walk in

any time.

Fuck.

"Yes, actually."

The man's hand drifted to his pocket and he retrieved his wallet.

Fuck fuck fuck fuck fuck! No!

The detective flipped his wallet open to reveal his badge. "I'm Detective Shearer, NYPD. Do you mind if I ask you a couple questions?"

The steady drum of nerves beat faster in Trevin. The office was hot. Too hot. They'd found something. They had to have.

"Sure," Trevin said. "Pull up a chair."

Trevin's knees buckled him into his high-backed chair. He skimmed his hand across the desk to sweep some papers onto his lap. He couldn't do this. This wasn't what he signed up for. Sure, on some level he expected it. But usually he just shoved a needle in his vein and that took care of that. No smack right now, either.

He'd never broken a single mirror or seen a black cat cross his path. Yet, here he was, unable to turn on the TV without seeing talk of Rory Nathaniel. When he turned off the TV, the thought of the Petersons and their stupidity consumed him. He couldn't escape. Now, this balding NYPD detective settled himself in one of the armchairs in his office, and he was about to have to talk the biggest game of his life without so much as a milligram of a Benzo in his system. This was plain unfair.

But why would the NYPD be here? They wouldn't be here, right? The Feds were investigating the Cradle Robber. It didn't make sense.

He smiled at the detective, who was opening a small notebook. "What can I do for you?"

Besides tell you anything about how I'm involved with the case of your career.

The detective glanced behind him at the open door. "I noticed you're a little short on office help, huh?"

Dirk's comment about Ollie being a loose end flooded Trevin's psyche and his eyes narrowed against his will. If he asked about Ollie, he'd give a fake name of his secretary. The dude couldn't have a search warrant on him, right? Could he get one while he was here?

Stall.

"Yeah. Business hasn't been so great lately. I'm starting to wonder if they outlawed divorce in the state while I wasn't looking, actually."

The detective quirked his head as if accepting his answer, though he didn't seem the slightest bit amused. "Mr. Worneck, how long did Ollie Favre work for this office?"

Shit.

Good thing he hadn't lied about her.

The papers in his lap curved in waves, damp from the sweat of Trevin's palms. Had Ollie gone to the police? "She worked here a little over three months when I had to let her go. Damn shame, too. Good girl."

Good. Now, there's a word I didn't know was in my vocabulary until this moment.

"Yeah, it's a shame all right," the detective said. He scribbled down a few things.

Something in his voice triggered a trip wire in Trevin. A lump the size of his addiction formed in his stomach. "Is Ollie okay?"

The detective looked up from his memo pad, grey eyes piercing. "Ms. Favre was killed, Mr. Worneck."

Now, Trevin's stomach clawed from the inside, trying to get out. This was bad. This was *really* bad. "What?"

The detective nodded, somber. "It looks like the standard mugging. She was on her way home from drinks with her girlfriends. The guy nabbed the credit cards and money out of her purse and a nice wristwatch. Still, we're obliged to look into these things. When a severance check showed up in Ms. Favre's mailbox, I decided it was best to be sure it was nothing. Mr. Worneck, it sounds cliché, but do you know if Ollie Favre had anyone who might want to harm her?"

Tears blurred Trevin's vision. The pressure inside of him pushed, hurting. "No. She didn't talk much about her home life."

Ollie had never spoken of her friends. There was no telling what they knew about him, and he had no names to check. True, when someone had come in and crushed her boss's nose, she hadn't gone to the cops. He wouldn't peg her for talking about her work much. But how to be sure? She'd mentioned a mother in the suburbs once, but from the few things she said that he paid attention to, he gathered they weren't exactly entering any mother-daughter beauty pageants anytime soon.

Fuck Dirk!

The detective closed his notebook and stood. "Thank you, Mr. Worneck. I'm sorry if I interrupted anything. Like I said, it's just standard for me to come by and meet you. I'll probably be in touch in the coming days, but when you have a chance, could you fax copies of any employee records, applications, things like that? It would be good for us to have those in our files."

The detective flipped a card onto his desk. Trevin stood, shocked, without picking it up. That was it?

"I sure will." Trevin managed to choke the words past the bile in his throat. If terror could come across as grief, he was the saddest man in the world right now. "Do you have any leads as to who might've done this to her?"

"Nah, not yet. Hopefully we'll find something. Lifted a print off the purse, so it's only a matter of that coming back from the lab," the cop said. "But whoever did it might not be in the system."

Dirk's ridiculous nitpicking at every drop off, the standard list of procedures he made Trevin follow to the letter for every kill flashed in Trevin's brain.

That's what you think.

"Right," Trevin said. The relief of a hundred Valiums poured through his tense muscles despite the withdrawal hot flashes setting in. "I'll fax those forms over this afternoon. Please, if there's anything else you need from me, let me know. I hate to think of whoever did this to Ollie running around out there."

The detective nodded. "I'll be in touch."

As he stood in the doorway and watched the detective walk out the glass door into the rain-splashed sidewalk, Trevin couldn't help but think of the poor bum Dirk must've lifted prints off of to use on that purse. Homeless guy, probably. Wouldn't even know what hit him.

CHAPTER 48

"I'M SORRY I'M late, Laurel. Traffic was insane. I hope I haven't kept you from anything," Sarah Peterson said as she ducked in the door of the salon, hanging her arm outside to close her umbrella.

Everitt had watched Laurel stock shelves for the past hour while she waited for Sarah to pick her up.

That's nice. She's sorry for Laurel. How about a nice, "I'm sorry I may be trying to sell your infant, Everitt"? That'd be novel.

"Oh, no. Nowhere to go, nowhere to be. You know me. Work, work, work," Laurel said in her classic above the clouds way.

"You should take a day off now and then, Laurel. Enjoy some fresh air," Sarah replied.

Yeah. Make like the almighty Sarah Peterson and trick girls into thinking they're helping a desperate couple. Life's a lot easier that way.

Damn. This woman could act so normal when she wanted to.

Everitt had been a ghost since her call to McKenzie McClendon. She'd wandered through her days, focused on finding more information. Occasionally, she broke into tears of frustration, which Laurel liked to call her "hormones having a tantrum." Now, she sprayed cleaner on the countertop next to Laurel's station and scrubbed the space, not looking at Sarah.

Everitt hadn't dared to try to call McKenzie McClendon again since the day in the bathroom. The reporter had been right:

she wasn't about to give her real name. Too dangerous. If she was wrong and the Petersons found out what she'd done, she'd have ruined everything.

It wasn't like she could've called McKenzie McClendon even if she'd wanted to. Or another reporter, the police, or anyone else for that matter. Something had Sarah spooked. She'd told Laurel that Everitt was not to make any phone calls at work due to "privacy issues" surrounding the adoption. Everitt's cell phone had since vanished from under the mattress.

Now, she was truly alone.

"Fresh air's for the upper class, Sarah. I don't need those kinds of luxuries. No, sir. Not me. I watch these snooty falooties running around town in their five hundred dollar tennis shoes, yet they'll cut in front of an old granny in the taxi line. Makes me wonder where my piece of that pie is and the whole nine yards. But I know the time'll come when those shoes won't help 'em. The Lord giveth, and the Lord taketh away."

Sarah chuckled. "Oh, come on, Laurel. Don't tell me you're one of those, 'Thou shalt not covet' types."

Laurel's red lips rounded into a shocked "O" before Sarah's genial smile told her the woman wasn't attacking her faith. "If you're asking if I go to church, the answer's yes. You don't read the Bible, Sarah?"

Sarah shook her head and tapped droplets off the tip of her umbrella onto the doormat. "I'm not a big fan of the Good Book, Laurel. I can't say I think it's much more than old men brainwashing people. I'm sorry."

What the——?

Everitt didn't move, didn't blink. She didn't give a hint of the freak-out inside her body at Sarah's words as the pieces of knowledge lined up in her mind. If Sarah wasn't a big fan of the Bible, then chances were she wouldn't leave a copy of the book in the guest bedroom for the surrogate.

Laurel stuck the last bottle of the new conditioner on the

shelf, looked at it, then held it out to Sarah. "Try this one out for me? And that's okay. I'll keep on keepin' on. I figure you'll open the Good Book when you least expect it."

"Don't bet your next pair of tennis shoes on that one," Sarah said. She winked at Laurel, the crow's feet contracting around her eye. She turned. "Are we ready, Everitt?"

On a normal day, Everitt would've had to fight her inner smartass to contain the snide comment about how *we* weren't ready for anything. Now, she stood to leave.

Sarah Peterson patted her awkwardly on the back. "Okay, then. We're off. We'll see you tomorrow."

"Yes, ma'am," Laurel's voice rang in Everitt's ears.

Everitt followed the gentle guide of Sarah's hand without speaking. What could she say? Unless she wanted to make a scene, she'd better keep her mouth shut. She couldn't afford to say what she was thinking. Not yet.

First, she had to get back home and tell Sarah she was so tired she'd better go straight to bed. If that Bible in the nightstand didn't belong to Sarah, it had to have belonged to someone.

And Everitt had to find out who.

CHAPTER 49

DIRK SAT IN his Mercedes in the parking garage for forty-five minutes waiting for Dr. Michael Burton to arrive at work. He didn't take the car out much. In fact, it had been in a paid lot under a different name for months until now. Still, when Dirk had decided to take this particular field trip, he'd figured the Benz would be right at home.

Finally, the good doctor parked the red version of Dirk's automobile in his designated parking spot beside the double doors that accessed the bridge to St. Alphius Hospital. Dirk pretended to talk on his cell phone even though Michael Burton would probably never notice him parked several spaces back. Even if he did, Dirk was content he'd disguised himself well enough.

After Michael Burton disappeared up the stairs, Dirk got out, catching the reflection of his newly bronzed skin and dusty brown hair in the shiny black of the Benz. He'd gone over and over it in his mind. There was no way the bitch knew enough to give anyone a description of him, much less have worked with a sketch artist. Still, he wasn't taking any chances. Sure, this was a lot harder than trying to sneak in as a florist or a food delivery guy, but the hospital was checking people like that left and right, what with the Cradle Robber still on the loose. They were scared he'd come after Rory Nathaniel. If they found out he was here, this would be the last place they'd check, and his plan would confuse everyone so much that they probably wouldn't ever figure out this was where he came in.

When he reached Michael Burton's car, Dirk pulled out his handy kit. He'd already scoped the area for cameras and found none. Stupid doctors parked their hundred grand cars in here, and not so much as a security guard was on duty. He sifted powder onto the car door.

The police aren't the only ones with fun toys.

The shape of the good doc's handprint materialized. Dirk applied the thin layer of cellophane-like contact paper to it. It lifted like a lover waiting for his touch. Perfect.

He took a smooth plastic card out of the satchel around his chest. Before coming today, he'd traced a perfect outline of his left thumb onto the card before cutting the plastic. Now, as carefully as he would perform surgery, he transferred the print to the card. Then, touching only the rims of the plastic, he slid his gloved left thumb into the elastic band—perfectly measured to fit right onto the top of his thumb like a ring—that was superglued to the other side of the card. Voila.

Supplies tucked back into the satchel, he headed across the bridge toward the hospital, disciplining himself to not smile. It'd been all too easy to find a way in. Hospital websites and their egotistical, braggart staff pages seemed innocent enough, but they also gave someone like him pictures of every doctor who had access to the hospital along with other information, like where they went to medical school. Tidbits like that led to pictures on social media sites of Dr. Michael Burton with his brand-spankin' new Mercedes. Why, that could be dangerous, especially for a hospital that held a girl who'd lived through such a heinous tragedy.

Don't they know there's a killer on the loose?

A camera was positioned at the entrance, but unless Dirk made a mistake, they'd never look. If they ever *did* look for the person who scanned in twice as Dr. Michael Burton, they'd see a guy enter the hospital the exact same way every employee did. They'd chalk it up to a glitch that Dr. Burton's thumb print registered twice.

And he wouldn't make a mistake.

Dirk held up his plastic-ed thumb to the scanner. A green light crossed the screen. A beep, then a click, and the door unlocked. He was in.

McKenzie followed Nessa Earley and Whitney Trias through the nerve center of the *Gazette*, hobbling as fast as her crutches would carry her to keep up.

The more she thought about it, anyone called the Galloping Gossip was unlikely to lead her closer to the black market baby ring. What was she doing here? She should be out chasing down more leads at the IVF clinic or talking to the jogger who found the Cradle Robber victim they'd dubbed "Fountain Girl."

Better here than home worrying someone's coming back to kill me.

"Here we are. The Gossip's Evil Lair. Now, he's kind of an asshole, so don't take it personally." Nessa Earley knocked hard four times. "Hey, Tubbo! I have someone here to see you. Open up."

Sheesh. Nessa Earley made Whitney seem as cuddly as a basket of kittens.

The door of the office swung open. McKenzie's jaw dropped.

No way.

In front of her stood her former editor, Morton Gaines.

Dirk could do this part in his sleep. He strode through the hospital, confident, belonging. A snake in the grass. Once, he let his head be turned by a nurse whose baggy scrubs couldn't hide her toned legs. That could be fun. But no. He was here to do a job. It was vital he get in and out, leaving as little trace as possible. Discipline here and now.

First, he needed a patient. A small boy sat in a wheelchair in the hallway hooked to an IV pole. No good. Kids remembered way too much and had a sixth sense. The elderly woman with the walker posed a similar problem.

Then, he saw the guy sitting on a bench outside x-ray, his tibia sticking halfway out of his right leg. Forties, in pain. He'd remember Dirk was white, maybe hair color, but that was about it. Adults made piss-poor eyewitnesses.

Dirk's phone buzzed in his pocket, but he didn't reach for it. As much as he wanted to take that call, the urge to slice into another pretty young thing spreading through him like a virus, he had to ignore it for now. There'd be time for the weasel later.

He rapped his knuckles on the door to x-ray. A doe-eyed technician appeared.

Lucky for you I'm working right now.

"What's the hold up?"

The radiograph tech blinked up at him as if he were speaking Dutch. "Sir?"

Dirk bit his own laugh and cocked his head toward the man with broken tibia. "X-rays. We need those pronto. I've taken over this case, and I have about four rooms backed up waiting on these rads. Can we put a rush on them?"

The girl blinked some more, stared. Then, she straightened her shoulders. "Certainly, doctor. I'm right on it."

"While you're at it, did they send his file down? I need to make a couple quick notes before I'm so bogged down I don't know the difference between his tibia and his sternum."

She nodded, eager. "Yes, sir. I'll grab it."

Look like a doctor, sound like a doctor. Wow. You must be a doctor.

A moment later the tech returned. She was a bit stocky for his taste, but my, did she have some lovely, refined facial features. Strikingly pretty.

"Here you go," she said, frazzled, as she handed him the random man's file. If HIPPA only knew.

"Thanks. I'll be down to review in about fifteen. That give you enough time?"

Her lips were smeared with plum. He could imagine the way the skin of her love handle looked under her shirt, the way it collapsed gently to make a crease against her pelvic bone. Dirk's back tingled. A knife would slice so beautifully through that fold.

She glanced at the pink Velcro watch on her wrist. "Yes. I think I can have them by then. I'll do what I can."

"Wonderful," he replied, glancing down at her hospital ID badge, "April."

April Gregory's plump mouth parted in a smile. It was all he could do to turn away. Later.

File in hand, he sped toward the nurses' station of the ICU floor, following the signs overhead. If he knew hospitals, the file he wanted still hadn't made it out of the ICU even if the woman had been discharged. Access to it could be a different story, but if Dirk played the part right, it wouldn't matter until days or weeks down the road. The police would've already obtained whatever copies of the bitch's records they were allowed. Chances were good that as soon as the cops had what they wanted, that little folder started to collect dust. It could've been as soon as the day the girl left the hospital.

Dirk forced down the bile that rose in his throat at the thought of her.

Control yourself.

The nurses' station in sight, Dirk strode with greater purpose. He'd been seen, so it was time to make sure he didn't drop any piece of the character, not even the twitch of an eyebrow. His gait was different than Dirk Harris'. His shoulders rested back farther, his mouth remained firm to smooth out the dimples.

The heavy-set charge nurse at the desk would be a bit harder than the tech fresh out of radiology school. That girl wasn't only charmed. She was scared of making a mistake. This woman, if he had to guess, was a vet. She required a different approach. A blitz. He broke into a dead run.

Take her down before she can take you.

Dirk reached the desk. Before the nurse had a chance to say a single word, he was talking faster than an ad man. "Crash cart on the third floor! We need a crash cart on the third floor! Crash cart up there is MIA!"

The charge nurse reacted as she was trained to, not even questioning why on earth she was hearing this from some random doctor she didn't recognize rather than on the phone upstairs.

Perfect.

"Room?" she called behind her, already jetting down the hallway.

He wouldn't have figured her as being able to move that fast. "Three-oh-o-two," he yelled after her, intentionally garbling the last digit. He knew she wouldn't waste the precious seconds to have him repeat.

As she sped away, he eased around the corner and into the nurses' station. If anyone in the circular ICU was looking, he was just any other doctor. Slots in the south wall held folders, apparently in admittance sequence. He yanked out the stack on the date they found the bitch in the freezer and flipped them open one by one, skimming for key words. There was a lot he needed to know.

The sixth folder down was money. "Stab wounds" and "premature labor" caught his eye. He undid the brads holding the notes in the folder and slid the papers out. Then, he retrieved the records he'd already removed from the folder belonging to the guy downstairs with the broken tibia and placed them into Rory Nathaniel's file.

He pocketed Rory's records, chuckling softly. He'd already dropped the tibia guy's folder directly into a Hazmat box on the fifth floor. If anyone found Rory's "new" records any time soon, they'd have one hell of a time tracking down the owner of file 908765, especially considering Dirk had called an administrator downstairs away from her desk long enough to pull up the file on her computer and make sure it no longer existed. And if those up here didn't know tibia guy or his contact information, chances were that so much time would've passed no one would remember his name, nor that a strange young doctor had ordered rushed rads on him.

Dirk slipped the stack of folders back into the wall in the same order he found them. He moved out of the nurse's station and into the stairwell. His skin practically exuded steam, his lips wet. If the record switch came to light and people around the hospital heard about the tibia guy, the only other person Dirk talked to face to face that could put him together with the tibia guy was the sweet little tech with the doe eyes.

Oh, April. Everything happens for a reason.

CHAPTER 50

INSIDE THE PETERSON'S dreary house, Everitt shucked the hideous puke-colored raincoat Sarah insisted she wear so she "didn't catch pneumonia." Sarah took the slicker from her and hung it on a hook inside the closet door.

"How about a bowl of potato soup? Warm you up?"

Everitt stared at the hardwood floors, then forced a yawn. "No, thanks, Sarah. I think I'll go to bed early tonight. It's been a long day."

Sarah's eyebrows pitched inward toward the bridge of her nose. Before Everitt could back away, Sarah's palm was plastered against her forehead.

"Uh-oh. You're not getting sick are you? Do we need to go to the hospital? I don't want you sick, Everitt. Maybe you're working too hard. We need to check into it if you're sick. It could endanger the baby."

Yeah. We wouldn't want anything to happen to your precious paycheck now, would we?

Everitt brushed Sarah's palm away. "I'm fine, Sarah. I'm just tired. Pregnant people get tired. It's normal."

Especially when their every waking moment involves planning escape routes from this hell-tastic pit of doom.

Sarah smiled, though Everitt had learned long ago that Sarah's smiles didn't always equal happy. "Okay, then. Go on up. But if you're hungry in the next couple hours, come on down."

I'd love to, except you'll lock me in my room as soon as I'm in there.

"Thanks," Everitt said. She trod up the stairs on heavy feet, a dull ache in her back.

Though Everitt didn't turn back, she'd have bet her very limited contact with the outside world that Sarah was watching her climb the stairs. She knew it with the same certainty she knew that Sarah would listen outside Everitt's room as soon as she shut the door. Sarah would listen for her brushing her teeth, turning down the bed, then wait for the light to go out. She'd inspect the crack underneath the door to make sure no slivers of light indicated Everitt was in the midst of enacting a shrewd escape plan.

This time Everitt didn't give a shit. For once, she had no desire to leave the house. Everything she wanted to know had to do with that nightstand drawer.

Inside the bedroom, she went through the motions. Donned her pajamas, washed her face, and flossed. A couple of nights this week she'd spent an extra few minutes in the bathroom making straining noises just to make Sarah uncomfortable, but she didn't waste her time tonight. She crawled under the heavy covers and pulled them up to her chin, then flicked off the lamp and waited.

As expected, she heard the tiny snick of a key turning the lock three minutes later. Everitt rolled onto her side. Head on her pillow, she stared at the bedroom door with wide eyes. She wasn't sure what was creepier: the shadow of feet in the lit hallway, visible under the crack in the door, or the slight twist of the doorknob as she was locked in from the outside.

When Sarah's footsteps padded down the hall and away, Everitt sat up. She felt around below her in the blackness for the handle to the nightstand drawer. Then, the Bible inside it.

She clutched the book tight to her chest at first, wondering who it belonged to before her. The first time she'd slept in this room she'd seen this Bible. Now, it could be the key to getting herself out of this clusterfuck.

She'd taken the penlight from a keychain in Laurel's purse

and hidden it in the band of her underwear, the only place the Petersons wouldn't find it. Now, she slid the light out of its hiding spot, ducked under the bedspread, and let the Bible's cover fall open. Her thumb found the button to click on the penlight. It illuminated the tidy cursive writing on the first page:

> *To anyone who is alone and finds themselves lost in the dark, I hope you'll find this useful. To be quite honest, it never helped me, but I leave it in hopes it will be of some comfort to you. Remember Psalm 23 and Philippians 4:13. Like I said, they didn't do much for me, but I hear they are good, even if you disregard parts or don't want to read the entire book. Peace be with you, and I hope you find your way.*

Everitt flipped to the back cover, closed the Bible, and opened it to look at the front cover again. No name, damn it. No name, and now all she had were some lousy Bible verses. Some help. Unless Psalm 23 happened to be a recipe for an invisibility potion so she could walk right out of the Petersons' house the next day, she had no desire to read something some old dude wrote because he thought he'd heard bushes talking while they were on fire.

Even so, ironic the note said "lost in the dark," when here she was, reading this in the middle of the night with a stolen penlight.

Psalm 23, huh?

^{1}The Lord is my shepherd, I shall not be in want.

^{2}He makes me to lie down in green pastures; he leads me beside quiet waters,

^{3}He restores my soul.

Everitt flipped through the Bible, skimming the books written across the top. Psalms was smack in the middle of the thing.

Her skin prickled uncomfortably. In the first verse, the word "want" was circled lightly in pencil.

```
⁴Even though I walk
      through the valley of the shadow of death,
I will fear no evil,
      for you are with me;
your rod and your staff,
      they comfort me.
```

What the hell is that supposed to mean?

It wasn't only the verse that confused her. Everitt squinted and stretched her neck back to view the Bible from farther away. Then, she leaned in until it was right in front of her face. Yes. Those *were* underlines, as faint as they were. They emphasized the words "fear" and "comfort."

What is this? The freakin' Da Vinci Code?

She needed a pen.

Everitt snapped the penlight off. She slipped from beneath the covers and tiptoed to the bathroom. Careful not to jostle the contents, she slid the drawers open one by one to look for something to write with even though she knew those barely-stocked drawers well enough to know she wouldn't find anything. Damn it.

Her eyes fell on a brown eye liner pencil. Sarah had bought a few toiletry items for Everitt, including razors, body wash, and a little bit of makeup. It'd have to do.

Safely back under the covers and light back on, she scribbled the words onto her left arm with the pencil along with the word "want."

Want

Fear

Comfort

She capped the pencil and kept reading.

You prepare a table before me
    In the presence of my enemies
You anoint my head with oil;
My cup overflows.

Everitt opened the eyeliner again and wrote the words "table" and "presence," which were both underlined in the Bible. Her head spun.

She scanned the page for other underlined words, even turning a few pages, but there were none.

Now what?

Back to the original note inside the cover. Everitt reread it, then flipped to Psalm 23 and reread *that*. Either she was totally misunderstanding, and this wasn't someone trying to leave a message, or the girl who had written this had forgotten to give her the key to this code.

She read through the note again. It *had* to be a message. The girl said none of the verses helped her, so she wasn't leaving passages of the Bible because she found Jesus. In fact, she said it twice.

On to Philippians.

Philippians was closer to the back than Psalms. Everitt flicked the pages until she saw the large number four.

¹³I can do everything through him who gives me strength.

This time, there weren't any words circled or underlined. There *were* marks over each and every "e" in the passage. A total of five of them.

Everitt turned back to Psalm 23 and reread the fifth verse over and over again. Nothing. It sounded like it applied, of course. Something about enemies made sense. But from what she could tell, nothing about the "e's" in that passage stood out, nor was there anything she missed. She penciled in "e" on her arm, then reread the Psalm again in its entirety. What could she be—

Then, she noticed it. At the top of the page, in the corner, there was something written under the header that listed the book and chapter the page went through. The header said Psalm 26:6. Everitt squinted to make out the tiny scrawl. It looked like an "o". No. It had a stem at the top. A "b". It was a lower case "b".

Her heart rate picked up, and she raced back to Philippians. Sure enough, markings smudged the header. The girl had circled the 4:4, traced over her circle, *and* underlined it. Beside the header she'd penciled in: = k.

Everitt glanced back up to Philippians 4:4, but nothing was written. Now, she had a bunch of words, some numbers, and some random letters. She marked "4:4 = k" and "b" on her arm, then she looked over everything there:

> *Want*
> *Fear*
> *Comfort*
> *Table*
> *Presence*
> *E*
> *4:4 = k*
> *B*

None of it seemed to go together. Reading it was giving her a migraine.

One piece at a time.

The freshest thing on her brain and the only thing on her arm with an equals sign, she zoned in on the 4:4. There were other numbers. The chapters and verses listed in the note, the chapters and verses as they appeared in the text. None had anything attached to them *except* the headers.

The header numbers equal a letter.

She eyed the lower case "b" on her arm. Hesitantly, she used the pencil to write a parenthesis after it with an equals symbol.

Want

Fear

Comfort

Table

Presence

e

4:4 = k

b (=)

But what number?

The Psalm in the header was 26:6. Everitt held the Bible closer to her face. She hadn't thought to look at Psalm 26:6 before. She found it at the bottom of the page. There, next to verse 1, an equal sign was scribbled along with "x2". At verse 3, a tiny equals sign linked to a "b" was drawn in, a blessing. She jotted 3 next to the b on her arm, her pulse fired up, and then wrote, "x 2."

Want

Fear

Comfort

Table

Presence

e

4:4 = k

b (=) 3

1 x 2

Unfortunately, the split-second of excitement deflated when she realized she still had no clue what she was looking for. She skimmed her arm list again. None of the words contained either a "b", a "k", or an "x." And did the letter "x" go with the number two or one? Or both?

Then, there was the letter "e", which wasn't attached to a number at all. This made no sense. She couldn't make any words with "b", "k", "x" and "e" in any combination.

But the "e's" didn't have equal signs. "E" didn't have a number.

Think, Everitt.

Whoever wrote this had taken great care to make sure that of all the numbers referenced, only the headers led to numbers with a letter value. The "e's" were even differently marked to suggest it.

Everitt blinked. She had overlooked another difference. On her arm, she slowly underlined the words "fear," "comfort", "table", and "presence", then circled the word "want." Now, they were exactly as they appeared in the text.

Want. The only circled word.

She read back through the verse where "want" appeared with a ring around it, but other than that one circle, nothing stood out. The answer had to be somewhere else. She checked both the Philippians' and Psalms verses again, but the word "want" made no further appearances. Everitt was lost.

Then, the original note popped back into her head. She opened the Bible's cover and re-read its message once more.

To anyone who is alone and finds themselves lost in the dark, I hope you'll find this useful. To be quite honest, it never helped me, but I leave it in hopes it

> *will be of some comfort to you. Remember Psalm 23*
> *and Philippians 4:13. Like I said, they didn't do*
> *much for me, but I hear they are good, even if you*
> *disregard parts or don't want to read the entire*
> *book. Peace be with you, and I hope you find your*
> *way.*

There it was, in the next to the last line: *want*. Her eyes drifted across the page, reading the sentence in which the word appeared. Her breath caught. Coincidence? Maybe. But…

Six words away from the word "want" sat a word you *could* make with a "b" and a "k", at least, if not the other letters. Book.

Everitt spelled "book" on her arm. Then, very deliberately, she penciled a tiny three over the "b". *b = 3. And 4 = k.* She drew a four over the "k" in "book."

Now, she was left with this weird "1 x 2". There wasn't an "x" in book. Then again, neither of the other equals signs were assigned to two letters. The others had used numbers already printed in the Bible with equal symbols drawn in. In this instance, the one was in the Bible text, with the equals sign drawn in, and the x2 written in. The one had to be the number associated with the "x." But "book" didn't have an "x," damn it.

"O" doesn't have a number. There are two "o's" in "book".

Everitt gasped and grinned. *X2.* The "o", the only letter without a value, was equal to one…times two. She drew a small one over both "o's".

Now, she took deep breaths.

Next thing, Everitt. What else is different?

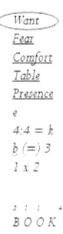

None of the circled words seemed to have anything to do with the word "book." The numbers went with "book." Then, there were the crossed out "e's". She crossed through the "e" on her arm. What was it about the letter "e"?

Then, Everitt bit her lip.

Letters.

Quickly, she jumped to the underlined words. If "b" was three, and there were no "b's" in any of the circled words, the numbers had to correlate to that particular letter in another way. First, she took the first letter from the third word. She continued on to take the second letter from the first word, the second letter from the first word, and the fourth letter of the last word.

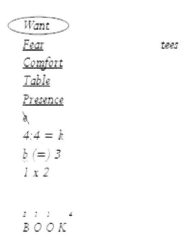

It was a word, but made no sense, not to mention it used nothing from the second underlined word at all. It couldn't be right.

She smudged the missed attempt from her arm, then started again. This time, she took the third letter from the first word. Next, she wrote the first letter of the second word. She almost wrote it again because of the "x2," but stopped herself. There were four underlined words. So instead of doubling the letter of the second word, she took the first letter of the third word. That used the one, times two. Her heart galloped as if it saw the end before she did. Yes, this was making a word. She took the fourth letter of the final word.

Yes!

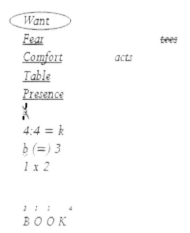

Acts.

Everitt hadn't read the Bible, but she did know that Acts was another section in the book. Eagerly, she thumbed through the ancient text, her insides a cocktail of nerves and anticipation.

When she reached the book of Acts, Everitt immediately saw more underlines on the very first page:

> [12]Then they returned to Jerusalem from the hill called the Mount of Olives, a Sabbath day's walk from the city. [13]When they arrived, they went upstairs to the room where they were staying.

This time, Everitt was armed with a code. Using the three, one, one, four method, she jotted the corresponding letters of the underlined words as they appeared through Acts.

> [18]With the reward he got for his wickedness, Judas bought a field; there he fell headlong, his body burst open and all his intestines spilled out.

229

She skipped a few paragraphs to the next time she saw underlines, which was in Acts chapter two.

> ⁴All of them were filled with the Holy Spirit and began
>
> to speak in other tongues as the Spirit enabled them.
>
> ⁵Now there were staying in Jerusalem God-fearing Jews
>
> from every nation under heaven.

Then, it skipped another few paragraphs.

> ¹⁴Then Peter stood up with the Eleven, raised his voice
>
> and addressed the crowd: "Fellow Jews and all of you
>
> who live in Jerusalem, let me explain this to you;
>
> listen carefully to what I say. ¹⁵These men are not
>
> drunk as you suppose. It's only nine in the morning!

Everitt skipped over to read the last underlined word, which was down at verse twenty-six, but she didn't need to. She already had the message from the circled letters in Acts scrawled on her arm. She sat stunned in the dark, afraid to move, even though she knew another answer—whatever it may be—was only feet away.

Bathroom drawer.

CHAPTER 51

"YOU HAVE TO be kidding me," McKenzie said, throwing her hands up and looking to the sky before leveling her glare on her former editor.

Morton Gaines stared back at her, eyes wide. The Galloping Gossip's loose tongue had lost its free-flowing nature.

"Aren't you going to say anything?" She'd worked for the man for years, and then he'd given her up in an instant. It wasn't like they'd ever been best friends, but McKenzie didn't think he wanted her dead. If there weren't witnesses present, she might have leapt over his desk and strangled him with his too-skinny black necktie

"I...I don't know what to tell you," Morton stammered. Sweat gleamed on his bare head under the fluorescent lights. His gaze moved to her crutches, her leg.

"Yeah, yeah, I'm a gimp. Are you just going to try to skirt over the fact that it's your fault?" McKenzie spat.

"I know what you're thinking—"

McKenzie's dry laugh cut him off. "No, Morton. Somehow, I sincerely doubt that you do."

"McKenzie, I didn't mean to—"

"Sell me out? Compromise my story? Get me shot?"

Morton gaped at her. For a second, he turned to Whitney, then to Nessa as if looking for help. Both women's stares trained on McKenzie.

She shook her head. He'd done what he'd done, and it didn't

matter why. Morton Gaines sucked at life, and that was all there was to it. Asking for personal loyalty was stupid and pointless right now, no matter how pissed she was.

"Look, Morton, while the thought of shoving the stupid column that almost got me killed down your throat is...*appealing*, that's not why I'm here. The shooting happened before your column came out. You're the only unhandled human who knew what I was writing. I need to know who you talked to before you wrote that column before the crazies invaded the clinic."

Morton fell speechless again. His mouth opened, closed, and re-opened as he tried to speak several times, a codfish out of water.

"I didn't tell anyone," he whispered.

The heat of McKenzie's anger surged from her ears and into her cheeks. "Don't mess with me, Morton." She didn't have a legal leg to make him talk, but she could and would make his life a living hell if he didn't tell her what she needed to know, and *now*.

Her former boss looked again at Nessa and Whitney as if willing them to help him explain. He looked back at McKenzie with watery, panicked eyes.

"McKenzie, I'm not messing with you. You can believe me or not, but I didn't tell a soul prior to writing the column. Whoever knew you were writing that article, they didn't hear it from me."

Everitt stepped as lightly as she could out of bed. Now, as she sat on the bathroom floor, she readied herself for opening the drawers—and the possibility of Sarah noticing that she was out of bed. The last thing she needed was for Sarah to suspect she made phone calls from a non-existent phone in the bathroom and insist on accompanying her for her visits to the toilet.

Technique would be the key. Pull the drawer slower or faster depending on which made less noise, but how to know without trying?

As if to bolster her courage, the baby kicked hard against her belly, a butterfly fluttering.

Really, kid?

In the softest whisper she could muster, "We're kind of in this together, whether I meant us to be or not. If I go down, you go down. I don't know if you realize that."

She plopped back on her rear end from where she was crouched to open the first drawer. Had she really talked to the fetus? She had. She'd talked to it.

All of this was all the Peterson's fault. Everitt had to find out what was in that drawer, and everything could go back to normal.

Okay. Here goes.

Right before her hand tugged at one of the side drawers, some instinct or other thing from a place she couldn't know stopped her. How many times had she looked in those drawers? She knew everything in them. They were too sparse to house anything she wouldn't have already noticed.

And yet, they were the only drawers in the bathroom. Had the message been referring to another bathroom in the house? Surely not. Whoever left that message knew if ever someone read it, how much danger that person was in, how trapped. She'd know the only chance to find a message would be to leave it here, locked in with her.

Everitt's hand drifted away from the drawer handle.

The message didn't say it would be inside the drawer.

She reached for the cabinet door. As slow as she could manage, she opened it. Everitt exhaled when it opened without a sound. She leaned into the sparse cabinet, which was stocked with only a few rolls of toilet paper, a bag of cotton balls, and toilet bowl cleaner. When her torso was far inside the cabinet, she shined the penlight up at the drawer bottom on the right. Nothing.

She shifted with difficulty to face the other side, careful not to knock into the cleaner.

Please let there be something. Please don't tell me I'm missing something.

But as her penlight skimmed the bottom of the left hand drawer, she knew she wasn't. There was writing, penciled onto the bottom of the drawer. How was she going to make that out? It was so tiny. She'd have to climb all the way into the cabinet. Eight months ago, easy. Now? Doubtful.

She squeezed forward, trying to make herself fit. Breathing hard, she was now as far in as she could possibly fit, her belly and balance prohibiting her from coming closer. She craned her neck and winced as a muscle pulled in between her shoulders. The penlight found the writing again, though, and this time, she was close enough to see it. Four sentences. Only four sentences, but what she read made goosebumps skitter over her arms.

> *There are lots of others besides us. Most are dead.*
> *If you can, get what's in the shades. Then, whether*
> *you can or not, RUN.*

As McKenzie's eyes bored into Morton Gaines, the burning in her neck intensified, spreading all the way to her toes.

Dear Lord. He's telling the truth.

"If you didn't tell anyone, who knew I was at the IVF clinic researching that article?"

Morton glared at her, his fear of facing McKenzie from a moment ago melting into righteous indignation. He wiped his brow. "Maybe nobody did."

"Now what are you talking about?" McKenzie replied. Why could nothing go right today?

"Maybe nobody knew you were there. Maybe the shooting had nothing to do with you," he replied.

McKenzie rolled her eyes. "Morton, you said yourself I was the cause. They came in shooting to stop me from investigating the black market baby trade."

Morton drooped his bald head to the right and raised an eyebrow. "Seriously, McClendon? Of course I said it was why. It made a good story. It was a theory nobody else had. A new angle makes an interesting article. You know that."

McKenzie's cell phone vibrated in her pocket. Normally, she wouldn't have dreamed of answering it in the middle of an "interview," but right now she was the exact mixture of confused and annoyed that she could use an excuse.

"I have to take this," she said. She stepped past the others, sped down the hallway, pulled out her blackberry, and punched the button. "Hello?"

"McKenzie?"

Immediately, McKenzie recognized the voice. '*Shannon.*'

"Shannon, what is your name? Who are the people you're with?"

The girl's voice was barely audible. "No time. Felicia Rockwell. Look at Felicia Rockwell at the IVF clinic. Felicia Rockwell."

McKenzie jammed her finger into the volume button on her phone as Shannon's line crackled with static. "What else, Shannon? What about Felicia?"

"Felicia…Peters…Ev…Feli…ersons."

Then, the line went dead.

CHAPTER 52

EVERITT SAT ON the floor next to the windows under the heavy drapes and stared at the pre-paid cell phone she held in her hand. Only moments ago, she'd used the phone she'd found in the drapes to call McKenzie McClendon's cell phone number, which she'd memorized the day she'd called it from Laurel's salon. She was the only person to whom she might be able to get enough information across to in exactly thirty-six seconds that it might be of some help. That was all the phone had left on it. Thirty-six seconds.

Thirty-six seconds could call 911, but not long enough to relay any information. No doubt Sarah and Rodney Peterson would cover-up any "issues" arising from such a phone call, and she'd have tipped her hand. The reporter, though, had to be expecting her to call back. And this time, she had to take her seriously, because it wasn't just the phone in those drapes.

A ragged piece of paper was wrapped around the phone. About thirty-five names were listed under the heading, "Known Names-Adopting."

Everitt had read the list over twice, something niggling at the back of her mind for a moment. She'd looked back and forth at the phone, trying to figure out how to use the precious few seconds a previous inhabitant had either thought to leave her or hadn't made it out in time to use. She'd almost cried at the thought of what desperation the other biological mother must've felt in this room. She knew how the girl must've felt, somehow gaining access to a cell phone, then to feel broken when she couldn't find a way out.

It was then that the day at the café had popped into her head, the day of the IVF clinic shooting. Laurel's voice saying, "I can't believe there are people who would do that at a place where there are pregnant women." The memory of throwing up as she thought of Zan being dead. Coming back from the bathroom and seeing McKenzie McClendon's name on TV, a crawling list of the shooting victims across the bottom. She'd read each name, feeling a kinship to each.

The tingling again. She recognized one name from the crawler on the piece of paper in the drapes. Felicia Rockwell.

Now, she squeezed the phone as though it were a life raft, even though it could do her no good anymore. She'd passed along the only piece of hope she had. All there was left to do was get rid of this phone and find some way to follow the second part of the girl's desperate message: run.

"With what can I help you today in lieu of doing my real job or anything I might consider leisure?" Jig asked on the other end of the phone.

"Felicia Rockwell," McKenzie blurted without preface. She leaned against the wall in the hallway of the *Gazette* offices. "Where've I heard that name before?"

She could hear Jig's keys clacking away. "Let me double check this, but I'm pretty sure you know it because she was one of the people dead on the floor near you in the IVF clinic."

McKenzie fell back against the industrial wall, crutches tucked under her arms. That was where she'd heard the name. One of the victims.

"I need…" She had no clue what she needed. "I need information on her."

"Anything specific, or would you settle for trouser size and favorite Journey song?"

McKenzie rolled to face the wall, leaning on her forehead. "I don't know."

Jig started to hum the theme from "Jeopardy!"

"Not helping," McKenzie growled.

"You don't give me enough credit, you know? I'm a full-time smartass, which means if I'm ever to get anything done, I have to be able to multitask. Here you go. Felicia Rockwell, age thirty-nine, nurse at Greater New York Fertility Specialists for five years. Went to school at Phillips Beth Israel School of Nursing in New York. Widowed once, divorced a second time, has one child, a girl named Tess. What else would you like?"

It was the awful choice between one too many leads or one too few. Right now, it seemed there were a thousand at the same time, so she opted for more. "Ex-husband's name, any other family she has. Daughter's age, birth date...in fact, tell me everything you can find about the daughter, and I mean everything, down to the shoe size and favorite Journey song."

"Trouser."

"What?" McKenzie replied.

"It was trouser size. Not shoe," Jig answered. "I'm on it. Will text you."

As McKenzie ended the call, Whitney's Christian Louboutins clicked toward her on the tile floor.

"What are we doing?" her new editor asked.

A worthy question.

McKenzie couldn't think what to say. They'd come to the *Gazette* offices to cuss out the person who wrote the article and gave McKenzie away. Come to find out, not only did Morton Gaines not cause the clinic to be shot up, but that the massacre may not have been because McKenzie was there at all. If "Shannon" was right and she'd stumbled into a black market baby ring Felicia Rockwell was involved in, it was entirely possible that Felicia was the primary target.

"The shooting at the clinic," she said sharply to Whitney,

"how many people were killed?"

Whitney blinked a few times, caught off guard. "Ah…eleven, I think. Eleven dead, thirteen wounded, maybe? I'd have to check. Why?"

McKenzie didn't answer, but rather, blitzed her with another question. "How many were nurses?"

"Huh?"

"How *many* were *nurses?*" McKenzie said again, this time emphasizing words as if she were talking to someone hard of hearing.

Whitney's nose scrunched up like she'd smelled rotted cabbage or someone beneath her. "McKenzie, I agreed to help you, but I'm your editor, not your research assistant."

She didn't have time for these games. McKenzie reached out and grabbed Whitney by her frail, Barbie doll-inspired shoulders. Whitney's eyes bugged out past her pointy nose, but thankfully, she was stunned to silence.

"Whitney, I need you to trust me. Smooth this thing over with the *Gazette* people for me. I need to check on something, but I have a tip. I'm on to something big, but I can't spend time schmoozing over this mishap with Gaines. I promise you, you will not regret it."

The editor took one large step back, wriggling free of McKenzie's grasp. Whitney's mouth twisted into a disgusted snarl.

Yeah, she's not letting me leave here unpunished.

"McKenzie, this is going to mess up so many lives…"

"Whitney, I know your adoption turned out well, but plenty *don't*. Some kids end up in bad situations like the foster homes you were talking about. Don't people like my friend Jonas have a right to know their child didn't get sold into some kind of sex slavery? It happens to kids, you know. I'm not saying everyone who buys a baby on the black market is bad, but some are. Someone has to make sure those kids are okay. When I write this, I promise I'll try to give both sides to the story, but it's important this comes out. If not for the parents, then for the children's lives that are at stake."

Whitney stared at her for a long moment. Tears welled in her eyes.

"Go," she said.

For a second, McKenzie stalled. Had Whitney said what she thought she had?

As if to demonstrate, Whitney flicked the back of her hand twice at McKenzie like she was swatting a tiny bug. "I said go. But if you don't have a suitable story on my desk by the time we go to print on Monday, find yourself a new job. Keyword there is *suitable.*"

No need to ask for further clarification. McKenzie hobbled toward the stairwell, then turned and took the exit to her right. Jig would get back to her about Felicia's relatives. If McKenzie's hunch was right, the daughter may well be the place she needed to dig next. She needed to research more about the victims of the clinic shooting, too, but first things first: she had to find Jonas.

CHAPTER 53

"So, THE REPORTER," Rory said, lifting a slice of pizza out of the box, "do you really work with her, or is that only to do with all of this stuff?"

Jonas grabbed a piece for himself and bit off half of it. He knew "all this stuff" meant the Cradle Robber, but he still wasn't sure how to answer. "McKenzie was a high school classmate. I hadn't talked to her in a while. But then this case came up. I had a feeling...I called her."

Think before you speak, moron. She's a human. *Not a case.*

"I had a feeling about the Cradle Robber victims."

You are really bad at this, dude.

Jonas backtracked again. "I tried talking to the police, but no one would listen. I knew McKenzie and thought I could call in a favor. Reporters dig up answers for a living and all."

They'd made it onto the screened in porch with the pizza. Day had turned to night. Crickets chirped, and a dog a block or two away barked twice, then fell silent. He should probably take off but felt uneasy leaving Rory alone. She'd said her husband would be home from work any time now, but he hadn't missed the gleam of tears pooling in her eyes. She was scared. Besides, it was nice to have someone listen without suggesting he start AA meetings.

Rory licked at a string of cheese on her lips. "Does she have any leads for you?"

Jonas shrugged. "You're the obvious lead. You've...you've

lived through it. I guess I'm—"

Don't say it. Too much pressure. Shut up.

Rory expelled a half laugh, half sigh, but mostly, it sounded like defeat. "You're hoping I'll remember something that'll help you find him."

Shame crept up from Jonas' toes, twisting the muscles of his back and shoulders. She'd invited him here for commiseration, and here he was, parading his own selfish wishes. "Rory, I'm sorry."

She smiled, though. She tucked a strand of hair behind her ear before shaking her head. "Don't be. I get it. I really do."

He wanted to press. His swallowed questions tasted bitter on his tongue. If the memories came back to her, they'd come on their own time.

As if he'd spoken his last thoughts aloud, Rory mumbled softly, almost to herself. "I don't remember much. All these people want me to. The police, victims' families, you. I want to so much, but I can't. The whole thing's like being in the middle of a dense fog, and I can't muster the energy to push through it."

Rory wrung her hands in her lap, the pizza on the table forgotten. This woman had been through hell. The only victim to live, yet the only person with her right now was a total stranger. No one really knew what they'd do in a situation until it happened to them. Even so, if Noelle had lived, no way Jonas would've let her out of his sight longer than five minutes for the rest of her life.

Rory kept whispering. "I need to remember. I want to. I need someone to understand. Someone in the world."

Before he had time to think about what he was doing, Jonas reached across the table and covered her hand with his. Her fingers were so small they disappeared in his grasp. Rory looked up at him through tear-spangled lashes but said nothing.

The energy between their gazes broke when Jonas' phone erupted in bass guitar in his pocket. "Sorry," he said.

He jerked his hand from atop hers and jammed it in his pants for the phone. He glanced at the ID.

Damn it, McKenzie.

"Be right back," Jonas said as he stepped onto the patio to answer.

"Where are you?" McKenzie demanded.

To tell or not to tell. That was the question.

Vague is good.

"I'm finishing up here," he replied.

"Well, finish up faster. I have a lead."

Excitement rushed through him. "The Cradle Robber?"

"Not exactly. I think I found out why the clinic shootings happened. It gives us another place to start looking for Gibb and the black market trade. So it eventually ties back to the Cradle Robber. Think big picture here."

The last time Jonas saw his baby was the morning Noelle left the house. Gibb's little round face, the way his growing belly had poked out of his too-small Elmo t-shirt. Now, he tried to picture the same face, pudgy and infantile, stretched into that of a toddler, then a school-age child. Unfortunately, the only image he could conjure along with Gibb's baby face was Noelle's, bloody and frozen on the cement.

"Don't you think we should talk to Rory Nathaniel some more? After all, she had to have seen the guy. The clinic's like detouring around our ass to get to our elbow. Why do that when we could just touch our elbow?"

"Jonas, she might not ever remember what happened. And if she does, she's still not likely to remember the guy's distinguishing features. Unfortunately, it's pretty common among trauma victims. The clinic lead is solid."

McKenzie's lead might be solid, but Jonas' gut—his heart—said he was right. Rory wanted to remember. He could help her. He *would* help her.

"I'll be tied up a while longer. Go check out your lead. I'll catch up with you as soon as I can, okay?"

He hung up without waiting for her response.

Now he's off on his own little quest. Job interview, my ass.

McKenzie might not know the specifics, but she wasn't that dumb. He was checking out a lead of his own. She didn't understand why he was hiding it from her.

Your loss, Jonas Cleary. I hope you realize that nondisclosure goes both ways.

McKenzie checked to see if she'd received the message she'd been waiting on from Jig while Jonas had been giving her the old one-two.

She had.

> *felicia's ex-husband is jerome kyler, lives at 2 brandon in astoria. working on the kid, but is harder than it should be. figures. keep you posted.*

McKenzie shoved her phone back in her purse. A small lead was better than none. Jonas or no Jonas, it was time to visit a dead woman's ex.

"What was that all about?" Rory asked when Jonas came in from the patio. He'd been talking to McKenzie McClendon. She was sure of it.

"Nothing important. McKenzie checking in, actually."

"Oh?" she replied, acting surprised. She had sort of wondered how Jonas had explained his visit to her to McKenzie. She hadn't invited the reporter over, after all. Rory wasn't trying to be rude, but she wasn't prepared to talk about what the reporter would want in a second interview.

Jonas sat back down across from her. "She thinks she has a lead on the clinic shooting. She wants me to help."

Rory couldn't help the reflexive raise in her eyebrows. "And you don't want to?"

Jonas leaned his head back and let his exhale blubber out through his lips. "I don't know what I want, Rory."

He seemed drained. Worn. She recognized that well. "Believe it or not, I understand how you feel."

"Do you?"

She nodded, hesitant. It always sucked when people said they understood something but really didn't have a clue, which was why she wouldn't do that to him. "I think I understand, yes. You're torn about the clinic shooting, right?"

Jonas dropped his chin to his chest. "It doesn't make sense to me that McKenzie's so stuck on it. If whoever shot up the clinic did it because they didn't want McKenzie to write about the black market for babies, fine. But unless they can hand me my wife's killer on a platter, and until I can get my son back, I'm not...I don't want to say, 'I'm not interested,' because I *am*. But—"

"But you're *more* interested in the killer and your son."

"Well, yeah."

His shoulders sagged. His eyelids drooped. Every line of his body read of his desperation for relief. Of exhaustion. This had been years and years of his life. She had to be able to do something.

"You know," Rory said, but then wavered. She didn't know Jonas Cleary that well. He might not take what she said the right way. Better to keep quiet.

And yet, what if he needed to hear it? Needed to realize he wasn't as stuck as he thought?

"What?"

Say it, Rory.

"I don't want to step on any toes. McKenzie's a great reporter. That's why I talked to her at the hospital. But you can always keep up with her and look around yourself, too."

Jonas stood and paced the porch, absent-mindedly running one hand along the screen. Lines stretched across his forehead in rivers of worry. His fingers, nails bitten to the quick, fidgeted with his pants legs.

He smiled, but there was no happiness behind the expression. "I don't know what to look for, Rory. I don't know where to look next, how to go about it. Unless you can help."

She bowed her head.

I figured as much.

Her eyes misted. She lifted her chin up toward him. He kept his hands stuffed in his pockets while he stared out the window, seeming to look for an answer he might never find.

Unless I can help.

"Maybe there's a way I can remember," she said quietly. "People do, don't they? They have ways of jogging memories, right?"

He faced her, concerned. "Hypnosis?"

Rory laughed. She couldn't imagine lying on some half-witted shrink's sofa while he waved a watch in front of her. "I wasn't thinking that, exactly. But aren't there ways to help call up repressed memories? I don't even know what I'm thinking of. My brain's in such slow motion. But I know there have to be ways."

Jonas considered this for a moment. "When I lost my keys, Noelle would always ask me where I was when I had them last. I'd tell her that if I knew that, I wouldn't be looking for them."

He smiled at the memory, this time a genuine grin. His gaze drifted far away from her back porch.

She took a deep breath. "So, you think I should retrace my steps?"

As soon as she said it, Rory bit her lip.

Can I really do this?

The widower's smile sank into a frown. "I'd never ask you to do something like that, Rory."

She had to try. For Jonas.

"You didn't," she replied.

CHAPTER 54

MCKENZIE STUMBLED OFF the subway at the very last stop in Astoria. It was a little late for a visit, but some things didn't wait for sleep. She moved as fast as she could through the streets, but using crutches to get around wasn't exactly as quick as she'd have liked to have been. It would've been nice to have Jonas tag along so she wouldn't have to walk through this part of town at night, but some things didn't wait for *Jonas*, either. At least she could use her crutches as weapons.

The apartment building on Brandon came into view. The pink blossoms of the neighborhood's Japanese magnolia trees might've seemed friendly, even family-oriented in the daytime. But like many of the more out of the way parts of New York City, with night came shadows and unlit alleyways, characters whose faces couldn't be made out in the dark. She slipped past a group of older women standing in their housecoats on an apartment patio, speaking in Russian. Number two was up on the second floor, around the side of the building.

The splash of her shoes and crutches in the puddles dotting the path were the only sounds in the alleyway. Cigarette butts littered the ground around the walls covered in graffiti. The alley opened up into another line of apartment buildings. A boy walked a stocky black bulldog mix in the tiny patch of open grass before the apartments, while a woman stood on the second floor stairway trying to burp her crying baby.

McKenzie climbed the stairs past the woman and turned onto

the hallway. The smell of urine made her stop for a second to overcome the urge to puke.

"Whatsa matter, *chica?*" a voice jeered. "That look on your face makes you look like you've been *enculada.*"

McKenzie whipped around to see the catcaller leaning against the wrought iron railing halfway up the next stairwell. He blew a puff of cigarette smoke out of his nose. His friends flanked him, one sitting on the stairs, the other on the top of the landing, laughing.

"She looks like that because she's here for her weekly *Criko*, eh?" the landing mocker replied, his voice scratchier and calmer than the first.

She backed away, then turned to keep going, but she sensed the men moving behind her, following.

"Oh, don't go, *Chica*! I don't have the *Criko*, but I have something better for you!" the first's slurred voice called from just behind her.

Shit.

McKenzie's skin tingled as she felt his breath on her neck right before he stepped in front of her, blocking her way.

I've been through worse than this. I can handle it.

But with the lead jeerer in front of her, his buddies behind, something in her overshadowed the strong, pissed off reporter who'd once fought a psychopath on a rooftop. She was small, insignificant.

Don't show them you're afraid.

She froze and stared directly into his eyes. The sleezeball in front of her leaned into her face. The pungent mixture of cigarettes and alcohol was an almost physical presence, threatening to knock her backward.

"You want *Crika*, *huera*? I can arrange a *pase de mecos* any time for you."

McKenzie had no clue what the words meant, but by his tone, it was clear they were anything but polite. She searched her brain for a comeback, but it wouldn't answer.

"Is there a problem, here?" a different voice sliced the air, cool and deep.

McKenzie's eyes popped open to see a black man in his fifties standing in the doorway of an apartment three feet from her, his gentle eyes assessing the situation before landing on the guy with the cigarette breath. This must be Jerome Kyler, Felicia Rockwell's ex.

The lead jeerer took a step back from her and lifted his hands as he faced the man. "We were just here for a little fun, old man. We can cut you in *pa-pi.*"

The man nodded but stepped farther into the hallway. Now, McKenzie understood why the jeerer had backed away so easily: the man with the gentle eyes was pointing a 9mm at him.

"Well, see that you have it somewhere else," he growled. "This is a family oriented building, so keep it that way."

The Latino's chest puffed and he raised his chin, but he didn't respond. He turned and left, his buddies following.

As soon as they were a few yards away, the man lowered the weapon but kept his eyes trained on them.

McKenzie blew out a sigh of relief. "Thank you."

The man turned to look at her, his face thoughtful. He gestured with his empty hand to the gun in his right. "It'd do you good to pack one of these if you're plannin' to walk around this late." He stopped, looking at her from head to toe, his eyes landing on her knee brace, her crutches. "Then again, you don't look like you come out here all that often if you think it's a good idea on those."

She shook her head as she read the number on the door behind him. "No, I don't."

"Then, get on in before those hooligans come back for a second round."

He stepped into his apartment as she followed in disbelief. People in the city wouldn't trust you if you told them you were collecting canned goods for the needy. Maybe it was the neighborhood, or maybe it was Jerome Kyler. Then again, maybe it was the added security of the 9mm.

Furniture and knickknacks obscured the walls of the one-bedroom apartment. A desk, complete with computer and printer, took up one side of the room, while a couch, loveseat, and well-worn leather recliner were all crammed together against the other two walls. McKenzie chose the recliner as she watched Jerome wander into the kitchen.

"Can I get you a cold beverage, young lady?" he asked.

"No, thank you," she said, her gaze roaming the unframed pictures tacked to the wall above the desk. Most were a younger version of Jerome and a pretty, young, dark-skinned girl. The two of them hugging for the camera in the park, a picture of them in front of a fake Christmas tree.

Jerome re-entered the living room carrying a can of Coca-Cola and a glass of ice. He popped the top and poured the fizzy drink into his cup, nodding at the pictures. "Yeah, that's Felicia," he said.

McKenzie jumped. "How'd you—"

He grinned as he wiped the rim of the glass where some of the coke had overflowed. "You're not a cop, and you're definitely not from this neighborhood. You've got Manhattan written all over you. And you're looking for me. Oh, not to mention your face has been plastered all over the news. You're that reporter."

She laughed, uneasy. "That I am."

Jerome sipped his drink and smacked his lips. "Yup. I knew it was only a matter o' time before the press found me. Even so, I didn't expect it to be you. We'll get it over with, then."

This guy had obviously never been eaten by a hungry school of reporters if he greeted them with a chair and a Coke rather than a boarded-up door. Still, who was she to question a willing victim?

"How long had you and Felicia been divorced?" McKenzie

asked.

"You don't waste any time, do you, then?" he shot back. There was no anger on his face, though. Only regret. "My talking to you—will it help anything?"

McKenzie met his gaze. Truth was better with this guy. "Maybe."

He took another swig of his Coke and swished it around his mouth as if to give himself time to think. After swallowing hard, he spoke. "Off the record."

Her mouth twitched a little, but she nodded her consent. Understandable. People involved with her had a tendency to either be in trouble or have trouble find them. Jinx didn't even begin to describe it.

"Okay, then. We divorced about ten years ago," he replied. "Not 'cause I wanted to, mind you. But there are lotsa things couples can't survive, no matter how strong they are."

McKenzie leaned forward, studying the pictures. "Like what?"

Jerome stood and moved toward the picture mosaic on the wall. He ran a palm over his tufted grey marble hair. "You have children, Miss...uh..."

"McKenzie. You can call me McKenzie."

"All right, then. You have children, Miss McKenzie?"

"No," she mumbled.

"Me, either, but not because we didn't try."

McKenzie's gut contracted like she'd been punched. Usually, it didn't bother her. She preferred not to think about it at all. Even so, she *was* pushing thirty, and the closest thing to a man in her life was a neutered Great Dane who slobbered all over the bathroom floor after drinking a bowl of water. Kids weren't even on the radar. Even if they were, if she so much as entertained subjecting something as innocent as a baby to her recklessness and constant fuck ups... She should be locked up for being an unfit mother for the mere thought of procreating. She couldn't keep anyone around her alive, much less *give* life to someone else.

Jerome untacked one of the photos from the wall and looked at it closer.

"Are you saying you and Felicia split up because you had difficulty having children?"

Felicia's ex-husband choked out a dry laugh. "Difficulty doesn't begin to cover it. We tried and tried. So hard. All kinds of tests done. Hormone treatments. Went through three miscarriages."

"I'm so sorry to hear that."

He waved her off. "No, don't be. Things happen. But the longer and harder we tried, the more I watched Felicia grow more depressed, more desperate. I was workin' as hard as I could, but the university doesn't pay enough for everything she wanted us to try. My salary wasn't the only thing that couldn't keep up, either. She was obsessed with having a baby. It dominated every moment of every day. Every aspect of her life. I couldn't do it anymore. Couldn't go through any more tests or treatments. I just wanted us to be normal again. I told her I couldn't keep doing it. When I did, she said if I couldn't, neither could she. Turns out, Felicia wanted a baby with or without me. She left the next day."

"That must've been hard."

Jerome hummed his assent. "Still is. And when I heard what happened to her, it hurt even worse. Still love her, even if I wish I didn't. Then I saw the *Gazette's* piece about the article you were writing about the clinic where she worked, about the black market baby trade. I couldn't help but think that yeah, she was desperate enough. It seems like a huge coincidence that this comes to light, and she has an adopted little girl."

At the eager reaction on McKenzie's face, Jerome shook his head, his eyes wide.

"Uh-uh, now. Don't you get me wrong. I don't know a thing about any of it. I just wouldn't doubt it if she was involved with something like that. I'm telling you, she wanted a baby bad. Real bad."

"So do you believe Felicia's daughter was part of an illegal adoption, Jerome?"

Jerome turned to stare her down. "Miss McKenzie, what do *you* think?"

She massaged her temples. If Felicia Rockwell had a child, she was one like Whitney, who had ended up in a home that desperately wanted her, and not for indecent purposes. But how did the Cradle Robber fit into any of this? "None of this makes any sense."

"What's that?" Jerome asked.

She lifted her eyes. "I'm sorry. I was just talking to myself. I have a million pieces to this thing, but they seem to all be parts from different puzzles."

Jerome stepped into the kitchen and returned with a can of ginger ale and another glass. He plucked it open and poured, then set it in front of McKenzie. "Care to share?"

Something about the invitation was intriguing. The fact that she didn't know him made discussing certain details a liability. But by the same token, his connection was obscure enough to make him one of the few relatively safe people for her to bounce ideas off of.

Yet again seeming to read her thoughts, Jerome said, "Look, I know I'm a perfect stranger, but you seem stumped. Frankly, I want these people brought down as much as you do. So let's chat."

It wasn't long before McKenzie was spilling a *lot* to Jerome Kyler—the Cradle Robber connections, as well as how she'd become involved in the first place.

"So, without going into too much detail, Jonas' wife's killer, this string of crimes, this trade, and the people involved with it who killed Felicia and the others in the clinic are all connected. In order to bring any of it down, I have to uncover at least one piece. The problem is none of those pieces are cooperating."

Jerome had listened while he played with the pull tab on the can, twisting it back and forth. "Hm. And you say this guy's wife *wasn't* pregnant?"

"Nope," McKenzie answered. "The baby was in a stroller. About a year old."

The tab popped off on the fifth flip forward. Jerome added it to the pile of tabs collecting on his coffee table. "That's a piece worth looking at."

McKenzie had been watching Jerome and his pull-tabs so long that she'd absently started to fiddle with her own. "How do you mean?"

"Well, if the Cradle Robber *did* kill your friend's wife and take her baby, that's very different from taking the babies from the womb. So, why the switch?"

"Obvious, isn't it? Once babies are born, they can be traced. There are blood type records, footprints, et cetera," she said, her gaze following his finger as it stirred the pile of tabs.

"Maybe. The obvious motivation would be that extraneous pieces become variables. The more moving parts, the harder it is to manage." His finger flicked the pile, sending tabs raining to the floor. He reached for one of the can tabs he'd been piling up and dropped it inside the can in front of her. He grasped the can, lifted it, and shook. The tab tinkled inside. "Fewer particles to contain if the baby's still inside."

McKenzie nodded. "Right. And less of a trail for anyone to follow if anything goes wrong. The baby being born is how we tracked Jonas' kid to the extent we did. But you can't track records of a handprint that doesn't exist."

Jerome had scooped up the soda can tabs and was now lining them up in a train from his Coke can to her ginger ale. "True. You have to consider the other aspect of the tracking, and I don't mean the baby. I mean the M.O. The aspect of it that has not a whole lot to do with the children."

Jerome, I think you've had enough caffeine for a while.

"How can they have nothing to do with it? The pregnancies are the whole point of why he'd somehow be involved with the trade."

He looked up at her from the line of tabs he'd formed. "I said they didn't have a *lot* to do with it. Not nothing. Consider, though, that when he changed his M.O., it was to streamline his process. That probably worked in more ways than one. When he changed, it was because something about the prior method wasn't perfect. The more he tried and learned, the more he morphed, right?"

"Right…"

"So, in theory," Jerome said, as he picked up the ginger ale tab, which was the farthest away from him at the very end of his tab line, "the more he learned his lessons, the more distant his methods became from *him*. This allowed him to go undetected much easier."

McKenzie watched as he brought the ginger-ale tab back toward him to his Coke can, lining the pull up with the place where it would've previously been held on. The ginger-ale tab was fatter than the place made for a Coke pull-tab. He shrugged and placed it back in its spot at the end of the procession.

Jerome picked up the Coke tab at the very front of the lineup, the closest to his can of Coca-Cola. "Which would mean that with the earlier victims, he was closer to being caught."

Well I'll be damned.

Her eyes widened as she watched Jerome Kyler fit the Coke tab to the original Coke can, a perfect match.

CHAPTER 55

"I SAW ON the news where police are still trying to determine which drugs caused her to go into premature labor," the med-surge nurse said.

Dirk tugged a stitch through the skin around a bullet wound. The bullet was gone thanks to his handiwork and a speedy nurse anesthetist who had the guy gassed down before Dirk finished scrubbing in. Now, he wished he'd let the victim bleed-out as, once again, the conversation turned to the girl the news boasted "survived the Cradle Robber."

"Tox screens still haven't come back?" a tech asked from behind a mask.

Dirk's hands shook a bit in anger. His fingers weaved the skin faster. He had to get out of here.

"The initial ones are back, yeah, but they didn't find much of anything. They're running more in-depth stuff that won't come in for a few days," the nurse responded.

They won't find anything, morons. That's the point, isn't it?

"Dr. Harris, are you all right?" the nurse asked.

Dirk suddenly realized his stitching had doubled pace. He focused on slowing to a normal rhythm.

Control yourself.

"Yes. Ready to be done is all. Hotter than Miami in July in here today."

The nurse and tech agreed. They yammered on about weather patterns and how the hospital made enough money to splurge on a higher air conditioner bill.

Dirk didn't really feel the heat. In fact, he felt nothing except the rage spilling into his gut. He had to force his hands to maintain a steady pace.

He tied off the final stitch and clipped the loose ends of the suture. He'd deal with other loose ends tonight. They couldn't wait any longer.

Everything happens for a reason, and Rory Nathaniel, you're it.

Following girls home wasn't the best idea, but Dirk wasn't in a research mood. Instead, he stayed on the opposite end of the subway, his face buried in a magazine. The pretty young x-ray tech he'd fooled to get Rory's medical records earlier got off in Washington Heights. He followed, careful to stay a good four people behind her in the flow of pedestrians.

When April turned onto a side road to cross into what must be her neighborhood, Dirk kept walking. The thought of her juicy chub meeting his blade made his mouth water, but no matter how urgent the need to rid himself of that last possible connection, he hadn't scoped this area. It was reckless for him to have come after her without a plan.

She is a connection. Remember that.

The thought brought back living legend, Rory Nathaniel. He had to focus on deep breathing. He couldn't make it through another night like this, not if he had to talk to Bonnie, work at the hospital, visit his mother in the nursing home, and be around other God-forsaken groups of people intent on discussing in detail the murder that went wrong.

He stopped at the next intersection, noting his current whereabouts and picturing them on a city map. The Excelsior Hotel was within walking distance, and it just so happened he'd met a lovely young girl staying there earlier in the week. Had to be a reason.

CHAPTER 56

THE HAIR WAS still in the door jam. No one had been here.

McKenzie unlocked her apartment door and collapsed against it. So much to think about and no clue which direction to move. She needed to pick a focus.

Carbon groaned his welcome and meandered to his food bowl. "Got it, buddy."

Don't got it.

She hobbled into the kitchen where she kept his food, scooped some out. How was she supposed to do this on crutches? "Come here, Carbon."

The Great Dane peeked around the corner, seemingly unwilling to leave his vigil over the dish until she brought his supper.

"Come on," she said, patting her leg.

He wandered around the doorframe and stepped gingerly onto the tile as he noticed the food scoop.

McKenzie opened the cabinet where she kept the bowls. No clean dishes.

"Sorry, buddy," she said before pouring the contents of the scoop on the floor in front of him.

Carbon, however, wasn't insulted. He vacuumed up the kibble with gusto, then ran back around to the living room where he lapped up the two-thirds of his water he didn't sling to the floor as he drank.

Thank God the water was full. I don't know how to carry cups or bowls on these things.

"Night, Carbon," she said on her way to the bedroom.

She peeled her clothes off and tossed them onto the dresser before hobbling into bed in her white bra and mismatched polka-dotted panties. Showers took energy; she had none left. Her knee was killing her, and her arms felt as if they might fall off. Anyone wanting arm tone needn't look for a gym when they could just sprain an ankle or break a bone and be on crutches a few weeks.

Jerome Kyler had given her a lot to think about. The problem with that was she needed more details about Noelle's death to know anything about her killer. Rory Nathaniel would call when she was ready to talk again. Until then, she was a dead end, too.

That mystery girl on the phone, Shannon, had given her the Felicia connection. Jerome didn't know anything about Felicia's potential involvement with the black market other than that it seemed possible, but Felicia's kid was still a lead worth following.

You can't do anything until Jig gives you more information. Your brain will put more together faster if you shut your eyes a while.

But her thoughts wouldn't slow down for sleep. She dozed, her mind full of Jonas, Noelle, the clinic, Rory Nathaniel, and faceless women on subway tracks and in park fountains.

She woke up to her Blackberry bleating a text message alert.

Jig.

She grabbed the phone from the nightstand and opened the message. Wrong again. It was from Whitney Trias.

Another dead girl. Call me.

McKenzie jammed the callback on her phone. After all, her boss had covered for her at the *Gazette*. Whitney answered on the third ring without so much as a hello. "New body found at the Excelsior, possibly the Cradle Robber. Went in to the M.E. for rushed autopsy ordered by the cops. No one has information other than that rumor. We land this, it's big."

McKenzie wiped the sleep from the corners of her eyes. "Wait. What do you mean by *possibly?* Either it is or it isn't, right?"

"You'd think so, given the way she was found sliced up in an elevator shaft," Whitney replied, "except for the fact that she wasn't pregnant."

McKenzie could practically hear the hope in Whitney's voice. She couldn't blame her. If the Cradle Robber had killed a woman and not for her child, it meant the story just took a step away from the baby trade.

"Let me see what I can do," McKenzie said.

McKenzie clicked off the call with her current editor, then immediately dialed her former one. This was about to be awkward.

For a second, she thought Morton wasn't going to answer. Finally, right before she hung up, he barked an indeterminate greeting into the phone.

"Morton, it's McKenzie," she blurted, talking as fast as she could. "I know yesterday was bizarre, and I'm sorry for accusing you of screwing me over."

Even though you did.

Morton Gaines grumbled gibberish. She must've woken him up.

"What do you want, McKenzie?" he growled.

So much for being pleasant.

"I need your contact at the Medical Examiner's office."

His laugh nearly blew out her eardrums. "No way. I don't work for the *Herald* anymore, McKenzie. And I'm not writing for greeting card companies."

She gripped her phone harder.

Make him an offer he can't refuse.

"I know things you don't, Morton Gaines. This could be a good situation for both of us."

Something crackled. She heard crunching on the other end. The man was never too sleepy or busy for a bag of Doritos.

"What you mean?" he asked between chomps.

This could be tricky. Throw Whitney under the bus—screwed. Don't make a deal with Morton—screwed. No matter what, she had to come out on top of both of them.

"*Meaning*," she said, making it up as she went along, "I have multiple pieces to this story. I turn up the information I need and take it to one angle, and you can have another."

Morton crunched, considering. "How do you know I don't have all of what you have?"

This time, it was McKenzie's turn to laugh. "Trust me or don't. The track record speaks for itself."

Silence and chewing answered her for a minute. Finally, Morton responded.

"Okay, McKenzie. But of the two angles, I get first dibs, or else I'll let out the dirt I doubt you have on your pal Jonas."

CHAPTER 57

"ARE YOU SURE you're ready for this?" Jonas asked Rory as they stood outside Grand Central Station.

Her hands shook harder than an eighty-year-old who'd missed two doses of blood pressure meds. Still, her face was painted with resolve. "Now or never."

Jonas put a hand on her back both to steady her and prompt her forward. She obeyed. She passed through the doors into the entryway, the golden ceilings towering above. Sunlight spilled through the tall windows. People bustled around them, all on their way to somewhere in a hurry.

Rory stood in the middle of the foyer staring up at the recreation of the constellations embedded there. If he hadn't known far better, he'd have thought the gaze was full of wonder, almost child-like. As it was, he had no trouble identifying it as the zombie-like state that takes over a person's brain when they're hurting from something beyond their mind's ability to cope.

He stepped to her side and touched her shoulder, a gentle reminder she wasn't alone.

"We went downstairs for food. To the bathrooms."

Jonas nodded and led her toward the corridor that would take them to the food court. As they milled with the stream of subway riders and tourists, Jonas glared into the face of every man he passed. His imagination went into overdrive as he pictured every one of them with knives hidden under their coats. A young man of about twenty listened to his iPod while an older gentleman in a NYPD sweatshirt and a red scarf played the trombone next to an open case. Anyone could be turned into a serial killer with a bit of imagination.

They descended the staircase past Junior's in the food court. The smell of hamburgers on the grill hit Jonas from all sides. Without speaking, Rory hung a left toward the bathrooms at the far south end. Jonas followed.

Don't interrupt. Let her remember at her own speed.

She wandered, lost, toward a wall in between the men's and women's restroom signs. Stock still, rooted to the spot, she again lifted her eyes to the ceiling, focused.

Please, remember something. Anything.

His damned cell phone rang.

Rory stood in Grand Central where she'd last stood with Bryce on *that* day. She stared at the ceiling, thinking, her mind zooming in and out like a kaleidoscope. So fuzzy.

"What?" Jonas yelled into his cell.

Try as she might to shut him out so she could reach out and touch the thought at the edges of her psyche, his words broke through and blocked her.

Fight it. Fight it, Rory! This is important.

"When?" he barked.

Rory begged her brain to hold onto the notion niggling at her, grappled to cling to it, until finally, it slid beyond her reach.

Damn it!

"I'm busy at the moment. I'll call you back as soon as I can, all right?"

Tears stung her eyes as she felt Jonas approach her. A drop trickled down her face onto her dry, cracked lips. She had nothing to say to him right now.

"Hey. You're okay," he said, apparently misreading her emotion as what she was remembering of this place rather than what she wasn't. "I've got you."

At that, she collapsed against him, letting the ever-threatening sobs rack her body. Her hands wrapped his broad shoulders and clasped them like she was falling off a cliff. She couldn't hold it back anymore.

His arms, at first unsure, found themselves, and he bear-hugged her. "It'll be okay, Rory."

He guided her toward a nearby table and chairs and sat her down before pulling up a chair for himself. Her butt was numb on the plastic seat as she stammered. "You don't understand."

Elbows on the table, she hid her face in her hands. Her back shook with her cries. Jonas' face peered under her arm.

"Explain it to me, then," he whispered.

"I've lost everyone," Rory muttered into her palms. Her sweat and tears were salty, disgusting, and they were only distracting her worse. With the back of her hand, she brushed tears out of her vision, her hands coming away stained black from mascara.

Jonas yanked a few napkins from a dispenser on the table and pressed them into her hand. "No, you haven't. Your husband, your friends..."

Her shoulders wobbled harder, reacting of their own volition to the unsure quality in his tone. He'd left off because he wasn't even sure she had any friends.

"Bryce doesn't love me," she wailed. Heat seared her cheeks as people stared. She was all too aware of the purplish color her skin must be taking on. She'd never been what people called a "pretty" crier. Still, there was only so much she could control anymore. She raised the napkin to her face and blew her nose hard. Then, she concentrated on lowering her voice. "He doesn't. I know everyone thinks he must because of everything in my life and how everything went down—damn it. He really can't stand the sight of me. Before I was pregnant he'd said he was leaving. He was having an affair with his secretary. I'm sure of it. Then, he stayed for appearances...the baby...but always he was with her.

Still is." The words ended on another painful wail.

Jonas sat there, dumbstruck, feeding her more paper napkins. Rory didn't blame him, after all. She wouldn't understand it, either, if she was him. She crinkled the last napkin and threw it in a ball on the table before taking a new one to mop her eyes again.

"I know," she hiccupped into her napkin-balled fist. "It sounds crazy. He looks like the doting husband." She gasped a deep, rattling breath, trying to calm her chest. "But he actually told me last night it would have been easier if I hadn't made it. If I'd just died, he would've been able to do what he wanted without feeling guilty."

"You're...kidding..." Jonas sputtered, though by his tone she could tell he didn't believe that she would joke about this.

Part of her wanted to tell him, the other part terrified of telling anyone. She sniffed into her napkin. Then so quiet maybe he wouldn't hear her, she whispered. "He hits me."

Jonas stood, his form looming over their little café table. "What?"

Rory reached for his hand but averted her eyes as she gave him a series of short fast nods. "He started hitting me about two years ago. First every now and then, but not often. Then, more and more. Half the bruises the hospital noted were from the Cradle Robber actually weren't."

Jonas collapsed back into his chair.

She laughed, dry. "I guess he would have an easier time being with his whore if I'd just died, what with all the media attention. Can't blame him for wanting me gone. He could drive over to be with her without anyone to make him look bad on the front page."

Jonas gaped at her. For a second, she dreaded the moment when he would try to talk her out of believing the things she said. But then, he surprised her.

"I know the feeling."

She peeked away from her makeshift Kleenex at him.

"What?"

He half-laughed. "Well, not the whore part and definitely not the being hit part, but I know the way it feels to sense loved ones would be better off without you."

Rory sniffled and dabbed at her damp cheeks. God, she had to be the most awkward sight in this terminal. "Noelle?" she ventured, hesitant.

Jonas' eyes misted, but he coughed to cover it. His hulking torso contorted, hunched. "Nah. Not exactly, anyway."

Rory blinked in confusion. "How do you mean?"

Jonas looked down at the table, concentrating hard on the discarded napkin in the middle. "I don't know that I really want to…"

He stopped and wrung his hands together on the table. Sunlight caught on the gold wedding band he still wore. Rory looked deep into his eyes, willing him to tell her what he was thinking. They could be at the same place on this hard journey. Her chest clenched painfully at the wave of anxiety that came from remembering she was in Grand Central Station.

As if he was reading her thoughts, he mumbled, "I'm asking you to tell me everything. I should be willing to give you some of my deep, dark junk, too. Shit. Okay. I was in prison once."

Rory's thought process capsized in a single instant.

It must've been the dropped jaw that gave her away, because Jonas' mouth quirked at the right corner. "Don't judge me too harshly."

Close your mouth.

Rory shook her head from side to side. "I'm not, Jonas. It just wasn't what I was expecting. That's all."

He smiled sadly, twisting the ring back and forth on his finger. "I can't believe I told you that."

Rory frowned, dropping the tear-soaked napkin and covering his hand with hers. "I'm…I'm glad you did."

They sat in silence for a few moments before Jonas spoke

again. "Aren't you going to ask me why?"

Her fingers left his hand and started to tear the most recent makeshift handkerchief. She did want to ask, but she was also probably the one person on earth who knew better than to pry.

She shrugged. "I figured you'd tell me if you wanted."

Jonas leaned back and rolled his neck in a slow circle. He glanced around at the patrons at nearby tables. "I do want to. But it may be another story for another time."

Rory sighed hard and nodded.

This time, he put *his* hand onto hers. "Really. I do. This isn't the best place."

At this, her tears cranked up again. She shrank in, taking his cue to notice the crowds around them. So many eyes. Looking. Invading. Grand Central may not have been the best idea after all.

"You're right," she whimpered. "Let's get out of here."

Jonas sat with Rory in his living room, Rory in a reading chair next to the window, he on the sofa facing the mantle. Bringing her to his house hadn't seemed the most prudent idea, but then again, neither did telling her his history in a public place full of public ears.

Now, as he talked, he searched her face for any hint of judgment or wariness. He saw only empathy in that face, her eyes wide in amazement and compassion. He told her about walking into his home and finding a man beating his father with a golf club.

"He was screaming that Dad was a piece of shit, hitting him over and over. Dad was balled up in a fetal position, not even fighting back. I didn't know if he was alive or dead, but I had to do something. I jumped on the man's back and pulled him away."

The memory was as vivid as if it were yesterday, down to the particular smell of the man's body odor. "We struggled. He had hold of my hair, but I had him in size by about forty pounds. I slammed him into the bedpost to try to knock him off me, but he didn't let go. I threw him into it again and again, and every time my anxiety upped a notch. Every time I was more sure my dad, who still hadn't stirred, was gone. I was so scared about my dad, so angry. I lost control. At some point, I stopped trying to get the guy off me and started punishing him for what he'd taken."

Rory's hand hovered in front of her mouth. She bit down on her pinky as if to keep from registering an opinion.

He went on, eager to spill it before he thought about it too much. "By the time I came to my senses, this dude I'd never seen was lying beside my parents' bed, bloody and broken. Dead."

Rory sat there, quiet. Thank God. Better silent any day than accusatory. She wasn't shrinking from him, either. He could tell. Her face registered only surprise.

He looked down at his hands. Before that day, he'd never known they were capable of such a thing. "Turns out, he *was* dead. My dad, I mean. The guy *and* my dad. They…they put me away for manslaughter. I called the police myself. Told them what happened. I thought somehow it would be considered self-defense, but it wasn't. Still not sure how all that works, actually. Either way, I was screwed. That was the year after I lost Mom. Breast cancer."

"That's awful," she mumbled.

It was fine. He probably wouldn't know what to say, either.

"Why was he there?" she muttered, her finger still in her teeth.

"What?" The image of the man he'd killed came to him, then his dad's blank face when he rolled him over to check his pulse, to give him mouth to mouth.

Rory took her pinkie out of her mouth and wiped it on her shirt. "The man. Why was he beating your father?"

"Dad owed him money. Gambling," Jonas answered. His father had always been a sucker for a bet, damn it. His mother had hated it, begged him to stop. At times, she'd threatened divorce, but Dad always knew she was bluffing.

"I see," Rory replied. "But…"

"What?"

"You said you knew what it was like to not be wanted around. Like people were better off without you. Who were you talking about?"

A lump rose in Jonas' throat. "Noelle. We were already married when it happened. She never once said she wanted to leave, never acted like she didn't love me. But I guess I always thought she should move on with her life while I was in prison watching *Where in the World is Carmen San Diego* reruns. Find someone who could actually be there for her. If she hadn't had the bad luck of falling for me, that is."

Rory laughed, though it sounded forced and watery. "Yeah. I've always kind of thought anyone bad off enough to be involved with me either deserved a preemptory medal or a pass to the nuthouse. Whichever. Both."

Her voice hit a note of pain. Jonas couldn't tell if this was about Bryce or something else. "Did you guys talk about this before…before the incident at all?"

She glanced sideways, seeming to look for an easier answer than the one she was apparently thinking. Her eyes returned to him, sad and longing. "No, not really. I knew about her, though. His girlfriend. I was dumb enough to think it was a phase. He didn't really love her. He couldn't. When he was bored with her, he'd be done."

Anger simmered in Jonas chest. He blew out a controlled breath. "When was the first time he hit you?"

Rory shook her head, cast her eyes downward. It wasn't her who should be ashamed. It was the lowlife coward who struck his wife.

"I don't remember," she said.

Jonas reached out, touched his fingers to her chin. He lifted her face up until her eyes met his. "Yes, you do. You think about it all the time. You have nightmares about it." How could a man have done something like this to her?

"I don't like to think about it," she said, looking back down.

Her fingers played over the tearstains on the bottom of her shirt. Jonas thought about the belly that had been there only days before, swollen with life, kicking...What was worse: losing the people you loved or losing yourself?

Rory shrugged, defeated. "I guess in the end, the truth is he never loved me. If he did, he wouldn't go elsewhere, would he?"

Looking at this soft, scared woman now in such pain, Jonas couldn't help but want to stab Bryce in his throat the next time they came into contact. "He sure wouldn't use you as a punching bag," Jonas said.

"That too," Rory admitted, though her shoulders slouched. "Jonas, can I ask you something?"

"Sure."

"Am I...well, this is going to sound really juvenile, but...am I pretty?"

Jonas blinked, leaned away from her. He hadn't expected this.

"It's just...I know I'm no model or anything, but I always thought I wasn't too bad. But he wouldn't leave me, go behind my back with another woman unless I was, well, hideous, would he?"

Jonas didn't answer. How could he? He would never have cheated on Noelle. Ever. He couldn't have, even if he'd wanted to. He belonged to her. That loyalty had nothing to do with her looks, though his wife had always been the most beautiful thing in his world. Then again, he wouldn't have *wanted* to. That was the whole point.

She looked up and offered the least cheerful smile Jonas had ever seen.

"See?" she said, folding her hands in her lap. "You know it, too. He's staying now because he feels bad. Same as before."

Jonas crinkled his forehead. "What are you talking about?"

Now, Rory let out a second derisive laugh, then shoved a

stream of tears off her cheek with the heel of her palm.

"It's why he married me in the first place. My family died in an accident when we were dating. I had nowhere to go, no one else. Bryce asked me to marry him, I think, on a whim. He was trying to be my hero." At this, she choked out the words as she alternated between sobs and maniacal laughter. "I was stupid enough to believe he could be."

That stupid, stupid man.

Jonas stood and crossed to her chair. He lowered himself to the ottoman and leaned forward, wrapping the crying woman in his arms. Her body fit strange, foreign there. She was close to the same size as Noelle had been, but where Noelle had seemed both feather light and yet fixed, rooted, Rory was more delicate. Her frame bent into him, awkward, as she hugged him back, her hunched form convulsing with torment. How could that asshole do this to her?

In the next second, something replaced the anger in him as he held tightly to the dainty woman quivering in his embrace. He pushed her out of his arms and looked into her face. At all the hurt sketched there. She blinked, her mouth slack.

Then, before he knew what was happening or who did what first, they were kissing. He drank her lips, salty with her own tears. Hers kissed his back, eager, desperate. Her arms wrapped around him, and she clutched his shoulders. Her face nuzzled into his neck as his hands, which he'd lost all control over, began to rove under her shirt and over the soft, pale skin of her back. She moaned softly when he brushed the back of his hand down her side.

When his hands reached the tender flesh of her belly, though, he froze. My God. What was he doing?

Rory seemed to know what he was thinking. She grabbed his hand and pressed it against her empty womb. She hugged him tighter, buried her head into his chest. The scent of her lotion caught him. He recognized it as baby lotion, the same smell of the kind Noelle had smoothed on Gibb's cheeks to heal dry skin from the windy city.

Rory would never know the smell of the lotion on her child's skin. A hatred for Bryce swelled in his chest. Some people took everything for granted. He'd been one of them once, but no more.

CHAPTER 58

EVERITT HAD TO get out and fast. The baby was due any day now. She couldn't afford to waste one minute.

This morning she'd managed to dispose of the prepaid cell phone by chucking it into a dumpster out back of the hair salon. The rest of the day she spent planning out what she would do tonight. It would be hard, tedious, and *drastic*. The Petersons watched her all the time and Laurel every other second. She had no chance of running away for help. She had to bring help to *her*.

The New York City cops ignored a lot of crazy shit, especially if they showed up at the house of a middle-aged, white-collar couple where the wildest thing in their cupboard was decaf coffee. Whatever Everitt did to attract help had to be something they couldn't ignore.

Finally, when her day at Laurel's was over, she tried the same routine as the night before. "I'm really pooped, Sarah. I think it's another early bedtime for me."

Sarah's forehead crinkled in what she was trying to make look like worry, but underneath, Everitt could see the irritation. "Are you sure you don't need me to call the doctor, Everitt? You're more and more exhausted these days."

Everitt waved off her concerns. "I'm more and more *pregnant* every day. Another of the many joys of pregnancy. Once this little one is out, you'll understand why he or she is keeping me so bushed!"

If you were actually planning to adopt the kid instead of sell it.

Sarah smiled a prim, polite grin. "I suppose you're right. Okay. Go on up. Let me know if you need anything. Cookies and milk, hot cocoa...anything."

Yes, Sarah. I'll let you know if I turn into a first grader while I'm upstairs, for sure.

Everitt waddled up the stairs holding her belly, rounded the corner, and entered the guest room. As soon as she was in, she moved around just enough before flipping off the light but didn't crawl into bed. She stood stock still at the door, waiting for Sarah Peterson to lock her in.

At last, the key turned. Sarah's footsteps padded down the hallway.

Now.

Everitt swiftly slid the bedding from the mattress. She stuffed the bottom of the comforter into the crack under the door. Next, she worked in the dark to drape the sheet over the curtain poles so it floated over the window, a sheer cover.

The bedside lamp was next. She gently dragged the nightstand over a few feet from the bed. Now, it split the center of the bed directly across from the window. She pulled off the lampshade and tilted the lamp onto its side. From here, it should hit just the right angle.

Everitt meandered around the other side of the bed where the footstool from the bathroom stood low on the floor. She pulled out the sash from the ugly bathrobe Sarah had bought her and secured it to the base of the ceiling fan.

This is the only way, Everitt.

It was time. Everything was set, and she was ready. She turned on the lamp, trotted around the bed, and climbed onto the footstool.

For one last moment, she cupped her blossoming belly in her hands. "I'm so sorry I got us into this mess. I'm sorry you're not even here yet and your life already has more drama than a bad Lifetime movie."

Everitt drew a deep breath, steeling herself for what she had to do. She looped the tie, already fastened to the fan, around her neck.

God have mercy on me.

CHAPTER 59

MCKENZIE HADN'T BEEN sure what to expect when she'd first asked Morton Gaines to set her up with the medical examiner. Still, here she was in the cold room filled with drab gray walls and matching grit-colored tile, in the middle of a journalist's wet dream as the M.E. prepared to examine the body of the latest Cradle Robber casualty. The fluorescent lights thrust a harsh glow on everything in the room, including the stainless steel slab on which the body lay.

Zacharias Bayle was anything but old school. The loop dangling from his eyebrow made him look like a Middle Eastern punk rocker right through the scrubs and mask. Zacharias looked younger than her.

Across the room, the body lay out on the table, so badly mangled she couldn't tell what it would look like once she moved closer. She had to be insane.

"You ever viewed a postmortem examination before?"

She shook her head, her eyes still on the body a few feet away.

"Figured you for a first timer," he answered. "It's not as bad as you might think. Just do me a favor and don't puke, okay? It'd be a real bummer if I had to try to cover up vomit as part of my report."

He clicked on his voice recorder before donning a fresh pair of gloves. He motioned for her to follow with a nitrile-covered finger.

Zacharias first wandered around the body of twenty-six-year-old Larkin Prater without touching her, making notes into his recorder. "Victim was found in a white cotton blouse, sleeveless. Black knee-length skirt. A-line, pencil. Material appears to be polyester, but will be determined." He turned to McKenzie. "Later, I'll make notes that involve the specific makes and numbers on any clothing tags, but first, preliminary findings I can see visually."

She nodded again, unable to stop looking at the way Larkin's body was crushed, like road kill scraped to the side. Bile, burning and acidic, scratched at the back of her throat. The antiseptic formalin smell didn't help. McKenzie had seen death before. Hell, she'd *killed* before. But not like this. Noah had killed. A lot. For a living. Maybe she—or anyone, for that matter—had the capacity to kill if they were backed into a corner or were defending themselves or those they loved. Maybe Noah was different because he killed people to protect others. But what sort of monster could make the leap from killing out of necessity to killing for pleasure? Arousal, even?

Bayle, however, seemed unfazed. No sweat beaded his forehead as it did hers. He didn't look as if he were swallowing excessively, fighting the nausea as she was. Damn him.

He recorded the number of lacerations, their sizes, and locations. He photographed every angle of each. In addition to sex, race, height, and weight, Zacharias made notes on things McKenzie would've never even considered. He called out everything on her body—or lack thereof: tattoos, piercings, jewelry, tan lines. When he mentioned the princess cut diamond ring on her left hand, McKenzie's chest clenched. Engaged.

He plucked some of Larkin's mousy brown hair, drew blood. Easier to watch Zacharias' hands than the girl's face. Still, so far so good.

That is, until the skin started coming off.

Underneath Zacharias' first incisions, he used forceps to peel back the top of her chest cavity. McKenzie wretched as she turned around.

Don't throw up. Don't you dare!

"If you need some air, take some," Zacharias said evenly.

McKenzie's feet, covered in the paper booties they'd made her put on along with the scrubs, carried her toward the door, one useful, the other dragging along with her as she moved on her crutches. She stopped twice to cover her mouth with her hands.

Behind her, Bayle said, "Don't feel bad. Nobody is good at it the first time."

Down the hall in the bathroom, McKenzie splashed cold water on her face. Damn. This was not normal. Crutches tucked under her armpits, she leaned against the bathroom wall, debating. This was one place no one else had access to. She couldn't afford to burn this contact. Still, the chances of her stomach making it through were about as good as the chances that the Cradle Robber would call her right then and give her his exact name, location, and zodiac sign.

As if on cue, her phone vibrated in her pocket. She reached under the scrub top and snatched it out.

What the hell?

"Jig?" Once upon a time, it'd been so tough to get in touch with Noah's former flame. These days, it seemed Jig called every time she turned around.

"Where are you?"

"Well, if you must know, I'm at the Medical Examiner's office watching an autopsy. I mean, actually, I'm in the bathroom at the moment, but—"

Jig cut her off. "Save the personal details for your *E! True Hollywood Story*. I'm about to text you the address. They'll probably fire me for telling you this, but I think I might've found your girl, I'm afraid to say."

McKenzie's heart rocketed. "What? What girl?"

But she already knew, even before Jig answered.

"The pregnant girl. The surrogate one. Neighbors called 911. Turns out the family she's living with are wanted in two countries for all kinds of screwed up shit. We've been looking for them a long time, and we found 'em because of her."

McKenzie tried to put together Jig's disjointed details. She blurted all her questions at machine gun speed. "Wait, wait. How do you mean you found them because of her? How do you know it's her? Why'd the neighbors call the cops?"

"Gotta run—work to do. Address coming. But yeah, neighbors called the cops when they saw the silhouette of a pregnant girl hanging in the window."

CHAPTER 60

THE RED AND blue strobes of a half dozen police cars lit the night sky, illuminating the gawking faces of people in pajamas and bathrobes on the streets. Already, helicopters circled in the inky darkness overhead, the whomp of their rotors echoing against the tidy houses of the normally quiet suburban street.

McKenzie had limped back to the autopsy room and told Zacharias Bayle of her emergency. Sounding bored, he said sure, she could call and go over the results with him later. Maybe he'd even been a little thankful to be left alone.

Now, she wondered why Jig had told her to come. She wouldn't get anywhere near the place. Several other reporters pressed against police lines, trying to collar someone with information. A news van was parked three houses down, its crew scurrying to set up a live feed for the late news.

As she had the thought, a hand with flamingo pink-lacquered nails grabbed her wrist across the tape that said, "Police Line, Do Not Cross."

"She's with me," Jig told the cop at the line as she held McKenzie's crutches for her in one hand and used the other to steady McKenzie as she hobbled into the inner circle with her.

"You're not exactly keeping your involvement with a reporter a secret," McKenzie said, rushing on her crutches to keep up with Jig. "Besides, you're a technical analyst. What the heck are you doing here?"

Jig pushed through a crowd of cops toward a trailer set up in the middle of the road directly across from what McKenzie assumed was the townhouse at the center of the frenzy. "I'm scrambling feeds to keep other morons of your persuasion—no offense—from having access to what's happening. If one of the neighbors decides he could make a quick buck, our lives become hell. I'm also trying to figure out this mess, and right now, you know more about it than anyone. So, here you are."

Jig passed into the main compartment of the trailer. Without a word to McKenzie, she looked to a guy in navy suit pants and an FBI vest. "Owen, this is McKenzie McClendon. She's the one I told you about."

McKenzie stared from Jig to the FBI guy. She couldn't afford to get in trouble for withholding information. *Had* she withheld information? No. She hadn't. Right?

But the agent didn't seem interested in reprimanding her. "Ms. McClendon, thank you for coming. I'm Special Agent Owen Holder, FBI. You know Everitt Armstrong?"

Everitt Armstrong. Shannon.

"Not exactly," McKenzie stammered. Did you know someone if they knew you? If you'd met in an OB/GYN's office one time? "We...we met once. I never knew her real name. She's contacted me since then, though. Regarding her circumstances."

"And she told you the people she was staying with may be involved with illegal surrogacy?"

McKenzie nodded quickly. "Yes. But she didn't tell me anything. No names, no addresses, nothing. That's why I didn't call the police."

Owen waved his hand as though he knew her concerns. "Ms. McClendon, we're trying to determine the mindset of the couple involved. We've profiled them to the degree we can, but we need to know more than what we've got so far. We don't know what to expect."

A piece of the puzzle clicked into place. They were outside

the house, watching. If the FBI was here to examine Shannon's—Everitt's—body, why were they out here?

"Expect?" she murmured.

Jig was seated at a station at the side of the trailer, pecking away at a laptop. "Yeah. Sorry. Forgot to mention. Cops were called when the neighbors phoned in the hanging pregnant girl in the bedroom. Banged on the door, tried to storm in. That's when they heard gunfire. We know Rodney Peterson put a bullet in his head. Sarah Peterson has a gun to Everitt's."

CHAPTER 61

JUST WHEN EVERITT thought she'd made it. Just when she'd thought it would pan out, the plan had gone to hell.

She'd stood in the light for what seemed like hours, but finally, Everitt had heard pounding at the front door. "Police, open up!" Splintering wood, footsteps, yelling.

Sarah screamed, "I knew it! I told you this would happen! They told you they didn't know which one she was!"

Rodney bellowed back. "I told them her name! Told 'em to take care of it! How was I supposed to know they'd take that to mean, 'make it look like a bunch of activist nutjobs shot up the clinic'?"

"You should've given them instructi—"

A gunshot.

"Damn it!" Sarah shrieked. Everitt's door burst open. "You!" Sarah screamed.

Before Everitt could react, Sarah Peterson had a pistol at her temple. "Clever," Sarah'd hissed in her ear.

Now, she stood in front of Sarah in the living room, eyes shut tight. She'd seen Rodney's body in the kitchen. Sarah had nowhere to run, no way to win. Everitt was the only thing between the devil woman and hell.

The baby kicked furiously inside her.

I know! I want to move, too, believe me. I would if I could.

Behind her, Sarah muttered to herself. "How much do they have? They couldn't know everything. Impossible. I could tell them it was all Rodney…"

Yeah. That'd work if you weren't holding a pregnant hostage right now.

Sarah's words grew more and more frantic as she thought out loud. "Yes. Rodney. Say it was Rodney. Tell them she's in on it. She wanted the money."

The baby jabbed Everitt again, begging her attention away from Sarah's whispers, the cold gun against her face. Her eyes fluttered open. Somehow, she expected to see the tiny imprint of a foot against her belly. Instead, her peripheral vision caught a movement that made the hair on her arms bristle.

To her left, beneath the stairs, was the door to the townhouse's crawl space. There, a tiny tube peeked out from the crack under the door.

McKenzie sat next to Jig in the trailer and filled Owen Holder in on what she knew. Based on her profile, he said Sarah Peterson was unlikely to negotiate.

"I should've homed in on what she'd told me. I should've found her before now. What if Everitt doesn't make it out of this?" McKenzie said. So strange to use this girl's real name as though she'd known her for years. Her stomach knotted as the faces of Levi and Uncle Sal clouded the edges of her memory, joined by a young girl with a rounded belly and a gun to her head. If Everitt and her child made it, could these two lives possibly make up for some of the damage she'd done? The lives she hadn't been able to save the last time she'd let a story consume her?

Jig clicked back and forth on her computer, managing internet traffic. "You couldn't have done anything different. We all tried. Besides, the best of the best are on the job. They'll get her out of there. The team in the ducts is snaking out cameras to see what angles we can get for a shot to take her down."

McKenzie pressed her forehead onto the cool Formica of the station beside Jig's. What would she say to Whitney *now*? Her editor had sounded so hopeful when they'd talked about the possibility that in the light of the newest murder, the baby trade might not be the Cradle Robber's sole motivation for killing after all. Now, this situation was about to drag a whole different aspect of the baby trade into the light, a cockroach caught when the porch lamp came on. Whitney would have no choice but to let McKenzie cover it, but at the same time, she'd promised her editor to report it fairly. To somehow explain both sides. Not to mention the unfortunate deal she'd made with Morton.

And now, another child's life was at stake right in the wake of her story.

This was a nightmare.

Owen Holder's voice echoed from the front of the trailer as he checked in again with the S.W.A.T. teams through his walkie. Each of the shooters reported their position.

"No shot. I have no shot on the south side."

Another voice clipped in. "No shot on the upper corner."

Everyone in the trailer waited to hear from the third sniper, but the silence only grew louder and louder. Nothing.

Owen Holder clicked his walkie again. "What's your status, Boss?"

No answer.

"Boss! Report status!"

Still nothing.

The air in the trailer thickened with each passing second. McKenzie's neck tingled in anticipation. Of what, she wasn't sure.

A shot rang out. A scream. Yells coming from outside the trailer.

Then, a crackle rattled from Holder's walkie talkie. "Boss here. Suspect down. Hostage secure. Clear."

The stillness in the trailer from moments before erupted into chaos. Agents scattered and rushed the trailer's exit. Holder barked commands, and radios chattered.

Everitt was okay! Right? Yes. That was what they'd said. She couldn't think of what to ask or who to ask it to in the bustle around her.

Next to her, what had been the one continuously moving person in the trailer had become the sole motionless figure. Jig's fingers stalled at her keyboard. After a second, they rose to her temple, where she rubbed her head in slow circles.

"Not again, Noah," Jig whispered.

Everitt had hit the ground hands first. She rolled onto her side and clapped her hands over her ears. It was like being on a plane, her ears under pressure. Everything was too loud and too quiet at the same time.

Sarah Peterson lay in front of her in a heap. Blood seeped onto the woman's face, her wild eyes frozen. Her normally neat hair clumped and matted weirdly at the crown. What was going on?

A man with a gun hung upside down from the broad fireplace, only his torso visible, as though he'd slid Santa-Claus style down the chimney headfirst. His legs dropped, and he crouch-landed in the ash. As he moved toward her, she read his jacket: FBI.

"Are you okay?" he asked, though she could barely make out the words. They were having some sort of weird, underwater conversation.

Everitt said nothing, just stared. Then, she looked down at her belly.

"Are you hurt?" he asked again through the tunnel of sound between them.

She couldn't speak. A moment later, paramedics charged in, came to her. They took over and started an IV line. One fastened a blood pressure cuff on her bicep.

Across the room, a policeman rolled Sarah Peterson's body over. A bullet had ripped upward through the base of her neck. Everitt's eyes drifted to the ceiling, where red liquid and chunks were splattered like a strange art deco painting.

The paramedics tipped Everitt onto her side and slid a board beneath her. She was in the air, being carried toward the ambulance. Her ears rang, and the world around her blurred.

At the last possible second, her voice seemed to remember how to work. She glanced over her shoulder at where the man from the fireplace now stood talking to another group of agents in FBI vests.

"Thank you," she choked, even though he was too busy to hear.

McKenzie followed Jig toward the townhouse, her stomach tumbling. Not only had she found Shannon—Everitt—but Noah Hutchins was here. Her ex was the hero of the night in his own ridiculous, rogue way.

Jig's leopard print peep-toes crunched on the pavement. "I know what you're thinking, believe me. I've been there. But now's not the time. He's in deep shit for this one."

What do I do, give off some kind of pheromone when I think about Noah?

Jig was right, though. Not the place. Damn, protocol was stupid sometimes. Sure, he hadn't been given the order to shoot, but Sarah Peterson hadn't been about to let Everitt walk out of there.

McKenzie hobbled after Jig toward the ambulance. Everitt sat in the back with a line of IV fluids dripping into her arm. Paramedics had brought her out on a gurney but had quickly seen that despite being terrified, she was okay.

The freckle-faced teen she'd met a few weeks ago at Dr. Schwetzer's office looked as if she'd aged a decade. Worry lines stretched across her forehead and her eyes glazed over with fear. She rested against the ambulance wall, her palms flat on her belly.

She's going to be so pissed at me.

Everitt looked up. A weary smile crossed her face. "How's

that for evidence?"

Jig took the cue that the two needed a minute. "I'll be back for you in a few. Don't go anywhere."

McKenzie watched Jig cross the yard before leaning on the side of the ambulance. "Everitt, huh?"

The girl kicked her feet awkwardly. "Just so you don't think I'm a complete idiot, I tried to sneak that in before the phone died."

McKenzie's memory flashed on their conversation about Felicia Rockwell. It was true. She'd tried to say, "Ever," at the end. Still, this girl had no right to think she'd acted like a moron.

"You did great," McKenzie said. God, she hated the patronizing quality of her voice. She didn't mean it that way. As far as she was concerned, the girl was a genius.

The medics came back with some papers for Everitt's signature. "Everything looks okay. We want you to come with us to the hospital to get checked out, but you're going to be fine. And the baby looks to be fine, too."

Except that you were held hostage by a lunatic, cut off from everyone you love, and now have loads of medical expenses you can't pay.

It must've been what Everitt was thinking, too, because she frowned. "Is it bad that I've got the whole 'nowhere to go' thing?"

They weren't exactly friends, but then again, this girl didn't have *anyone*. She hadn't for a while.

"Stay with me," McKenzie blurted out, her tongue moving faster than her brain.

Oh, damn it. What've you done now?

Everitt stared at her, eyes hooded. Distrustful.

Can't blame her.

"What's in it for you?" Everitt asked.

Still, there was no hostility in the question. Only conversation.

McKenzie shrugged. "Nothing. Everything. Depends on how you look at it. Either way, I'm writing your story, and you're out a bedroom. You might as well use mine. Besides," she said, nodding toward her crutches, "we're both sort of temporarily on the disabled list. May as well help each other out. You can use the hell out of me while I use the hell out of you. Win-win, I'd say."

Everitt glanced around at the flashing blue lights, the fray of scared neighbors and hungry journalists at the police line. "I wouldn't say any of this is a win-win, but yeah. I guess you're right about the living set-up."

McKenzie took in the girl's dirty hair, the lack of sleep that shadowed her face. McKenzie had so much to do, so many angles to check out, yet all she wanted to do right now was make Everitt a cup of chamomile tea, let her take a hot shower, and listen to her. That part of her that had first fallen in love with journalism ignited. People, and her interest in them, had drawn her into this industry in the first place. Something about the mystery of why some people lived, some died, some fought, and some gave up: those were the reasons she wanted to tell true stories and in the process, maybe figure out a little bit more of how life in general made some sense.

"It's a deal, then. Let me see if I can find out when you can come home."

CHAPTER 62

AN HOUR LATER, McKenzie was on her way home. Jig had appropriated a police car to drive her and Everitt back to her apartment. On the way there, Everitt's head rested against the glass of the cruiser, her eyes wide open, staring in front of her. McKenzie knew that look all too well. Disbelief.

Once inside her place, McKenzie sat quietly across from Everitt while the girl ate a bowl of ramen noodles. When she was finished, McKenzie grabbed Everitt fresh towels from the linen closet and showed her the spare bedroom, complete with the kitten comforter from her college days on the twin bed. At first, after his death, she hadn't had the heart to move any of Pierce's things. After a while, she hadn't had the heart to leave them. He probably wouldn't have cared either way, but her stomach somersaulted at the thought of someone stepping into the sacred space.

Then again, Pierce would consider Everitt worthy after all of this. "It's not much, but I suppose it's something."

Everitt plopped on her back on the mattress without bothering to take off her shoes. From this angle, McKenzie couldn't even see her face for the mound that was her stomach.

"Trust me," she said, "I couldn't be more thrilled."

McKenzie searched for words, questions about the ordeal. Finally, she swallowed all of them. "Get some rest. We can talk tomorrow."

Everitt muttered an okay, and McKenzie exited, pulling the door closed behind her.

She collapsed against the closed door.

Jesus, McKenzie. You have the latest almost-victim of a black market baby trade in your guest room, a clinic shooting to investigate, and a medical examiner to call about autopsy results. What village of orphans did you save to land in journalism heaven? And where on Satan's book did you sign to turn it into hell?

So many angles. What to do first? And after that? Call Zacharias Bayle. If it was anyone else, she'd figure he'd have long since gone home, but something about this guy told her he didn't *like* going home. He was too fond of his weird little dungeon of cadavers. She pulled out her almost drained phone. After she plugged it into the wall, she sat on the floor next to the outlet and made the call.

The M.E. answered on the fourth ring. After confirming again that all of the information was off the record until the official report was filed, he started talking.

"Well, we'll have to wait for toxicology labs to come back, but initial findings suggest she had drugs in her system. No puncture wounds to suggest needles, injection sites, that sort of thing. It's looking like the same M.O. of the other Cradle Robber victims. I'd take a guess and say those tox screens will come back positive for scopolamine and DMSO, or something similar, but don't quote me on that. Same cutting pattern, depth of wounds. Some of that was hard to determine because of the level of—er— *damage* done to the body, but from what I could tell, it was consistent."

"Damage" seemed an understatement when describing being crushed by an elevator. God. She did *not* want the answer to her next question. "Was she alive at impact?"

"Yes."

"Right," she replied, stiff, and she scribbled a few notes on her legal pad. "And she definitely wasn't pregnant?"

Bayle chuckled. "Unless someone slipped me some scopolamine before the dissection, I'm pretty sure I checked the right uterus."

McKenzie winced. "Okay. Anything else of note? Anything different from the other victims?"

"Not really. All the other victims were of varying ages and ethnicities, so not a pattern there to compare. Nothing crazy I found either. Just the usual notes. Some scar tissue in the abdominal cavity, probably from where her appendix was removed. Normal chest, lungs. Healthy liver. Looks like she didn't drink a day in her life. Contents of her stomach mostly empty except some nuts and swallowed gum that hadn't passed or digested yet. Pretty everyday findings, actually, unless you count the whole flattened-by-an-elevator thing."

M.E.'s had to be a bit eccentric to go into the field they did, but the guy could at least try to hide his nonchalance. "Right," she answered. "Thanks. I may call again if I think of any more questions."

He laughed again. "Thank you. I may answer if I feel up to it."

With that, he hung up.

She dialed Whitney, but stared at her phone for a long minute before hitting call. She really wasn't ready to have a talk with her editor yet about how she planned to balance the Cradle Robber's latest kill and the hostage situation with the Petersons.

Finally, she pressed the send button. Whitney answered in short order.

"So, the M.E. does say the latest victim wasn't pregnant," McKenzie said. She took a deep breath.

Get it over with.

"I'm putting together a small piece on it, but I'm waiting to see how exactly the killer and the Petersons tie together before I move forward with the bigger piece since I still have a couple days."

"How do you mean?" Whitney said, her voice sharp, all traces of the vulnerability she'd shown to McKenzie in her office the day she'd confessed her background gone.

"How do I mean what?"

"What do you mean figure out how the killer and the Petersons are tied together? Who says they are?"

McKenzie caught a glance of her surprised face in the stove's reflection. "Um...Whitney, someone is killing pregnant women, the babies are living, an IVF clinic has been shot up, and now, people buying a baby have held a woman hostage. Call me crazy, but if they *aren't* related, this is a bigger coincidence than finding a sopping wet cat right after a fish bowl's been knocked over."

"We don't report stories *you* think are related, McKenzie. We report facts," she snapped.

"I know that, Whitney, but I—"

"I suggest you know for sure before you put a thing about it being connected in your article. When it lands on my desk, I won't ask for changes. I'll veto it outright. Understand?"

McKenzie mouthed a curse-word. Whitney's feelings on the subject were understandable, but at this point, they were a serious conflict of interest. "Got it."

Next task was Jonas. He may have made her mad, but sooner or later, she'd have to talk to him. And when she did, casually mentioning that Everitt was staying in her spare room as an afterthought might not be wise.

Dread spread through her like wildfire as she pressed the button to dial Jonas.

Get ready, buddy. You're about to get caught up.

CHAPTER 63

TREVIN ROCKED HIMSELF back and forth on the bench near Strawberry Fields. To onlookers, he was any other junkie, but he knew better. Paranoid schizophrenic was closer.

As soon as he'd seen the Petersons on the news, he'd gone into complete and total freak-out. They were both dead, sure. But there might be something in their house. Something that pointed to him. What about phone numbers in their cell phones or address books or fucking rolodexes or wherever people keep their phone numbers? The cops would be on to him any time now. Not just the local cops, either, if the NYPD could be called 'local'. The Feds. If they knew he was the Peterson's lawyer, he was screwed ten brand new ways unknown to the Kama Sutra. He knew multiple modern translations of that one.

Or hell, even if he couldn't worm his way out of it, the time would be skim. Maybe only fines, probation. Assuming they didn't find out who he *really* was, anyway.

The girl was the fucking problem now. The day the damned Petersons had walked into his office to draw up the new set of papers, he knew he was screwed by the entire Belgian national football team. Still, he'd thought he would find his way around it, have time to sort it out. Now, she was God-knows where with God-knows who telling them God-knows what, and all it would take would be one little mention...

Fuck!

He'd also heard about the most recent dead girl, the one that wasn't pregnant. He'd known it would happen sooner or later, but he'd forced himself to ignore it. But now he'd lost control, whatever little control he might have had. No more income, too much media, and the monster on the loose. Dirk killed loose end Ollie. If his secretary was a loose end for that psycho, what did that make *him*?

No. Even Dirk isn't that crazy. I'm too tied to him. They'd find him. Neither one of us wants to be linked to the other.

A couple walked past, hand in hand. The guy noticed Trevin and stepped around his lady friend to shield her from the creepy rocking guy. Their paces quickened. Trevin burst into deranged laughter.

That's it! Run away!

Trevin swayed back and forth on the bench, overcome with the hilarity of it all. There were odds and ends strewn all over the place he had no way to keep in check, and more he wasn't even aware of, for sure. Yet, Trevin hadn't touched a single girl. Not one.

He rolled onto his back on the bench. His guffaws sounded robotic, foreign in his ears. His feet slammed the metal seat to punctuate his laughter. It was so damned ridiculous.

The one guy who could put him away for life was the one responsible for killing them.

Rory lay on her right side, facing the wall, her turquoise nightgown draped over her. It was her favorite. Not particularly pretty, but it covered all of her just right, complete with a modest neckline. She'd never had the cleavage to make her want to show it off, but since she'd been pregnant, her breasts spilled over the lace trim ever so slightly.

The door creaked open and shut. Rory breathed evenly as she listened to Bryce's wallet and keys hit the dresser, his spare change clink into the jar on the nightstand. Two or three receipts he didn't need to save would remain by the change jar. She'd sweep them into the trash bin tomorrow as always.

Silence as he changed into his pajama bottoms. When they'd been dating, he'd slept in only boxers.

In the bed beside her, he smelled of cigars and brandy, though she knew he didn't drink it at home. So different from the scent still lingering from Jonas.

What had she been thinking? Jonas had told her today all about his past, his stint in prison. He was, for all practical purposes, a convict. Even if she wasn't happy, she couldn't do this. Shouldn't do this! Things between her and Bryce had been awful. But he was still Bryce, wasn't he?

Rory rolled over, the smooth skin of her husband's back directly in front of her face. She pressed her dry lips to it and closed her eyes.

"I thought you were asleep," he whispered, his voice blurred at the edges from alcohol.

"No," she breathed. What do you say to a man sharing your bed when you've kissed someone else? "Where have you been?"

Bryce inhaled deep, but he didn't turn over. After a few silent seconds, he replied. "Finishing up some work."

Rory exhaled the breath she'd been holding. The usual answer. A tear slid down her cheek. She let her lips graze the skin over his spine once more. Her eyelashes fluttered against him as she willed him to say something else to her. Anything.

His light first snore told her he wouldn't. Rory turned back over, her hand lingering over the place where days before, his baby had been growing.

All that work must be exhausting.

She closed her own eyes and drifted into uneasy sleep, thinking about how maybe she'd never really known Bryce at all.

CHAPTER 64

MCKENZIE PACED THE living room. It'd been almost two hours since she'd called Jonas. She'd been through another dead girl, Felicia Rockwell's ex-husband's theories, and a hostage situation since she'd last seen him. What the heck was he doing?

Finally, a knock sounded on the door. McKenzie flung it open. "About time—"

She stopped midsentence.

"I'd have been here sooner, but I didn't want to come empty handed," Noah Hutchins said. He held up a plastic bag full of paper Chinese-food boxes. "I come bearing gifts."

McKenzie stared at the former SEAL without taking the food. His hair was longer than when she'd last seen him, his ice blue eyes a little more rested. He was also a little more clothed.

"What are you doing here?"

Noah pushed past her into the living room and set the bag on the coffee table before flinging himself onto the couch. He took one of the boxes out and opened it, not bothering to grab silverware or chopsticks. He tipped noodles straight from the box into his mouth. Chewing a mouthful, he said, "Gee, Mac, I missed you, too. Sorry I'm not waiting on you. I know it's rude, but believe me when I say being grilled for killing a perp should have to wait until after dinnertime. I'm starving."

She shook her head. After all, why wouldn't he come by? They were both in the same town for once. They'd come from the same crime scene.

Dear God. Some people have magazines or movies for common interests.

"You're right. I'm sorry. I'm expecting someone..." her voice trailed awkwardly.

Please don't let him catch that. Please don't let him think—

"Oh!" A grin broke out across Noah's face. "Gentleman caller, eh? Well, then. I'm right on time!"

How had she ever loved this asshat? "Noah, it's not like that. Jonas is a friend."

Noah still smiled ear to ear in that all-too-familiar, "Let me be the judge of that," sort of a way. He sat back and cracked his knuckles.

As if on cue, Jonas' hand stopped hers right as McKenzie went to close the door.

Kill me now.

"Okay, please tell me what's so important that you've resorted to stalking me?" Jonas said.

His gaze hit Noah on the couch, and Noah stood. The SEAL dialed down his shit-eating grin to a smirk. "You must be Jonas."

Jonas' eyebrows scrunched together. "Who are you?" He looked to McKenzie.

McKenzie fought for composure. "Jonas, this is my friend and former big story, Noah. Noah, this is my friend and current big story, Jonas. And for the record, you both give yourselves way too much credit. And also for the record, Jonas, you called *me* for help, remember?"

Now, though, it was Noah's turn to narrow his eyes. "Whoa, wait a sec. This dude is involved with..." he jammed his thumb toward where he knew the guest room—and Everitt—to be. Someone, apparently, had filled Noah in on her temporary adoption of a pregnant woman.

McKenzie gave a quick shake of her head. So much for smoothly catching Jonas up to speed. "So, yeah. About that. The pregnant girl who called me for help because she thought the couple adopting her baby were black market psychos? Yeah. Well. She's in the guest room."

"What?" Jonas yelled.

"You've missed a little," Noah supplied.

For the next thirty minutes, McKenzie filled Jonas in on everything. Noah made her stop to give details on everything from before he'd become involved. Each time she did, Jonas waved his hand as if to urge her on, irritated, but McKenzie wasn't telling Noah anything out of kindness or to be polite. She told him because she knew his skill set.

She told the two about Felicia Rockwell's ex-husband, about how he had nothing to do with her adoption of a child, but that he felt sure the possibility of the black market was strong. The rest of the conversation with Jerome Kyler still niggled at her mind, but for now, she skated over it. The important details were out of the way.

"Jig's looking for info on the kid, but nothing so far. Then, we got a little sidetracked. First we found out about the Cradle Robber's most recent body, which, by the way, was minus the cradle robbing. Then...this..." she said as she pointed toward the guest room door.

Jonas sat there as though he'd been struck dumb.

Noah kept his eyes on McKenzie. "Okay, so if this Felicia has an adopted kid, what's the progression? I mean, say we find information on the kid. What does that tell us?"

McKenzie propped her crutches against the wall. She used the coffee table to ease herself to the floor across from Noah and opened a box of noodles. Maybe food would help after all. "Good question. I have a lot of leads, but no straight line. Everything bleeds together."

"Figures," Noah replied. "Let's make it linear, then. Forget the adopted kid for a second, since we don't have that info yet—"

"And who are you, a Hardy boy?" Jonas cut.

Noah glared at him but didn't bite back. He wouldn't. Noah

understood Jonas' mindset better than Jonas thought. "You know how it is. You shoot someone holding a hostage without orders, get suspended. Gotta pass the time somehow."

"They suspended you?" McKenzie asked. She wasn't sure why she was surprised. Maybe because Noah always seemed to be out of the reach of rules like those.

"Pending an investigation."

"I still don't understand why you need to be here," Jonas said.

"In case you haven't noticed, Brainiac, Mac's shot, and both your faces are all over the news. You want your son, you need someone who can get in places you can't. Anyway, we don't have Felicia's adopted kid, but what we do have are the Petersons. They were connected to Felicia Rockwell. In some way, shape, or form, the Petersons and Felicia are connected to the Cradle Robber if he's selling babies to the black market. That is, unless there are two separate baby trade rings operating in New York City at the same time, which is almost…well, it's doubtful."

McKenzie followed. "So, who is he connected to, though? The Petersons were using Everitt and surrogates. Where does a serial killer who takes babies come in?"

Jonas piped up. "Has to be a degree of separation, right? The Petersons selling babies are one aspect. They do it a different way."

Noah's glance shot toward Jonas. "Yes. It's the same as black market weapons, organs, et cetera. Baby trafficking is like any other organized crime. Organized."

The words conjured images of horse heads in people's beds in McKenzie's mind. "What are we talking here? A mobster of some sort? The Manhattan Godfather?"

Noah wobbled his hand back and forth as if to say 'sort of'. "We may not need to look that far. I'm sure there's a higher up. The connection we're looking for is somewhere further down the chain."

Jonas took a box of noodles out of the bag even if they weren't for him. "Did any of the Cradle Robber victims know Felicia or the Petersons?"

"Doubt it. I doubt the Cradle Robber knows about the Petersons or Felicia. Vice versa, too," Noah said.

McKenzie's head hurt. She needed a flow chart. "So, since we have no clue who the Cradle Robber is, and we *do* know the Petersons—ish—we should try to find out who they were connected to?"

Noah nodded slowly. "I'd say that's the best course of action."

"I know where to start," a voice said.

McKenzie, Jonas, and Noah all snapped their attention toward the guest bedroom doorway. Everitt rubbed her eyes, red and sick-looking. She looked at them each in turn, her brain seeming slow to catch up to her previous words.

"I met the Petersons pretty recently, but I can take you to someone who's known them a lot longer."

CHAPTER 65

AS THE SUN peeked over the tops of the skyscrapers, the weird group approached the door to a shop bearing neon-green lettering that said, "Hair if You Dare."

Jonas bit back his comment about how a salon was the last place he needed to be right now. He'd just made out with a woman for the first time since his wife was murdered. They would've done more had she not just given birth. She just happened to be a victim of the same murderer who killed his wife. On the scale of one to fucked up, that had to rate off the charts. Still, Rory was asleep, and he needed McKenzie on his side. If he couldn't talk to Rory anyway, he might as well be with McKenzie and a girl connected to this baby trade thing.

He followed McKenzie and Noah as Everitt led them all into the shop filled with women who looked like they belonged at a Lady Gaga fan club meeting. From the teens to the forty-somethings, all had some kind of funky hairdo—fuchsia stripes in their hair or a spiky bob that looked more like a startled porcupine.

Everitt led them to the largest station, where a tiny blonde woman painted violet paste onto the head of a lady in her chair. The hairdresser glanced up as they approached, curious but unconcerned. Everitt had called to warn her they were coming.

When they reached the station, Laurel finally put down the wand she used to dole out the violet and hugged Everitt, comically calm under the circumstances. "I'm so glad you're all right. I had no idea anything like that was going on, Everitt. I swear, if I'd known, maybe I could've helped."

Everitt gestured to the group. "Laurel Jeffries, meet McKenzie, Jonas, and Noah."

The blonde turned back to her work. "Nice to meet you all. Not sure how I can help you. I already told Everitt everything I could think of as far as the Petersons and the whole nine yards. Always seemed like a nice lady. Can't believe I was so wrong about someone."

The woman in the chair listened, curious, but didn't speak. How did women talk to hairdressers the way they did with all these people around?

"That's okay, Laurel," McKenzie said. "We just wanted to come and pick your brain a bit, see if you could tell us about the Petersons before Everitt met them. You told Everitt they had another surrogate before her. What do you know about her?"

Laurel smoothed her spatula over the foils in the lady's hair. She crinkled her brows in concentration. "Let's see, here. Her name was Tiffanie. She was young like Everitt. Didn't have a last name. Gorgeous honey-colored hair. Ruined it, putting that frost on it like we did, but she wanted to try..."

Hair color. Of course, we need vital information, and we get hair color.

McKenzie seemed un-phased. "Did Tiffanie work for you, too?"

Laurel shook her head as she pulled a plastic shower cap over the lady's purple cone head. "Nope. Only came in for a hairdo every now and then. Though, now that I look back, it *does* seem like Sarah brought her in when she needed to run an errand and couldn't take her with her." She shrugged. "You know what they say about hindsight."

That it lets you know you're a fucking moron?

"And she was the only surrogate that you know of?" Noah asked.

Laurel nodded, leading the woman back to a machine that looked like it was designed by aliens to suck out the brains of human beings. The woman sat down, and Laurel hit a switch. "You have five minutes."

She returned to the station, scooping up the opened packets of color and mopping up the droplets of purple on the counter. Everitt grabbed the bowl and took it toward the back room. Jonas heard water running.

"Thanks, doll," Laurel said. She pursed her red lips. "I was trying to think. Tiffanie went to school around here. NYU, maybe? No, that wasn't it. She mentioned *wishing* she could go there. Maybe it was that she was planning on applying there." She grinned at them. "You said you wanted to pick my brain, but it's already a little picked!" Laurel laughed at her own joke and shook her head.

What was he doing here, listening to this woman who sounded as if she'd had some of that hair dye to drink? He should be somewhere finding out why Rory had been targeted, finding out why Noelle had been. What Rory and Noelle had in common. For more reasons than one.

"What about Felicia Rockwell? Does that name ring any bells?" Noah asked.

Laurel stared at the ceiling. "Nope. Don't think I've ever heard of her. Was she a surrogate?"

No one answered. Instead, McKenzie asked another question. "Did Sarah Peterson ever say anything about her doctor or the Davidsons? Hall Davidson? Melissa Davidson?"

Jonas tensed at the mention of the people who'd "adopted" Gibb. Laurel couldn't have been more relaxed if she were being asked about her tofu preferences.

"Nope. Nothing there. I knew a Monique Davis one time, but that's about as close as I can come. I can give you her phone number if you like."

"That won't be necessary," McKenzie replied.

Jonas had been around McKenzie long enough to recognize the set of her mouth indicated severe frustration. If Laurel didn't start talking soon, Jonas wouldn't have to worry about getting away. McKenzie would jump ship, too.

"She went to a lot of doctors, it seems like," Laurel said. The way she looked at the air while she talked, Jonas wondered if she saw her own thoughts written there.

"Any names?" McKenzie prompted.

She searched the air in front of her some more, then above before repeating her favorite word. "Nope."

McKenzie balled her fists at her sides. Jonas would've laughed if the lull in the conversation hadn't allowed his mind to drift to worrying about Noelle. What would she think if she knew about him kissing Rory? Would it make it better or worse that she was connected in the way she was?

The phone rang, and Laurel apologized for needing to take it. She grabbed the handset to answer it. Jonas watched from the side as McKenzie and Noah huddled.

"She's a dead end," McKenzie said quietly.

"Maybe. I still feel like we could finagle some more names out of her, though. Talk to her more about Tiffanie's details. She could remember something, and…she's not coming clean."

Laurel's voice on the phone mixed with the whispers. "Sure thing," she was saying. "I have a ten o'clock and a two on Monday. I would move you sooner this week, but I'm cancelling my book Friday to go to that funeral of my client. Yeah. Poor thing. Lost her job and mugged in the same week, and the whole nine yards. Yeah. The lawyer she worked for didn't have enough business and decided to close up shop and the whole nine yards. Yeah. Okay, girl. Sounds good. See you then."

Laurel hung up the phone, her back to them. "If I think hard, maybe she said something about a doctor in New Jersey. Or was it New Hampshire?"

Behind her, though, the entire group had fallen silent,

including the lady under the dryer. A client of hers had been murdered this week? One who worked for a lawyer?

"Laurel. Your client—the funeral. What lawyer did she work for?"

Laurel stared back at them, wide-eyed. "I don't really know. I try not to pry into people's business too much. Knew she worked for one from what she said, but I never asked for names or anything like that. Ollie's mom called me to fix her hair for…you know. Otherwise, I doubt I'd have known anything about it…" Her eyes widened as her mouth swirled into an "O." "You don't think she's involved in this whole thing somehow, do you?"

McKenzie and Noah exchanged glances, then McKenzie said, "Laurel, how can we get in touch with Ollie's mother?"

CHAPTER 66

BONNIE STOOD IN the bedroom doorway holding a towel around her naked skin. "Dirk, this is getting old. Doesn't your phone have a calendar in it?"

Dirk forced the bile back down his esophagus. "I know, Bonnie, but it's not my fault. That damned Chief of Staff has it in for me."

He'd just informed his girlfriend he had to pack and immediately fly out to California for a medical conference where he'd been scheduled to speak, which didn't fit well with her plan to seduce him. Now, her twig-like frame trembled as she tried to control her anger, her non-existent chest heaving with the effort. Damn. It was almost skeletal. Repulsive.

Still, he hadn't exactly done it on a whim. He'd known the past few days he'd need to finish up what he'd started. This had simply sped things up.

"How can they do that? Normal people have work schedules. They have to adhere to your schedule. It has to be some kind of labor law, right?"

Dirk picked up his carry-on, which he'd brought in for the sole purpose of opening to pack a jacket he'd left at her place a few nights ago. It was always good for them to see that you were packed and ready to go.

He pecked her on the top of her bird-like head. "Not in the medical profession, hon."

She crossed her arms over her towel. "Well, just know you'd

better not ever take me to one of those big hospital functions, because if I run into the Chief of Staff, I'll give him a piece of my mind."

Noted.

He pulled her into his free arm and let his head fall against her the way he'd seen couples do before. Made them seem close, intimate.

"I'll remember that," he whispered truthfully. "See you in a couple days."

Who were all these people in her house? She'd come home from work at the hospital, but no one was here. What had happened? She'd changed out of her scrubs...

April Gregory's eyes blurred all the moving bodies together. She couldn't make out a face. Above her, a clearer face hovered over her. The guy's eyes were coal black. He had a day's worth of scruff on his face. His mouth was moving, but her brain wouldn't process what he was saying. Why was he here? As she stared into his coal eyes, the color of her childhood teddy bear's, another pair of eyes shot to her mind. Hazel eyes. That guy! She'd met that guy. He'd come to her door. Brought a package that had been delivered to his place by mistake. Such a good-looking guy.

She moved her lips to try to tell the coal-eyed man she couldn't understand him. She was floating, just her head. Her body didn't exist. Where was it?

They'd talked awhile. Somehow, he'd ended up asking her on a date. She'd said yes, excited. Handsome, clean-cut. She hadn't been on a date in so long.

The coal-eyed man left her vision. She stared at the ceiling, trying to both think about the hazel-eyed man and pick out some of the sea of distorted words at the same time. Hazel eyes. He'd shown up to pick her up for their date. Asked to use the bathroom. So nice. Polite.

A prick in her arm. She barely felt it, though. Distant, like when the dentist shot her up with Novocain before a filling.

What?

April urged her eyes to focus, to look down for the source of the poke. There, a needle ran from her vein, and a tube snaked from her arm. She couldn't follow the tube, though. The red bloody matrix that was her arm caught her attention. Cuts. So many of them, and yet, she didn't feel them. Nothing.

Coal eyes flitted back into her line of vision. He spoke again, and this time, she could make out his words better, though he still sounded like he was talking to her through glass.

"We're here to help you, April. Don't worry. You've lost a lot of blood, but we're giving you some medicine to make it better."

How do you know my name?

Her lips wouldn't form the words. She closed her eyes. It would be okay. Whatever it was, it would be okay. They were worried over nothing, even though at the same time, she knew that thought didn't make sense. She had seen her arm. It should be scary. But it wasn't. It didn't hurt.

"This won't hurt at all."

April's eyes shot open at the memory of the hazel-eyed man's words. She was suddenly very aware of who the coal-eyed man was and why he was here.

Panicking, she tried to flail her hands. Scream words. Nothing. She blinked rapidly, her eyes the only part of her she could manage any control over.

Look at me!

The EMT wasn't looking, though. He was busying himself at her IV, a full syringe at the port.

April watched him plunge the medication into the IV and her veins. She could do nothing but beg with her blinking eyes for him to stop.

CHAPTER 67

"THE MOST RECENT victim was found in her Washington Heights home after an urgent 911 call was made from a pay phone nearby. Authorities suspect that the perpetrator himself may have made the call, but FBI agents have refused to comment on what this may mean about the assailant's pathology."

Rory sat an inch away from the TV, bundled in the afghan as she watched the report. Her reality show had been interrupted by the breaking news of the possible Cradle Robber victim, and she'd been drawn to the TV like it was magnetized to her. She inched closer and closer until finally, she was near enough to grab either side of the set with her hands.

She could feel Bryce standing in the doorway before he spoke. "Shut it off, Rory."

Rory didn't answer. The news was too entrancing, terrifying.

"We do not yet know the identity of the victim, but we do have unconfirmed reports that the resident of the home in question is twenty-five-year-old April Gregory, a technician at St. Alphius Memorial Hospital in New York. Authorities have yet to—"

Bryce's finger jammed in between her shoulder and her face to turn off the set, but it was too late. Rory had heard the last words, and her respiration sped to a pant. "He can't..." she stuttered. "...he knows! I can't! He can't!"

The scream that escaped her throat sounded like it came

from someone else, but by the way Bryce grabbed her, held her fast to him, she knew it was her own.

The Cradle Robber killed someone at St. Alphius Hospital! He's looking for me!

Bryce backed away from her but held her shoulders still, forcing her to look at him. "Deep breaths. I need to make some phone calls in the kitchen, okay? Sit here. I'll get one of your anxiety pills."

He ushered her to the wing chair where she'd been before the breaking news came on, tucked the afghan around her, and disappeared into the kitchen. When he came back, he handed her a glass of water and one of the little orange tablets. She took it as he disappeared back into the kitchen.

Rory watched for his back to turn, then tucked the tablet under the chair cushion. As much as she needed it, what she needed more was the ability to run if she had to. She needed to not feel sluggish. She needed to feel she could fight.

The long ride crammed into the car with other people made Jonas more anxious. He'd have loved to have taken a separate vehicle, and would've just to have the free time to think if they didn't have to go all the way out to Jersey. No cabs were willing to travel from New York City to Jersey. It was sometimes even hard to find a car service that wanted to. The thought of finding the lawyer that was handling the Petersons' illegal adoptions was intriguing, but it didn't feel like it was bringing him any closer to finding the Cradle Robber.

Jonas stared at his phone, willing Rory to call him. Text him. He'd somehow feel better if he knew she wasn't freaking out about what they'd done. Or hell, if he knew she *was* freaking out. The *knowing* part was the key.

The car turned into a driveway leading toward a home that looked like it was built with flat stones. A dark-haired lady stood in the glass doorway on the porch, arms crossed. As McKenzie paid the driver, Jonas' phone lit up.

"Hello?" he answered despite McKenzie's glare.

It was Rory. "Jonas, I don't know if you saw, but there's been another girl killed. Jonas, she——" she paused, wretched. Cleared her throat. "She worked at the same hospital where I was after the attack. St. Alphius."

Jonas' chest clenched painfully, and his blood sped up in his veins. "Is Bryce with you?"

Rory choked a sob. "Yes. But he's calling around, trying to find someone to stay with me while he goes in to the office. I don't...I can't be around just anyone right now, Jonas!"

He put a hand on the driver's shoulder, held up his finger to indicate one minute. Next to him, McKenzie stared at him incredulously. Noah and Everitt were probably doing the same behind him.

"Hang on. I'm on my way," he replied.

"What the heck, Jonas?" McKenzie demanded. Here they were, in Freehold, New Jersey to interview a dead girl's mother, and Jonas was saying he was turning around and leaving. This was *his* idea! He'd been the one who had wanted her to do this story in the first place.

"I have to go," he said as he climbed back into the car.

McKenzie stood in the way of the door. "Jonas, what on God's green earth could be more important than this? What the *hell* are you not telling me?"

Jonas' gaze fell to his shoes, then to his wedding band. "I've been talking to Rory Nathaniel."

"You what?"

He had been in communication with the one living Cradle Robber victim since they interviewed her and hadn't told her? While she was almost getting raped in Queens looking for Felicia Rockwell's ex-husband, he'd been withholding vital information from her?

"Chill out a minute," he said softly. "She hasn't remembered anything. We've been trying to retrace her steps, though. See if she *could* remember anything."

He has to be kidding me!

"And you didn't think this was worth sharing?"

Jonas shrugged, his eyes clouding over. "I would've told you if there was anything worth telling, but you seemed to think Rory was a waste of time until she remembered something that would benefit you. To you she's just another source for your story. I thought I could help her, though. As a living, breathing person who's been traumatized. A person, not a story. She needed someone who would understand."

McKenzie thumped her crutches on the pavement. "Well, for God sakes, far be it for me to deny you playing shrink while I'm out digging through the craziest, most screwed up maze on earth for *you!*"

Jonas barked a sarcastic laugh. "For me? You're such a martyr, McKenzie. You have no idea what it feels like to be left behind to pick up the pieces by a nutcase like that."

Her gut clenched like she'd been punched by someone twice her size as his words brought forth the *exact* feeling of how it hurt to be the only one left standing when everyone around her, everyone she loved, had died because she was more ambitious than she was worth. "Oh, yeah. I'm really clueless—"

"Maybe Rory does need a shrink. Maybe I need one. But we both understand what this is like. I need to be there for her." He stared her down, challenging her, daring her to refute him, his eyes burning with intensity she couldn't quite peg.

Unbelievable. "What could she possibly need you for that is so important it can't wait another minute?"

The look on his face gave him away before he could answer. The distant hurt in his eyes, the same pain that shadowed them when he talked about Noelle. "Someone else was killed?"

Jonas nodded. "Yeah. Not only that, but someone who

worked at St. Alphius Hospital."

Shit.

"He's looking for her, then," she whispered.

Jonas grabbed the door handle. "Looks like it."

McKenzie flattened her palms against her slacks next to her crutches.

Reason with him. Be calm.

"I know you want to help her, Jonas, but the police should really handle—"

"Handle what? Handle protecting her? They couldn't even hide what hospital she was taken to."

McKenzie looked to Noah, pleading.

In answer, Noah stepped toward Jonas. "Man, she's right. Believe me, I know what it's like to want to take things into your own hands, but this is better left to the pros."

Jonas's hand shook ever so slightly on the cab door. A vein pulsed in his neck. "And when it was you, you didn't leave it to the pros, did you? You had to do it on your own. It wasn't a choice, right?"

Noah's jaw clenched. He didn't answer.

"I might not be an FBI sniper, Noah, but I'm a man just like you are, goddamn it."

With that, Jonas slammed the car door. McKenzie, Noah, and Everitt stood in a stranger's driveway as the cab sped away.

CHAPTER 68

MCKENZIE STOOD IN the driveway, unsure what move to make. A new body. Another one.

My God.

She caught Mrs. Favre standing in the doorway watching them, waiting on them. Finding the lawyer involved with the Petersons. That was the next step. "Okay," she said, both to Everitt and Noah as much as to herself. "I have to make a quick phone call, then we go inside and interview Ollie's mother."

She scrolled through her phone until she reached Zacharias Bayle's last call. She hit the send. The M.E.'s voicemail picked up.

Well, makes my decision easy, I guess.

McKenzie left Bayle a quick message asking him to call her back, then shoved her phone into her purse.

"Ready?" Noah asked.

"As ever," she replied. They headed up the steps toward Mrs. Favre.

Mrs. Favre was younger than McKenzie had expected. From far away, the woman's posture had screamed osteoporosis, and the silhouette of her short, poofy haircut had reminded McKenzie of Sophia from the *Golden Girls*. But now that she was up close, the hair and posture didn't match the smooth, flawless skin without so much as a hint of crows' feet. If McKenzie hadn't known she had a daughter in her twenties, she'd have thought the woman was closer to her own age.

"I'm sorry to keep you waiting, Mrs. Favre. We had a

personal issue. Thanks for seeing us on such short notice."

Mrs. Favre looked McKenzie up and down, then did the same with Noah and Everitt. Finally, she turned back to McKenzie, acknowledging her as the ringleader of the group. "What is it you know about Ollie?"

Good question.

"We're not sure, Mrs. Favre. Let me explain."

She detailed—sort of—the connections among the IVF clinic, the Petersons, and Everitt. For the moment, she left out the Cradle Robber. The woman looked overwhelmed as it was.

Mrs. Favre pinched the bridge of her heavily made-up nose and closed her eyes. Had she caked on all that foundation because strangers were coming over? Did she even realize she didn't need it? The only thing this woman's face had to hide might be the lost hours of sleep the mother had suffered, but even that didn't show in bags or puffiness. It was more something hollow in her pupils.

"Let me get this straight," she replied slowly. "You don't think Ollie was mugged. You think someone killed her because she was involved in organized crime?"

McKenzie inhaled.

How to explain this?

"Not exactly. You see, we think she may have worked for the lawyer involved in this ring of—"

"You mean Mr. Worneck?" the woman asked. Her eyes had popped back open and her gaze now travelled from McKenzie to Noah to Everitt and back.

"Was that her boss' name?" Noah asked.

The lady nodded furiously, clearly eager for more information. "Yes. Worneck. I can't think of his first name. Ollie never called him by it."

"No, no. That's great, Mrs. Favre," McKenzie said. She cut her eyes to Noah to silently ask him to Google the name. He was already on his iPhone. Maybe he'd think to message Jig, too.

McKenzie was about to ask another question when her own

phone buzzed. Zachariah Bayle.

"Excuse me, I have to take this. Work..." she said. Ollie's mother waved her hand that it was fine.

As she headed to the porch to take the call, she heard Mrs. Favre comment to no one in particular, "He always seemed like such a nice man from what Ollie told me about him."

"They always do," Everitt replied.

Trevin plugged the numbers into his pre-paid phone in every combination he could think of. Nothing.

He'd known there wouldn't be any response. Not anymore.

The office wasn't safe, nor was his home nor anywhere connected to his name. The police had been by, but they were only half the problem now that Dirk wasn't answering to anyone. No more Petersons. No more Dirk. No more babies. No more money. The Jap would be back.

Trevin sure as hell wasn't hanging around where the henchman could find him. Luckily, the old neighborhood and the old gutters didn't come with a street address. You either knew them, or you didn't.

As he wandered the back alleys in the Bronx neighborhood where he'd grown up, he passed the familiar bulky bodies scrunched up on the side of the pavement. At least the ones shaking with DTs were alive. The others could be asleep, overdosed, murdered...no telling. Most people didn't give a rat's ass. Easy to blend in here.

There were people here who could help him, and not just because they had juice. What he needed most now was to do what any good rat backed into a corner would do: be a motherfucking rat.

CHAPTER 69

"WE'RE TALKING WAY too often here lately," Zacharias Bayle said after McKenzie answered the phone. "Yes, to answer your question, I'll to be here late again tonight. Bodies to dissect...reports to dictate."

"You have her yet?"

"Not quite," he replied in his casual monotone. "The Feds are transporting her as soon as the paperwork's squared away. I went over to the hospital ER to walk the scene. Took some notes and everything."

"She was in the ER?" McKenzie repeated, confused. Usually these girls were, well, unquestionably *dead* by the time they were found.

"Oh, yeah," he replied. "For sure. Off the record?"

McKenzie cursed under her breath. "Of course."

"She was still alive when the medics got hold of her. Cause of death to be determined."

This was a first. "Blood loss?"

Bayle tsked into the phone. "Did you not hear me? I said I don't know yet."

"Right," McKenzie replied. "My fault. Can I come by, then?"

"Aw, sure," he answered. "I'll put on the chicken."

She remembered Noah and Everitt inside with Mrs. Favre.

Shit!

Feeling like a twelve-year-old, she asked, "Can I bring a friend?"

Or two.

Bayle laughed hard. "McKenzie McClendon, this is an autopsy, not middle school play practice. I'm letting you in against protocol as it is, and only because I'm a lonely, depressed nerd, and you're an attractive female in my age bracket who happens to like talking about dead bodies. I'd say other people are pretty much off limits."

"Okay. I respect that. I'll be around in about an hour."

"Looking forward to it," Bayle said.

Autopsy dates: all the rage. Now, what to do about Noah and Everitt?

As if he'd heard her thoughts, Noah stepped through the glass door and onto the porch. "What's the news?"

McKenzie gestured to her phone. "The M.E. says I can come in for the examination of the new body. He doesn't want anyone else present."

Noah shrugged. "Just as well. Mrs. Favre and Everitt started talking. I think they're about to become best pals."

"Heard from Jig?"

Noah shook his head. His face was fuller than she remembered. He'd been eating more, but the change was subtle. Maybe a five pound difference, but either way, a healthy one. "She hasn't had any luck turning up the name Worneck. If Mrs. Favre knew anything at all about Ollie, we'd probably have more information, but she's flying blind."

The way his lips moved when he talked warmed her. Tickled memories of the way they'd felt pressed against hers, warm and hard and—

Focus.

"Maybe you two can hang around here and see if you can leech out any more memories. I'll head to the M.E.'s office and get the skinny on the DOA."

McKenzie flinched at her own wording.

She wasn't dead on arrival, though. She'd been alive.

"Sounds like a plan," Noah replied.

His eyes held hers a second longer, his mouth quirked in an affectionate smile that made McKenzie's heart flutter. She smiled back as he turned to go inside.

Zacharias Bayle already had the latest victim on his table. He glanced up from the body. "McKenzie McClendon. So glad you could make it!"

Like we're meeting up for frozen yogurt and a movie.

"Thanks for having me, I guess. So, what do we have?"

"Ah, April Gregory, an unfortunate x-ray technician who caught the eye of our city's current psycho-in-chief." He glanced up at McKenzie and raised one eyebrow. "*Not* pregnant, before you ask."

Whitney will be happy. Too bad that doesn't help April Gregory's family much.

"How do we know she's a Cradle Robber victim, then?"

"The same little symbol is carved in her arm like the others," Bayle replied without looking up.

McKenzie whipped out her legal pad and pencil and jotted notes as Bayle recorded his own. "Any idea how she died? Was it blood loss?"

At the glare he shot her, she re-phrased. "I mean, do you *think* it was blood loss?"

Bayle scraped at a piece of skin on April's thigh, then took a few pictures of it. He cut a tissue sample to be sent to the lab. "Nope, I don't think it was blood loss. She was bleeding a lot, sure, but not...hm. Not nearly enough for the amount of wounds she had. I could venture a guess here, but I might be wrong."

McKenzie jotted another note on her paper. "Oh, come on, Zacharias, since when are you modest?"

He cocked his head, still examining the place on her leg from which he'd taken the sample. "Well, never. Okay. If I had to guess, I'd speculate she didn't die from blood loss at all. I'd guess she died because she wasn't losing *enough* blood. Or the *reason* she wasn't losing the amount of blood she ought to have been given the circumstances, that is."

McKenzie stared at him. "Are you the Cheshire Cat all of the sudden?"

He looked up from where he was using a pair of tiny forceps to lift a section of skin from her other cold thigh. Bayle wiggled his eyebrows. "Do you want me to be?"

She swatted the air in his direction. "Go finish your autopsy, you sick little man."

Bayle laughed, then put his blade back to April Gregory's skin.

Here we go again.

"Okay," he said, "what I mean is, my hypothesis from what I can tell, which isn't much at this stage, is that she may very well have died from a blood clot that caused her to stroke out."

"What?"

"Yep. My theory is that it was all part of this sicko's 'see if they die' game he likes to play. I think this time, he shot her up with a drug or two that would interact with the drugs the paramedics would give to almost any trauma patient at risk of bleeding to death on their way to the ER. One of those drugs, tranexamic acid, a.k.a. TXA, helps keep patients from bleeding out because, while it doesn't assist blood clotting, it keeps blood clots from breaking *down*, if that makes sense. Works really well for patients losing a lot of blood. If this guy anticipated her receiving tranexamic acid, he could pre-dose her with something that would make her blood predisposed *to* clot, so the TXA would cause fatal blood clotting."

"Jesus Christ working at a Starbucks," McKenzie breathed.

"I don't know. This guy's probably worse. I bet Jesus makes a divine cup of coffee."

The autopsy went on. McKenzie made notes as best she could between her gag reflexes. Damn. She was *not* cut out for this.

Bayle was in his element. He sliced open organ after organ with manic energy. April's heart and lungs were normal. Bayle also pronounced her stomach empty, her bladder full. He took a urine sample for the lab.

The girl had only one ovary, it turned out. Zacharias said it looked like the other had been removed rather than been a birth defect. Her other reproductive organs were intact.

"Ironic, isn't it?"

"What's that?" McKenzie replied. Something had been tickling the back of her mind, but she couldn't pull it up.

He stared at the cadaver, his scalpel working diligently. "Well, I mean, she was killed by the Cradle Robber, and she only had one ovary. I don't know. I guess it's not that weird. Random thought."

She nodded, chasing the escaped thought. A similarity or difference. Something she should be seeing, damn it. "Is there anything you've noticed that's significant in comparison to the others?"

Bayle shrugged. "I wish."

"Is it possible to look through the reports? I mean, of the other autopsies?"

The M.E. glanced up at her, amused. "You should really get out more, you know?"

"So, how was your prom date?"

He chuckled. "Okay, okay. Yeah, I can let you take a look. Run—or hobble—out there and grab the clerk. I'll have her fetch the file. Knock yourself out. The records cannot leave this building. Lucky you. You get to spend some more time with me."

Everitt followed Mrs. Favre upstairs to Ollie's old bedroom, which turned out to still be full of boy band posters, framed high school achievement certificates, and pictures of friends, despite the fact that the girl had moved out years before. Stuff popped from every nook and cranny. The room was so busy it might burst.

"So Ollie moved out at eighteen?" Noah asked from behind her.

"Yes," Mrs. Favre answered. "She was ready to before that. Always a free spirit. But yes, the day she graduated high school, practically."

If Everitt had walked in this room today without knowing anything about its owner, she'd have thought Ollie still lived in it. Post-it notes stuck to the bureau mirror, change on the dresser. Only the pillow shams in front of the regular pillows, perfectly undisturbed on the lavender comforter, gave away that this room had not been lived in for a long time.

The little guest room at the Petersons' flashed in, so sparse and unwelcoming. The names on the list left by a former surrogate crossed her mind, then the shapes of the faceless girls that had come before her. That room had only looked like it hadn't been lived in. More like a holding cell on death row.

She shook away the thought and focused on Ollie Favre's bedroom. Sarah Peterson's face jumped in, angry, her voice hissing in her ear. Then, her body crumpling on the ground next to Everitt, blood and brains spattering both Sarah and her.

Stop thinking about it, Everitt. Stop it now!

Everitt forced her gaze to the photos lining the room, which were plentiful. Ollie smiled from most of the frames, usually with another person or two. The electric blue shocks in her black hair were her signature even at a young age.

Ollie at Disneyworld in mouse ears. Ollie with friends on the beach. Ollie with friends in a cap and gown. Ollie painting her room the mint green it was now over the old, stark white.

Mrs. Favre crossed the room and picked up the picture of Ollie with the paint roller.

"She made me take this. She was always making me take pictures if she was the only one there to witness something and couldn't take them of herself. She took pictures of everything. Looking at all these frames you'd think she'd set out every picture she'd ever taken, but she didn't. We have boxes and boxes in the attic, and that's before pictures went digital."

Everitt stared into Ollie's happy-go-lucky eyes in the photo. She wore denim overalls, a nineties staple.

Before pictures were digital...

"Mrs. Favre, did Ollie still take pictures? I mean, after high school. Do you know if she was still an avid photo-taker?"

"Oh, definitely," Ollie's mother answered, her voice threatening to break "Bought her a digital camera for her birthday a few years ago, so no more boxes of film. But yeah, I can't imagine her ever stopping taking pictures."

As Everitt suspected. "Do you know where she kept her photos? On her computer maybe?"

Everitt followed Mrs. Favre's gaze to the ceiling, which it turned out was covered in even more pictures. Everitt imagined Ollie lying in the bed, gazing at a starry sky of her friends and good times.

"Probably so. I haven't really looked to be honest. I haven't had the strength to go through that much. She had to have had them on there somewhere. She'd send me a picture or two of different events. Weddings and things. Oh!"

Everitt's gaze left the ceiling pictures and returned to Ollie's mother.

Noah echoed Everitt's thoughts. "What is it, Mrs. Favre?"

The woman had already turned to leave the bedroom. "I remembered something."

Everitt and Noah followed her back downstairs, where she sat at the desktop computer in the kitchen and started clicking away furiously.

"It has to be here somewhere," she muttered.

Mrs. Favre was searching through her old e-mail account, opening every e-mail from Ollie that contained an attachment.

Finally, after at least twenty e-mails, she gasped. "Here! Here it
is."

A group of people at what looked like a Christmas party of
some sort appeared on the screen. They all wore the loopy grins
of one too many glasses of spiked punch. Each sported an ugly
sweater bearing some bad symbol of the season, like a reindeer
with lighted antlers or a giant candy cane. Ollie sat on the left, a
red plastic cup in one hand and her other hand making bunny ears
on the man next to her.

"An office Christmas party at the law firm before the lawyer
opened his new offices," Mrs. Favre said. "I remembered it
because it was when Mr. Worneck first asked Ollie to come and
work for him. She was only a temp at the other firm and didn't
know him at the time. She was surprised he'd invited her."

She pointed to the man sitting next to Ollie. His eyes were
glassy as he made fake bucked teeth underneath her bunny ears.
"That's Mr. Worneck."

Everitt stared at the lawyer knee-deep in this entire mess.
Ollie's mother's words became lost amidst the bumbling train of
her thoughts.

No way.

"His name isn't Worneck," Everitt mumbled.

For a second, she hadn't realized she'd said it out loud.
Then, Noah was tapping her shoulder, trying to get her attention.
She blinked up at him, barely able to tear her eyes away from the
picture.

"How. Do. You. Know. That," he asked slowly, deliberately.

She turned back to the picture, still unable to believe it.

Small damn world.

"Because," she replied, studying his face to be sure, even
though she already was. "I know that guy."

CHAPTER 70

MCKENZIE SAT IN a metal chair with the files the clerk brought her. Bayle was still busy making notes she didn't want to miss, but she was glad she had something to focus on other than the sounds of saws cutting through flesh and bone. She'd asked the clerk to pull a few other chairs inside the door, which she now used to categorize the files in any way that made sense.

So far, she'd stacked them according to where the victims had lived, which borough they were last seen in, where their bodies were found. None of those led anywhere. Something physical, tangible connected them, she was sure of it, but she hadn't found it yet. Ethnicities were across the board. Hair colors, maybe because of the Laurel connection, but she tried it anyway.

"Pattern. Where's the pattern?" she said to herself.

Bayle spoke up from the other side of the room. "I'm sure the FBI is asking the same thing."

He might be right. People way more qualified than her were looking into this thing, but they weren't telling her anything. She divided the folders based on heights, weights.

That doesn't make sense, moron.

For a short moment, her excitement rose.

Look at their livers—maybe they drank at the same place.

But none of the autopsies had significant findings about the livers.

But it's something like that. Come on, brain. Tell me what you were trying to nail down earlier.

The sound of a cell phone tone bit the air. She glared at Bayle mischievously.

"What?" he asked. His phone, in the pocket of his coat where he'd taken it off across the room, rang to the beat of "Another One Bites the Dust."

He shrugged and smiled, but made no move toward the phone. "Can a medical examiner not have any fun?"

Back to the files.

Think, McKenzie!

Livers. Hearts. Lungs. Smokers? No. What else did people do besides drink and smoke that they'd have in common?

Again, the air was broken by a ring. Only this time, it was her own. She glanced at the glowing face. Noah.

"Do you mind?" she asked, but her finger was already on the answer button.

"By all means," Bayle said.

"Putting you on speaker," Noah said before she had a chance to say anything.

Voices rumbled vaguely in the background, then Noah's voice again. "Can you hear me?"

"Yeah," she replied. "What's up?"

"We found the lawyer," Noah answered.

McKenzie dropped the file she was holding on the chair in front of her. "How?"

"Mrs. Favre had a picture. Well, Everitt can tell you—"

Everitt's voice cut in. "The scumbag used to show up in the neighborhood where Zan—my baby's father—lived, looking for smack. Tried to steal from a guy I knew once. He was chased out of the 'hood and never came back. I would've never pegged him as a lawyer. Ten to nothing would've told you he was your typical junkie."

McKenzie drummed her fingers on the top file, nervous. Could they have found him? Have a name, find this guy, maybe find who all he was associated with? "Who is he?"

"I don't know. I know his name isn't Worneck. I can't freaking remember it now, but I know it's not that. I'd remember it if I heard it. I'll send you a copy of the picture, just so you'll have it."

Suddenly, the tunnel sound disappeared, and Noah's voice filled her ear. "Thought you ought to know we have a possible connection. Keep ya posted."

"Okay," she replied. She switched off the phone and gazed blankly in Bayle's general direction.

"Bad news?"

McKenzie shook her head, confused. "More like too many directions."

He squirted the syringe of blood he was holding into a glass tube. "Tell me about it."

Her stomach rolled, and her leg throbbed. If only more pain medication didn't mean less clarity. She needed out of this room, needed fresh air. Perspective.

But the files...

"I'll be back in ten. Gonna walk outside a minute, clear my head," she said, struggling to stand.

"'kay. We'll be here," Bayle said, delight in his voice. "Don't daydream about me too much out there."

"I'll try to contain myself."

CHAPTER 71

Jonas reached the threshold of Rory's home and stood on the stoop for a moment before knocking.

What exactly are you planning to do here, numb nuts? Tell this guy not to worry about finding someone to sit with his wife? Tell him to head on to work, that you'll take care of her?

Then again, who cared what this loser thought? He was the one leaving his wife alone with her attempted-murderer on the loose.

Jonas banged his fist on the door.

A moment later, Bryce Nathaniel's chubby face appeared in the doorway. His close-cropped haircut, his too-perfect, tucked-in polo irritated Jonas for some reason.

Bryce studied Jonas with beady eyes, seeming to recognize him but trying to place from where. "Can I help you?"

Behind him, Rory cowered in the hallway. The afghan from the other day draped her shoulders like a cape, her tear-stained face turned toward the floor.

Jonas pushed past Bryce into the man's own house.

Don't let him know she called you. You'll only make things worse for her.

"Yeah. I'm a friend of Rory's. I heard the news and came to sit with her."

Bryce turned to Rory, and his eyes narrowed. "Rory, what is this?"

Rory didn't look up, but instead, wiggled her socked toes.

"I...um...I..."

The red patches rising on Bryce's face, the way his jaw clenched, made Jonas' gut tighten. Rory had told him about Bryce's temper. His marbles weren't all in the bag. Sure, it had to be confusing, annoying, and maybe even a little frustrating for a guy you didn't know other than meeting him in relation to an article about your child's death to show up at your house to keep your wife company. But this reaction—the balled fists, the twitching in his temple—this wasn't the reaction of an understanding guy. Nor was banging your mistress when your wife was recovering from trauma. No, those were the signs of a philandering abuser.

"I know you have work to do, so I thought I would swing by and see if Rory wanted to grab a cup of coffee," Jonas said. He sounded good to himself, in control. "Sorry for barging in like that. I didn't mean to intrude."

Jonas looked at Rory, willing her to accept the invitation. He could take her out of this house here and now, no more words said. They could talk about how to deal with Bryce's temper later. About how to get her away from him.

Rory glanced at Bryce, then at Jonas, and back again. She held her husband's gaze, a strong current of something like contempt hanging between them. "I think I will go have a cup of coffee, Bryce. I'll be back before late."

Bryce's chewed his cheek as Rory threw the afghan off her shoulders and onto the bench in the foyer. She passed Bryce. Jonas followed her out the door.

Outside, Rory stopped on the pathway leading from the steps. "Oh, shoot. I have to go back. I didn't bring my purse."

"I have it covered," Jonas said.

"No, really. I need it. I feel naked without it," she replied, already doubling back toward the door.

"Do you need me to come in with you?" He stopped himself from adding, 'so your husband doesn't give you a black eye.'

She shook her head, but he could see the fear in her eyes. "I'll only take a sec."

Probably worse if he went in with her, come to think of it. So, he stood outside and watched her walk back in.

The minutes seemed like hours, so much so that Jonas checked his phone three times to see how long it had been. Each time, only a minute or two had passed, but dang, it was an eternity. How long could it take to grab a purse?

Okay. If she's one more minute, I'm going in.

She reappeared on the stoop, unscathed, her shoulder bag across her chest.

"You okay?" he asked. His gaze roamed her body. Not a mark on her.

"Fine. Let's get out of here."

Jonas sat across from Rory with his black coffee, dumped three sugars into it, and poured creamer until the cup nearly overflowed. He definitely didn't seem like the coffee type. This proved it.

"You know, if you order a latte, you can have your coffee the way you like it and keep your hands from being scalded," she said.

He smirked. "Not as much of a challenge."

She sipped her own ginger concoction and let the warmth of the cup seep into her hands. Nice to be out of the house again. How easy to pretend all was good in her world sitting here drinking in the café atmosphere, surrounded by coffee aromas and chatting women dressed in Gucci, women whose biggest problems were which nanny to call on the regular nanny's day off.

Her real world had become too surreal to think about, with her flat stomach and healing bruises now the color of rotting red cabbage.

I have a serial killer after me.

"Why does this shit always happen to me?"

Jonas stirred his coffee, then downed half of it in a single gulp. "Believe me, I've had the same thought plenty of times."

She chuckled a little, despite herself. "Seems like we've had this talk before."

"Eh, maybe we're not meant to have families. There are other worthy goals in life, right? The Peace Corps? *The Amazing Race?*"

The palm holding his coffee cup was twice the size of the mouth of the mug. God, it would feel nice against her face, with the roughness, the calluses. What was wrong with her? She shouldn't be thinking about anything but Bryce, the baby…the Cradle Robber.

"You're an optimist now?" she replied.

Let yourself be. It's okay for five minutes.

"Damaged widower by day, optimist by, um, coffee. Yeah, I tried to make that work." He covered the awkward moment with another swallow from his cup. "So, you never told me what *did* happen to your family."

Rory stared into her drink as the images flooded her. So much screaming.

"There was a fire. At my house." She twirled her finger in her latte. "I don't know why I hate telling people that, exactly. I think it's because most people expect me to say, 'car accident.' When I don't, they act like I've told them golden retrievers can talk."

Jonas shoved his hand through his hair. "Oh, I know what it's like. Try telling them your wife was murdered."

Rory sat, her finger still in her cup, and stared at him. The statement had wiped every sense of coherency to her thoughts. Flatline.

"Oh, damn," Jonas said, "I'm sorry. I didn't mean to…shit."

The curse words broke her reverie. She shook herself and removed her finger from the coffee. She dabbed it dry on the napkin on the table. "Oh, no, no. Don't worry about it."

Jonas scooted his chair around to the corner of the table. He leaned in. She caught the scent of his deodorant or after-shave. Something spicy. Masculine.

"By the way," he said, "it doesn't take ten minutes to get a purse. You had me worried."

He'd notice, of course. He was that kind of guy. Still, a girl could hope she wouldn't have to talk about it. She propped her elbow on the table and rested her chin in her hand. "That obvious, huh?"

"Well, if I hadn't seen his face ten seconds before, maybe, but as it was, I didn't think you guys were playing a game of gin rummy in there."

He hadn't asked her to elaborate, decent fellow that he was. She needed to, though. It would be easy for him to get the wrong idea.

"He yelled at me. Grabbed my wrists. Yelled mostly," she said. Tears leaked from the corners of her eyes, but she blinked them away.

Do not cry anymore. Enough is enough.

"That's enough," Jonas said, echoing her thoughts. The bitterness bit the edges of his voice like a cold snap after spring. "You're grieving. He shouldn't talk to you like that, but he definitely shouldn't physically threaten you. You've been through hell. A man kidnapped you. You need to feel safe. Comforted."

Rory closed her eyes. It was the same thing she'd heard before, and yet, she never had a good answer. She opened them again and looked into his concerned face.

"It'll be fine, Jonas."

Jonas' eyes narrowed. "Maybe you shouldn't go back until it blows over."

"I'm not," Rory admitted quietly. This time, the sobs slipped out of her despite her best efforts.

Jonas leaned forward, covered her hand with his. "What do you mean you're not?"

"Bryce…he kicked me out." The tears rained harder, her

voice choked. "And there's a psycho after me. The last thing I needed was to piss off Bryce and have him kick me out."

She bit back the tears now as best she could, annoyed with herself. He had to be annoyed by now, too.

He wasn't, though. Jonas clinked his mug back onto the table, his eyes firmly holding onto hers.

"Rory, come and stay with me."

She didn't even try to tell him no. She couldn't. As soon as he said she could go with him, something in her told her that she would. After all, it was like she'd told him: she had nowhere else to go.

Dirk had lied a lot in his day, and even he didn't believe his own eyes, nor did he trust them to recount the events he had witnessed. He knew he shouldn't. It broke his own policies, but he pulled out his phone to snap a picture.

It had taken a little digging to find Bryce Nathaniel's home in the suburbs. Turned out, the golden boy hadn't bought the place himself. Daddy Dearest assisted him a great deal, and Daddy Dearest's name was on the deed.

The people on the street probably never noticed him, nor considered that it wasn't garbage day. It didn't matter. It was like every other non-pattern he used: you could only kill a garbage man and pose as his replacement once. He would only *need to* once, and this bitch would be out of the picture.

Now, he stared at his phone, double-checking his facts before he deleted the damning evidence. Surely, he was wrong.

But no, he wasn't. Rory Nathaniel had left the house with another man, a man that wasn't her husband. It was too horrible and delicious to be true.

For anyone else, this would be a very, very bad thing. Patterns were bad. It was part of the rule book.

And yet...it was true. Rory Nathaniel had walked out her front door with none other than Jonas Cleary, a man Dirk had seen in the news years ago. He remembered Jonas well.

Everything happens for a reason.

McKenzie hobbled up and down the road outside the ME's office. The air wasn't exactly as fresh as she'd made it out to be. It smelled more like the fresh leavings of the poodle across the street. Still, better than formaldehyde.

While she hobbled, she mentally ran through facts. Noah and Everitt were still at the Favre place, working on the lawyer. Jonas was talking to the Cradle Robber's only living victim, trying to backtrack her steps. She was here, watching April Gregory's autopsy and putting folders into stacks. The Petersons' other connections, Felicia Rockwell and her maybe illegally adopted child, the Davidsons, Gibb...all those things still dangled like unfinished items on a to-do list.

What had she been thinking before? It infuriated and frustrated her that the memory wouldn't come.

She sifted through the victims' names and profiles in her mind. Every single one had been pregnant up until the elevator girl. Something had happened to make him stop targeting pregnant women.

Then again, he hadn't gone for them. Not at first. Jonas' wife hadn't been pregnant. Gibb was a baby in a stroller when he was taken. Her conversation with Jerome Kyler flashed in, his analogy of dropping the Coke tab into the can to show why the killer took the babies while they were in utero. His train of pull-tabs from the ginger ale can to the Coke can.

The dead girls aren't pregnant now, and they weren't before.

They weren't at first.

The thought struck McKenzie like she'd been slapped hard in the face. She'd known for a while that the pregnancies weren't the pattern, but rather, a source of profit for the killer. But she'd been so focused on what the pattern *was,* if it wasn't the pregnancies, that she hadn't stopped to think how the pregnancies *impacted* the pattern.

Jerome Kyler implied the killer deviated from his earlier M.O. to streamline his process, leave fewer traces. McKenzie had taken that thought and latched onto it, sure that if she trained her sights on the girls, a pattern would show itself. The nickel dropped for her. Even if Jerome Kyler thought the pregnancies weren't as important, they were, in fact, *the* most important thing. The Cradle Robber had altered his previous method to make for a better process, yes. But if his earlier attempts weren't as good and he felt he *needed* to streamline, it had to be for a reason. People didn't fix things if they weren't broken.

McKenzie whipped out her phone. She had to talk to Jonas. She needed him now, no matter how much she didn't want to after the way he'd acted. The phone rang and rang. She cursed.

"Come on, Jonas," she said, tapping her toe.

He didn't need to retrace Rory Nathaniel's steps. They needed to retrace Noelle's.

CHAPTER 72

TALKING JONAS INTO leaving Rory Nathaniel wasn't easy.

McKenzie had told him to bring her along, but he insisted she was too tired and still recovering. Probably true. Still, McKenzie managed to convince him that if he'd turn his attention to her for a little while, they'd have some answers. Then, she'd hung up and uncrossed her fingers.

She met him at his house, where he'd taken Rory to lie down. Rory didn't want to miss any of their talk, hell-bent on hearing every detail McKenzie had discovered. McKenzie understood and didn't care if Rory hung around. Jonas insisted she rest.

"I swear, I'll tell you everything," he said, ushering her up the stairs to the loft.

As he trotted back down the stairs, he looked more alive than he had in days. Rory Nathaniel, however wilted she was, did that to Jonas.

Jonas must have caught the look on her face. "I told you. She's only staying here because her husband is a bastard with a temper. Those two don't mix when you're drowning in unwanted attention from press and serial killers."

McKenzie shook her head. "I didn't say a thing."

"Sure you didn't."

She held up her hands.

It's none of your business, McKenzie.

"Okay, so Noelle."

Ugh. Bad transition.

Jonas sat down across from her. "Backtracking my wife's steps is a little broad, don't you think?"

McKenzie yanked out her legal pad from her purse. She'd jotted notes on the way over, ideas of where to start. "Maybe. Maybe not. What did she do all day? Who did she hang out with? You know, her routine that day. Any day."

"God, I don't know. I mean, I do know. I just don't know. Not that much. She took care of the baby. Went for groceries. To be honest, that's really about it after Gibb was born, except the yoga classes..." Jonas narrowed his eyes and tilted his head. "Now that I think about it, as far as I know, it was the last place she went before she died."

A burst of adrenaline coursed through McKenzie. "Where did Noelle take yoga, Jonas?"

Jonas lifted his head out of his hands. "The gym a few blocks away."

"When Noelle was found, police questioned people at the gym that day, right?"

"Well, yeah, I mean, everyone was questioned. Why? What are you thinking?"

McKenzie's brain tingled. Too many things wrestled with each other in there to all fit.

"I don't know. I think we need to go talk to the people at the gym. That was her last stop, and if it was one of the only places she went with the baby, I...I don't know, Jonas. I think if she went there with the baby, that's probably where he saw her." She cut herself off before the last thought slipped off her tongue.

Or met her.

If she wanted to work out, McKenzie wouldn't be caught dead in a place with the clean, crisp air of Moroney's. She'd much rather put on sweats and go for a walk. No one in here sweated. They glistened stylishly.

To one side, a class of women did crunches on giant rubber balls. In the room to her left, a row of treadmills hummed, each occupant in his or her own world of earbuds and iPads. They'd already explained who they were at the front desk. The skinny teenager with braces had run off to fetch a manager.

A man appeared who resembled a telephone pole in height, build, and posture. His helmet of beetle-brown hair shone in the lights, and his nostrils may have been rounder than his eyes. His thin-lipped smile was clearly forced.

"I'm Elton Childs, managing director here at Moroney's. How can I help you?" he asked in the same disinterested way a waiter would ask someone if they wanted sparkling water or flat even though the girl at the desk had to have already informed him of why they were there.

McKenzie tried not to stare at his nose as she introduced herself and Jonas. "I'm writing an investigative article about the death of Noelle Cleary a few years back. I was wondering if I might ask you a few questions about your gym at the time that happened."

Something flashed in his eyes at Noelle's name. It had clearly been the source of some tension—and annoyance—for a long time. His perfect pink lips thinned.

"Moroney's is a health club, not a *gym*," he said. The last word made his face constrict as if he'd eaten something sour. "Either way, we have cooperated with the police."

No wonder your nostrils are so fat. It has to be hard to breathe with your head so far up your ass.

McKenzie mustered composure. "I realize that, Mr. Childs, but I'm looking at a new angle, and I'd be very appreciative if you would humor me. We'll only take a few moments of your time, I promise. But it does require asking you to check your files."

Elton Childs looked over Jonas, who glared at him with enough contempt to crush a small country. And while Childs was taller, Jonas outweighed him by at least fifty pounds.

Childs must have concluded the same thing. "All right then, but I do have to keep it short. I have a meeting."

With the admissions committee at Harvard, no doubt.

They followed Childs through the metal turnstile and past several rooms filled with exercise equipment and grunting, perspiring bodies. Finally, they reached a small hole in the wall between the Men's Locker Room and a broom closet. Childs' office. McKenzie looked for a chair, but the small room had none, save for one folding chair behind to Childs' desk. She and Jonas stood in the tiny room as Childs sat down.

He typed a password into his computer. "What do you need to know?"

"I know that the police looked into everyone at the gym the day Noelle Cleary was killed, but I was wondering if you could check if there was anyone enrolled in the mommy and me yoga class she was taking who *wasn't* in class the day of the murder," she replied.

Elton Childs hit a few keys. He hadn't asked for the date.

Wow. He's still all over this.

"That's odd," he replied. He stared at the screen that had appeared and scrolled up and down through the list.

"What's that?" Jonas growled.

Elton looked up at him, then at McKenzie. "Well, she's not in any of the class records. She wasn't enrolled."

McKenzie stepped closer to the computer so she could read the names. Childs, stricken by the discrepancy, was too busy gaping to stop her. Sure enough, Noelle's name was not on the list.

Jonas muttered something under his breath from across the room. McKenzie looked at him leaning against the wall, arms crossed, deep in thought.

"What'd you say, Jonas?"

"She wouldn't have been," he said, this time louder and surer.

At McKenzie and Elton Childs' blank stares, Jonas continued. "She had a membership, but her membership didn't include classes. Regular access to equipment. That was all it entitled her to. One of the instructors was really into these protein drinks they made at the health chain Noelle worked at before she was pregnant, and they made a deal. He traded getting her into classes for her discount at Health Nuts."

The moment he said the stupid name of the shop, a fuse lit in McKenzie's brain. Noelle's obsession with health food and exercise. The contents of the girls' stomachs in their autopsies. Her conversation with the pharmacist about her mythical daughter. He'd said not to worry about DMSO, that it was a dietary supplement sold over the counter in health food stores.

Gentle Jewish Jesus.

They'd found him.

CHAPTER 73

MCKENZIE SPEED-DIALED Jig the moment she stepped out of Elton Childs' office.

"Your friendly neighborhood tech analyst here. What favor can I do you today?"

"Jig, can you cross reference the gym employees at Moroney's with customer debit card purchases and records at Health Nuts in Manhattan from the months leading up to Noelle Cleary's death? It's him. It's the connection," McKenzie said. Her heart pounded, blood threatening to burst her veins. This was it!

"Okay, okay," Jig said. "Unclench your butt cheeks, already. I'm on it."

Keys clicked. Seconds ticked by.

"You do realize if I come up with a name, the FBI gets it, too, right?" Jig said, stating the obvious.

"Yes," McKenzie answered, "as long as you realize I'm running with it."

"Don't you tip him off," Jig said, pecking more keys.

"Get him fast, then," McKenzie answered with a smile.

"Coming up now," Jig answered. "One result. Employed by Moroney's Health Club as a trainer, frequent buys at Health Nuts over a period of about six months. Sweet Mary and her fertile womb. He's a doctor. Dr. Dirk Harris."

Jonas tapped his fingers while he stood next to McKenzie as they both waited for Jig to relay more information.

"What?" McKenzie yelped into her phone beside him.

"What's happening?" Jonas asked.

She held up a finger to him. "I'm putting you on speaker, Jig."

McKenzie punched the button. Jig's high pitch filled the hallway. "Dr. Harris didn't exist until three years ago. If you want to get technical, he *did* exist, then he died, then he was apparently reborn or resurrected. Whichever term you prefer."

"What do you mean?" Jonas blurted.

"I mean Harris isn't Dirk Harris. He's a fraud. He's been using Dr. Dirk Harris' identity for three years, but before that, I'm not sure who he was. Though we're about to find out."

Jonas watched McKenzie drop her crutches and slide down the hallway wall onto her rear end. She laid the phone on the floor. He mimicked her. They both stared at the phone, waiting.

After a long minute, Jig's voice echoed again. "Ha! The current Dirk Harris' fingerprint on file is with Jessup Memorial Hospital—he works there. Employee fingerprint match coming up. His name's Dylan Whitfield. Oh, my. No wonder he grabbed someone else's identity. Kid spent his entire teenage lifespan in juvie for—oh my God. For tying his sister up in the woods behind his house and slicing her up with a letter opener."

The look in Noelle's eyes, far away and gone, popped into Jonas' mind. His gut wrenched painfully. "Are they arresting him? Like, this minute?"

"On their way to his residence now," Jig replied. "With any luck, we'll have him before the day is out."

Jonas couldn't speak. Prison. A trial. It was too good for this monster.

McKenzie was on another wavelength. "What detention center, Jig? I want to check something."

"Will I regret this?" Jig asked.

"Do you regret me finding out who the Cradle Robber is?" she countered.

"Ah," Jig said. "Touché. Hudson County. You didn't hear that from me. Incidentally, what are we checking on?"

The reporter lifted the speakerphone and spoke fast. "Someone hired this guy to gut infants out of women. I'd be willing to bet it's someone who knew he'd not only do it, but that he'd enjoy it."

Despite her bum leg, McKenzie was already up and heading down the hallway. Jonas followed.

The Hudson County Detention Center was only a few miles from where they were now. They made it in record time. For a place that housed kids—even awful ones—it seemed like a wasteland. She didn't see a soul on the grounds after they spoke with the guard at the front until they reached the reception area.

The lady behind the desk looked like she'd been faced with a choice to either take this job or become a housewife who knitted sweaters for her nineteen cats. The woman gave them a kind smile before asking what she could do to help.

"We're looking for...I don't know what we're looking for," McKenzie said. She looked to Jonas for help, but his face was scrunched in concentration. He was obsessing over the Cradle Robber being caught, she knew, but in that second, she wished to high heaven Noah was here with her instead of on a wild goose chase with Everitt to find some strung out junkie lawyer.

"I'm looking for records from when a kid named Dylan Whitfield was here."

The woman stared at her in disapproval, already shaking her head.

Please, no.

This was McKenzie's only chance to make things right. To do something worthwhile with this mess she'd made she called a career.

We have to find Gibb.

"Look, I know this is unconventional, but maybe we can go

about this another way. I'm looking for someone—"

The woman cut her off. "I knew I shouldn't a done it. Knew he was lying even when I did. But I did it anyway, and now everyone thinks they can come in here and tell me a story like that and look at records."

Someone had been here to go through the records. Someone had beaten them to the punch. Another reporter? Had Whitney gotten wind of this already? Or had somebody else always been one step ahead of her?

McKenzie couldn't give up. The Cradle Robber had a file here. This woman was about as good at keeping secrets as Carbon was at ignoring a sandwich lying on the coffee table. McKenzie had to wheedle it out of her.

Risk versus benefit.

"Ma'am, this is extremely important. It may be a matter of life and death. I'm investigating a murder. The person who came in here looking for those records may be tied to it. I need you to tell me anything you can remember about who it was."

The woman didn't seem to find it strange that McKenzie didn't show identification or tell her she was an "investigator" from the start. She snapped to attention, the word "investigating" seeming to have lit a fire in her. "I can't tell you who he was, but he came in to look at his brother's file. I can tell you that."

"Can you show me the file?"

The woman stood. No more questions needed, apparently.

"Is it that easy?" Jonas whispered.

"Count your blessings."

The lady returned a moment later with a folder, muttering as she walked toward them. "You could tell they're siblings, too. Looked exactly like the brother, this guy. If that helps you any."

She laid the folder open on the table.

McKenzie pushed away the images of Levi as a child driving his little red jeep in Uncle Sal's driveway from her mind and stared down at a picture of a younger, less tired Worneck. Only, his name in the file wasn't Worneck. It was Ivanson.

Trevin Ivanson.

On the way back from the detention center, both McKenzie and Jonas were silent. After all, there wasn't much to say until they heard back from Jig with information on Trevin Ivanson. McKenzie's mind reeled. What to do about the article? Morton would take his cut she'd promised him for sure. Then, she had to somehow write the article she wanted to while at the same time not doing exactly what Whitney feared.

She wanted so badly to prove she could write a good piece without ruining lives in the process.

"Do you think you should call Rory and let her know we found the Cradle Robber?" she asked absent-mindedly. Maybe it would feel somewhat fulfilling to be able to tell one person she could make her life *safer* and not more awful.

"We'll be there in just a few minutes," Jonas said.

"Unless we hear from Jig and need to chase down Trevin Ivanson…"

"Oh, right. I guess I could."

McKenzie leaned back and closed her eyes. For the next few minutes, maybe she could block out all of the bad things and just relax, knowing things were going to look up from here.

Rory picked up her phone. If this was Bryce, they were about to have a bad connection.

Jonas's voice burst from the receiver.

"Rory, we've found him. We have a name. They're going to catch him."

Her heart jumped into her throat and slid back down again. The Cradle Robber. Caught?

The adrenaline rush lasted only about five seconds. Suddenly, the room began to spin. Everything shifted, blurry.

What the—

Her gaze followed the phone's fall from her hand to the floor. The cover, broken. A piece next to the bed, the other across the room.

That's when she realized she wasn't alone.

CHAPTER 74

RORY OPENED HER eyes and blinked. Something was caught in their corners. Dust, maybe. What had happened? A fall...

Then he stepped into her vision. The man looked more like an Abercrombie model than the devil himself. Chiseled. Perfect. The epitome of tall, dark, and handsome.

Rory tried to move, but she was stuck, almost like she was in a human-sized glue trap. Only, nothing held her down.

Mother of God.

The flat blade of a scalpel traced her bicep as his lips tickled her ear. "You sure don't learn from your mistakes, do you, *Rory?*"

The mocking way he said her name chilled every inch of her body. She tried to force words out of her mouth, her brain darting around the room for help. She'd dropped the phone. Surely Jonas would've heard. He would come. "Why are you doing this?"

He laughed mirthlessly, the quality of the laughter scaring her more than the scalpel blade threatening to slice her at any moment.

God!

"We have to finish what we started, right, *Rory?* We can't leave business unattended. That would be lazy. Half-way. Surely you of all people don't want to only go half-way, do you?"

Say what he wants you to say.

"No...no...I..."

That cold laugh hit her ears again. "Of course you wouldn't."

She screamed as the blade dug into her arm. Tears sprang to

her eyes. She wanted to rub them, rub out the scratchiness, but she couldn't move her hands. While her skin could feel everything, her muscles were practically paralyzed. Her body felt inflated. She pushed her foot as hard as she could. She heard it brush against the floor, but she couldn't feel it moving.

Help me!

God, where was her phone? She scanned her surroundings, though she couldn't turn much. The phone was on the floor, where she was now. It had to be.

"Oh," he said, holding up her phone, "I took the liberty of pressing 'end' on your call. I didn't want it to use up your minutes."

New tears that had nothing to do with her burning bicep streamed her face.

No!

He pocketed the phone. "Poor Jonas. You really ought to have left him out of this, you know. After all, he'll go through it all over again. Tsk, tsk. Oh, well. He'll live, I'm sure. Now, *Rory*, let's see if we can do this right this time."

His scalpel moved to her other arm.

Do something. Even if you feel nothing, do it!

With every ounce of force she could gather, she shoved her arm upward and connected with his forearm. The scalpel flipped out of his hand, nicking his arm as it flew backward.

"Bitch!" he yelled, grabbing the cut.

In that second, she did the only thing she could think of: she forked her two fingers like she was in grade school and jabbed at his eye sockets. He yelped and stalled. She rolled. So groggy.

Come on, legs!

Like an inch worm, she scooted across the wood floor on her stomach toward the door. It was so far away. She'd never make it.

A hand clenched around her ankle, the door sliding away in front of her. She couldn't see what was coming. Breathing hard, she let the momentum roll her onto her back.

Use it!

He pulled her into him. As he did, she curled her leg to her chest and kicked out, aiming for anything she could hit. By luck, her bare foot crunched into his nose. He fell back. His grip on her leg slackened. She wiggled her foot away. Some of the feeling was coming back. Maybe she could stand.

She clambered to get up, but her leg collapsed under her. She landed in a heap.

Phone!

It had fallen loose from his pocket at the kick. She dove for it, fingers clenched around it. They grappled for buttons as she felt him scrambling to his feet over her. She hit some keys, which ones, she couldn't be sure.

Then, she was off the ground.

He'd hefted her over his shoulder. His breaths came hard, like a rabid wolf. "You are such a serious pain in the ass."

Through the door, toward the loft steps.

Don't let him take you anywhere!

She grabbed the doorframe, but her strength was nothing. He pried her loose with only a slight tug. "Should've just died the *first* time, Rory."

I can't die. I can't. I won't. Not after all this.

She sank her teeth into his ear, the only thing she could reach. He growled, staggered as his salty blood met her lips, the metallic taste gagging her.

Don't think about it.

She held on, her teeth deep in the skin. Rory whipped her head back hard, ripping the tender flesh, the texture in her mouth causing vomit to rise in her throat.

He screamed, then lurched backward from her, throwing her away from him as if she were something hot he'd touched.

Her puke—and the piece of his ear—flew out of her mouth onto him as her back connected with the hallway wall. She slammed the ground, but didn't let herself think about the pain or the disgust.

Stairs!

"Sick!" he gasped behind her.

She was already on her stomach, using her arms to belly crawl to the stairs. Momentum going, she slid down the first two. Her chin bashed the third step, and she bit her own tongue hard. Dazed, she tried to regain her bearings.

That was when an impact struck her gut. The room spun again as she flew down the rest of the staircase. She reached through the hole between the banister and the stairs to try to grab hold, try to stop herself, but her hand met the mantle of the faux-fireplace underneath. Everything she tried to grab wasn't attached. Knick-knacks rained to the floor below her. Glass shattered as picture frames hit. Her head caught the banister at the very end. She could hardly see.

"Enough is enough," he said behind her.

His feet plodded down the wooden stairs after her, his voice loud in her ears. God, her head hurt. Something stirred far away. Sirens? She wanted to be still, to listen.

But she needed to move, to get away. She pushed herself to her hands and knees, but everything toppled to one side in her vision. Rory crawled a few feet. So dizzy. She looked down, waiting for the world to right itself.

Below, the glass frame containing the handprint of Jonas' baby was broken into a dozen pieces, the sad little print ripped in half on the floor.

Please, no.

He was behind her, gaining. "Everything happens for a reason, *Rory*," he gasped, winded.

That it does.

She whirled on her knees to face him, her vision skewed.

She found his eyes, the potent blend of raw fury and desperation driving her as she mustered all the strength she had to dive at him with the shard of glass in her hand. He caught her by the wrists, forcing her weapon upward.

"It's all over, *Rory*," he said.

A loud thwack. The impact to his head caused Dirk Harris—the Cradle Robber—to slam to her left into the floor. He was still.

Behind him stood McKenzie McClendon, weight shifted to her good leg, one crutch on the floor, the other in both hands.

"You're right. It's all over," McKenzie said.

She swung her crutch high above him and hit him twice more.

CHAPTER 75

MCKENZIE STOOD THERE and caught her breath from hobbling into the house once Jonas finally made it inside. His phone battery had died as soon as he'd started trying to call Rory back when they'd heard the sounds of a skirmish, so he had been on the cab driver's phone with police when they'd turned onto Jonas' street. McKenzie had jumped out of the taxi in the driveway and despite her injuries, had stepped fully onto her leg using just the brace for support to half-run, half-hop toward the house.

Now, blue lights flashed outside behind the blinds, and paramedics, having finished checking Rory, eased McKenzie into a living room chair. They worked to sew the stitches she'd ruptured putting so much weight on the injured leg. To think she'd once sewed a similar injury of Noah's in a beach house.

To keep the thought from turning to other, worse ones, she diverted her attention to where across the room, Jonas knelt next to the sofa where Rory lay. Red splotches on Rory's face were quickly turning shades of blue and purple. Bloody cuts covered her arms and legs, and her right eye was nearly swollen shut. Remembering the sneaky way the Cradle Robber had killed April, McKenzie had already warned the medics against giving Rory any TXA, just in case he'd shot her up with the same drug he'd used to kill the poor radiation tech.

McKenzie's gaze fell to the side of the couch. Jonas and Rory's hands clasped together, fingers entwined. She nodded.

Good for him.

Out of the corner of her eye, a policeman stepped into the house, the same one who had led the stretcher flanked by several other cops that had carried the unconscious Dirk Harris outside.

"Is he dead?" Rory asked.

The officer shook his head. "Right now, no. But he's in critical condition. The ambulance is taking him to the hospital. I had no idea crutches could do that kind of damage," he said, sliding a furtive glance at McKenzie.

She shrugged at him. She and Rory hadn't exactly told him about the two extra swings she'd taken for good measure. He'd probably find out if he didn't realize already, but she couldn't care less. He deserved it.

As soon as the police finished taking their statements, they let them know they'd be in touch and left the trio to be in peace. The paramedics did the same with the stipulation that if either of them had any problems to call them ASAP or go to the nearest hospital.

When everyone was gone but the three of them, Rory leaned back and squeezed her eyes shut tight. "Oh, God, oh, God. Where have you guys been?"

"Finding the Cradle Robber's accomplice, a.k.a the lawyer who hired that monster to attack you so he could arrange for your baby's illegal adoption," Jonas answered.

Rory's face went blank. McKenzie could imagine what it must feel like to have one assailant caught, only to find out another part of her nightmare still walked free.

"Did you f-f-find him?" she stuttered, her lips chattering.

Jonas pulled the blanket on the couch up around her shoulders. "Not yet. We're working on it. We found the lawyer's real name. Now we're waiting on Jig."

Rory nodded.

"Rory, do you want one of us to call Bryce?" McKenzie asked.

Rory's eyes widened. She shook her head, fast and furious. "You can't. You wouldn't, would you? Jonas, she can't."

McKenzie held her hands up. Jonas had mentioned Bryce and Rory were on the outs, which was somewhat understandable. Losing a child could do something to relationships. But they were still married. She just wanted to help. To be such a controlling husband, he sure had kept his distance. Thank God. "Rory, don't worry. I'm not going to do anything without your consent. I just thought you might want him to know—well, no matter what's going on with you two, I thought this might be a moment you'd want him to know where you were—"

"Nobody's going to call Bryce," Jonas said, squeezing Rory's hand and shooting a glare at McKenzie.

Rory visibly relaxed, but then, started violently shaking her head again. "But the lawyer. You're looking for him?"

"Don't worry, Rory, we'll find him. When we do, there's every chance he could lead us to your baby," Jonas said.

Rory collapsed her head onto the arm of the couch and hugged the throw pillow to her. Her knees curled to her chest as she cried and cried and cried.

The day turned into night as they waited for Jig's call. McKenzie had checked in with Noah and Everitt, who had decided to check out parts of Everitt's old neighborhood. Between the two of them, Noah had told her he didn't expect them to find much, but that Everitt seemed to need to keep moving, that it was the only thing helping her cope.

If anyone can understand that, it's me.

There would be a time later when Everitt would climb under the covers and never want to come out again. Heaven knew McKenzie had those days. But right now, Everitt was in the phase where nothing would make all of the wrongs feel even remotely acceptable unless she put one foot in front of the other to try to make sense of it all. She would have to attempt, at the very least, to find the truth.

The more time that passed, the worse Rory seemed to become, more restless and in pain. The medics had treated her at the house, but despite their urgings that she be checked out at the hospital, she had begged not to go. Not that McKenzie could blame her; the hospital would dredge up all kinds of feelings from her last stay there.

Still, a few hours later, Rory was practically whimpering constantly, shifting to try to get comfortable. With every moan, the cuts and bruises seemed to darken, deepen, and look more alarming.

She dozed in five-minute intervals before waking back up. Finally, when Rory's eyes drifted closed for one such slumber, McKenzie tugged Jonas into the kitchen.

"I know she doesn't want to go, Jonas, but look at her. She needs medical attention. More than they could do here. What if she has internal bleeding? What if she's clotting up?"

Jonas hung his head and rubbed his eyes. "I know. I've been thinking the same thing the past half hour. I don't know how to convince her to go."

"We'll have to be honest with her. Or you will, rather. Tell her you're worried. She'll listen to you. I hope…"

"Damn it," Jonas said. "Okay. I'll talk to her when she wakes up."

McKenzie filled a kettle and set it on the stove to start a cup of coffee. They could both use one. "I know you don't want to, but somebody really needs to call Bryce, too."

"No way," Jonas answered.

"Jonas, he's still her husband, even if not for long. He should know she's been attacked."

Jonas wrung his hands in his lap. "He knew the first time and didn't do a damn thing to help."

McKenzie shrugged. He had a point. Bryce was Rory's call. "At least ask her if she wants us to call him when we go back in."

Jonas nodded but didn't speak again. He sat at the table, twiddling his thumbs.

McKenzie smiled. "I didn't know people did that anymore."

"What?"

"You're thumb-twiddling. I didn't know anyone still knew that was a time-waster."

He stared at his fingers, which stopped moving, and laughed. "Yeah. Picked it up from Noelle."

McKenzie poured him a cup of weak Maxwell House and set it front of him before taking the chair across the table. Funny how in the last few days, with the bourbon out of his system, she was starting to see places where his old self—the Jonas she'd known—peeked through.

"You really loved her," she remarked.

Did I say that out loud?

"I did," he replied.

A groan from the living room broke in. They both rose from the table. For a second, Jonas stood there.

"You can do this," McKenzie replied.

"Right," he mumbled.

Then, he turned and headed toward the kitchen door. McKenzie followed him down the hallway. She stood in the doorway of the living room as he took a seat next to Rory's limp form on the couch.

"Rory, I'm really worried. I think we need to take you to the hospital. I know how you feel about that, but you could have injuries we don't know about…"

Rory didn't protest. She must've been in more pain when she woke up, because now, she whimpered quietly. Her hand squeezed Jonas'.

"Okay," she whispered.

CHAPTER 76

EVERITT SAT IN a taxi with Noah. Both of them were silent. They knew exactly what they were about to do, the ramifications it could have. But as soon as she'd had the thought, she had known there was no going back. If this worked, it would change everything. As the cab sped through midtown, she leaned back, trying to process the day. All the emotions.

She'd walked with Noah through her old stomping grounds. "I thought you said he didn't hang around in this neighborhood anymore because he got run off."

Everitt had glanced sideways at him as she'd passed the bike rack where she'd tried her first hit. The alley where she'd taken money from her first john. So many screwed up memories of this little corner of hell. Still, her associations here didn't compare a bit to the comfortable home where she'd been held hostage.

"I did," she'd replied. "I told you. I need to do something. Something useful. Maybe someone down here remembers him."

They'd talked to her old friends, but none could remember the guy she now knew to be Trevin Worneck. Ivanson. Whatever his name was.

Her phone had rung in her pocket. She'd considered not answering it, but then thought better of it with everything going on. Good thing.

"Everitt? Thank God!"

"Who is this, please?" she said, not quite able to place the voice.

"Jig," the voice said on the other end. "I've tried to reach McKenzie, Jonas, and Noah. None of them is picking up, and I can't text it—records. But I found a number for Trevin Ivanson. I need to get it to them. I'm busy as shit with another case that came down the line, so I can't keep trying to call. Can you make sure they get it?"

Everitt dug a pen from her purse. "Yeah, I'm with Noah, but I can try to keep calling McKenzie and Jonas. Shoot."

She took down the number, mumbled, "Sure thing," to Jig's thanks, and hung up.

"What's that?" Noah asked, eyeing the paper.

"What we came here looking for."

Now, the images rushed through Everitt's brain faster than she could catalog them. Funny how things got clearer when you stepped away from them.

McKenzie went with Jonas to take Rory to the ER. She was whisked off for a CAT scan, leaving McKenzie in the waiting room with Jonas, who barely squeezed into one of the plastic arm chairs there.

Less than ten seconds after they'd taken seats in the lobby, the glass doors across from where McKenzie sat opened, and Whitney burst in.

She saw McKenzie almost immediately and crossed toward her. "So you *did* hear?"

"Huh?" McKenzie said, all dignity forgotten. Things were happening so fast she couldn't force her brain to process the events or characters quickly enough.

"The Cradle Robber. It's all over the news. They're keeping most reporters back at Vincent Street, but I sweet-talked that cop from the sting case by promising him I would keep his name out of the articles about it…that's not the point. I came as soon as I heard. Figured you were off trail-blazing and didn't know. I'm glad to see you didn't let the ball drop."

McKenzie blinked. Then, her head caught up. Whitney didn't realize she'd been the one to nail the Cradle Robber.

"Drop? McKenzie dropped *him*," Jonas said from behind her.

Whitney's gaze snapped from McKenzie toward him. "And you are?"

Talk about two people with different agendas.

"Whitney, this is Jonas Cleary. He's the friend I told you about whose son I've thought—*we've* thought..." She glanced at Jonas. How to explain? "The Cradle Robber took his son years ago. Killed his wife. We caught the Cradle Robber tonight at his house."

For a moment, Whitney stood silent, mouth agape. "I'm so..." She looked at Jonas, scanned his entire form up, down, and back again like a small child seeing the person behind the puppet strings for the first time. A mix of amazement and horror.

"How long has it been since you've seen him?" she whispered.

Jonas cleared his throat. "Close to five years."

McKenzie stared at them, a successful, well-adjusted product of the black market baby trade meeting a father destroyed by the very industry Whitney so desperately wanted to keep under wraps. Her throat constricted, the power of the moment holding her gaze to both of them as if their sheer proximity to each other would cause a spontaneous combustion.

Whitney nodded, never taking her eyes off him. "You've never stopped looking for him, huh?"

Jonas shook his head. "Never."

Whitney half-laughed, though the reaction held no mirth. "I've always assumed my parents wanted to get rid of me. Didn't think twice about it."

McKenzie glanced back at Jonas, whose gaze was fixed on Whitney.

"Maybe they thought about it more than you think," he said. The look in his eyes drifted somewhere McKenzie couldn't see, then back to the present. "So, you think about your parents?"

Whitney nodded, then seemed to realize she hadn't mustered a verbal answer. "Yes," she choked out.

"A lot?" he asked.

A tear slid down Whitney's cheek. "Every day." She wiped her cheek with the back of her hand, then looked down at the ground.

When she looked back up, it was toward McKenzie. "Write the story. Do what you have to do. Be ready to go with it Monday."

McKenzie watched Whitney's curls bounce as she walked away, back through the sliding doors.

Jonas returned to the waiting area and squeezed back into one of the tiny chairs. McKenzie followed.

She wanted to say something, to lighten the moment, but something told her this wasn't the time. Instead, she perched on the chair next to his.

Her cell vibrated. She pulled it out and glanced at the number. Not one she knew.

"McKenzie McClendon," she answered.

"Where is my wife?" a voice bellowed.

McKenzie's heart skipped. "Excuse me?" she said, even though she'd understood every word.

Jonas' nostrils flared. He could hear the other end of the line, too.

"I said *where* is my wife, Ms. McClendon?"

"How did you get this number?"

"You gave it to me, remember? In the hospital that day. Now tell me where she is. I know you know. She hasn't been home in days, and given the circumstances, I have a right to know—"

Jonas ripped the phone from McKenzie's hand. "You don't have *any* rights here—"

McKenzie snatched it back just in time to hear Bryce say, "Who the fuck is this?"

"Bryce, I'm not in the position to give you any information your wife doesn't choose to give you herself…"

"She has been through hell, Ms. McClendon. She's not thinking right," he replied, his voice edgy.

While his words were true, everything Rory had told Jonas said she'd go through even more hell if Bryce found her. "I suggest you cool off, Mr. Nathaniel—"

"Oh, so I'm Mr. Nathaniel now!"

"*Bryce*, you need to calm down. I'm sure your wife will call you when she's ready to talk."

"So you *do* know where she is?"

McKenzie's pulse pounded. For all the crazy situations she'd been in before, this was one she didn't have any experience handling. "I didn't say that."

"Look, whatever she's told you, she's not in the state of mind to be alone. You don't even know if she's coherent. For all we know, the roofies or whatever could still be in her system making her think wrong—"

McKenzie put up a finger to keep Jonas from spewing whatever venom was going through his head at the moment. This was hard enough to process without controlling him, too.

"I'm sorry, Mr. Nathaniel, but I can't help you. If you're concerned about your wife's whereabouts, I suggest you speak with the police and file a missing person's report," she said quickly, then hung up before he had a chance to argue.

"Great," Jonas mumbled. "The police know exactly where she is."

"I didn't know what else to say. Besides, maybe Rory could use their help, because I know if he's looking for her, he could be dangerous," McKenzie replied, distracted by a vague thought her brain couldn't quite hold still long enough to analyze.

"He doesn't even act like he lost a child," Jonas seethed, though now it seemed he was talking more to himself than to her.

Jonas fidgeted, every moment growing visibly more

irritated.

"It's all The Cradle Robber's fault. All of this."

McKenzie put a hand on his shoulder. "Gibb will know you didn't give him up. I swear it."

Jonas hit the chair arm hard. "Even if he does, it won't be the same."

After shifting several times to force a better fit, he threw his hands up and stood. "I can't sit still, here, McKenzie. I can't."

He walked away from her, and she scrambled up to follow him. "I'm coming with you."

"I'm not going anywhere," he growled.

She swung her body through her crutches with every step to try to quicken her pace and keep up. "The hell you're not."

He whipped around to face her. "What is that supposed to mean, exactly?"

"I know you've thought about it, Jonas. I'm not an idiot."

Jonas glared at her but said nothing. His fists clenched, unclenched, then furled again. Finally, a defeated look spread over his face, and the manic gleam in his eye dissolved.

"Fine," he said. "Let's find a drink machine. If I don't have some more caffeine soon, it'll be a liquor store."

"Okay," she said as she fell in stride with him again.

Whether Coke or liquor, she supposed either was better than him finding the Cradle Robber here in the ICU.

After days of trying to find information, here it was, coming to Trevin. It wasn't like he'd hoped. He'd seen it on the news crawler in Times Square before the phone rang. He'd hopped a bus to go see someone about it when the phone call came.

A raspy voice trailed through the line, half a whisper, half in pain. A chill ran up his spine. "I swear to God, I will find you and cut your heart out."

Fuck.

Trevin didn't answer, but his stomach turned over. This

wasn't good. He was talking. The news said critical, and Trevin hadn't been as worried. But he wasn't gone. He was alive. Talking. Alive.

And pissed.

"When I make it out of here, I'm going to find you and cut your heart out for turning me in. Know that."

The phone clicked.

Fuck.

CHAPTER 77

DIRK BLINKED INTO the overhead light. This couldn't be. He'd done everything right. Everything.

The small ICU whirled, shifted around him.

What the hell?

He looked into the face staring down at him. Blurry.

Unbelievable.

Muttering. His own. Far away in his own ears. "They'll realize it eventually, you know. It wasn't open. Too closed. Much too closed. They'll look. Realize."

He knew he was talking out of his head even as he said it. But it made sense. All of it did.

"Even the closed ones were open," he breathed.

Then Dirk's arm stung. A tingling sensation crept up to his bicep. Fire ignited under his skin, burning slowly at first, then faster and faster like acid eating at him from the inside out. His breathing quickened, his screams muffled by the pillow held over his face.

He thrashed against the bed as the blood in his very veins seemed to boil within him, the handcuffs binding him to the bed cruelly preventing him from clawing at his searing flesh.

His cries died, the pain too intense to speak or even scream. The pillow moved. He looked one last time into the face above him. Someone would notice it had been too closed. Everything happened for a reason.

But he couldn't see the reason. Not now. The pain ripped

through him, and yet, no one had realized. Not yet. The pain tore him piece by piece, dragging him off to hell.

Trevin entered through the doors of the emergency room and nicked scrubs from the supply closet. That had been the easy part. The next would be much trickier.

Still, he'd underestimated what police would overlook if you looked like everyone else who worked here.

He stepped off the elevator onto the floor of the ICU, already sweating through the stiff blue material. Dirk was the only person who could still implicate him. He was sure. He'd made sure all other records that connected the old name were destroyed. Only Dirk could tie Trevin to Dirk.

Not to mention, Dirk would slit his throat. There was no way around it.

The syringe was in his pocket, full of nothing but air. But, as any good heroin addict knows, those air bubbles in the right place could be fatal.

He moved into the circular hallway toward ICU room number ten. Fifteen more steps, and he'd be there. This nightmare would be over.

Something was wrong. Across the hall, ICU room ten was empty.

Where could they have taken him?

Hands grabbed him, shoved him to the floor. His cheek met the linoleum as his hands were yanked behind his back.

"Trevin Ivanson, you're under arrest for the murder of Dirk Harris, and God only knows what else after that. You have the right to remain silent. Anything you say can and will be used against you. You have the right to an attorney…"

The words were mush in his ears, the far too clean blood in his veins pounding around him.

"He's not dead yet!" he screamed into the shiny, bleach-scented floor. "I haven't killed him yet!"

Panic. His throat constricting. Why wouldn't they understand?

The syringe dropped from his pocket as the FBI agent hoisted him from the floor. His foot brushed it as he tried to gain his footing underneath him. Another agent surged forward to pick up the weapon with a gloved hand.

"You don't understand! I didn't kill him!" Trevin yelled into the face of the agent holding him.

The agent pushed him toward the elevator. "Sure you didn't, buddy." Then, the guy lowered his voice. "But if you weren't a rat that crawled out of the same gutter he did, I'd congratulate you."

CHAPTER 78

EVERITT'S NEXT TASK was even harder: getting answers from people who didn't want to give them.

If she could find more information about Noelle's killer by backtracking, maybe she could do the same thing to help find Jonas' child too. And Everitt had seen a list of names, names left to her by someone who'd been like her and tried to research what the Petersons had done. She'd read those names. All of them.

The Davidsons had been on that list.

Thinking back, all of those people had to have come into contact with someone who knew about the Petersons. If Felicia Rockwell and the Davidsons had both been involved at the same IVF clinic, and Felicia had an illegally adopted child, Felicia had to have told the Davidsons about the baby trading ring. Or, the Davidsons had told *her*.

Now, Everitt sat across the living room from Felicia Rockwell's mother, Noah Hutchins next to her. When they'd showed up at her door, Lorraine Rockwell seemed to know from the second she saw Everitt's belly why they were there.

She turned to the little girl lying on her stomach coloring in her coloring book. "Tess, go in your room for a while and color, okay?"

"Okay, Nana."

The little girl's pink-beaded braids bounced as she stood and picked up her book and box of crayons. She dropped a few loose ones as she tried to fit them all in her hands, then stuffed them in the box. Tess half-ran, half-skipped on the tips of her toes toward the back of the apartment.

Now, they sat in a stalemate. Everitt had asked Lorraine about Felicia's relationship to the Davidsons, if and how she knew them. Lorraine stared at her, cold. "I can't tell you anything. I won't."

"It'll come out," Noah said. "Even if you don't say anything, even if you try to keep it secret. They have the names. It's only a matter of time."

Lorraine Rockwell's eyes misted, then she doubled over and wailed. "I know! I just can't bear to lose her. She's all I have left. Felicia's gone, and the baby is all I have."

Everitt leaned in toward her. "How do you think Jonas Cleary feels?"

Lorraine peeked through her fingers at Everitt, then down to her belly. She gestured a finger toward it to indicate the baby. "Boy or girl?"

Everitt rested her hand on the bump that was her child, the place where the first labor pain would hit. So would motherhood.

"I don't know," she whispered.

Lorraine nodded and stood. She paced the room back and forth. Her right hand drifted over her heart. "I wonder if Tess' mother knew."

Everitt watched the woman cross to the small area where a table and chair set for two lingered in the corner in place of a dining room. She picked up the Cinderella bowl there and carried it to the sink. She dumped the handful of soupy Cheerios out of the bottom. Lorraine gripped the sponge off the sink and started scrubbing. Hard. Fast. Then harder.

"Felicia became good friends with them. Melissa Davidson and she went through IVF at the same time," she explained. Her hands worked at the already pristine bowl. "I don't know if Felicia got her information from the Davidsons. I could lie to you and say I did. But I don't. I know where they were, though. I know where they are now, too."

Noah helped Everitt into the cab, then climbed in himself. He could take Mac her answer, and maybe finally, once she gave her friend back his kid, she'd let herself off the hook for what had happened to Levi. "This is just unreal. All of these people adopting children they either coerced the parents into giving up or who were kidnapped? Do they have no consciences?"

Noah and Everitt had sat in Lorraine Rockwell's living room as she had explained the Davidsons' situation to them over tea. Hall and Melissa Davidson wanted a child badly, had tried for years, but ultimately were unable to conceive. That was when Melissa was diagnosed with breast cancer. It didn't exclude her from the adoption process entirely, but it meant she'd be much further down the list to receive a child looking for his or her forever family. That's when they found out about a couple working in the city who, for a price, could make their dream family come true."

"They felt stuck. Like they had nowhere else to go," Everitt said, rubbing her ever-growing belly.

"But the Davidson's knew they *bought* a kid," Noah argued.

Everitt shook her head. "All they knew was that the baby meant everything to them."

"Even so, they're crooks. All of 'em."

Christ running on a hamster wheel.

Everitt suddenly squealed.

"What's wrong?"

She took a deep breath, bit her lip, grimaced, and let it go. "I...I think I'm in labor."

CHAPTER 79

MCKENZIE AND JONAS met Noah and Everitt as they walked in through the set of double doors of the maternity ward, just a quick elevator ride two floors from where they'd been sitting in the ER, waiting on Rory to be wheeled back from her CT scan. Noah had called from the cab to say they were on their way, to insist they meet them, and that he had more information about Gibb. McKenzie had been unable to get more out of him, though, as his every other word was peppered with his asking Everitt if she was okay.

Now, Everitt's face was scrunched up in pain. Noah's sweat-beaded pallor and the grim line of his mouth betrayed his horror. This man had killed people, but he'd clearly never been present for the birth of one. He lingered behind Everitt, his hands still at his sides rather than swinging the way one's arms normally did when walking, as if he thought that at any moment, the baby might come slipping out and he'd have to catch it.

"How far apart are your contractions?" McKenzie asked, falling into stride with Everitt as best she could without both legs. Luckily, a very pregnant woman didn't move much faster than someone on crutches. They walked toward the OB assessment area. She wouldn't understand any answer Everitt gave since she'd never had experience with a woman about to give birth, but it was a question everyone and their cousin knew to ask, so she was at least able to show concern.

"Six minutes or so. I don't know. I don't know if I'm timing them right," Noah answered for her.

"You're not," Everitt said through gritted teeth. "You time them start to start, not end to start."

Noah muttered an apology, and McKenzie had to stifle a laugh.

Everitt checked in with the desk. The nurse sent her on back while the rest of them were required to produce their IDs to record their visit in the maternity ward logbook. Until a few weeks ago, McKenzie would've thought this a stupid policy, but now, it seemed vital.

She dug her driver's license out of her purse. "What'd you guys find out?"

Jonas' breathing caught slightly behind her.

"The Davidsons are still in Georgia," Noah said, the color returning to his cheeks now that Everitt was no longer his responsibility. "A different part, but they're there. Macon, Georgia. Felicia Rockwell had gotten chummy with them. They kept in touch. Felicia's mother didn't have an exact address, but she does have a cell phone number. Jig's working on a trace of the account now."

McKenzie limped around to look at Jonas, fighting tears. Her high school sweetheart stood, stunned, his plastic ID frozen at his side.

"Sir?" the nurse working the intake booth prodded.

Jonas wordlessly handed her his license, staring at McKenzie. She could only imagine what was going through his head right now. His heart. After all, Gibb wasn't even hers, but her own chest seemed to be severely malfunctioning in both the heartbeat and breathing departments.

"You folks can go on through to the waiting area," the intake nurse said, passing their IDs back to them.

Jonas, however, stood rooted to the spot.

"You can't go now, Jonas. I know you want to, but you need to do this right. If you do anything stupid, it could jeopardize your getting your son back. You need to take the right steps. Go through a lawyer," McKenzie said.

Jonas nodded but didn't move. His eyes shined.

Whitney's words about ruining lives popped into McKenzie's mind, thoughts of how the faceless Davidsons had probably fought so hard to keep their secret so they could have Gibb as a part of their family. A family they loved. Levi's face flashed in, then his mother screaming at her at his funeral. She'd caused so much pain for so many people.

But unlike Levi, this time, even if the Davidsons lost, someone was going to win. Jonas.

And now, even Whitney knew it.

McKenzie smiled and reached for him. "I know." She squeezed his hand. "I know."

Jonas lowered himself to the chair next to Rory's hospital bed and smoothed back her hair. This woman had been through so much.

At his touch, she opened her eyes, slow and sleepy. Then, panic crossed her face.

"It's okay. He's dead. The Cradle Robber's dead, and the lawyer he'd been working with has been arrested," Jonas whispered.

He brushed his lips against her forehead, careful not to touch the cut there.

She stared at him, confused. "What kind of drugs do they have me on?"

He glanced to her arm, where a tube with plain saline solution snaked into her vein. "None. You're sober as can be. They're gone."

Her chest rose and fell with the sigh of relief. "I can't believe it."

"It's true, but we're not entirely out of the woods. Bryce called McKenzie," he said, talking faster as she opened her mouth to protest. "Don't worry. She didn't tell him where you are or anything. But I do think we should talk about what to do where he's concerned. He's probably going to talk to the cops, if he hasn't already."

A shadow crossed Rory's face. Fear.

"Try not to think about it now," he whispered. It was probably wrong, discounting a woman's husband. But given Bryce's history, his empathy was seriously lacking. "We'll deal with it when you're better. Together. I'll help you."

She reached for his hand, squeezed it. "Thank you."

He nodded, unsure of how to put into words everything else he had to tell her. "I have other news. We know where Gibb is."

Rory gaped, shocked. Then her eyes lit up as she smiled. "Oh, Jonas. That's so wonderful. I'm...congratulations."

Jonas looked down at the bedside rail. How to ask something like this? After all, she was still legally married. Still a woman with obligations to someone else.

He'd thought of asking McKenzie, but Everitt's contractions were getting closer and closer, and since McKenzie was all the poor girl had, she'd begged McKenzie to stay with her. But he didn't want to do this next part alone. Couldn't, maybe.

Jig had not only found the Davidsons in Macon, but she'd gotten her director to put in a call to the local police department regarding the situation. Jonas started talking, still looking at the floor rather than the pale, bruised face of the woman lying in the bed in front of him. He told Rory how McKenzie had called a lawyer contact she had while they'd waited upstairs for Everitt's labor progress to be checked. How he was now all set to begin the long, complicated proceedings to get his son back.

He kept reminding himself he was one of the lucky ones. Felicia Rockwell's little girl, Tess', blood sample was being compared with DNA from a missing persons database, but since the police had found that Trevin Worneck had destroyed most of his records, the chances that Tess' birth parents would be found or get her back were miniscule.

So many black market babies, and yet most of those parents would never see their kids. Some people could consider it a good thing. Lorraine Rockwell and those others who currently had custody of one of these kids would probably sleep more soundly knowing their beloved little family member couldn't be taken away from them. But Jonas couldn't help but think of all of the parents of missing babies who would never have closure. Some had never even *met* their babies. At least he had a chance at getting his back.

Unfortunately, the situation wasn't so simple. He couldn't just waltz down to Georgia and pick Gibb up. There were legal matters to fix, paperwork to go through. Courts to appear before. DNA tests to confirm, although Jig and that tattered little handprint Noelle had made had gone a long way toward cutting the red tape.

Given the situation, the police department had contacted the Davidsons. Gibb would remain in their care for the present for the best interest of the child under the stipulation that the Davidsons were not to leave the city and would remain under surveillance.

However, Jonas' lawyer was able to arrange a meeting between a court liaison, a social worker, Jonas, and the son he hadn't seen since before he could walk.

Now, Jonas looked back up at Rory. "The doctors say your injuries are pretty minor, and as soon as the paperwork has been processed, you'll be free to go. I know it's a lot to ask, and given everything you've been through, you're probably not up for it. It's probably not appropriate—"

Rory put a finger to his lips. "Jonas, just spit it out."

"Will you go with me? To meet...I mean, not meet...see...to see Gibb. Will you come?"

Rory raised her eyebrows, then laughed out loud as she said, "Yes. Of course, I will. I'd be honored."

Finally, he would have Gibb back. It didn't seem real. It was too good to be true. Tomorrow, he would see his baby boy.

CHAPTER 80

MCKENZIE BIT HER nails in the chair next to Everitt's bed. Whitney might've more or less given her blessing to the story, but the article was going to have to wait. Jonas and Rory had left eight hours earlier to head to Georgia. Lucky them. The monitor next to the girl beeped incessantly, strange lines spiking in time with the girl's grimaces.

"Are you okay?" McKenzie asked for the millionth time. Why the hell couldn't she think of anything better to say at a time like this? Of course the girl wasn't okay. She hadn't planned to keep this baby, but nonetheless, she was about to have to push it out of her body. It couldn't be the highlight of her universe, especially now that no one was waiting in the wings to adopt the child.

"Peachy," Everitt said as she blew out a breath.

Pierce's face popped into McKenzie's memory, his humor and fondness for puns. "I'm impressed. You're in active labor, and still, you're making Georgia jokes."

Everitt panted and laughed a little, even though she looked anything but amused. "Have they landed yet?"

McKenzie shook her head. "Haven't heard. My cell reception in here is shit. Want me to check with Noah and Jig?"

Come to think, it *had* been a long time. A *really* long time. McKenzie couldn't imagine how it must've been for Rory when she'd gone into labor while the Cradle Robber had her. She might've gone through less trauma because he didn't excise the baby from her stomach for that reason, but still, if she'd had a labor this long with a serial killer present, it had to have been the scariest ordeal imaginable.

Why the heck would the Cradle Robber be willing to wait that long?

"No way in hell you're leaving me here. Just get the nurse to tell them to come in here, too," Everitt said.

"What?" McKenzie asked, shaking herself from the train of thought. Surely she'd misheard.

Everitt rolled onto her side, biting her lip hard, then releasing it as the monitor registered the contraction's end. "Why the hell not? It's not like this is some perfect birthing experience to be featured on *A Baby Story*. We might as well add awkwardness."

McKenzie shrugged and jammed the call button on the side of the bed. When the nurse responded, she told her Everitt would like the two others waiting in the lobby to join them.

A moment later, Noah appeared in the doorway, peeking in like a child, unsure of whether or not he was allowed to come in the room. Jig shoved past him.

"How's it goin' in here, rockstars?" she asked.

"Swell," Everitt mumbled, the monitor again registering a surge of cramping. "What's the latest on Operation Get the Kid Back?"

"Flight to Atlanta took off and landed on time. I got a text about two hours ago that their E.T.A. to Macon was an hour and a half. I'm guessing by now they're in their jammies with visions of sugar plums dancing in their heads," Noah said. He'd walked in quietly behind Jig and plopped down on the wooden rocking chair in the corner. He scanned the room, his gaze lingering on the little warming station set up beside Everitt's bed. "So how long before the...um...the—" he gestured toward Everitt, his hand rotating in a get-on-with-it sort of motion.

McKenzie glared at him, but Everitt half-laughed. "I'm hurrying, I promise. If I'm keeping you from something—"

Noah held up both his hands, innocent. "No, no. Take your time. You just keep doin' what you've gotta do."

"Thanks for the blessing."

A nurse rapped on the door as she walked in. "How are we feeling, Everitt? Do you need anything for pain yet?"

Everitt's face scrunched again. She didn't answer.

"Keep breathing. Panting can help. You're almost in transition. It's the worst part."

"Really? I'd have thought the worst part would be pushing the baby out of your—"

"Noah!" McKenzie yelped, cutting him off.

Everitt still said nothing but did as commanded and panted like Carbon after a fast-paced walk in June. When the beeps slowed and the monitor's line leveled out, she shook her head. "You're not drugging me up. I can't risk not knowing what's going on."

McKenzie's chest clenched. "Everitt, if you need something, we're all here. We're not going to let you out of our sight."

"The kid either," Noah agreed.

At Noah's statement, McKenzie's heart galloped. She'd have never thought he'd be this way.

Everitt grunted, shifting to her other side. "No offense, guys, but my trust scale is a little off kilter. Don't get me wrong, though. I'll totally take you up on hands to squeeze and people to cuss out coming soon to a hospital room near you."

Jig sidled up to the bed and offered her hand. "Just don't break the nails. I just had them done. You can break the *fingers*, but no nails."

The nurse ripped a printout from under the monitor and glanced over it. "Everything looks good here, Everitt. Hang in there, and let me know when you start feeling the urge to push, okay?"

"Oh, don't worry. You and everyone in a fifty mile radius will hear about it."

"Contractions are about every four and a half minutes, so you're getting close. We'll be back to check your dilation in just a few minutes, so if you change your mind about something for pain, now's the time, okay?"

Everitt gave a thumbs up with the hand not holding Jig's. "About how much longer?"

"Could be minutes, could be another couple hours before you're ready to push. But the way you're progressing, I'm thinking another hour or so. Hang tight," the nurse said. Then, she walked out the door.

"In that case, I'm gonna run call Jonas and make sure they've arrived safely. I'll be back in a flash," McKenzie said, following the nurse outside.

McKenzie couldn't help but think that as rough as it was to sit there and watch Everitt in so much pain, the squirm of excitement in her stomach surprised her. In a few hours, they'd be meeting a new little person just as Jonas was getting ready to meet his own.

CHAPTER 81

RORY WALKED THROUGH the neighborhood only streets away from the hotel she and Jonas had checked into. She'd had to wait until he fell asleep to sneak away. With luck, she'd be back and in bed without him ever realizing she was gone. But she had had to go, to find out where Gibb was. It would devastate Jonas to get there only to find out Gibb wasn't there anymore or, God forbid, was exceptionally happy with his family and didn't *want* to go with Jonas.

But Rory could save him that fate if she got to him first.

She didn't know much about the safety of the neighborhood, but considering the way these streets were nearly deserted, she would see any strangers coming from far off. Besides, the one man on earth who wanted to harm her was gone now. Why should she be afraid? At least, that's what she kept telling herself.

The GPS on her phone told her to make a right on the next street, which she did. It took her across the interstate, then into another little neighborhood full of cookie cutter houses. If she was right, the Davidsons lived in this area a few streets over. In just a little while, she would save Jonas any heartbreak he might have coming, and she could head back to the hotel without him being the wiser. It was all for his own good.

The phone woke Jonas on the third ring. He grabbed it off the pillow next to his. McKenzie.

"What's up?" he groaned.

"Are you asleep?"

"Not anymore," he said. He rolled over to look at the clock on the nightstand between the two double beds. The other bed was empty.

He ignored the talking in his ear as he stood and crossed the room. A note lay on the sofa. He picked it up, scanned it.

"Hello?" McKenzie's voice registered again.

"Oh, yeah, sorry. I was reading this note Rory left. Says she couldn't sleep, so she took a walk. Not to worry. Sorry, it distracted me."

"Is that safe?" McKenzie asked.

"Oh, probably. I wish she'd woken me so I could've gone with her, but the area's nice enough. I don't think she'll go far. She probably didn't wake me since I was so antsy before and actually *did* manage to fall asleep. How's Everitt?"

"It'll probably be a few more hours. I'll let you hit the hay again before you wake up all the way. Just checking in."

"Ten-four," Jonas replied.

He climbed beneath the covers and closed his eyes. He did wish Rory had woken him. She was a grown up, sure, but you couldn't be too safe these days. She of all people should know that.

When McKenzie returned to Everitt's room, the wailing had turned up a notch. Everitt now screamed and writhed in pain, cussing at everything from the ugly floral curtains, to Noah, to the beeping of the monitors.

"I think we'd better get a nurse in here," Jig said, her fingers white from blood loss where Everitt was squeezing them. "It's either close to time to push, or Everitt needs some serious Prozac."

"Got it," McKenzie said, leaning onto her crutches. But Noah was already halfway out the door.

"Going to find one," he said.

"We've called them with the button already, but they're taking their time," Jig said.

"I meant a Prozac," Noah replied.

Everitt spewed a stream of words that made even McKenzie blush. Damn. Feeling helpless, she stretched the cup of ice chips toward Everitt. The girl dug her hand into the cup and popped a few chips into her mouth.

"Did you get Jonas?" Jig asked.

"Yeah. They're in Macon. He was sleeping. Rory's out walking or something."

"What?"

Everitt swallowed the ice, then squealed through her gritted teeth. "This baby is coming! They better get their asses here, 'cause I don't know what I'm doing! But it's coming."

"Oh, Jesus," Noah said from the doorway.

Jig glanced at him. "Just plain Jesus?"

Noah shook his head, his eyes fixed on the lower half of Everitt's body, which was still covered up by a sheet but twisted back and forth with the girl's pain. "I think I should probably wait outside for this…"

"Oh, hell, no!" Everitt said, glaring at him. "You *will* watch this. You, as a man, *will* watch this and have to see what this is like. I don't care if you're not the father. It's symbolic."

"That's exactly what I'm afraid of," Noah said. He took one step inside the door but otherwise stayed as close to the wall as possible.

"Someone tells me we think we might be ready to go in here," a nurse said as she bustled in.

"*We* are definitely ready," Everitt replied.

The nurse shooed the others outside to check Everitt's progress. When she reopened the door, she pronounced it was, in fact, time to push. Jig manned one side, McKenzie the other, each grabbing a hand. Everitt scooted to the end of the bed and propped her legs in the stirrups.

It was all McKenzie could do to keep from laughing at Noah across the room. He leaned against the wall, shaking his head slowly back and forth as though he couldn't believe he was there.

The nurse instructed Everitt to try not to push, whatever the heck that meant, while she fetched the doctor. So, instead of cheering her on to push, McKenzie and Jig tried to keep straight faces as Everitt cussed Noah up and down the wall, occasionally nodding at her to encourage her.

"You tell him," Jig said.

"I could never get away with this," McKenzie said.

Jig nodded her approval. "Why do you think I'm so glad she's doing it? Nobody messes with a lady in labor. This is the first and only time in his life Noah's been dressed down and not given it right back."

Noah had taken to his phone, scrolling through God only knew what to try to ignore Everitt's steady stream of male bashing. "Oh, man. They found a new Cradle Robber victim."

"Impossible," Jig said.

Everitt yelled something that sounded like, "Go to hell," and threw her head back toward her pillow.

"No, it was an old victim's body, just one they apparently didn't find until now. Decomposed some. Rats had gotten to the body. Ramona Crabtree. Let's hope she's the last."

"Sick," Jig replied.

"Was Ramona Crabtree pregnant?" McKenzie asked.

"Can we *please* not do this right now?" Everitt muttered, but it was so quiet, no way Noah could've heard the request.

"Was," Noah said. "No more details yet. Your new BFF the M.E. can probably tell you more."

McKenzie heard her phone ringing from across the room, but she was a little too busy to answer. Then, a voicemail ding. Next, the chime of a text message. With every sound, McKenzie looked in the direction of the phone.

"You let go of this hand, I'm cussing at you next," Everitt

said between pants.

"Hey, Noah, grab my phone and check it, will you?"

Noah fished McKenzie's phone out of her bag. "It's Morton. He's been seeing on the news about a possible death and arrest related to the Cradle Robber—wants to know what he can run with so he doesn't lose the inside scoop. What do you want me to tell him? You going to hold up your end of the bargain and give old Morton a piece of the pie?"

"Do I have a choice?" McKenzie replied.

"Are you McKenzie McClendon?"

She laughed. "Yes, Noah Hutchins, I am. I'm as honest as a Girl Scout."

"I've known a lot of seriously deranged Girl Scouts," he said. "So, should I reply?"

"Well," McKenzie said slowly, "I want you to tell him something. I'd rather not give him a choice."

"Of course you wouldn't."

"Can you two please get this wrapped up so we can focus on more immediate things?"

Just then, the nurse and doctor whisked in. Another nurse took over at McKenzie's spot at Everitt's hand, so she let go and moved to Noah.

"What can I say? The newspaper business waits for no one." She snapped off a text to Morton.

"What'd you give him?" Noah asked.

"The lawyer and the black market, because oddly enough, I'll still get to do the lawyer and the black market. Two sides of the same coin, really. I couldn't pass up the trade between the killer and Noelle. Yoga classes for health food. No one guessed at the connection. Besides, I have less firsthand knowledge on Trevin." McKenzie glanced across at Noah, then at Jig, who was standing out of the way for a technician to inject something into Everitt's IV line. "Maybe if *someone* had called me back, I could've been onto Trevin sooner and up there to watch them arrest him. But that's okay. I know things get busy."

Despite the squeals and groans coming from the bed, Noah and Jig both stared at McKenzie like she had suddenly turned into the lady in labor and had grown a belly before their eyes.

"What are you talking about?" Jig asked.

"You," McKenzie replied. "You didn't ever call me back about the Trevin stuff. I didn't know until after Dirk Harris—or Dylan Whitfield—was dead and Trevin was arrested that he—"

McKenzie stopped talking at the lift in Jig's eyebrows. She and Noah exchanged an awkward glance.

"I know I didn't call you. I had Everitt do it," Jig said.

"Everitt didn't call me."

All glanced at Everitt as if to give her a chance to defend herself, but her eyes were shut tight, her face twisted in pain as she pushed, the nurse beside her counting.

McKenzie looked back at Noah. "She's kind of busy. We can ask her later."

"We don't have to. Everitt did call you," Noah replied. "I was with her."

McKenzie picked up her phone again and scrolled to her call log to the night the Cradle Robber had broken into Jonas' place. She was sure she hadn't gotten a call that night.

And yet, sure enough, there it was. Everitt's call. McKenzie glanced to the time of the call. She'd been in the kitchen with Jonas at the time.

Sweet cartwheeling Jesus. What the hell.

Something clicked into place in her brain.

Rohypnol.

Bryce had mentioned roofies in Rory's system. Could be conjecture, but…

She whipped her phone out and, on a whim, hit the button to dial Jonas again. No answer. He'd probably gotten smart and turned his phone on silent to sleep.

While Rory was out for a walk.

"Jig, if you'd just been attacked by the Cradle Robber, would you go on a walk by yourself in a strange town?" McKenzie ventured.

Everitt breathed heavily through her nose as behind them, the nurses told her to rest through the next contraction.

"Not unless I had a head injury," Jig said with a sarcastic chuckle.

Exactly.

McKenzie scrolled through her contacts looking for Rory's number, but it wasn't there. Her stomach plummeted. "I'll be right back."

Jig glanced at Everitt, then back to McKenzie, eyes wide. "Where are you going?"

McKenzie didn't answer. She needed to find Rory, and fast.

She threw open the door to the stairwell and took them as fast as she could hobble back down toward the emergency room. When she reached the triage desk, she clapped her hand right on the shoulder of the nurse beside it.

"Which way to CT? My daughter is there," she lied.

The nurse pointed toward a set of double doors to the right. "I'll buzz you through these two doors, then take a right to the dead end, then a left. CT is at the end of that hallway, but you can't go into the room until the scan is over. There are a couple chairs outside for guardians to wait."

"Thanks," McKenzie said, frazzled.

Through the double doors, to the right. She'd been through enough with hospital administrators to know that if you wanted information, they were not the place to find it. They had it, sure, but it'd take you twenty minutes longer that way. She had a better idea.

She turned left at the dead end. The door to CT was open, luckily, so no scan was in progress. A scrawny, red-haired guy who would've looked like he'd just graduated high school last week if not for the deep set worry lines in his forehead stood across the room at a keyboard, punching buttons. He glanced up.

"Can I help you?"

"I know there are tons of rules about this and everything, but I came to you because there's no time to lose. You know how the bureaucrats are. A new friend of mine was in here a while ago for a scan, and she was released from the hospital. But now, she's off by herself, and no one knows where, and it's just…after a traumatic head injury, we're all worried about her. She's been through a lot recently, so she's changed her cell number, and I don't have the new one yet. I was hoping you could look her up for me real fast so I can call and check on her."

The redhead shook his head. "That's against hospital policy, ma'am—"

"I *know* it's against policy, but don't you have some sort of policy against letting people with head injuries run around on their own? Couldn't you guys get sued if something bad happened? Better yet, how are *you* going to feel when Rory turns up dead from wandering into traffic or something right after you all told her she was okay enough to leave the hospital?"

"Ma'am, if her doctor deemed her fit to be medically released, then there's no reason to panic—wait, did you say she was in here just a few hours ago?" The technician's face went from one of professional calm and reasoning to downright puzzled.

"Right. Rory Nathaniel."

The tech shook his head again, his previous stream of thought obviously forgotten. "You must be mistaken. No one by that name has come through here today."

"What?"

"I haven't had any Rory today. Or yesterday, for that matter."

"But—"

McKenzie looked at her feet, wiggled her toes. What the hell was going on? This guy had to have a head injury of his own.

"Never mind," she said. She turned back around and traced

her steps back toward the ER and to the stairwell. Rory was out on a walk somewhere, and Jonas wasn't answering his phone.

Everitt's face was practically maroon as she pushed, her legs bent all the way up to her torso. She held a nurse's hand on each side, but Jig stood beside the nurse on her right, giving her a pep talk.

Talk about bad timing.

McKenzie sidled up behind her and tugged her sleeve.

"Jig, I need you to do something for me."

Jig turned her head, mouth wide open. "Now?"

"Yeah, now. It can't wait."

Jig glanced back as if to check Everitt's reaction, but Everitt's eyes were closed tight with the push. Jig shrugged. "Doubt I'm helping much anyway, but what could you possibly need done right this instant, McKenzie?"

McKenzie pushed away all the scary thoughts trying to encroach. The only way to do anything about any of them was to get in touch with Rory before anything bad happened. "Is it humanly possible to get access to Jonas' cell phone contacts? I need to find Rory. Immediately. Like yesterday."

Jig bit her lip. "Contacts? I don't know. Maybe. It'd be easier just to send everything on Jonas' cell phone to yours. Why?"

"No time to explain. We have to move. You can do that? Send Jonas' stuff to my phone?"

Jig shook her head, but she was already moving toward the door. "Not exactly, but I think I can help you. Be back in five."

CHAPTER 82

RORY STOOD ACROSS the street from the two story brick house where the Davidsons supposedly resided. She could just walk over there. Knock on their door. But no, she wasn't here for that. She was just here for reassurance that Gibb wouldn't further complicate Jonas' life.

So instead, she sat across the street at a bus stop, watching them from a safe distance. Their blinds were open, so she could see everything going on inside. Her heart beat faster and faster the more time went by as the anticipation of the moment she'd first see Gibb drew closer. She hoped he wasn't already in bed asleep.

Her heart thundered as most of the family entered the living room from the kitchen. Melissa Davidson's back was turned toward her in the kitchen. The mother seemed to be washing plates by hand. Hall Davidson plopped into a recliner and opened his newspaper. Two children sat on the floor with a board game. Checkers, perhaps? Did kids still play that? Rory's heart skittered faster.

She watched and waited, thinking. After a long half an hour, the parents followed the kids upstairs. Rory sat and twiddled her thumbs. Another ten minutes passed, and Hall and Melissa came back down alone.

Tucking them in, maybe?

Then, Hall Davidson walked toward the first window, and the blinds flitted downward. Then, the second. Rory's view was no more.

She gripped her phone, her pulse racing. She had to say something to Jonas, but the words wouldn't come. If she didn't word it just right, it would be horrible. Hell, it was going to be horrible no matter which way she sliced it, but better this way than if she said nothing. God, she couldn't think clearly. Why had this had to happen? Why couldn't anything just be simple?

Of course, she could go back to the hotel and tell him in person, but she didn't think she could stand it. Maybe her past had simply made her too afraid of someone's reaction to something like this. God knows she'd had enough run-ins with men with tempers to last her a lifetime.

He's going to hate me if I don't tell him in person.

Then again, he might hate her either way. Safer to do it now. Here. That way, if he wanted her to check on anything else before she returned to the hotel, she could. She'd do any leg work *for* him so he wouldn't have to be involved in the nightmare himself. It was the least she could do.

She picked up her phone and typed.

"Eight...nine...ten," the nurse counted. "Great job, Everitt. You're doing fine. We're almost there."

McKenzie's muscles relaxed. Ever since she'd come back to the room, her body had developed some weird synchronization with Everitt's. Every time Everitt pushed, McKenzie found that she tensed everything she could tense as well. She'd offered a hand for Everitt to hold, but the girl hadn't even heard her. It was just as well. McKenzie didn't feel qualified for any sort of midwifery-related task, even the lowly art of hand-holding. The baby would be better off born without her assistance, considering her help usually turned into a disaster for everyone involved.

She turned the phone Jig had given her over in her hand. Still no messages, despite her willing them to appear every minute and a half. She'd checked over and over, but to no avail.

According to Jig, the spare cell phone Jig had fetched from

her car would now receive any and all phone calls or texts sent to Jonas' phone number. When McKenzie had asked her how the fuck she'd managed that, Jig had provided the helpful explanation that if McKenzie ever asked about how this was done or even breathed a word that she'd done something like this, she would lie through her teeth, then give McKenzie's phone number to every single telemarketer on the planet.

Which meant that now, all McKenzie had to do to find Rory was wait for Rory to contact Jonas. She just hoped Rory *would* contact Jonas while they were apart. If she didn't, McKenzie would have to wait until Jonas woke up, and that could be hours. It was a long shot, of course, but it was the best they had.

"Nine...ten...Good, Everitt. Really good. We're almost there," the nurse said.

"Get it out of me!" Everitt shrieked. She flailed and tried to detach a stray piece of hair matted to her face.

McKenzie's breath caught in her throat as Noah stood from where he was seated beside McKenzie and walked across the room toward the bed. He brushed the sweaty strands out of Everitt's eyes. "Better?"

Everitt nodded but closed her eyes and scrunched her entire face with the force of the next contraction.

Noah stilled like a rabbit in the middle of a lawn, seeming not to know whether to stay put or move back to the couch. In the next instant, Everitt jerked forward, the contraction compelling her to push. As she did, she grabbed Noah's bicep.

"One more push, and we'll see the baby's head, Everitt. You can do it," the doctor said from the stool in front of Everitt.

"That is definitely *your* opinion," Everitt gasped. She clenched her eyes shut again.

McKenzie's entire body stiffened, bracing along with Everitt. "One...two..."

Three. Four. Five. McKenzie flipped the phone over in her hand.

She jumped when she saw the blinking light on the phone. "Six…seven…eight…"

Jonas, you up?

McKenzie's typed as fast as she could:

Where are you?

"The baby is crowning," the doctor announced.

"Don't you think I can fucking tell?" Everitt shot back.

The phone lit up again.

Oh, Jonas. I'm so sorry. I came to the Davidsons. I needed to make sure you weren't going to get hurt.
Oh, Jonas, I'm so sorry.

McKenzie's stomach knotted. None of this made sense, but with every breath, she was more sure. She typed back again.

Sorry for what? Rory, what's going on?

"The baby's head is out. Just one more big push, Everitt, and he or she will be here."

The light blinked.

Oh, Jonas. Lorraine Rockwell must've been wrong. Gibb isn't here. The people here. I watched them. They have two kids, but both are girls. He isn't here, Jonas.

McKenzie blinked. Behind her, Everitt groaned, then yelled. In the next instant, the tiny cry of what sounded like a baby dinosaur filled the room.

"It's a girl!"

Goosebumps sprang up on McKenzie's arms as she turned to see the doctor laying the little goo-covered bundle on Everitt's belly. Had Levi looked like that when he was born? She hadn't been able to save her little cousin from a cold-blooded murderer, but she'd saved this child. Something in her heart that she hadn't known was frozen unthawed a little. A life for a life. Not a bad trade.

Everitt stared wide-eyed at the breathing mound on top of her as the nurse checked to make sure the baby's mouth was clear and the doctor worked at the end of the table to clamp the umbilical cord. The corners of Everitt's mouth turned up in a tiny smile. She laughed and wiped away a tear.

McKenzie's eyes welled up. Good, God. Everything this case had dragged all of them through, yet something about that tiny baby girl cooing quietly on her mother's belly made it all seem okay.

"Do you have a name?" Jig asked.

If Jig hadn't spoken, McKenzie might've forgotten there were other people in the room. McKenzie looked up to see Jig grinning, her eyes fixed on the baby now screaming at the top of her lungs. The nurse wrapped the tiny person in a blanket and handed her to Everitt.

Everitt smiled, her stare never leaving her child's face. "Not really. Hadn't planned on needing one. I thought during the labor if it was a boy I could always use Noah since he was so useful to punch for the past few hours, but for a girl—"

At this, McKenzie glanced at Noah, expecting some snide remark. He said nothing. Just stared at the little one, his face completely blank with shock.

When he didn't react, Everitt finally shifted her gaze to him and beamed. "So, what do you think? Worth hanging out of a chimney for?"

Noah swallowed hard, eyes still set on the baby in Everitt's arms. Then, he let out a single chuckle. Relief.

"She's...perfect," he whispered.

Everitt turned back to the baby, brushed a tiny cheek with the back of her hand. Everitt hadn't yet mentioned what she planned to do now that the couple adopting her baby had turned out to be money laundering freaks, but she didn't have to. The tender look in her eyes as she leaned forward to let the baby close the round "O" of her mouth around her pinky finger told McKenzie that this little mother wasn't ever letting this baby out of her sight again. Not with the kinds of whackos they all knew to be in this world.

Jonas!

"Oh, shit, that reminds me. I got a text from Rory." McKenzie relayed the message, her heart thumping. They'd come so far, and now, when Gibb was closer than ever, it could all be ruined. "Noah, Jig, we need anyone—everyone—you know at the FBI. We have to get someone to the Davidson house, ASAP. We also need someone to go to Jonas' hotel. No time to lose. If anything's happened to Gibb, I have no idea what Jonas is capable of."

CHAPTER 83

JONAS JOLTED AWAKE at the banging on his door. He glanced at the glowing clock face on the night stand, then at the other bed in the room. Rory still wasn't back. God, he should've gone with her.

What if something has happened to her?

He slipped his t-shirt over his head, crossed the room toward the door, and yanked it open. A uniformed policeman stood in front of him. "Jonas Cleary?"

Jonas nodded, glancing at the badge the officer held up. "Yeah, I'm Jonas. Can I help you?"

Ironic, really. The cops had never helped *him*, so he just assumed they needed something he could offer.

"I need you to come with me, sir. It's about your son."

Rory stayed put at the bus stop, trying to answer all of Jonas' questions as he texted her. It was vital she get every single detail right, lest he wonder. So far, she'd counted the windows in the house so they could analyze if it was at all possible Gibb could've been already sleeping behind one of them the whole time Rory had been there. Then, she sent Jonas the license plate numbers of the cars visible in the open garage, though she tried and tried to tell him that would be something McKenzie and Noah and Jig would swear they had already checked out and that they were obviously wrong.

She jumped as she saw headlights coming down the road

perpendicular to the one on which she'd stationed herself. Almost simultaneously, the porch lights of the house in front of her came on. She should leave. They might've noticed her sitting there a long time. That wouldn't be good for anyone.

She cut to the block parallel to where she saw the headlights just as the car turned onto the street where the bus stop was. A police car.

Now, she couldn't leave. She needed to know—not just for Jonas, but for herself. She stepped into the shadows cast by the shed three homes down and watched as the cop car turned into the driveway of the house she'd been watching.

Then, the motor cut off, and a policeman stepped out of the car. The back door of the car opened, and Rory's breath caught as Jonas himself climbed out of the back seat. He must've called the cops, figuring the Davidsons had run.

She glanced at her phone, expecting a text from him at any moment to ask where she was. To tell her to meet him at the house. The phone was blank, though.

Jonas stood in the driveway of the brick house so foreign to him but not to his own son. Would Gibb even recognize him? Would he have any kind of family resemblance at all?

The policeman stepped into the garage in between the expensive black sedan and the white SUV. He knocked on the door. Jonas couldn't hear the rapping, but he might as well have. His own heart echoed it, after all.

A dark-headed man opened the door, his face somber. So, this was the man his little boy had called Daddy for years instead of him.

The hatred bubbling in his gut for the other man was knocked out of him along with the breath from his lungs. A blonde boy with a bowl haircut peeked from behind the man.

A boy with Noelle's porcelain skin, her oval face. Her high cheekbones.

A boy with his eyes.

The horror of the past few weeks seemed to drain from him, and a smile broke over his face. He couldn't have controlled it if he'd tried. Years of waiting, hoping. Years of wanting revenge, and yet, all of that in this moment seemed far away. The Davidsons may have called him Blair, but Gibb was only yards away.

They'd taken a lot from him, but one thing they hadn't been able to do was change Gibb's eyes.

Rory watched as the cop knocked on the door. A middle-aged man answered. A moment later, a small blonde boy stepped sheepishly from behind the man at the door.

Rory couldn't see Jonas' face from where she stood, but she could only imagine the way his heart must be feeling. As if it would burst. A tear dripped down her cheek and chin. She couldn't believe what she was seeing.

A family.

McKenzie sat on the couch at the hospital, squeezing the phone in her hand tighter and tighter as though doing so could cause news to come faster to her through it. She'd only tied up the line briefly to get someone on the way to Bryce's house to explain what was going on. It was the least she could do for the poor guy. Stupid, really, since any news would come to Jig or Noah and not her, anyway.

Across the room, Everitt cuddled the baby to her bosom, sing-songing words of gibberish. Jig and Noah were both outside scrambling their contacts.

McKenzie's grip on the phone relaxed a hair. Despite herself, she smiled, the image of Noah staring down at the baby glowing in her mind. For the past year, she'd thought only of Levi and how she had failed him. Any time she'd dared to even think of children, it felt like a demon walking into a church sanctuary.

She'd been so sure she wasn't capable of caring for a child, and even if she was, she had no one to have one with anyway.

She'd write the article, and she would include everything. The entire true story. Both parts. The dark, horrible side of the baby trade, and also the dark, horrible side of evil people that had nothing to do with the trade. Her promise to Whitney wouldn't be that hard to keep after all. Some of the bad guys were running an illegal baby trade, but at the same time, some of the bad guys were just plain bad.

"You know," Everitt said, the baby talk voice transitioning smoothly into her normal, gritty tone, "I think I'll call her Mona. It's kind of a combination of McKenzie and Noah. You guys did save us, after all."

"What about Jig?" McKenzie joked.

Everitt bit her lip and tickled the baby underneath her chin. She looked back at McKenzie. "Middle name."

Just then, the door opened, and Noah came striding through. "We got it done. Jonas is with Gibb. The Davidsons were at the house. No sign of Rory."

McKenzie let out the breath she'd been holding. Rory wasn't around, but then again, she'd stopped answering texts a while ago. McKenzie had no way of knowing what exactly had happened, but she could imagine.

She picked up the phone Jig had cloned to take and send messages from Jonas and composed a text. She flipped the phone around toward Noah to let him read it. "Good enough?"

He skimmed the message. "It's true enough. Go ahead. Hit send."

McKenzie pressed the button to transmit the message to Rory. Part of her regretted sending it, but the other part of her knew that at some point, she'd want to finish this. After all, it *would be* one hell of a story.

She stared at the phone, waiting for a return message, but none came. She knew it wouldn't. It would end with her own words.

> *You've realized by now this isn't Jonas, and like the coward you are, you've run. But you can't run forever. If you think you won't be found, just remember I found you this time.*

EPILOGUE

THE TERM "SOCIOPATH" doesn't scare me. I've known for quite some time that I am one. Maybe it was the day I set fire to my parents' home in Long Island that gave it away. No. I knew before then. Long before. It was probably the day I looked at my mother and knew I was supposed to feel something for her but didn't. I knew something was wrong with me. Different. Since then, I've learned to embrace it and let it work the way it has to, the only way I know how. For someone who is starting to tap his potential, however, here are my fundamental truths:

Liars aren't made. They're born. Do I know if my kid would've been a liar? No. I don't know if it's genetic. If my mother and father were any indication, probably not. They truly loved me. That's why they're dead. Because I was born a liar without a conscience.

A lot of talented liars think that because they're born liars they're good at it. Lying is a craft to be practiced and shaped every bit as much as painting or writing. Or acting. In fact, lying and acting can go hand in hand, perfect lovers.

The second truth is the eyes. Your eyes can betray you faster than your tongue. Why do you think so many poker players wear sunglasses? Over the years, I learned what eyes look like when people are sad, scared. It's my default eye position. I don't have to think about it anymore. They just go there. When I was younger, though, it was a different story.

Don't get me wrong. I didn't set the fire because they knew.

Quite the opposite, actually. I didn't plan to do it at all. They were useful, at times. But I was bored, and I needed a way to get what I wanted—attention from Bryce. The fire was the idea that came to me in the moment. Which brings us to where I am now. Where you are now.

The last truth is the most important of all. It's a rule, so pay close attention.

I walked through Grand Central Station the last day I was pregnant. I took a train to Staten Island, where I booked the hotel room I would stay in for the next several hours. The Cradle Robber was the answer to all my problems, this dratted pregnancy I'd never wanted in the first place. Plus, this situation would give me the exact same thing my parents' "tragic deaths" had given me years before. The only attention better than the attention people lavish on you when you've lost someone is the kind they shower you with when you've lost someone *and* become a victim. I hadn't anticipated that I'd piss off the most prolific murderer of the century and have him come after me. I didn't think that far ahead, I guess, even though I thought I'd planned well.

Which is why I'm looking into the eyes of the man next to me on the Greyhound bus line, searching for that thing I see when I look in the mirror at my own. I'm searching for that same thing I saw in Dirk Harris' eyes when he showed up to confront me. Seeing that had let me know I'd have to leave, even before Jonas' kid turned up and put the nail in that coffin. I'd gone to the Davidsons' house, thinking maybe I could convince Jonas everything had gone wrong and he had no one but me. I gave all the right details, so that way, he'd believe me. He'd be devastated, but he wouldn't check anything for himself. Not tonight. Best case scenario, I could've tipped off the Davidsons, and they'd have run just like every other time. But seeing as how they'd come under surveillance, the best plan now would be to either get rid of Jonas' son or convince Jonas he was still out there somewhere and not here. Then, it would be just me and Jonas on the hunt. I'd become all he had in the world.

At the time, I didn't know how I'd keep McKenzie McClendon from screwing everything up, but somehow, I'd make sure to keep her in the dark. After all, I'd done it before. I've always been a master at keeping people where I want them. Everyone except another like me.

Right before I plunged the potassium chloride into his IV, Dirk Harris had pointed out my fatal mistake: the freezer van I was found in was a closed environment. Anyone looking hard enough could've seen closing a victim in a moving van wasn't the Cradle Robber's M.O. He was a watcher, and he couldn't have watched me die in a travelling freezer van.

Once the Cradle Robber was dead, people might've never noticed the tiny insignificant detail that would point out the truth. They might still never see the surveillance tapes from the stadium that would show me walking into the game, baby bump gone completely from where I'd delivered in a hotel room the night before. They might never know I closed the freezer van's door after climbing in, all ready for the driver's first scheduled stop. They might never notice that the drugs in my system weren't exactly the same ones Dirk Harris used on his other victims. They might never look in that box in the very back of the hotel freezer. Even if they do, they might not be able to trace where it came from.

But as soon as I saw Jonas step out of that police car, I knew it had gone wrong. Then, when he didn't text me to meet him at the house, I realized I hadn't been talking to him the entire time. That bitch had somehow found out. There was nothing left to do but leave or let the cops find me. No brainer.

Bryce won't miss me. Now he can spend all his time at the office. Heck, maybe he'll take up with his secretary and make all the things I told Jonas true. After everything I've put him through, he could use a good lay.

The man next to me on the bus is probably in his seventies.

He could be my grandfather. The best part of it is he doesn't know me from anyone else on the bus, and I don't see any trace of that thing in his eyes. You know the thing. That blank slate. The one that means your eyes can be anything you want them to be.

"I'm Mac," I say to him, because it's the first name that comes to mind.

He smiles and introduces himself, no clue I'm Rory Nathaniel. He has no reason to think I'd lie.

Don't lie to another liar, because they know the rules of the game, too.

ACKNOWLEDGMENTS

EVERY TIME I sit down to write acknowledgements to say thank you to all of the people who have made a book possible, I'm one part giddy and happily overwhelmed by the amount of support I have in the publishing professionals, family, friends, acquaintances, and enemies who have in one way or another lent a hand to this book coming to life. I'm another part daunted and terrified I will slip-up and forget to name an important someone, hurt a cherished friend's feelings, or make some sort of foolish mistake in which I call an Aunt an Uncle or a friend named Bob, Billy instead. So, if that gaffe happens to be you this time, please know it wasn't intentional, and that even though I somehow missed you during my scatter-brained moment, that I am ever so thankful for you and your help in bringing this novel to life.

First and foremost, I have to say thank you to Pat Shaw, my lovely editor. This book would not be without you. You are truly my biggest champion, die-hard fan, and my wonderful friend. So many people hope if they are one day published that they will be lucky enough to have a relationship with their editor in which they and their editor hit it off from the beginning, share similar tastes, visions, and style preferences. But most of all, they hope their editor is tough but encouraging, supportive of the author's vision but thorough, inspiring yet practical, and realistic while always somehow managing to rally the author when he or she needs it most. Unfortunately, most authors are not this lucky. At best, they are assigned an editor they get along with…most of the time. But I hit the jackpot, because I got every single one of those things in Pat and then some. Thank you.

To the Stairway Press team of Stacey Benson, Chris Benson, Guy, and the big guy, Ken Coffman—thank you for continuing to take a chance on me, giving me an opportunity to share my thrillers with the world, and being willing to send my books out there for all to see. I'll never forget what you've done for me.

Thank you to Matt Stine and 27Sound Entertainment for my wonderful website, including SWAT, the coolest thing I could've hoped for in website design. You guys are awesome! Also, a big thank you to Circle of Seven Productions for both the Chain of Command and The Trade's trailers. You did a wonderful job, and they fit the books beautifully. To PensiveDragon.com for the wonderful cover for THE TRADE that captures perfectly the scene of this book that is the essence of what I think of when I imagine this story, thank you.

To Katie and Khal for your wealth of information involving the medical field and for being willing to risk being placed on watch lists for your Google searches as you helped me determine how to drug someone, I am forever in your debt. As always, to Dr. Richard Elliot for his expertise in forensic psychiatry and for helping me to diagnose these crazy characters and make them realistic, I thank you. To the Possum who shall remain nameless, who always gave a hand when it came to weaponry, I bow to you. To Señor Lindell Saloom and his house guest, for verifying the Spanish speaking portions of this novel: muchas gracias! To Dawn Brose for her insight into the wild, wacky world of a hairdresser: I couldn't be more thrilled with a character than the one in this case. Thank you! To Zach Broome, "plant expert," for one late night helping me to remember what sort of tree I was talking about: I'm grateful to you! And for Courtney Hatlee and her nursing knowledge, I am thankful. My dear, you are greater than Stoney.

A thank you to my wonderful read-along-ers, who were my first line of defense before I sent it to anyone in the industry: Danielle, Courtney, and Lizzie. I couldn't get through any of this without my wonderful Purglets, my Pitizens, or the fabulous group of Bryn, Kelly, Jenn, Jenna, Ami, Robert, Norma, Tracey. And an endless thank you to George Berger, who read this book at warp speed, and when I wasn't even confident in myself, reminded me that he loved the book exactly was. Thank you, G.

Personally, I would be crazy without friends outside writing, too. A huge thank you to my theatre and dance families at Theatre Macon, Macon Little Theatre, Hayiya Dance Theatre. I'm also thankful to my new friends at The Central Georgia Alzheimer's Association for the ongoing help in my research for an upcoming book.

To everyone who supported *Chain of Command*, but even more, those who took it upon themselves to go above and beyond to spread the word about *Chain of Command*; Kim Bagley Bryant and Kate Crumbley in particular. Without you guys, I couldn't get the word out nearly the way I've been able to, and your help is so valued.

To Will, for always being there to answer a question or let me vent, I thank you. To ChristaCarol and Alaina for allowing me to use Alaina's name and have her be a special inspiration for a scene. Thank you to "my brother" Meg, for letting me call or text night or day, and for making me laugh throughout the entire process. I also appreciate you letting me name my first victim after you. I love you.

To Ashlee, who is my Chief of Staff. Without her, books wouldn't get here, because I would be too much of a mess to get them onto the page. She keeps me sane...grounded. For wandering the streets of NYC with me to find locations "to murder people" for this book. I'm sometimes afraid of how much I love her.

To my Mom and Dad, thank you for raising me exactly the way you did: to go for what would make me happy and to never settle. I've never been happier in my life, and I hope more than anything that I make you both proud. It's not until you're older that you realize how precious your parents are to you, but I'm so glad that I've realized it. I love you both.

And to the littlest member of my family who is sound asleep as I write this just like the little one was when I wrote the acknowledgements for *Chain of Command*, thank you for being a bright spot in every day, the big smile I see if ever I'm frustrated, and the hug that can remind me that if nothing else, to you, I'm the greatest thing since sliced bread. I love you, Shmoopie!

To David: There was a time in my life when I thought I might quite writing. You changed all that. I couldn't have asked for someone more perfect for me. For all the nights you stayed up late with me writing, pulling out my hair, all the nights of edits you wiped my tears and told me to scream if I needed to, then brought me chocolate and Mountain Dew and helped me regroup. Thank you for being my biggest fan, and thank you for being my rock, my confidante, my everything. I love you.

And to my readers who have picked up this book, I hope you enjoy it, I hope it thrills you, entertains you, shocks, and surprises you, but mostly, as always, I hope it keeps you reading late into the night.

If you loved this book and have a moment, I would be very grateful for a short review on the page where you purchased this book. Your help in spreading the word is very much appreciated. Reviews make a real difference to help new readers find an author's work. Thank you so much.

To read more about future books, please stop by my website at http://colbymarshall.com/

ABOUT THE AUTHOR

Writer by day, ballroom dancer and choreographer by night, Colby has a tendency to turn every hobby she has into a job, thus ensuring that she is a perpetual workaholic. In addition to her 9,502 regular jobs, she is also a proud member of International Thriller Writers and Sisters in Crime. She is actively involved in local theatres as a choreographer as well as sometimes indulges her prima donna side by taking the stage as an actress. She lives in Georgia with her family, two mutts, and an array of cats that, if she were a bit older, would qualify her immediately for crazy cat lady status.

Turn the page for more from Colby Marshall

CHAIN OF COMMAND
A McKenzie McClendon Thriller

The road to the Oval Office is paved in blood...

The simultaneous assassinations of the President and Vice President catapults the Speaker of the House into the White House as the first female President of the United States. Evidence points to a former Navy SEAL as one of the assassins.

Relegated to writing sidebar stories instead of headlines, journalist McKenzie Derrington composes a scathing story about the Navy training killers, igniting the fury of the alleged assassin's former partner.

Former Navy SEAL Noah Hutchins doesn't believe his partner could have committed the heinous crime. They'd endured the horrors of Afghanistan together. His buddy was a hero, not a murderer.

No one who knows the truth is safe...

Thrown together in a search for the truth—and a career-making story—McKenzie and Noah must unravel a dangerous web of lies that includes a radical foreign faction, a violent ultra-feminist group, and corrupt politicians willing to kill to keep their secrets. And an assassin who is still on the loose.

His next targets are already in his crosshairs...

Turn the page for an excerpt of CHAIN OF COMMAND

CHAIN OF COMMAND

CHAPTER ONE

Zero Hour
California

HIS HEART RATE never rose above sixty as he looked through the scope of his .50 caliber sniper rifle at the unfortunate soul caught in his crosshairs.

He kept his breathing even. He inhaled deeply, slowly, so he could hold his breath as long as it took when the moment came. Then, he controlled his exhale equally. Hold. Breathing when he pulled the trigger could affect the shot's precision. He had done this a time or two. Actually way more than that. But this one was different.

This one he knew.

Still, no reason to worry. Stick to the protocol. He fixed on the target's head in the center of the scope. The perfect kill shot. Just the way the United States military taught him.

Beside him sat a cell phone, the prepaid kind you could buy in any discount store and pay cash for so it could never be traced. Only one person had the number to this phone.

He sucked air into his nostrils, noting the feel of the air temperature as he watched the glowing face of the phone, the clock flicking in time from 8:59 to 9:00 PM. The phone vibrated against the cement. He turned it on and listened in his earpiece.

"You good to go?"

"Yep, have to go now. Target locked."

"On my three," said the voice. It was important their shots go off at exactly the same time so the message would be unmistakable.

He heard the voice count it off at the other end of the phone. "One..."

His finger tightened on the trigger. His eyes bored into the skull of the man he was about to blow apart. He was lucky he still had a clear shot, but then again, his plans rarely went wrong. Amazing that something so incredible and horrible could be counted off in the same manner as ripping a Band-Aid off of a five-year-old kid's knee.

"Two..."

His finger tensed just the right amount and held there, ready to fire.

"Three."

As he squeezed the trigger, through the phone he heard the shot at the other end of the line.

A blast right on top of my own. That's a new one.

Even as the recoil slammed his frame backward, he was already back on his feet and disassembling the rifle. He thrust the pieces into his case in less than thirty seconds, then ran down the stairwell, calm but in a hurry.

And he was right to be in a hurry. He'd not only just heard the gunshot that killed the President of the United States. He had just executed the Vice President of the United States.

Day 1: Early Morning
Washington D.C.

The phone rang. The shrill cry of her mockingbird ringtone crowed in the air demanding an answer. Try as she might to ignore it, it just wouldn't stop.

"All right, all right!" Fifty-three-year-old Elaine Covington rolled over in her bed and pulled the receiver to her ear. This had better be good.

"What?" she barked into the phone. The numbers on the clock beside her four-poster bed read 12:44 A. M. Who the hell would be calling at this hour, and what was so important they felt like they needed to wake her up?

"I'm sorry for the lateness of the hour, Madame Speaker," said the voice on the other line, tension seeping through the cracks of his tone. His first words were too fast, his last few too slow, as if he didn't know what to call her. "But it's an emergency. This is Bert Royal."

She knew him, though her staff spent more time with him than she had. There weren't many occasions when her position required her to interact with President Seymour's Chief of Staff. Elaine clutched the phone tighter as Bert spoke..

"The president and the vice president have been shot. Both are dead. Madame Speaker, you're the first Congressperson, um, former Congressperson to know."

Through the white hailstorm in her mind, the lists of what to do, what to say, in what order, and to whom battled for dominance. She had to get dressed, had to get out of this room, out of bed, damn it. "Give me ten minutes. No, make it fifteen. Get that new bimbo press secretary we just hired. Meet me at the back office."

"No, Madame Speaker. I'm sorry. I've got orders to send a car with a special detail to take you to a secure place."

She swore. What her exact words were she doubted she'd remember. She agreed to be ready within the hour. She dropped her cell phone back on the nightstand, her knuckles still white from clenching the phone.

She lay back on her pillow. Surely she was in the middle of a dream. A nightmare. Congress would assemble; she would have to preside for hours over a debate about whether or not to attack the country responsible.

Suddenly, her eyes flew open. She sat up straight in her bed. She hadn't been asked to show up at the Capitol. She had been told she'd be taken to an undisclosed location where she would be debriefed.

It was as if she'd been slapped across the face the same way her grandmother smacked her once when she talked back to her at age ten.

President Seymour was dead.

Vice President Tifton was dead.

The Constitution dictated the next person in line.

Elaine Covington blinked twice. She was now the President of the United States.

Elaine's heart pounded as she was ushered into an unmarked black sedan. It sped through town without yielding to a single traffic light or stop sign. It pulled into an underground parking garage, but Elaine couldn't tell where they were. She'd tried to follow the maze of turns the car made from the moment the Secret Service closed her inside, but she'd lost track. She only knew they hadn't driven too far, so they must still be in DC.

Two Secret Service Agents hustled her into a dark corridor. The men on either side of her were supposed to make her feel safe, but somehow they only made her more edgy. Sweat seeped into the silk blouse she'd thrown on underneath her charcoal gray suit. She fought to breathe evenly. To present a calm facade.

As she came to the end of the tuneled hallway, low lights streamed into the corridor from one side. The agents steered her inside the room. She found herself standing face to face with President Seymour's Chief of Staff, the president's National Security Advisor, and the Secretary of Defense, along with a handful of other people she didn't recognize right away. A rip tide of whispers surged around the space. Nerves crept up her neck like a wild electrical current threatening to catch fire.

Another person standing in the room caught her eye, though he was off to the side and not part of the general buzz of conversation. He stood next to the wall, alert, in his Navy uniform. The briefcase he held was handcuffed to his wrist. Elaine's chest clenched, but somehow she swallowed down the moan that threatened to escape her lips.

The nuclear "football" was a forty-five pound briefcase that held, in essence, the ability of the President of the Unites States to unleash a nuclear response to any threat to the nation. The briefcase, always handcuffed to a high-ranking military officer, was never more than a few feet from the president at all times.

And now, the power to detonate those weapons was in this room, only a few feet away from Elaine Covington. This was no dream. No action movie scenario. This was real.

The briefcase still held Elaine's attention when a voice reminded her others were present in the room.

"Madame President," Ronald Garrety, the National Security Advisor, said.

The silver hair receding from Garrety's round face swam in Elaine's vision. Some part of her understand the words were addressed to her, but hearing him refer to her this way made it harder to pay attention to the words that followed.

"I know this must be a difficult evening for you, but we have much to discuss." He gestured to a chair across the table. "Please."

"Of course," she said, straightening her jacket. "Ladies. Gentlemen." She sat down, giving a nod to the two other men who'd not yet spoken to her.

Elaine licked her lips. What would a president say?

"Do we know anything?" Her face burned with how stupid she sounded as soon as the words tumbled out of her mouth. She should have been more tactful.

Bert Royal slumped in his chair. The short, dapper man looked for once like he had dressed in the dark, thrown on whatever clothes he'd worn the previous day. Bert had not only worked as President Seymour's Chief of Staff; he was also a good friend. This couldn't be easy for him, having to continue to do his job while acting as if his emotions weren't all over the place.

The National Security Advisor shot a glance toward Royal, but then quickly returned his stare back into Elaine's eyes. "Not a lot yet," he said, "but our people are on it, covering it from every angle. Vice President Tifton was killed as he was leaving an auditorium at University of California, Berkley, where he spoke to some college students. President Seymour was shot getting into his car. He'd just returned to Washington from his trip to Alaska. He was visiting the region hit by the earthquake." Garrety's eyes once again flicked toward Bert Royal, then back to Elaine.

"And other than that?"

"That's all we know. We know it was professional. Deliberate. The timing was too precise for it to have been a coincidence, so the two shootings must be connected. We're going to have to wait for further investigations to yield some results. At this point we have no leads. We just know we're dealing with two sick bastards who are damned good shots."

"Terrorists? Foreign country involvement?" she snapped back.

"Given the plotting and precision of the attacks, you'd think so, but we can't be sure. No one has claimed responsibility. We haven't picked up on any communications, though we are watching that situation closely."

Bert Royal, who until now had been sitting at the end of the table, silent, finally piped up. "Isn't that unusual? There should have been plenty of whack jobs lining up to tell us it was their brilliant idea to kill the president and the vice President simultaneously."

"What that tells me," Garrety said, "is this wasn't an attack on the American way of life. These aren't your typical terrorists who want martyrdom and infamy. These killers wanted to get the job done without being caught."

Garrety leaned forward, folding his hands on the table between them. "Most of the demented bastards who pull stunts like this want their names in the paper. They're proud of what they've done. Our killers, they aren't like that. They executed their mission and then disappeared. Which means one of two things: they were guns for hire or they have another agenda. Or maybe both," he said.

"In other words," Bert said, "professional assassins."

"Exactly," Garrety replied.

Coming September, 2013 from Stairway Press
OPERATION: GENOCIDE
By Yvonne Walus

An inhuman agenda…

In 1982, Annette Pretorius lives a life of privilege afforded to those of European descent in South Africa, but when her husband is murdered, she discovers a shattering secret: he'd been commissioned by the whites-only South African government to develop a lethal virus aimed at controlling the growth of the black population—already oppressed under the cruel system of apartheid.

A clandestine organization…

The murder came with a warning to Annette from a secretive organization: keep our secrets or you too will die. Captain Trevor Watson, Annette's former boyfriend, is appointed to lead the investigation. Watson's loyalty is tested as the evidence stacks against his high school sweetheart.

And the killing isn't over yet…

When the investigation points in a terrifying direction, Annette and Watson face a wrenching choice: protect those they love or sacrifice all to save innocents from racial extermination.

Turn the page to read an excerpt of

Operation: Genocide

Pretoria, South Africa—One Year Earlier

Professor Adelbrecht of the Biotech Research Agency for Vital Operations felt bile rise to his mouth as he watched one of the government's highest ranking officials wipe red stickiness off his fingers and extract cotton balls from his large, protruding ears. The whop-whop of the ceiling fan added a bizarre sense of ordinariness to the scene.

"I'm listening," the minister said. The cotton balls fell into the waste paper basket with an ominous absence of sound.

Adelbrecht talked fast.

"Brilliant. You sure it'll work?" The minister's question hung heavy in the sizzling African air.

The professor's mouth went dry. "Yes."

If genocide is really what you want.

"This office has full confidence in you and your team. We understand the Ebola virus was both an unfortunate and unforeseeable accident."

Spoken like a true politician, yet the professor felt the atmosphere in the room turn as thin as the ground under his feet.

"That's correct, Minister."

"Right. What guarantee do we have this new virus won't go ape-crazy?"

"With all due respect, Minister, Ebola was transmitted through *any* personal contact. The new virus we're proposing will be contagious only via sexual relations. Nothing else."

"So an infected maid will still be able to cook for you, but won't pass the virus on?"

"Hundred percent correct, Minister."

Assuming you don't sleep with her. But that was illegal, forbidden by the Immorality Act.

"Goes without saying that this discussion never took place."

"Yes, Minister."

"Even the Prime Minister doesn't know about this project."

Like hell he didn't.

"The limousine is at your service, Professor. The driver will take you wherever you desire."

Relief washed over him. He started rising from the sofa, ever the obedient puppet.

"Oh, and Professor?"

"Yes?"

The Minister With No Official Portfolio rose, his shoulders blocking out the sunlight of the summer day outside.

"This is your final warning." Suddenly, he didn't sound like a politician anymore. "Mess this up, and you'll wish you were dead."

Chapter 1—Saturday Night

IF IT LOOKS like an elephant and walks like an elephant, it's an elephant, thought Captain Trevor Watson.

For some reason, though, the higher powers within the South African Police weren't buying the wisdom.

He stood at the entrance to the rich man's garage, the smell of car fumes still tarnishing the night air. He scanned the confined space.

"This exactly how you found it?" he asked Jones.

The pimply constable stood to attention. "Yes, sir."

To the left side, a Ford Cortina with a teddy bear on the back seat. A silver BMW to the right. An expensive status symbol car for him, a practical one for her, Watson noted. That in itself said something about the dead man. A garden hose extended from the Beemer's exhaust to the driver's side window.

They had all the garage doors open now, airing out the interior before proceeding with the investigation.

"Your thoughts, Constable?"

Let the youngster learn on the easy ones.

Jones shrugged. "Looks like a suicide to me."

"Right." Did to Watson too, but obviously the brigadier had a different take on it to call him when he wasn't up on the rotation. Watson knew better than to complain. After last week's crap-out session, his job was hanging by the proverbial thread, except in his case the thread was thinner than a hair and more brittle than a dry twig from a thorn tree.

Officially, he'd been in the right. A white property owner had the legal right to shoot a black burglar, provided a warning shot had been fired first. The way some policeman worked, they would fire that warning shot themselves when they arrived at the crime scene and found only one spent cartridge. Some policemen, but not him. A week ago, Watson had been called out to a shooting scene: one dead burglar, one shot fired. Only one shot. Instead of fixing up the scene after the fact, he had chosen to obey the letter of the law, arrest the white homeowner for culpable homicide. The result? The guy who shot the burglar without warning got off with a smack on the wrist. Watson, given the history of his employment in the South African Police, came out with excrement stuck to both boots.

Remember whose side you're on, Watson, the brigadier's words kept ringing in his ears. One false move. Just one, and you're finished. I'm watching you.

So. Saturday night, and he'd been pulled out of bed to investigate *yet* another suicide. *Yet* another white middle-aged guy whose life of luxury had blown up in his face. Watson remembered the outline of the man's sprawling mansion, eyed the BMW, tried to understand. No go.

"Word has it, he's some sort of big shot. That right?" Jones swatted at his forearm, brushed off the dead insect. "Bloody mozzies."

"Far as I know, the victim hasn't been positively identified yet. Both cars and this residence, though, are registered to a scientist doing classified work for the government. That's why all sorts of trip wires sounded the alarm the moment the call came in."

"Live by the sword, die by the sword, hey, Captain?"

Watson waved a mosquito away from his own arm. Shook his head. "It's not as though the victim..." his memory was still sluggish from the sex marathon he'd had only half an hour before, "this Gordon Pretorius..." He paused, found his train of thought. "Not as though he died of poison, or a bomb explosion, or whatever it is government scientists create in their labs."

Annette Pretorius sat in her bedroom, facing her dressing table. Her gaze bounced off the freshly polished mirror and the bottles on the dust-free surface without taking them in. The words of the typed note she'd found behind the BMW's windscreen wiper flashed in her memory.

BURN ALL THE FILES, OR YOU DIE, TOO.
DON'T TELL THE COPS.
YOU HAVE TILL MONDAY.

Not a coward by nature, Annette wouldn't have been bothered by the threat, not even with Gordon slumped in the car seat less than a metre away. Ever since her first baby took his first gulp of air, though, her life wasn't her own anymore.

If she died, who would look after the children? Her mother? Annette shuddered at the prospect. She couldn't let it happen. To live, she had to do what they wanted.

She'd hidden the note in her bra, because her evening dress had no pockets. The paper's hard folds had stabbed her skin as she bade the party guests goodbye and rushed upstairs. The stiff corners kept biting into her flesh, yet she made no move to take it out.

What files? Where would she find them? How would she prove that she'd destroyed them?

Enough.

She didn't recognise the helpless person she'd become. Whatever happened to the rebellious redhead who used to read banned literature and, on one wine-filled evening, had set fire to her sensible beige bra?

Get yourself together, silly. Look for the files. Read them. Throw them in the fire.

She straightened her spine and, on still-shaky calves, walked over to Gordon's nightstand. Yanked open the top drawer.

A memory stabbed her right through the heart. Her old vitamin pills. What on earth were they doing in Gordon's drawer? She'd started taking them over a decade before, feeling run down after the birth of her second baby. Gordon had brought them back from work, an experimental pill that would make her feel better.

It had made her feel stronger, if a bit dreamy and untroubled by reality. But then the miscarriages started, and she felt weak and depressed no matter how many of those vitamin pills she took. In the end, she'd flushed them down the loo, but in her mind the sparkly blue pills that looked like sapphires would forever remind her of the five babies she'd lost, each of them as small as the tube of blue vitamin pills.

And now the vitamin pills were back, one tube almost empty, two untouched. She slammed the drawer shut. Opened another. Still, the questions gnawed at her like a termite in skirting.

Had Gordon been taking the blue pills? Why?

At least the dead scientist didn't kill his family.

The thought echoed in Watson's mind as he closed the internal garage door behind him and stared at the portraits of the man's three children in the entrance hall to the mansion.

At least he didn't kill the family.

The way these suicides usually worked, the bloody bastard shot his wife and children before turning the gun on himself. The change was refreshing. Still, a small part of Watson's self-interest wished the scientist had waited till morning. That way, he wouldn't have to face Charlene's accusing glare when he got back home.

A domestic servant appeared in the hall.

This time of the night? Shouldn't she be asleep in her own quarters?

"*Baas,*" she said instead of *good evening.*

Watson didn't waste time on social graces, either. "Where is the lady of the house?"

The whites of the maid's eyes gleamed under the chocolate-coloured lids. No reply. Didn't she understand?

"Your madam," he rephrased, consulting his hastily scribbled note. "Annette—Annette Pretorius?"

He'd known an Annette once, long ago. Her hair glowed red as though fashioned from all the fires of hell. She'd made him fail three maths tests in a row. Back then, he'd have walked barefoot on melting pavement for Annette LeRoy.

Watson shook his head. Annette LeRoy had long been gone

from his life. It was another woman he'd left in the snug bed when the call came to investigate this case. Peeved by the call-out, his lover had probably gone home.

Damn.

He wouldn't allow his life to interfere with work. Not now. Not when he'd finally regained his lost rank and status.

He stepped past the still silent woman into the spacious hallway, coated with the smell of stale cigarette smoke. "Call the madam." Harsher than intended. His patience ran in short supply tonight.

The servant averted her gaze. A cultural convention, he knew, not a sign of a guilty conscience.

"The madam is asleep." Her voice carried a gracious, educated quality. "First she tells everybody to please go home and then she goes upstairs."

"She—what?" The cop in him was fully awake now.

Asleep, hey? Curious.

You didn't go to bed when your husband killed himself. You fainted. You cried. You pretended to faint or cry. But go to bed? Then his brain caught up with the other titbit of information. "What do you mean, she told *everybody* to go home?"

The maid gestured towards the open door, through which he could glimpse kitchen counters with smudged wine glasses, squashed beer cans and dirty plates. "I'm washing up after the party when she comes up from the garage—"

"Your madam? Madam Annette?"

A nod. "She says to the guests, 'You will have to excuse us. Gordon is not feeling well. I think it's best if we called it a night.' And then she says she's so very, very sorry."

He was glad the maid spoke good English. Thanks to the government policy of limiting the duration and quality of Bantu education, few black people did. "What's your name?" he asked.

"Hester."

"What happened then, Hester?"

"Madam tells me to call the police, she says the number is on the phone pad, and to tell them the master gassed himself dead in his car."

"And then?"

"Then she is sick all over the kitchen floor." A false note in Hester's voice. Triumph? Glee? "To the master, she pretends she doesn't eat. Coffee for breakfast, a leaf of lettuce for dinner, that's the way he likes it. But tonight she throws up steak and prawns and potato. And chocolates."

"Thank you, Hester, you may go now." A new voice, soft and slightly hoarse, came from the staircase. "You'll finish the dishes tomorrow."

"Yes, missus." The black woman shot him one direct frightened gaze before she withdrew.

His tired brain decided to file it under follow-up-sometime, as he turned his attention to the widow.

Annette Pretorius. Red-rimmed eyes, fever-red cheeks, and red hair fashioned from all the fires of hell.

His Annette. Annette LeRoy.

Hester's feet fell lightly on the floor tiles as she crossed the kitchen floor and locked the back door behind her. The sky was as black as the inkwell she had used at school in an era where white kids used ballpoint pens. This late at night, with most residential lights out, the blackness was studded with the glimmer of many, many stars. As many stars in the sky as there were freedom fighters down here, on this sun-baked soil of Africa.

Find the files, the leader of her resistance cell had told her at the last meeting. *Those who aren't with us, are against us.* Hester didn't waste energy philosophising about loyalty and trust. Her action had nothing to do with grudges or her people's struggle against apartheid. The leader had asked and she had promised. It was as simple as that. With Master Gordon dead, the task had become trickier or trivial, depending on the madam's reaction.

The door to her quarters, in the far corner of the garden, stood open for air circulation. Now Hester closed it behind her and surveyed the cement floor for snakes and scorpions. She repeated the procedure with her narrow bed. Columns of bricks under each leg added extra height and guarded against the evil spirit, the Tokoloshe. The leader said that's nonsense, a myth invented by the witch doctors to scare the people into giving them money. Still, Hester reckoned you couldn't be too careful. Master Gordon hadn't slept on a bed raised by bricks, and look where it got him.

Trevor!

The air, thick as treacle, stuck in Annette's lungs, threatened to explode in her chest.

Trevor. An old school friend. An ex-boyfriend. The only man who knew her the way she really was, because he himself awakened the very worst inside her.

His presence should have made the situation better. It made it infinitely worse. She'd never been able to keep a secret from him. Now she had to.

Adrenalin propelled her forward, one gluey step after another.

"Annette."

She cleared the rasp from her throat. "Trevor Watson." She made herself walk faster, her bare feet registering the coolness of the terracotta. "I'm so glad it's you." One more lie for the evening—what did it matter?

"Annette," he repeated. His voice was fuller now, his face all grown up. "You haven't changed a bit."

You have no idea.

On perfect-hostess autopilot, she took his hand in both of hers and led him into the lounge. Her knees were jelly, and she still couldn't remember how to breathe.

"I'm sorry we meet under these sad circumstances," Trevor said. "Your husband…"

The remainder of the sentence slid off her earlobes without reaching the eardrum. She couldn't concentrate. They stood in the middle of the room, his hand still in hers, until her upbringing took over. "I'm sorry. I can't seem to concentrate."

Trevor started talking again. She watched his lips, and again couldn't distinguish the sounds, as though he spoke in a foreign language. Shell-shocked.

Is that what soldiers meant, this inability to use your senses?

If only her brain worked properly!

She wasn't stupid, contrary to what Gordon sometimes said—shouted—during his lapses of temper.

She let go of Trevor's hand, rubbed her forehead.

"I feel so—" she broke off. What did she feel? Wrapped in cellophane? Guilty? Lost? All her life, she had trained hard to suppress her emotions, to please first her parents, later her husband. Tonight was an exception. "Please," the words escaped before she could bite down on them. "I don't know what to do."

"What do you mean?"

BURN ALL THE FILES…

Should she show Trevor the message?

DON'T TELL THE COPS.

Somehow, she didn't think so. She forced her face into a mask of a helpless female. "What's the protocol, Trevor? Do I call the funeral home? Do the police do it? How do I tell people?" The mask immobilised her face. Oh, dear Lord, she had to tell the children.

Trevor's gaze became more focussed. "And your worry, at this point in time," he accentuated the last word, "is *protocol?*"

No, her mind screamed, my worry is the children's reaction, their tears, their future without a father. My worry is money for Monday's dinner, and for the Monday after next. My world has screeched to a halt and derailed, my ears are ringing and all I want right now is to wake up from this nightmare.

BURN…

Her mouth hurt to form words that suddenly grew a hard edge. "Nobody taught me how to be a widow." True enough. Somehow, her voice came out cool, calm and collected. Thank the Lord for small mercies.

The pause stretched forever before Trevor broke the silence. "Did your husband have life insurance?"

Insurance?

Annette tried to remember whether Gordon had ever mentioned the subject. She forced her lips to form words again. "I don't know."

Exhausted by the effort of speaking when she wanted to scream, she sank onto the sofa, allowed herself the luxury of leaning into the creamy upholstery. She gestured Trevor to sit, too. "I just don't know anything anymore."

"Did your husband have any enemies?"

Enemies?

Her vision tunnelled, then broadened with alarming speed. "What am I going to do?" She stared down at her lap where her trembling fingers kneaded the material of her skirt. They refused to settle.

The sofa hissed under Trevor's muscled body. "You loved your husband that much?"

Annette flinched. The question, in all its absurdity, penetrated through the fog in her head. "I beg your pardon?"

Trevor must have misunderstood her reply. "I'm sorry," he said. "My comment was inappropriate."

Was it?

Annette couldn't tell. He was the investigating officer. Surely he had the right to ask personal questions. Still, nobody had the right to hear the truthful answer to this one. "Of course I— loved…" she trailed off.

Even to her ears, it sounded weak and false. She tightened her lips against her teeth, blockading the emotion she kept deep inside. "Without Gordon, I don't know how I'm going to live from day to day. He took care of the finances. Tomorrow is pay-day for the staff and the children need bus money on Monday…"

The arrangement of the husband looking after finances was commonplace, yet Annette felt sick with shame. Why had she allowed herself to become ignorant about her family's money matters?

"Did your husband keep any cash in the safe?"

Annette tried to concentrate, though it was growing harder to do so. Her spine burrowed further into the couch.

"Documents, I think. And some gold collector coins. Not money, though."

"Do you have your own bank account? Your own chequebook? Credit card?"

The questions came fast. Annette couldn't keep up. The adrenalin rush died away, leaving her spent. Due to her punishing diet, she never had much energy these days. "I—I ..."

BURN ALL THE FILES, OR YOU DIE, TOO.

The room swooped into a spin. Sounds grew muffled. She would not faint. She would not allow herself that pitiful way out. "Perhaps we could talk—tomorrow? Please. I'm not feeling myself..." She grasped for control. "The children—are with Mother. Safe—Yes. Quite—safe now."

The last three words had come out slurred and soft. Watson had to strain to catch them. Annette's head fell back, and for a moment he thought she was asleep.

Her normally milky skin, though, looked even paler than usual; felt clammy when he touched her wrist to count the beats. Pulse under fifty. Not asleep or faking—she had fainted.

He lifted her legs onto the sofa and lowered her head onto the armrest. He noticed how skinny her limbs were. Must have lost weight since high school, not that she'd had any puppy fat to begin with. Small, more like a child in size. This was not how he usually conducted a suicide investigation, but then, he did not usually meet Annette LeRoy on the job. Should he hand over the case? Absolutely the proper and correct thing to do, and what he liked best in life was to do things properly and correctly. Not because he was saintly—because life was simpler that way.

He needed this case, though. And Annette meant nothing to him—now.

"Captain?" The constable's eyes flickered from the sleeping woman on the sofa to Watson, then back again.

"At ease, Jones. What do you have for me?"

"HQ radioed twice for an update. Are the preliminary

interviews completed?" Jones glanced at Annette again, more pointedly this time.

Watson ignored Jones' implied question.

Interviews?

The guests had been sent off, the kids had evidently spent the evening with their granny, and the lady of the house had fainted. He needed to think.

"Go touch the car's engine, Jones. And check the level of petrol left in the tank."

"Yessir."

Why would HQ need an update already? Big fish scientist or not, that's not how they did things. Watson rifled the pages of his notebook again. Pretorius, Gordon Pretorius. A common enough Afrikaner surname, a bit at odds with the British first name, but such things happened. Pretorius? It rang a bell. His memory flicked through its neat catalogue of facts until it settled on the list of ministers. No Gordon Pretorius there. Not a political figure then, thank his lucky stars.

Jones rapped on the doorjamb.

"The engine is still warm, sir, and the petrol tank almost full. The boys from the lab will be able to do an exact measurement."

He thought some more. "Was the engine running when you got here?"

"Negative, sir."

Watson stood up from the sofa, careful not to disturb Annette, and took out his radio. He knew Jones had toned down HQ's request. They didn't *want an update*. They demanded his immediate attention, utter deference and brilliant conclusions.

When his superior answered, Watson's gut twisted. The old fox, at HQ, on a Saturday evening? The case must be huge. "Watson here, Brigadier."

He wasn't allowed to say more. For the next ninety seconds, he listened.

Most officers loathed landing high profile cases. The potential glory wasn't worth the hassles with the influential family members who were more than used to throwing their weight about.

Watson was unlike most officers. It'd been six years since he was allowed to lead a case of any substance. Tonight, his luck had changed.

"You can count on me, Brigadier," he said.

When he disconnected, he looked straight at Jones, channelling his bafflement. "I'll be damned," he said. "HQ wants us to treat this as a murder case. Not a suggestion, an order. Have the team dust for prints."

"Yes, sir."

"Photographs?"

"Just the corpse."

"Take snaps of everything. The hose, the exhaust, the petrol gauge, the garage doors, the spiders on the ceiling. Is the medic here?"

"Should be arriving any minute, sir. Said he's not in a state to drive, it being a Saturday night, so we sent a car for him."

Watson forced a laugh. "Let's hope he's not too drunk to give us an initial opinion. The suicide—or the victim, if we're to accept HQ's theory—was one of our top scientists working on something super secret."

"Which was?"

"They won't tell us."

Jones scratched his head. "Did they say why we're treating it as a murder?"

A deep breath to steady the hammering in his chest. This would be his big break. His way up. If he solved it. "Because it's happened before."

"With respect, Captain, we get a fair share of suicides."

Watson knew it only too well. Suicide, often preceded by family murder, was on the rise. Heads of families unable to cope with stress, too proud to seek professional help when depression struck or when things went awry at work—sometimes they chose to end it, no matter what they heard in church every Sunday.

"Suicide happens," he said. "But when it happens to the second top scientist in less than five weeks, HQ sits up and takes notice."

Jones exhaled a whistle.

"Hold the amazement, Constable. You don't know the best bit. The other dead scientist was also called Pretorius. Pieter Pretorius."

"A coincidence?"

"No. His father."

Annette Pretorius woke with a start. Something was wrong. The light. Artificial and hard on the eyes. Also, not her bed. Not a bed at all.

BURN ALL THE FILES, OR YOU DIE, TOO.

Memories flooded back, crushing. She buried her face in the leather of the sofa. No escape.

"Annette."

If she kept very still, perhaps he'd go away. The approach usually worked for bullies: Gordon, her mother—mainly Gordon.

"Annette, listen to me. I need to ask you a few questions, and I need you to answer them. Please. It's important."

Important?

Important was a word reserved for things that had to do with Danny, Julie and Beth. Homework. Swimming galas. Protecting the children from Gordon's temper. Those were the important things in life.

"Annette?"

Like a slap. She sat up, shielding her eyes from the harsh light of the chandelier. Fury rose acerbic to her mouth. She was done living by somebody else's priorities. "Don't you use that tone of voice with me again, Trevor Watson. Not ever."

His Adam's apple moved up and down several times. "I apologise, Mrs. Pretorius." Nothing personal in his voice now, a textbook example of a policeman. "Please understand. Your husband," a slight pause, "passed away in unexplained circumstances, and it is my sad duty to investigate it. Should you prefer, I could have you escorted to the police station for official questioning."

It didn't make any sense. "But Gordon—I saw him—the hose." Images blazed in her mind, sharp and absolute. No ambiguity in the horrid garage scene. Gordon had taken the coward's way out.

Anger pooled in her head. She had to ask Trevor to repeat what he'd said.

"Was it you who found the deceased, Mrs. Pretorius?"

The *deceased*. She pushed the word away. "Yes."

"What did you see?"

She cast her mind back. The stairs—the door—*the deceased*. A sharp ringing, like the TV signal once transmission had ended, filled her ears. All she managed was a small shake of her head.

"All right," Trevor's voice softened. "Please tell me about the children. You mentioned they were out of the house? With your mother? Or with your mother-in-law?"

"With my mom. She lives nearby."

"How many children do you have?" The question had a spike at the end.

"Three. Danny's thirteen, Julie almost twelve, and Beth's just a baby." With every word, tranquillity spread through her. She looked at the family photographs displayed over the mantelpiece. When she rose from the sofa, she thought her legs might cave in before she reached the wall.

One by one, she moved the frames of the photos until they were all askew, hanging at haphazard angles to one another.

She surveyed the end result, waited for its impact.

No use.

"Mrs. Pretorius?"

Unfair. For fourteen years, she would align photo frames on the walls with an aluminium level and place the mugs in the pantry rims down, so dust wouldn't get into them. She would turn the standing fan a precise thirty degrees inwards whenever she switched it on, place the toilet roll the correct way in its holder and always squeeze the toothpaste tube from the bottom.

For fourteen years, her life had been filled with rules, small and big rules, bloody annoying rules, Gordon's rules.

Every day, for fourteen long years, she would rush around

the house ten minutes before he came home, straightening photographs, putting away toys and pulling down the blinds for privacy.

"Mrs. Pretorius."

Now that Gordon was dead, she thought it would give her pleasure to turn the mugs over, to squeeze the toothpaste tube where she damned well pleased and to leave the cap unscrewed too. But the experiment with the photo frames had proved futile.

Was Gordon's imprint on her psyche too deep? Had his way become her way now, too?

The hell it had.

"Mrs. Pretorius. Please tell me about your movements earlier tonight. You had a party? You asked the guests to go home?"

She wanted to throw Gordon's photograph across the room. But even with Gordon dead, now was not the time to give in to her impulses. She needed to come across—what? Sympathetic. Yes. And weak.

No problem. Fourteen years with Gordon could have made a wooden dummy an Oscar-winning performer.

The pale blue of Watson's police shirt was getting darker—and decidedly wetter—from Annette's tears. Her head rested on his chest. Watson loathed himself for noticing how close her body was to his. The dead were not the only victims in a house of mourning—their families suffered emotional wreckage, too.

And yet, if this wasn't a suicide?

Watson knew how often, how bloody amazingly often, the murderer was the one who reported finding the body. Not very likely if this vic's murder was linked to his father's, but still.

Shit.

He heard Jones's embarrassed cough. "Captain? The medic wants a word. It may be nothing, sir—"

Annette's physical closeness held far more appeal than any breakthrough in the garage.

"So why—" He checked his tone. "Sorry, man. Shoot."

"Sir." Jones cut his gaze to Annette. Clearly, the matter was not for civilian ears.

"Go ahead, Jones."

Jones lowered his voice. "The deceased was holding something in his fist."

Watson's hopes skyrocketed, trumping—for the time being—the warmth of Annette's skin. "A suicide note?"

"No, sir. A white unicorn."

Those who knew what his job entailed sometimes asked the The Minister With No Official Portfolio how true the rumours were. About South African security forces participating in exchange training programs, learning interrogation methods in Italy and swapping torture stories in Argentina. The minister always smiled his honest smile and said, "I know of no incident in which my people ever tortured a political prisoner."

It was true. His people mopped up the blood in the prison's dungeons, sluiced away the body fragments, disposed of the mangled corpses. The actual torture he always administered personally. Not because he had a taste for it, quite the contrary, he abhorred pain. Consequently, he had no right to ask anybody else to inflict it. Some things, though, simply had to be done, and so he did them. For the fatherland. To keep South Africa white.

"Daddy? Daddy?" The cry of his three-year old daughter pierced the thick night air of his mansion.

He glanced at the security screen. The guards were alert but not anxious, the alarm circuits not triggered. Monsters under the bed, most likely. "Coming, honey."

His wife stirred, her pregnant belly protruding through the thin summer blanket. He planted a kiss on her cheek, warm and soft with sleep. "Shhh. I'll handle it," he told her.

He'd handle it. His daughter's nightmares and the threat hanging over the country's future. For her, and for his unborn children, he would do wrong things to get the right result.

"Daddy?"

"Just fetching some anti-monster spray. Daddy's going to get rid of all the monsters."

Those under the bed and those threatening their country.

CPSIA information can be obtained
at www.ICGtesting.com
Printed in the USA
LVOW10s2310040517
533267LV00004B/847/P